PADLOCKED

PADLOCKED
By p.m.terrell

Published by
Drake Valley Press, a Division of P.I.S.C.E.S. Books, LTD.
USA

This novel is a work of fiction. Any other resemblance to actual persons, living or dead, is entirely coincidental except as noted under "A Note from the Author." The characters, names, plots, and incidents are the product of the author's imagination. References to actual events, public figures, locales, or businesses are included to give this work a sense of reality.

ISBN 978-1-935970-57-6 (Trade Paperback)
ISBN 978-1-935970-56-9 (eBook)
ISBN 978-1-935970-58-3 (Hardcover)
ISBN 978-1-935970-59-0 (Large Print)

Author's website: www.pmterrell.com

Padlocked *[pad, läkt]*
When the gates are locked in the afterlife, and only one's soul can open them.

What reviewers have said about p.m.terrell's historical books:

"Terrell introduces a new level of excellence to the historical novel. Using the mastery of an artist, Terrell paints colorful word pictures and descriptive phrases that are so exquisitely well-chosen that the reader is magnetically drawn into the plot, taking on a role as an active participant in the intrigue of the story." – Richard R. Blake, *Midwest Book Review*

"Wow. *Padlocked* will take your breath away. It is gut-wrenching and disturbing, but there is a glimmer of hope that clings to every page. It is a brilliant story and one I highly recommend." – author Maggie Thom

"P M Terrell's historical novels spring to life with vivid characters and descriptions. She is an artist, using words instead of paints to create her masterpieces. Her ability to merge fact and fiction makes reading about history an awesome adventure into the past." – Reviewer Sherry Fundin, *Fundinmental*

"I felt as if I had been to Ireland after I read this book *[April in the Back of Beyond]*. I got so engrossed I even went to my computer to read more about some of its history. Don't get me wrong; this is not a dry history book by any means. It's a story about its wars, its people and its beautiful scenery. It's one of those tales you just don't want to put down. The kind you keep looking at the clock thinking "just 15 more minutes" and pretty soon it's been a couple hours." – *Our Town Book Reviews*

Special Thanks

This book was a labor of love, and I deeply appreciate all those who encouraged me along the way, including:

Martha Dunlop, author of *The Starfolk Trilogy*,

Glenna Mageau, aka Maggie Thom, author of suspense and nonfiction,

Reverend N. Neelley Hicks,

And world historian and scholar Rob Stere.

1

January 27, 1945, Auschwitz-Birkenau, Poland

The day dawned like any other, but ended like no other.

Hank Mullins was a long way from home. He'd left his family behind in North Carolina to travel the world as a roaming photojournalist and war correspondent, and he thought he'd seen it all. He'd covered the Spanish Civil War and had arrived in Guernica after Hitler's first *blitzkrieg* test, an event that could still revisit his dreams, causing him to awaken in a cold sweat, as if the enemy were on him.

After Spain, he'd been trapped in Poland behind enemy lines when Nazi Germany invaded in 1939. The atrocities had piled up until he could no longer count them, nor did he wish to. Despite enormous challenges, he'd continued to perform his duties, even when it meant compromising his ethics, working with the enemy while simultaneously connecting with the underground resistance, all the while trying to get back home.

But as he rode in an open military vehicle, driven by a Red Army soldier, no less, his brain had difficulty processing what his eyes observed. He found himself in utter shock as he stood in the back, braced against the metal, as the vehicle crawled behind a long line of tanks and armored trucks, his camera steadily snapping. Through the years, he'd never had to force himself to take pictures, as it came naturally. Today, however, his arms kept dropping as he stared at the barbed wire fencing that effectively contained an entire city of barracks, factories, and buildings. Somehow, it felt as though he were violating the prisoners' dignity by snapping their pictures.

Reluctantly, he reminded himself why he was here and raised the camera once again, his heart rate increasing with his rising anxiety.

"What the devil?" The words were in English, the voice unable to mask an elitist Spanish accent, the kind that had become a target in his native Spain under the dictator Francisco Franco.

"Are you taking notes, Rafe?" Hank asked his coworker. He tried to keep his voice steady, though it began to break as he said his coworker's name. He glanced sideways at the younger man, noting his widened russet eyes and black hair tousled by the chilly wind.

"You haven't been giving them," Rafe Cabrera answered without looking at him.

"Read my mind."

"The whole world has been under the control of the evil one," Rafe continued as though he hadn't heard him. "But the ruler of this world will be cast out. John, chapter 12, verse 31. But I paraphrase."

"You're not reading my mind."

The vehicle slowed to a stop. Major Misha Volkov was waiting for them. He stood calmly with his back to the fencing, smoking a cigarette, as if he were casually awaiting them in front of a restaurant or hotel. His crisp uniform of the 60th Army of the First Ukrainian Front stood out amongst the privates. His deep dimples made him appear to be smiling even when he was not, a contradiction not lost on Hank as he struggled to understand the place to which the Red Army had taken them. Misha motioned for them to join him, and Hank and Rafe hopped over the side of the vehicle.

It was three o'clock in the afternoon, barely two hours before the sun would set. Light was already waning with the cloud cover. Hank knew the delay couldn't be avoided, as Allied soldiers had spent the day securing the camp, but he was concerned. Even if they allowed him back tomorrow, the action was today.

"Remember what we discussed," Misha said. He offered each of them a cigarette, which they accepted. As they lit them and looked past the major at the scenes unfolding all around them, he continued. "Though our troops have gone through the camp, there may still be boobytraps or holdouts. Stay on the main roads for now."

Misha turned around to face the camp, his expression fixed but his eyes wider than usual. "We have some informants identifying guards and other employees of the Third Reich. We have already rounded up several who attempted to blend in with the prisoners."

Hank raised his camera and shot through the fencing to capture scores of people so skeletal that it seemed like a miracle they could stand, let alone walk. He knew he would never be able to forget them, their eyes enormous within emaciated faces intently watching him. Some wore blankets over thin, nearly bare shoulders, emblazoned with the Red Army insignia, as medical personnel fanned out to usher them into the courtyard.

"There are only seven thousand or so still here," Misha continued.

"*Only* seven thousand?" Rafe asked incredulously as he wrote down the figure in his reporter's notebook.

"I'm told the camp's capacity is roughly 150,000," he answered impassively. "I want as many photographs as you can take. The soldiers are attempting to assemble the prisoners in the courtyard, there." He pointed to an open area. "They'll soon be transported to proper medical facilities, so you'll have to hurry."

"Matylda is there," Hank blurted as he watched her rushing from one patient to another, her crisp nurse's cap slightly off-kilter from her efforts.

"Yes," Misha answered as he looked at him pointedly. "We need every medic, especially those from the Polish Home Guard. We have too few soldiers who can speak their language."

"What's happening over there?" Rafe asked, pointing to a different area by the fencing where a group of men and women were being rounded up under guard.

"Those are Nazis," Misha said. He spat on the ground in disgust.

A sense of foreboding rose up inside Hank as he tamped down a wave of nausea. "Come on," he said. "We're wasting time."

"Don't feed the prisoners!" Misha called out behind them. "Doctors' orders."

"Does he think we're at a zoo?" Rafe spouted. "These are human beings, for Christ's sake."

Hank's senses were overwhelmed as he hurried through the wide gate with Rafe on his heels. First and most curiously, there was a stench that made his eyes water and forced many of the rescuers to don facial bandanas. Despite Rafe's comment, the only thing he could liken it to was the profuse odor that greeted visitors as they strolled into a zoo. This smell, however, was a thousand times more pungent.

Then there was the visual onslaught of so many men, women, and children who were clearly starving, their appearances gut-wrenching. Some acted as if they had dissociated from their environment and the actions unfolding all around them, their eyes blank and unseeing even as their feet moved them forward.

Others begged for food and water, and Hank and Rafe were compelled to tell them that it was coming. Still others kissed the ground before them, crying while they thanked them for being there. Still others knelt on the ground, their hands clasped in prayer, thanking God for their liberation from evil.

As if the scenes were not enough to overwhelm them, the sounds were deafening. Even those prisoners who spoke were oddly hushed, but the military rescuers were barking orders in every direction, causing men to scramble and repeat the orders throughout the camp. Other soldiers called out when they discovered something critical, the voices seeming to come from everywhere at once. It was a scene of organized chaos, soldiers and medics rushing in every direction.

"What's the plan, boss?" Rafe asked as he came alongside him. He dabbed at perspiration across his forehead, despite the winter chill, pausing for a moment to close his eyes against the unfolding scene.

Hank peered around them as he attempted to focus on the job at hand. "We'll follow this road first. I'll narrate while I'm taking pictures, as usual."

"Got it." Rafe already had a notepad in his hands and his pencil at the ready, as he always did. They had become a well-oiled team ever since Hank met Rafe during the Spanish Civil War. He'd initially been assigned as his driver and translator, but as the war raged on, he'd become more than a valuable assistant. He felt joined at the hip. When the war ended in 1939, and Franco targeted Rafe's family, Rafe followed Hank's reassignment to Poland while his parents and siblings fled to southern France. Little did they know that they would be trapped a few months later when the Germans invaded.

They made their way past each building at a crawl, stopping to snap pictures of the crowds that had gathered to gawk at them with the largest eyes in the smallest faces that Hank had ever witnessed. Soldiers often interrupted, instructing the prisoners to gather in the courtyard, their Polish words often stilted as though they'd rehearsed specific phrases. They worked swiftly and politely, though Hank felt they were intruders with no right to take their photographs. He wished he could explain what their orders had been the night before, that they had to take pictures to share with the Allies so the world would witness the atrocities committed there. But he couldn't. He could only try to tamp down the catch in his throat and keep snapping, dictating specific descriptions and key phrases to Rafe so they could later add them to the text with the photo.

"What the fuck?" Rafe asked suddenly, his voice sounding brash and incredulous. "Is that Max?"

Hank whirled around, following Rafe's pointed finger. Soldiers surrounded a short man in a business suit so soiled and wrinkled that it appeared he'd been sleeping in it. He seemed to be searching the crowds for someone, occasionally pointing at specific people, who were then arrested and disarmed, including an unusually tall, ramrod-straight female guard.

Hank snapped pictures of her as the prisoners descended upon her, pummeling her with their fists, removing her baton, and cracking it over her, as she writhed on the ground. The soldiers did nothing to stop their attack. By the time the prisoners began to back off, she was bleeding profusely, her hair pulled out by handfuls, and one shoe was missing.

As the woman was frisked for weapons, and several knives and whips were recovered, the soldiers decided to strip her to her underwear. While they marched her toward the front fence line, others continued to check her discarded clothing for all the hidden weapons.

The man in the dark suit turned around, and Hank caught his breath. "I'll be damned," he said. "You're right; that is Max." He took a step further, then stopped. "Wait. Is that Agata?"

Rafe followed his line of sight. "Agata, from the village?"

As Hank's eyes descended upon her, he felt a sinister chill rise through his spine. She was dressed in a guard uniform, and she appeared to be searching the crowds for someone. At Max's instruction, soldiers surrounded her, pushing her to the ground to check for weapons. Unlike the earlier guard, the prisoners did not surround her but remained a few yards away, warily watching. They discovered only a baton. She cried out involuntarily as they tied her wrists behind her and grabbed her by her forearms to lift her to her feet.

Hank continued snapping pictures until his film ran out. Cursing with the delay, he tossed the spent cartridge to Rafe, who efficiently plopped it into a canister and labeled it. Hank couldn't get the new film in fast enough, and he rushed after Agata as she was led away. Max was also being escorted toward the front, and Hank struggled to keep sight of both of them through the growing crowd.

"Has the world turned upside down?" The question was directed at Rafe, but his mind was spinning.

"You mean, Agata as a guard and Max helping the Reds?" Rafe continued without waiting for a reply. "I think that's fairly obvious."

While the prisoners were directed toward the courtyard, Hank followed the guards to the area beside the barbed-wire fence. Soldiers efficiently, though often brutally, lined them up as they arrived. Agata and the other female guard fell in beside the male guards, many of whom had been beaten and were in various stages of disheveled undress. Hank watched as a male guard was directed to the other side of Agata before he began taking photographs. Though he was seasoned, it didn't take experience to understand this was a momentous historical occasion, and the pictures of these cruel Nazi guards would be analyzed for generations to come, as if a mere photograph could unravel the mystery behind their brutality.

Agata failed to look at him, and he dared not acknowledge her in front of the others. She stood with her eyes downward, her shoulders slumped, her face bleeding from her encounter on the ground. Her hair was tousled, the strands escaping the bun at her neck. While other guards appeared defiant, guilt was written across her face. Hank took several pictures of her, silently begging her to look up, but she kept her gaze on the ground.

A soldier's megaphone broke through the commotion, and he turned to listen.

"All media," the young man bellowed as he stood atop a platform, "are to reconvene beside the first building." He pointed in that direction. "All media, you are urgently needed."

"They must have found the bodies," one guard laughed. Hank snapped his photograph, sickened by his callousness.

As the other guards chuckled or snickered, a prisoner in the crowd called out, "Agata!"

Hank's eyes swept the crowd to land on a woman in a striped uniform so oversized that it threatened to fall from her thin shoulders. Others in the crowd gathered, chanting, "Agata! Agata!"

"I'll check it out," Rafe said as he took long strides toward them.

Confused, Hank turned slowly toward Agata. Her eyes were still downcast, her face immobile, but a long tear raced down her face to drop on the dirt beside her. As he continued to turn, he heard a gasp, and he looked from Agata to Max, who was standing only feet from him.

Max was clearly startled to see Hank. His eyes were wide, and his hand went instinctively from his side to his chest. As Hank followed his movement, a heavyset male guard who towered over Max stepped forward just behind him and withdrew his hand from his pants pocket. As he quickly removed the pin from a grenade, Hank shouted. Max turned in the direction that Hank was pointing, and Agata looked up and met Hank's eyes.

What followed was the most terrifying sound Hank had ever heard. There was no warning hiss, as a pineapple grenade might make. This one was instantaneous. He could no longer see as the air around him filled with black smoke. All the camp sounds abruptly ceased—the megaphone, the clamor of soldiers and vehicles, and prisoners who had shouted Agata's name.

My eardrums have ruptured, he thought.

2

Hank

Hank opened his eyes to a strange, misty air. He expected to smell the acrid scent of a smoke grenade, but the air was oddly devoid of odor. He was lying flat on his back, the smoke obscuring his view of the skies.

His first thought was of Rafe. He called out his name, but his voice sounded odd, and he received no response. He tried to remember where his friend had been standing when the grenade detonated and was relieved when he recalled that Rafe had moved toward the prisoners. He prayed that it had placed him out of harm's way.

Hank placed his palms against the ground and tried to pull himself into a seated position. He was astonished to observe the length of his body and discover that his legs were missing. That's strange, he thought. They were there just a moment ago. He felt no pain, though he could clearly see that his pants were in tatters and covered in blood. It was odd seeing half a body, and he wondered how he would manage to get anyone's attention if he couldn't get off the ground.

The smoke appeared so pervasive that he wondered if there had been subsequent blasts. He hoped that Rafe was alright. He tried calling his name again. He should have been able to see the guards who had been lined up in front of him and the soldiers beside him, but they seemed to have disappeared. Maybe the medics had already taken them away. Maybe they were coming back for him.

He had the urge to look behind him. When he managed to twist around, he found himself staring into a massive white light. He thought the Soviets had turned on a floodlight to cut through the smoke, as the light appeared too large and solitary to be headlights. At least he now knew the direction to move toward to find the others.

It wasn't until he saw the gates in front of him that he realized he'd been wandering toward a light that appeared to be moving upward as though the terrain was changing. Startled, he peered down at his body. Oh, there they were. He shook one leg and then the other. He chuckled rather nervously and wiped his forehead. He must have been stunned by the blast and only thought they were gone. He felt a rising desire to reach the gates to hold onto them as if he might stumble and faint without their support. His head didn't feel quite right.

He was astonished to reach the gate to find it padlocked. Misha told them during the briefing that a Ukrainian soldier had fired his weapon into the lock until it had fallen apart and slipped to the ground. It had happened hours before Hank had arrived. He had even taken photographs of the prisoners' gaunt faces through the open entryway. Why would the soldier have shot off the padlock only to replace it with another?

And his camera was gone. Now he was irritated. The photographs were undoubtedly some of the most important of his career, and he'd lost his camera. Perhaps it wasn't lost, but only misplaced. Maybe Rafe had it, and Rafe had the first spent film canister.

Hank tried to peer between the bars to the other side, but the smoke obscured everything. He held onto the bars with both hands, and as he looked upward, he realized the German words he'd photographed, *Arbeit Macht Frei,* were gone. His eyes drifted to an odd carving of a young woman's face. Ah, he thought. That explains it. In his confusion, he wandered to a different gate. The soldiers hadn't removed the padlock from this one yet. All he had to do was find his way back to where he'd been.

"You might want to take things slow." The voice was pleasant but authoritative, much like a doctor's voice. "You had quite a jolt."

"Yes," Hank answered as he stared into the area where he thought the voice originated. "My head doesn't feel quite right. I might have a concussion."

The smoke had dissipated, leaving swirling colors in its place that reminded him of the Aurora Borealis. Eventually, he made out the figure of a man with dark hair and olive skin, seated casually only a few feet away. For the briefest of moments, he thought it was Rafe. But, as the skies grew brighter, he realized the facial features were very different. While Rafe's nose and jaw tended to appear chiseled, this man's were not, and his eyes seemed larger and darker.

"Do you know where Rafe is?" Hank asked. "My partner. He's a war correspondent," he added.

"Rafe was not injured," the man answered. "He reached the prisoners and was well beyond the blast zone."

"And the prisoners? Were they injured?"

"They were not."

"That's a relief."

"Rafe will live a long life," the man continued casually. "He'll marry after the war, relocate to America, and have five children. The first will be named after you."

"That's a good joke," Hank answered. He mopped his brow. He thought it would be sweaty, between the blast and his anxiety, but when he withdrew his hand, it was dry. "And you are—?"

"Joseph," the man answered.

"Well, it's good to meet you, Joe," Hank answered. "I'm—"

"I know who you are," Joe interjected smoothly. "You might want to sit down, Hank." He gestured toward a stone that jutted out from a stonewall fence adjacent to the gate.

Hank didn't care to sit down; he preferred to find Rafe and his camera. Yet, as he stared into the eyes of the man seated nearby, he found his hands groping for the stone seat. It was cold to the touch, and when he sat down, he had the strange sensation of energy emanating from it. "How do you know my name? Have we met before?"

"You're on the other side, Hank."

He glanced at the gate and then outward, as though expecting to see prisoners and Allied soldiers filling the courtyard. "Oh. Then, where is everybody?" He glanced at the skies. He shouldn't have been able to see the Aurora Borealis in the afternoon. "What time is it?"

"No, Hank." Joe's voice was patient. "You're on the other side of life."

"The other side of life," Hank chuckled, "is death."

"Some might say that."

"That's a horrible joke to play on someone," he said sadly. "It was nice to meet you, Joe, but I have work to do." He rose and took a few steps away from the gate, but found he could go no further. There were no physical barriers between him and his destination, but his foot became so heavy that he could not lift it to keep moving forward.

"Perhaps, it was your time." Although Joe was seated further behind him, his voice seemed to fill the air.

As Hank continued peering ahead, the colorful skies appeared to part, revealing a circle with a hazy outline. It was as though he was standing at the edge of a cliff and staring over it into a scene that was starkly different from the brilliant skies surrounding the gate. It appeared to be shades of brown, gray, and drab green. As he watched, he discovered four bodies lying prone on the ground with a growing number of uniformed people surrounding them. Medics, he thought. He'd certainly seen enough of them in his career. They obscured his view of the injured, and his eyes swept over the growing circle to find a surreal mix of skeletal people, many with blankets around their shoulders, while fit and robust soldiers rushed all around them.

Regardless of how long he stood there, he could not see beyond the circle.

Finally, he turned around to find Joe still seated on the stone beside the gate. "I can't be dead," Hank said flatly.

"You certainly are not," Joe answered smoothly.

"Well, that's a relief."

"The soul is eternal, Hank, and you have entered a different dimension."

"No," Hank said. "You don't understand. I can't be here. I have a wife and three children—"

"Dottie will be fine," Joe said. "So will your children, Mary, Susanna, and Ray. Funny how both Ray and Rafe have the same birth names. Raphael, isn't it?"

"How do you know their names?"

"I know all about you, Hank. You were born Henry Mullins in a little town in North Carolina called Lumberton, back in 1898. You weren't born in a hospital, but your three children were born at Thompson Hospital, weren't they?"

Hank placed his hand above his heart, expecting it to be thumping out of control. Oddly, he felt nothing. He did not want to see any more of the prison courtyard. He returned slowly to the stone seat opposite Joe and sat numbly.

"You married Dottie just before you enlisted in the military. It was 1916, wasn't it, Hank? And the 'war to end all wars' was raging. You were eighteen years old when you landed in Europe, and you soon discovered your calling was not to carry a rifle but a camera." When Hank did not respond, Joe continued, "The war ended, but your wanderlust had just begun. And, sadly, the

Great War did not end all wars, as you discovered. Shall we go back in time, Hank?"

~~~~~

April 1, 1939, Madrid, Spain

It was April Fools' Day as Hank strode quickly down the narrow hotel corridor. Although he was turning 41 this summer, he moved like a much younger man. He was slender and wiry, his shirt sleeves rolled up to reveal sinewy muscles tanned from years spent outdoors. In one hand, he carried a typed message he'd just picked up from the front desk, and in the other, a twenty-dollar American bill.

He heard the sound of men's voices long before he reached the hotel bar. It was a cacophony of accents, perpetually seeming as if everyone spoke at once, with no one listening. Any one or all of them were likely to pop up at any moment and rush from the room, a constant adrenaline rush of breaking news and urgent deadlines.

One voice rose above the others. He spoke perfect English in a cultured Spanish accent, but with the edge of too many drinks. "I swear it is true," he was saying. "Planet Earth is the battleground for good versus evil. Revelation 12, verses seven to nine. When Satan was cast out of Heaven—and I paraphrase—he was hurled to Earth and his angels with him. The battle continues here, my friends."

Hank burst through the doorway. "Don't listen to a word he says," he announced as several grunted their greetings or held their drinks high in tribute. "He
~~~~~

is a baby-faced youngster not yet schooled in the ways of the world—and a Catholic to boot."

"Go to hell," the other man said.

Hank slapped him on the shoulder. "According to you, I'm already there." He dropped the twenty-dollar bill on the table in front of him.

The younger man picked up the bill and held it in front of him. "Care to explain?"

"I do, in fact." Hank pulled out a chair. "Dario, drinks all around!" He settled into his seat as his eyes wandered over the appreciative crowd. He hesitated as his eyes landed on a man in the far corner who seemed oddly familiar. He appeared to be alone, his dark hair and skin blending into the shadows, as he quietly watched him. He glanced around the room, but when he looked back, the man was gone. He took a breath and turned back to his friend. "You have won a bet again, Rafe, and I always pay up. Twenty for you and drinks on me. The war is over."

"I knew the war was over days ago."

"Yes, but Franco just announced it. It is now official." He raised his voice so all could hear. "The Spanish Civil War is over, and Franco has declared himself the leader of the country!"

As the bartender set glasses of ale on the table in front of them, Rafe said, "I don't know why you sound so fucking happy, Hank. Evil has won yet again."

"Be careful with your voice," Hank chided, but he was only half-joking. He leaned forward. "There are spies everywhere."

"Don't I know it," Rafe grumbled. He ran a hand through his abundant black hair, but a lock fell stubbornly across his brow. His thick brows were knit, and his dark eyes troubled.

Hank grew somber. "Are your parents well?"

Rafe shrugged. "Last I heard from them. The mail is nonexistent, as you well know."

"They are still in France?"

He nodded. "Four months now. They are safe there, safe from Franco. He will seek retaliation now, and there will be nothing in Spain left to stop him."

"Will you join your family in France or cover the aftermath?"

Rafe took a long swig of his ale and wiped his mouth with the back of his hand. "France has officially ended *La Retirada*. In only the last four months, nearly half a million of my people have fled Spain for France, and they have declared the camps overflowing."

"But your family is not in the camps."

"It makes no difference. Spaniards are *persona non grata*."

"Then you'll cover the aftermath?"

Rafe shook his head. "I am marked, *mi amigo*. I have not been kind to Franco and his forces. As long as there is a newspaper still in print with my name in it, it is a death sentence for me here." He peered into Hank's eyes in the gloom of the bar. "What will you do, *mi amigo Americano*?"

Hank slapped the piece of paper onto the table between them, patting it as though it were a friendly dog's head. "Orders just in. I am going to Germany—after a rendezvous with Dottie."

"Are you crazy?"

Hank shook his head. "For seeing Dottie? It's been—"

"Of course not. You should have gone home long before now, and you know it." Before Hank could respond, Rafe continued, "But why Germany? It's like jumping from one fire to another—and Hitler is far more powerful than Franco could ever be. Remember Guernica."

"How could I ever forget it? Anyway, the magazine wants me on the front lines. With the war ending here, the lines have shifted."

"What front lines? Memelland?"

"Memelland is done. My editor has it on good authority that Germany will soon invade Poland."

"They wouldn't dare."

"The code name is Fall Weiss."

"Code name," Rafe repeated, taking a hefty swig of ale.

"That means the source is someone in Hitler's inner circle. No one else would know it," Hank said conspiratorially.

"Or it was made up for a twenty." Rafe shook the bill before returning it to the table.

"Why do you always have to be so cynical?"

"I am a realist, Hank. I have just seen my entire country destroyed. It is every man for himself." He called for another drink. "And why are you returning to Europe? The war is over here. You should be on your way home to America to your lovely wife and children. Kick back, Hank. Relax. Take it easy for a change."

"But the job is here. And," Hank added with a flourish as he patted the piece of paper in front of him, "there is a job for you as well."

Rafe froze with his glass halfway to his lips. He set it down carefully. "Doing what?"

"Same thing you've been doing here," Hank answered. "Besides, between the two of us, we have all Europe's major languages covered."

Rafe shrugged. "Not all, *mi amigo.* Not by a long shot."

"Close enough, for where we're going."

Rafe frowned. "Why would you want to set foot near the German border? You saw what the Nazis did to Guernica."

"Yes," Hank said. "I saw what they did." It had been Guernica that had changed Rafe. Before Guernica, the Spanish Civil War had been a cultural war between opposing ideologies. On the far left were the Republicans, a mishmash of socialists, communists, and anarchists. They counted among them the majority of the rural population, who had become enraged at the excesses of the wealthy elite while toiling seven days a week and still struggling to survive. On the right, led by Franco, were the Nationalists, fascists who believed in an elite ruling class and dictatorship.

Guernica had not only changed Rafe but had changed everything. With Hitler and Mussolini supporting the fascists, Hitler had sent his *Luftwaffe* to bomb the city indiscriminately, killing over 1,600 civilians at a time when the population numbered only 7,000. The town was demolished within three hours. The terror from above was something the world had never witnessed before, and it was said that two years later, the survivors were still traumatized by the horror unleashed on them. The atrocity had garnered international condemnation, but had done nothing to stop the fascists from rising across Europe. It was then that Rafe became convinced that Europe was not heading into a period of differing cultural and political opinions, but rather a battle between good and evil.

"So," Rafe was saying, "why would you possibly want to go into the lair of the lion?"

Hank finished his drink and leaned back in his chair. He rapped the table absent-mindedly. After a long moment of thought, he said, "We know what Hitler is capable of doing. We have seen it with our own eyes in Guernica and elsewhere. We know that Spain was a test for fascism, and now the fascists have won. If this truly is the battle between good and evil that you have been going on about for two years now, someone has to tell the world." He tapped the camera that always hung around his neck. "I trust myself, and I trust you, to tell the story accurately and honestly."

Rafe nodded unconvincingly and stared at a spot on the floor.

"I leave at daybreak for America," Hank said. "I'll be back in one week. And I want you to go with me."

"You'll supply the car?"

"The magazine will supply everything."

"And how do you propose getting me across the border?"

"Ah, you of little faith. The magazine has also thought of everything." Hank stood and carefully replaced his chair. The buzz in the bar was constant, gaining volume as the hours crept past. He leaned forward so only Rafe could hear. "Daybreak. Will you drive me to the airport? The taxis are not dependable at the moment."

"You will still be drunk at daybreak."

"I plan to be. But you, my friend, must sober up, because you will drive me while I sleep."

As Hank began to leave, Rafe said, "I'll be there."

"And Germany?"

"I'll go there, too."

"Don't you want to know what they're willing to pay you?"

Rafe shrugged. "I would have gone for free."

3

Agata

The skies were a color that Agata had never before witnessed. They appeared to be all the colors of the rainbow at once, and yet swirling like the river she'd fished in as a child, as the trout converged in the late afternoon. She thought she almost saw the trout as she stared, but as the moment dragged on, she realized she was seeing the colors of circling clouds that eventually converged into a dark, ominous gray.

It was silent. There were no songbirds joyously singing as if every moment was a cause for celebration. Unlike her childhood expeditions, no frogs or crickets were emerging at dusk. There were no voices, though she slowly began to realize that people surrounded her. Their mouths moved all at once as they frantically rushed in, their eyes revealing a peculiar jumble of horror and satisfaction.

Agata remembered now. She remembered the Jews crowded a short distance away, chanting her name. A tall, burly man with more weight than she'd seen since the early war years had demanded something in Russian of those who had been unceremoniously gathered. Someone else had translated his words into both German and Polish. "Which one of you is Agata?" he demanded.

She couldn't remember if she had responded. At that moment, a deafening noise had rocked the earth under her feet. She had a brief memory of being thrown into the air, all arms and legs, and then others' arms and legs intermingled with her own, interspersed with pieces of fabric, shoes, and blood.

Agata attempted to hear the men shouting just inches from her before realizing that the explosion had deafened her. She tried to look at their faces; she attempted to turn her head to look into the crowd, for surely Elsa had been there only moments ago. Her mind cried out for the men to look for Elsa. She could not be hurt. She could not have died. Not now. Not after everything they had survived.

But her voice never reached her lips.

She attempted to raise herself onto her elbows and was surprised to find she could. In fact, she felt surprisingly light as she had when she swam in the river. She was buoyant.

But as she came to a seated position, she looked down at her body to find that she was gushing blood. Once more, she attempted to cry out, for she could not sustain such a massive blood loss. They had to act quickly.

They were moving away from her, and with the words she longed to shout still frozen somewhere inside her, she tried again to get their attention. She stood quickly and effortlessly. Amazed at her strength and endurance, she exhaled in relief, only to recoil when a strangled voice beneath her rasped. Agata turned to find her body still on the ground. She lay flat on her back, her eyes wide but unseeing, a rattle in her throat expelling a mixture of blood and mucus.

It was then that she noticed the fog rolling in. It was heavy and furious, as though the storm clouds that she'd witnessed only a moment before were descending to earth. She could no longer see the throngs of people in their threadbare clothing, their faces smeared with months of dirt and grime, their bodies no more than skeletal remains, that somehow managed to keep breathing. She could no longer hear them chanting her name. The others that had been gathered around her were gone as well, as were the soldiers who had demanded they stand in single file, as she had commanded the prisoners so many times.

The air remained silent as it closed in around her. She was sickened by her body lying on the ground, the red liquid continuing to pool as though the ice and soil demanded every last drop of her blood. Cod at the fish market was treated better, their bodies resting on slabs of clean, fresh ice, not the churned, desecrated camp mud.

A blinding white light stung her eyes. As she shielded herself from it, she realized it was cutting through the gray clouds with pinpoint precision, opening a path for her.

She did not wish to leave. Elsa was here. She had to see to Elsa's welfare. She had to make sure she was still alive. Survive, Elsa, she wanted to shout. All you have to do is survive another day. You can do it, Elsa. You have to do it.

Then the gray clouds were gone, and in their place was a tunnel beckoning to her. She seemed to rise, but try though she might, she could not see the vast complex of dusty red barracks and the scores of people who she knew were there. The endless smoke that rose from the crematoriums was gone. The sickening stench was absent. There was nothing, nothing but her soul trying to reunite with her body so she could find Elsa.

She didn't remember her journey. She didn't recall when she could no longer see her body lying on the ground, and when the white, thick fog enveloped her completely.

Agata only knew that in the next instance, she stood in front of a pair of gates. They were not the ugly black gates at the entrance to the camp that proclaimed "Arbeit Macht Frei," or "work sets you free." These gates pulsed as though they were made of energy. She attempted to grasp the pickets, but her hands stopped just short of touching them. A padlock hung where the two sides met. As she stared at it, it transformed from pearl white to glowing silver, then morphed into oscillating gold.

Unable to touch the pickets or the padlock, she tilted her head back to view the top, but the gates did not end. Instead, they stretched for miles into the sky until a mountain of white, frothy fog obscured them. An image of her childhood swirled through her mind. She sat beside her mother in a church with stained glass windows and rich, dark wood, her eyes riveted on a cross behind the altar as the priest spoke of the pearly gates of Saint Peter. It was a homily that her father scoffed at when he heard it, which cemented his decision never to attend the church services with them.

Yet, here she was, a world away from the camp and her life in Poland, away from the filth, the mud, the stink, and the cruelty. All that existed now was her soul before these gates, and they were locked.

"I've been padlocked," she breathed, surprised that her voice had returned. "I committed murder."

"What did you say?"

The voice startled her, and she whirled around. "Where are you?" she demanded.

"Over here," the voice responded calmly.

The fog parted to reveal a woman sitting on a log. Her hair was short and white, framing a face with enormous brown eyes. She wore a gown that undulated in white, silver, and gold threads. It reached from her neck, covering her entire body, including her feet.

"Who are you?" Agata breathed.

"I am Celeste."

"Celeste," she repeated. She did not recall an archangel named Celeste.

"Celeste," the woman also repeated. As if reading her mind, she added, "And I am not an archangel. I am your guide."

Agata managed to chuckle wryly. "My guide. You know nothing about me."

"Oh, but I do." Celeste remained seated, her voice both commanding and quiet. "You were born Agata Goldberg."

"This is a dream," Agata said, holding her head in her hands. "I've been knocked unconscious. Wake up, wake up, wake up."

"I can assure you that this is not a dream."

"Wake up, wake up," Agata repeated.

"You prefer to be known as Agata Heinrich. It is the name on your forged identification."

Agata sucked in her breath. She dropped her hands to stare at the woman.

"It was your mother's name, was it not?" Celeste smiled patiently. When Agata did not respond, she continued, "You were born in 1922 in a German town not far from the Polish border."

"Fürstenwalde," she said flatly.

"It is a beautiful town, is it not? There is a very important train station there. Trains and beer gardens."

"There's a lot more to it than that."

"Of course, there is. Your father, Ira Goldberg, worked as a janitor at the port there, did he not?"

At the mention of her father's name, Agata's heart grew heavy. Her father had been an avid reader with a voracious appetite for knowledge. He could pontificate on ancient Greeks and Romans, emerging medical advancements, and algebra and geometry. Yet, he worked the night shift mopping the floors of warehouses situated along the Spree River. Founded in the 13th century, Fürstenwalde had always been a vital port for goods moving up and down the river. Since the 19th century, a constant volume of crates had been transported into warehouses for further distribution by rail. Beer and other goods were also stored in the warehouses before they were loaded onto ships. Her father often arrived home after the sun had risen, his back bent and feet swollen from hours of mopping, yet she had never heard him complain.

At school, however, all the children knew that her father was a Jew in a lowly job, and the harassment was often more than she thought she could bear. She was swift to point out that her mother was not Jewish and neither was she, no matter what they said. Had not been Jewish, she corrected herself.

"At the age of six, your sister was born," Celeste continued, bringing her attention back to the conversation.

"Elsa."

"Yes. Elsa. Shall we go back to the day of her birth?"

"I don't need to." Agata straightened her back. "I lived through it once. I don't need to again."

"Ah." Celeste seemed to grow larger as she studied Agata, her gown billowing out so it became one with the mist. "But, you see, this is how it works here."

"How what works?"

"Every event in your lifetime has been lived through the filter of your own beliefs and convictions. When you reach this side, you must revisit those events through the emotions and repercussions of those you impacted."

Agata's head began to pound as her emotions started to spin. The words "every event" echoed in her mind. She could not relive some events. She had spent a lifetime building walls to protect herself, particularly since the rise of Hitler and the invasion of Poland. She could not relive them. She simply could not. "Is this hell?"

Celeste cocked her head. "Did you think hell would look like this?"

She glanced at the padlocked gates. "No. But why would you punish me by forcing me to relive my life?"

"It is not punishment, my dear. They are lessons in understanding and compassion."

Agata opened her mouth to protest, but Celeste was gone in an instant. In her place was a long, immaculate hallway that smelled of disinfectants and cleaning solutions. On either side of the hallways were open doors, and the muffled sounds of coughs, groans, and moans. As Agata made her way down the hallway, she knew where she was, and she recognized herself before she reached the end, where half a dozen uncomfortable wood chairs were neatly arranged.

The young Agata sat alone, as she had for hours, a thin picture book gripped in her hands, her palms covered in perspiration. It was an oppressively hot day, and although the windows were open in the hospital rooms, there was no cross breeze to speak of.

She wore chunky black shoes, neat socks, and a dress that had been recently ironed but was now wrinkled from hours of fidgeting. The book and the pictures had long ago been memorized, and Agata could think of no other way to entertain her mind. She needed to use the bathroom, but there did not appear to be one in this hallway, and she had been told to remain seated there.

Sometime earlier, Agata thought her wait might be nearing an end, as her mother's two sisters, Gertrud and Herta, had arrived. They had passed her in a flurry without acknowledging her presence, whisked along by a nurse in a crisp blue and white uniform with a starched white cap perched atop her short chestnut hair, her shoes oddly silent on the polished floors as Gertrud's and Herta's rudely clopped along.

Agata thought she heard a baby's cry, but the sound was distant and weak. She thought this would be a joyous occasion, but the longer she sat there, the more frightened she became. She wiped away the tears that spilled along her cheek and longed for her mother's kind embrace and reassurance that all was well.

A movement caught her attention, and she glanced to the end of the hall. A nurse was just about to go through a set of double doors when she turned around and smiled at her. She looked oddly familiar with her white hair and kind expression, but she couldn't place where she might have seen her. Agata had never been to a hospital before. Then, the woman was gone, but something about her presence lingered in the air.

When no one emerged from her mother's room down the hall, Agata worked up enough courage to stand, set her book in her chair, and inch her way down the corridor. It was dreadfully long, and she was frightened of the open doors. She felt their pain and discomfort as she moved along; the acute spasm of a man coughing over an open pail, an elderly woman longing to tell the nurses that she was still in agony despite the medication, but who was unable to speak.

Agata felt everything acutely, and as she neared her mother's closed door, the air became heavier. She quietly pushed open the door enough to peer inside.

Her mother was covered in sturdy, white sheets that reached over her chest. Her father, Ira, stood on one side of her, grasping her hand and muttering something she couldn't quite hear. On the other side were Gertrud and Herta, both of whom were sobbing.

Then her father's voice became amplified in Agata's mind as he cried, "Anna, Anna, come back! We need you, Anna, your girls need you!"

Agata opened the door a little wider. A crib was near her mother's bed. The nurse she had seen escorting her aunts leaned over the lowered rail, briskly working over something inside. Agata tiptoed across the floor behind her aunts' backs as she peeked inside to discover a tiny baby swaddled in white linens as the nurse finished cleaning her face and placed a pacifier in her minuscule mouth.

The nurse abruptly looked up to find her standing there. "You shouldn't be in here!" she snapped.

Agata's aunts whirled around, and Ira rushed from the other side of the bed. He placed both hands on Agata's shoulders, but instead of marching her back down the hall as she expected, he led her to a chair set against the wall.

"Agata," he said. He repeated her name at least twice more. He was a handsome man with thick, dark hair, kind brown eyes, and a wide forehead. Though his eyes remained tender and warm, they also conveyed intense suffering. In that moment, Agata felt his heart shattering, his soul inconsolable.

Herta left Gertrud's side and came to stand beside Ira. They both dropped to their knees in front of her. As Ira sank his head into her lap, each sob wracked her small body, and she longed to stand and rush to her mother's side.

"Agata," Herta said sternly, "you must listen to me." Agata forced her eyes from her father to her aunt. Herta was a large woman who towered over most men, her buxom figure commanding attention and respect.

Her honey-brown hair was cut short and styled in finger waves, appearing oddly immaculate amidst the turmoil surrounding them. Her hazel eyes were red and puffy as she spoke. "Your mother is gone. She isn't coming back—"

"Don't!" Ira cried out, raising his head to lash out at Herta.

Agata focused on the tear stains in her lap as Herta continued.

"She must know. There is no sugar-coating what just happened. Agata, look at me." As Agata dragged her eyes upward to meet her aunt's, she continued, "It is time that you grew up."

"She's six!" Ira protested.

"You must grow up, Agata, because there is a baby in that crib and your mother is gone. You must be that baby's mother. Your father cannot do this alone."

Agata's attention became riveted on her aunt's words. She vaguely felt her own tears rolling down her cheeks.

"You must take care of yourself now, Agata, and you must care for your new little sister. There is no one else."

Gertrud stepped to the crib. Cradling the newborn, she set her into Agata's lap, arranging her hands to support her. "This is Elsabeth," she said. Gertrud was shorter and thinner than her sister but with the same reddened, hazel eyes. "Your mother chose the name." She began to choke on her words as all three adults struggled to contain their emotions. After a moment, she continued. "Your mother would want you to take good care of her. We'll find a wet nurse, but you must keep her clean, her diapers changed, and well fed. Do you understand? She is your responsibility now."

Ira stood. "Surely, you can't think that a six-year-old—"

"You must leave, Ira," Herta said, also rising.

He pointed to his wife. "Anna is here!"

"She won't be for long, and we can't protect you anymore."

Agata felt the life in her lap, but her attention was riveted on the adults.

"Ira," Gertrud said, her voice softer than her sister's, "you were tolerated because of our father's position. Now that Anna is gone, we can't protect you anymore. You will be fired from your job. You can no longer live in our home—"

"But the girls! Surely, you can find it in your hearts to help these defenseless little girls!"

"They are Jewish now, Ira."

"They are half-Christian!"

"Not in Germany. They are Jews. And it has only been our father's position that has held back the community from expelling you. Now that Anna is gone, you must leave."

"But—"

"You must leave," Herta said sternly. "You must do it for these girls."

Agata stared at the newborn in her lap. She was swaddled in a linen wrap so that only her head emerged. She had red, chubby cheeks, a wide stub nose, and a delicate covering of short, dark hair. Her pacifier slipped from her mouth, and as she struggled to turn her head back toward it, her lips were tiny and pink. She looked like a little angel. And Agata hated her.

In that instant, Agata wanted nothing more than to jump up from the chair and hand this bundle over to somebody else. If she got rid of it, it would bring her mother back. It was this package in linen that had killed her mother, but there might be hope yet that Anna would return to her. She had to return. She was six years old, and she needed her mother.

Then the baby turned its eyes on Agata. They were enormous, dark eyes, and they seemed to contain a wisdom that was not possible in a human, let alone a newborn. She opened her mouth to reveal hard little gums, and she waved her head this way and that in search of a nipple.

Agata balanced the child on her lap as she reached for the pacifier and placed it back in the child's mouth. The baby cooed. Her eyes seemed to fill with love, a love that became threads that bound the two of them together, wrapping Agata in its invisible embrace. "Elsa," she breathed. "I am your mother now."

4

Max

The smoke filled the air. At times, it was so heavy that Max Kursell was sure it would leave thick black soot all over him. He had seen from afar smoldering ruins from hard-fought battles, and this was certainly heavier than any cannon fire, much less a handheld grenade. He wondered if the grenade had only been the first of several explosions.

Max tried to shout for help, but he could not find his voice. He placed his hand on his throat and was horrified to discover that when he pulled his palm away, it was covered in blood. He hadn't felt any pain. In fact, he didn't feel anything at all.

Panic set in as he realized that complete silence surrounded him. He had heard stories of a formidable soundlessness in the camp, as it was against the rules for any prisoners to speak, lest they be punished. But this was different.

There should have been a great deal of noise. The Soviets and Ukrainians had arrived in large numbers in clamorous tanks and trucks. Military officers should be shouting orders. Those affected by the grenade should be screaming for assistance. Unless, he thought, they were all too wounded or stunned.

He realized he was standing, wandering aimlessly through a fog of war. He looked down to find that his legs were unscathed; so were his arms. He patted his torso, moving up to his throat again. It was dry. When he pulled his hand away, there was no blood on it, not even from his first contact only a moment before.

Max laughed, the sound reverberating around him. He had evaded being wounded. He'd made it through the war! He had survived and even thrived in Poland for six years of Nazi occupation. Now, he'd been able to convince the Soviets that he was on their side.

He nearly ran headlong into the gate. It had not been there a moment ago; he was sure of it. Perhaps it had been. He felt confused and disoriented. He found the padlock and swore under his breath before he grabbed the gates with both hands and rattled them. "Unlock this gate!" he shouted, his voice echoing as if he stood in an amphitheater. "Unlock it, I say! Right this instance!"

"Does it look like the camp gate to you?"

The voice startled him, and he whirled to the right and then to the left. The voice had seemed to come from all around him, encompassing him, encircling him. It was deep and guttural as if a wolf had suddenly found the capacity for words.

"Who are you?" he demanded. "Where are you?"

Max was met only with silence. He began to feel as if his torso was becoming constricted, and he struggled to breathe. "Do you know who I am?" he bellowed.

After another moment of contained stillness, the voice responded. "Of course, I do, Maxwell Erich Kursell."

Max froze. As the disembodied voice had spoken, the air around him had filled once more with odorless smoke the color of pitch. A senseless terror gripped him with such force that he struggled to remain in control of his faculties.

"Go ahead," the voice continued. "Look again. Does it resemble the gate to the camp?"

Haltingly, Max looked upward from the padlock. "No," he said. "It does not. The words are gone. But," he added, "I have been wandering. Perhaps I am at a different gate." He had no sooner spoken the last word than a cherub's face in the top center of the gate began to morph. It turned crimson and grew larger, the serene expression contorting into a monstrous image with a sinister smile, the tongue extending outward. He recoiled from it, dropping his grip on the iron pickets. He stumbled backward. "Where am I?" His voice had lost its studied command and sounded uncertain in the dark, swirling smoke.

"Perhaps, you have died, Max Kursell." The voice sounded throaty and silky now, like an animal stalking its prey.

"If I have died," he swallowed, forcing himself to assume control once more, "then are these the gates of heaven?"

A sinister laughter cackled around him. He felt as though someone had pinched him, but when he spun around, no one was there. He swiveled this way and that until dizziness overtook him. It was a head wound, he thought. I have a head injury. I must get help.

"Show yourself," he commanded.

"Ah. The last command you will ever utter." The smoke seemed to be pushed back and away until he found himself staring at a figure only a few yards away. He leaned in and squinted in an effort to see it more clearly. It must be a man, he thought. The voice had been too deep to be a woman. He appeared to be sitting, but his height was evident even while perched. He wore a cloak the color of graphite, which was so long that it covered his shoes and so high that it almost appeared to reach the brim of a head covering. The covering itself was odd; it was neither a hat nor a hood but both, concealing the face entirely. As Max watched, the smoke appeared to merge with the heavy fabric, creating an undulating mist.

"Who are you?" Max asked.

"I am Abaddon."

"Abaddon." He took a breath. He must remain in control. "And what is it you do here, Abaddon?"

The figure rose, and as it did, Max shrank away. It appeared to be at least three times his size.

"I hold the secret to the gate."

When Max found his voice again, it sounded weak and small. "Are you Satan?"

The figure remained in front of him, vibrating as though it had become a part of the coal-black air.

"There is some mistake," he continued. When Abaddon did not respond, he swallowed and continued, "I can give you whatever you need to open the gate."

"Whatever I need?" The cackle began again. "What is that, Max? Your money? Your material possessions?" The arms became outstretched, reaching at least ten feet in each direction. "At the moment of your death, your money ceased to exist. Everything you ever owned has disappeared."

"But—"

"Money and possessions are nonexistent here. No, Max. All that remains is your soul. Your soul is the key to the gate."

When Abaddon's words eventually faded away from echoing and circling him, Max said, "Then, I have faithfully attended church services every Sunday. You must know that."

"Was your soul there to worship, Max?"

"Well, of course," Max stammered. "That's the only reason people go to church."

"Is it?" When Max did not respond, Abaddon continued, "You see, Max, you cannot bargain with me—nor with anyone on this side. We see through to the essence of your soul. It was not your actions that decided your fate. It was the purpose and meaning that served as the seeds to your actions."

"Purpose and meaning?" he gasped. "My purpose was to survive. My purpose was to remain outside of the camp as a free man, not inside as a prisoner, no better than a caged animal."

"'No better than an animal?' And who made them 'no better than an animal,' Max?"

"Surely, you don't—I—I was only following orders."

Abaddon chuckled. "If you only knew how many times I have heard that."

"But I was—"

"Remember, Max." At the sound of Abaddon's voice, Max became mute, unable to continue. "You cannot bargain with us here. Whatever power you think you have is worthless here. It means nothing, just like your money."

After a long moment, Max found his voice had returned. "Surely, you must know that I never killed anyone."

"'Never killed anyone?' Do you think killing someone requires you to pull the trigger yourself, Max?" A glint of red shone from the depths of the head covering, as if the creature's teeth were the color of blood. "Killing someone sometimes requires a chain. An order, a declaration, a pointed finger. At any point along the chain, the act can be stopped; the chain can be broken. How many people did you select for slaughter?" When Max did not respond, Abaddon continued, "And when you cried and declared you were unable to do it, how many others did you order to participate in your stead?"

"I was too far down the chain to make a difference. Besides, how was I to know what happened in the camp?"

"Ah. Perhaps you thought they would be treated like kings." When Max fumbled for an answer, Abaddon continued, "Of course not, Max. The purpose was to make an example of them. The intent was to make them suffer. Each one had a soul, Max. And each one's soul was no less than your own but equal to your own. Everything else was a façade, Max. Their nationalities, their languages, their cultures... all a façade."

"Who are you?" Max breathed. "Are you God? Are you Satan?"

"It matters not who I am. What matters is who you were, who you became. What matters are the people you harmed, the souls whose lives you ruined, the reverberation of your deeds."

"You said my soul is the key. Then I demand that you open this gate."

"Open the gate, Max? And do you know what lies on the other side?"

As Max peered between the pickets, Armageddon loomed before him. On one side, he witnessed flames and death, shouting and cries, suffering, mayhem, and chaos. Too far on the opposite side for him to see clearly were lights, shields, and—he squinted to see more clearly—were those arms upraised?

"Your demands are worthless here, Max," Abaddon said. His arms seemed to encircle him, and yet, his arms were not solid but black, putrid smoke that threatened to enter his nose and mouth. "There is only one way to open that gate. And we must begin by going back to every moment in your life."

"Why? I have already lived it! Unless—yes, allow me to make different decisions—"

"The decisions have already been made, Max. The moments have already passed. It is time now for us to see them as God does."

"But—" His words were cut off as the arms spun him like a tornado. His breath was wrenched from him, his eyes were blinded, and a deafening roar enveloped him.

~~~~~

The apple hit eight-year-old Max in the forehead as he rushed along the busy street. He felt momentarily stunned as his head jerked backward from the blow; the images of the dusty street and rows of brown brick apartment buildings were replaced by a dizzying array of black spots. His legs and feet took on a life of their own as they stumbled rearwards before righting themselves and jerkily propelling him forward. A steady trickle of blood ran down his forehead and into one eye, nearly blinding him. He barely heard the boys' laughter, an echoing series of guffaws and taunts as he attempted to hurry beyond their range. He knew better than to respond, though he wanted more than anything to call them names and shake his fist. To do so would bring them from their open window above him down a narrow staircase into the street, where they would pummel him until he could bear no more.

And he was late already.

He burst into the Mond-Weiss Bakery, the door hitting the wall before slamming behind him in his haste. The Widow Weiss stood behind the long glass counter. She was a portly woman with a round face and kind, sparkling eyes. She always wore an apron covered in flour and always smelled of spices and fruits. Her daughter, Celina, was a teenager and looked, perhaps, like a younger Mrs. Weiss, her chocolate eyes dancing, and her shoulder-length bob dark and lush. She turned
~~~~~

around from dusting the shelves to greet Max before hesitating as she took in his appearance.

"Max!" Mrs. Weiss exclaimed. She grabbed a towel and hurried around the bakery counter. "What happened to you, dear?"

"I fell," Max answered. He hated to stand still for her to clean the wound on his head, but as she pulled away the towel to fold it over for a fresh spot, he noticed the bright red blood. His heart calmed as she continued. "Celina, bring me another towel, a wet one, please."

Celina rushed to the sink to get the towel wet and carried it to her mother. "Oh, Max," she said sadly, her voice tinged with affection.

Mrs. Weiss continued to clean him up properly. He could not allow his Mama to see him injured.

"Again?" she asked. "Dear Max, my dear child, you mustn't hurry so much that you fall again. I will wait for you, just as I do every evening. I promise you that." Finished, she leaned in to hug him. "Now. I have a special treat for you."

She rushed behind the counter. When she emerged a few seconds later, she motioned toward a bistro table. "Sit, sit, my dear Max. I have a *strucla* for you."

Max dutifully sat on the heavy wood chair while Mrs. Weiss placed a small plate and a cloth napkin in front of him. The aroma of the pastry wafted up, and he closed his eyes as he inhaled. It smelled of almonds, sugar, butter, and cinnamon. He accepted the fork she handed him and dug into the petite slice. He knew from experience that it was three bites, and he savored each warm, delectable piece as long as humanly possible.

"The bread is just coming out of the oven," Mrs. Weiss said from the back of the bakery. The ovens were in full view, positioned directly in line with the front door—a deliberate placement that allowed the aroma to waft through the open door onto the sidewalk beyond. As if remembering that Max had slammed the door behind him, she pulled the bread from the oven, placed it onto a cooling rack, and, while it cooled, she opened the door and put a brick at its base to keep it propped open. There were only a few who could resist the mouthwatering scent of her baked goods.

She took her time moving back to the bread, her eyes wandering to the scrawny little boy sitting with his head tilted back, his eyes closed, the tip of his tongue occasionally jutting out to lick his lips. Max Kursell might be eight years old, but he appeared closer to five. He was shorter than most and so gaunt that a brisk wind might carry him away. But he had a full head of fair blond hair and icy blue eyes, and who knew but someday he might be quite a looker.

Max was just finishing his *strucla* when she finished wrapping the still-hot bread in a thin piece of cheesecloth and placed it in front of him.

"Better take this to your mama," she said as she collected the plate, fork, and napkin. She hesitated. "Do you have food to go with this, Max?"

Max nodded but averted his eyes. "Mama is making soup."

"Oh? That's good. What is in it?"

He shrugged. "Radishes. Maybe a carrot!" He looked up and smiled.

"Do you think she might have a need for a piece of fish or two?"

"Fish?" His eyes gleamed.

"I had too much delivered today. She would be doing me a monumental favor if she took two pieces off me."

Max nodded and kept nodding as she quickly wrapped two pieces of food in a separate piece of cheesecloth. They were coated in such thick layers of crust, he knew they might never taste the thin slice of fish within, if there indeed was any. But it didn't matter. The crust itself was delicious. He knew it would be.

Mrs. Weiss walked him to the door as he held the two packages in his tiny hands. "Now, don't run too quickly," she admonished gently. "You don't want to fall again and split your head or spill the food."

As Max hurried down the sidewalk, she walked into the street, now deserted as suppertime approached, and made sure the boys in the next block noticed her. Folding her arms across her stout body, she continued walking toward them, narrowing her eyes. As Max approached that apartment building, they ducked inside and did not emerge even after he had passed beneath them.

~~~~~

Max hunched next to the living room radio as he carefully rolled the dial to receive a clearer signal. The radio was a monstrously large piece of furniture and something they would never have been able to afford, but his mother had received it as partial payment for sewing numerous items of clothing. It appeared to have been damaged, its wood marred, and the reception left
~~~~~

much to be desired. But it had opened up a new world to him.

He was eighteen years old now, his pale blond hair cropped short and his blue eyes sharp and riveting. He hadn't become tall and muscular like the movie stars that were all the rage now; his growth had been stunted at barely five-foot-four, and his body was just a slightly older version of his spindly childhood physique. He carefully listened to the phrase on the radio and attempted to repeat it verbatim. "Thank you," he said in English with a contrived British accent. "You're welcome."

"What are you saying now?" his mother asked from the dining table a few feet away. The table was piled high with bolts of material on one side and semi-finished clothing on the other. In between, Felka Kursell peddled the old sewing machine, her back hunched over the needle as she joined two pieces of fabric together.

Max repeated the phrases in their native Polish language.

"I don't know why you bother with all that," she said.

"I am learning both English and German," Max said proudly. "Germany and Great Britain are going to join forces to rule all of Europe."

"Hmph," she said, her voice blending in with the whir of the sewing machine. "I imagine the other countries will have a thing or two to say about that."

It had been this way for as long as Max could remember. He had no memories of his father, though a picture of him remained in a place of honor on the small fireplace mantle. He had been a slender man with rounded shoulders, his hair so pale that it almost appeared white. He had worked at a dairy on the outskirts of town. One day, when Max was barely two years old, his father had been kicked in the head by a cow. It had muddled his brain and speech, so that neighbors had said he'd been kicked silly. The injuries had been extensive, but he'd managed to linger for a few months before passing away.

With his father gone, Felka had become the sole provider. She had already been sewing clothes for the wealthier people in town, including Mrs. Weiss, who also owned the apartment building where they lived. After her husband's death, she took to sewing almost every day. In the evenings, she left home to work overnight in a small factory that manufactured pipes.

She set the piece she'd been working on to the side and moaned under her breath as she stood. She placed both hands in the small of her back as she attempted to stand up straight. While Max continued to repeat phrases he heard on the radio, she crossed to the mantle and retrieved a jar. Rifling through it, she extracted several bills and ironed them out with her hand before returning the jar to its place on the mantle.

"Max," she said, "please stop by Mrs. Weiss's bakery on your way to work today." She placed the bills on top of the radio. When she spoke again, she sounded weary. "Please tell her that I'll have the rest of this week's rent tomorrow."

Max took the money and shoved it into his pocket.

"You're going to be late for work, Max."

"I won't," he said, though he stood and turned off the radio. He rehearsed the phrases he'd learned in

English as if he were speaking to someone. He held a small, weathered English-Polish dictionary in his hands that he'd purchased from a library sale for a pittance, but he rarely opened it. It seemed like a lot of gibberish to him.

"Why do you bother with that language? You speak German and Polish. That is all you need."

"Someday, I might speak to someone from England."

She snickered. "They will have to come here. There is no possibility you will ever travel there."

Max moved to the door. "See you in the morning, Mama."

Felka followed him. As he opened the door, she leaned in and kissed him on the cheek. "Stay safe, my darling Max. I love you."

"I love you, too, Mama."

"When you get home later, there is some cheese on the counter and leftover soup in the kettle on the stove. You'll need to reheat it. It won't be any good cold."

"Thanks, Mama." Max held the door for her as she slipped through. She did not wear a coat, though it would be chilly when she left work in the wee hours of the morning before daylight had begun to peak through the night. She'd once owned a coat, but Max suspected that she'd sold it years ago to buy food. Poland was frigid in the winter, and though she would have the sniffles all winter long, she would continue to go to work. She also did not carry a pocketbook or wallet, as she had nothing in either.

Max followed her down the steps. When they reached the street, she waved to him as she hurried off toward one end of town, while Max took a more leisurely stroll to his afternoon job in the opposite direction. He had plenty of time, as it was close, and he preferred to put off getting there until the last possible minute, as he had grown tired of sweeping the shop floors and the street in front of it about as quickly as he'd begun working there.

As he rounded the corner, he was surprised to discover a large crowd forming in front of the general store. He made his way past the people to the source of their interest. The shopkeeper had set up a television in the window and turned up the volume so everyone could hear.

It was not the first time Max had seen this television. It was the only one he knew that existed in their bustling town of Będzin. It was as sturdy and large as their dining table, a piece of furniture as well as a place to show moving pictures. The picture itself was grainy and flickering, its quality alternately improving or worsening depending on how the shopkeeper adjusted the rabbit ears. Despite the volume, the voice was muffled through the plate glass, and Max leaned in to listen more closely.

The event was the annual Adolf Hitler March of German Youth, or the *Adolf-Hitler-Marsch der deutschen Jugend.* The imagery was like nothing Max had ever seen before: row after row of boys in matching shirts, shorts, socks, and shoes with neat ties. They marched with their arms and hands precisely folded over their torsos. As they neared the *Führer,* their leader—a boy who appeared younger than Max—issued a command, and they stopped, turning their faces in unison toward Adolf

Hitler and giving the Sieg Heil salute in perfect synchronization.

Hitler responded in kind, and with a slight wave of his hand, the group continued onward. Wave after wave of young boys repeated the march and salute before Hitler began to speak. His voice was low and calm, almost a monotone. Then, a few moments into the speech, he lifted his hand and punched at the air. His voice became more rapid, his movements more animated. As Max watched, mesmerized, he worked himself into a frothing, passionate, animated speech filled with rage and indignation.

The problem, he said, was the Jews. They owned everything. They owned the stores, the banks, and the cultural centers. They were a separate race, inferior to the Aryan race to which Germans belonged, and yet they prevented Germans from doing better because they controlled everything.

Several women clucked as they left their places in front of the store. They were followed by men shaking their heads. Yet, Max remained, transfixed. It was only when he realized that time was passing and he would be late for work that he managed to pull himself away from the television.

As he hurried down the street toward the bakery to give Mrs. Weiss the only money they had, he knew what he wanted to do with his life. He would not go to work at the dairy to pull on some cow's teats, and he wouldn't spend the rest of his life sweeping a rich man's floor.

No. He was going to be one of Hitler's Youth.

5

Hank, North Carolina, USA, August 1939

Hank sat at the head of the dining table, his wife beside him. She hadn't changed much in twenty years; she was still as attractive as ever—at least to him. Her strawberry-blond hair was shoulder-length and pulled back from her face into gleaming curls meant to imitate Ann Sheridan, her favorite actress. Hank didn't have the heart to tell her the style looked nothing like the actress, and he would have loved it just the same if it had been drooping in the rain. Her eyes were bright and alert, and he couldn't get enough of them. Although he carried her picture with him, it was black-and-white, and he missed seeing those gorgeous blue eyes.

His gaze wandered to their eldest, Mary, who sat beside her mother and was the spitting image of her. His heart ached as he realized Mary was soon to be nineteen years old; in all his travels, she'd been frozen in his mind as nine or ten, her little hand held in his as they walked to the ice cream parlor or the general store for penny candy.

As Dottie and Mary spoke about a dress Mary had seen in the store's window, Hank's attention roamed to the opposite side of the table, where Susanna and Ray were bickering good-naturedly. Susanna was two years younger than Mary and was more prone to live in her dreams than her older sister, who tended to be serious and mature. She also had a significant crush on Clark Gable and had the refrigerator calendar marked for the January release of *Gone with the Wind*. Hank imagined she'd strut around like Scarlett O'Hara for months. She already had the book dog-eared and worn and had dutifully followed the nationwide search for the movie role.

Ray was soon to reach the status of a teenager. His face was round and smooth, reminding Hank of his younger years before war and a hard life outdoors had weathered him. While Susanna read the behemoth *Gone with the Wind,* Ray was consumed by comics. His favorite character, like most boys his age, was Superman. He imagined himself as Clark Kent and even selected black, heavy-framed glasses like his. His bedspread contained the Superman logo, which had been challenging to find, but Dottie managed to get it for him last Christmas. Hank thought she discovered it in the Sears catalog.

"May I be excused?" Mary asked, bringing Hank back to the present.

"Yes, dear," Dottie answered. She turned to the rest of the family. "Whose turn is it to clear the table and wash dishes?"

"My turn to clear the table," Mary answered, "but I switched days with Ray. Buck is taking me to the county fair tonight."

"And I'm doing the dishes," Susanna added in a melancholy, singsong voice.

As the children rose and began clearing the table, a shaggy black-and-white dog lumbered out from under the dining table.

"Don't give so much to Rufus that it makes him sick," Dottie said.

"We won't, Mama," Susanna said with a sideways glance.

Hank rose from the table. "Care to join me, lovey?" he asked Dottie.

"I would love to."

They made their way through the dining room into the hall, partially dominated by the hardwood stairs leading to the bedrooms, with an intricately carved railing in dark mahogany. The front door was open, as it always seemed to be, allowing the summer breeze to roll through the screen door, down the hall, and out the back screened door in the kitchen.

Dottie and Hank settled into the porch swing. Hank grasped Dottie's petite hand. They were silent as they listened to the bullfrogs along the creek that ran on the opposite side of the road. It was after seven o'clock, and the sun was setting in a blaze of red and orange.

"Tell me why I ever left this," Hank said.

"It was part of the deal, as I recall," Dottie laughed. "You needed a woman who could deal with your long absences. I was the only one silly enough to agree."

"You've done more than deal with them. You've thrived, Dottie. You've done such an amazing job with raising the children—"

"They're only on their best behavior because you're here."

"I think you're selling yourself short there, Dot. Raising kids all alone and working, too."

"Well, it isn't like I'm not getting your paycheck in the mailbox every week, you know. That pays the bills and then some."

"Is it enough?"

"It certainly is. I work because I want something to do."

"How's the textile factory doing?"

"Very well. It takes me all week to put together payroll for the previous week."

"You're not working full-time, I hope."

"You hope, do you?" Dottie needled him. "I'm up to 30 hours a week now that the kids are getting older. How many hours do you put in every week, Hank?"

"How many hours are in a day?" He mused. "I'm always at work." He sighed before continuing. "I've been thinking, Dottie."

"That's dangerous."

"I think after I do this assignment in Germany, I'm quitting the overseas crap."

She leaned forward so she could look him in the face. "You love working overseas."

He shrugged. "I used to. And I still enjoy photography and writing. But a lot is going on in America, too, and it's safer."

"There isn't much going on here right now," she admitted. "Politicians are pounding their chests, saying we're heading for another war, which nobody wants, believe me. It's nice and quiet here. Days are predictable."

A black Ford with whitewalls pulled in front of the house, and Mary stepped outside. As she made her way across the porch and down the steps, a young man with close-cropped brown hair made his way around the car and opened the door for her. "Hey, Mr. and Mrs. Mullins!"

"Hey there, Buck!" Hank answered. "Have her back by midnight, son!"

"I'm eighteen, Dad," Mary said, rolling her eyes as she slid into the front seat.

As they pulled away, Hank asked, "Do we know if she's safe with him?"

"Stop it," Dottie said, slapping him playfully on the knee. "You checked him out the last time you were here, and the time before that. Buck's a good kid, Hank."

"Is he working now?"

"Same place he worked all through high school. But now, he's made manager. He's also enrolled in night classes."

"College?"

"College."

"Hm. Good for him."

"So, you were saying this is your last overseas assignment? I don't know if I believe you."

"It is, Dottie." Hank turned serious. "I feel like I'm getting too old for this."

"You're only forty-one!"

"Well, it's not like I plan to retire, that's for sure. But I want to come back home. Maybe the magazine can find me some assignments in the States. Even if I had to travel, I could get back home more often, and it wouldn't take me forever to get here."

"How long are you here for, Hank?"

"A week, ten days, tops."

"And your next assignment?"

"A month, maybe, if that."

"So, you're saying you'll be back home for good this fall?"

"Would that be a bad thing?"

"Oh, it would be horrible." She tried to tweak his arm, but he dodged her. "I give you until spring. By then, you'll be itching to go where the action is." She hesitated. "No, I think the first of the year."

"Cut it out," Hank said, pushing the porch swing a little higher. As Dottie squealed, he wrapped his arm around her. "Hey, I have an idea."

"Oh, Lord. The last idea you had gave us Ray."

"Let's go to the county fair."

"What?"

"It's a beautiful night. The sun is setting. The whole thing will be lit up. We can stroll around, get cotton candy, maybe I can win you a prize."

"You know what? Stop this swing, so I can get off. You just got yourself a date."

6

Max, Będzin, 1939

Max paused at the door as his eyes adjusted to the meeting hall's gloom.

The sun had shone brightly just a few minutes earlier, as he'd made his way from the shop. The shopkeeper had not been pleased that Max had wanted to leave a few minutes before they closed, but Max had dutifully cleaned the floors, swept outside, and even swept into the street in front of the store. He'd walked three blocks and up two flights of stairs with an armful of groceries for Mrs. Bosko, because she couldn't be bothered to leave her flat at the age of 97. And he'd even crawled into the darkest corners of the cellar because someone claimed to have seen a mouse escape from the fruit section into a hole by the cellar door. He suspected the customer wanted food at a discount, but the claim could have shut them down. As the lowest-ranking employee, he was a no-brainer to send after the phantom mouse. He was so pissed that he took a piss in the cellar's back corner.

His day changed when he entered the meeting hall for the monthly meeting of *Jungdeutsche Partei*, the Young German Party. It was a clandestine gathering that took place each month in a different location, lest ever-vigilant but narrow-minded intelligence services discover them. Members were sworn to secrecy, their backgrounds carefully investigated. Above the surface, he was just another young Polish man at the lowest rungs of society, still living with his mother, unable to find suitable employment, too poor and academically challenged to attend college. Here, he was somebody.

Several young men, most still in their teen years, greeted him by name as he pulled his Nazi armband from his pocket and placed it around his arm. His heart soared at the two Nazi flags draped against the front wall, flanking a makeshift podium, before making his way around the room, shaking hands, joking, and making small talk. Here, he was treated like a business leader, a member of a valued society, someone to be trusted with their deepest, darkest secrets and aspirations.

"Hello, Max." The voice was silky with a touch of mischievousness breaking through.

Max turned to find Stella Kowalska standing in the doorway. His heart skipped a beat, as it always did when he laid eyes upon her. She was seventeen years old, with ash brown hair that cascaded over her shoulders to curl around firm, round breasts. Her eyes were the color of seafoam, her lips richer than rubies. They had taken their assessments at the same time, which involved sitting under bright lights while their eye and hair colors were appraised and their noses measured, all while they were asked rapid-fire questions about religion and lineage. Both had been assessed as Nordic, the highest possible. It had taken several long months before either had been admitted, while their backgrounds were subjected to lengthy analysis.

"Stella," he said, straightening his spine. "How nice to see you again."

"I am waiting for you to chair a meeting," she said with a sly smile. She brushed a lock of hair away from her forehead.

"I will. I will."

"And get a good speaker. Someone to inspire us all."

"Oh, yes." He couldn't think of anything else to say, so he stood there woodenly, a smile plastered on his face, and was thankful when they were interrupted.

"Please, everyone, take your seats," a young man announced at the front of the room. "We have a very special speaker this evening."

Max half-turned to see the young man, a teenager of perhaps fourteen or fifteen, conversing with an older fellow, possibly in his twenties. Max was probably the oldest among them there, except for Leonard Gorski, who typically scheduled the meetings and chose the venues. With his age came respect.

It wasn't difficult to find an empty seat. There were two dozen set out, but he counted only ten in attendance. Max gallantly motioned for Stella to slip into an aisle first, then proudly sat next to her. Leonard eased into the seat on the other side of him. Leonard might have been twenty-five, practically an elder in the *Jungdeutsche Partei*. Like Max and Stella, he had been assessed as Nordic.

They exchanged pleasantries while the speaker passed out leaflets, and then Leonard leaned in to whisper to Max. "Are you looking for a meaningful job?"

"Always," Max answered. "What do you have?"

"City government."

Max's eyes widened, then narrowed. "Not cleaning streets or picking up garbage, I hope."

"Not by a long shot. It's an assistant to the mayor."

"The mayor?" Max sat up straighter.

"It's not much, but it's a foot in the door. You'd be delivering documents, getting people on the phone, grabbing the mayor's lunch—"

Max groaned. "A gopher." He sighed. "Women's work."

"I said it wasn't much, but you wouldn't be sweeping floors. And, hey, do a good job, and you could be recognized. It could be a start. Plus, you'd be well-positioned for us."

"What do you mean?"

Leonard shrugged. "You never know when the Nazis may decide to take over. There's been talk of it for months."

"What does it pay?"

"Twice what you're earning now, I wager. You still living with your mother?"

"She lives with me," Max answered, bristling.

The speaker began to talk, and the buzz of voices quieted.

"See me afterward," Leonard whispered.

He nodded and leaned back in his chair, his eyes set on the front of the room, and his hands held neatly in his lap. As the speaker was introduced, Stella eased her hand onto his lap and squeezed his hand. He turned to find her staring at him and smiling.

"This is a wonderful opportunity," she said. "You have been on the ground floor of the Nazi party here. You are practically a founding member! I can feel your importance in the party growing."

He smiled slightly and nodded. Yes, he thought. Stella is right. Perhaps my time has come. She did not remove her hand, and he placed his free hand over hers. Her hand was not soft, as he had imagined, but calloused. It didn't matter. He was going somewhere, and perhaps Stella would be on his arm as he climbed the ladder in the Nazi party.

7

Agata, Warsaw, 1939

September 1 began like any other day. The overnight temperature had dropped from the oppressive summer heat, and the high was only expected to reach the mid-70s Fahrenheit. It had every indication of a perfect autumn day in Poland's capital, where everyone had attempted to focus on their individual view of what was normal, despite the emerging threat at the border.

Agata, Elsa, and Ira had moved to Warsaw eleven years earlier. Agata had carried little Elsa in her lap on the train, and they had managed to pack all their possessions into two suitcases. Ira had decided to leave most of Anna's belongings with her sisters, though Agata had insisted on a few items so she would not forget her mother. Wedged among her clothing was a Bible with the New Testament, her mother's pearl-handled comb, a photograph of her mother in a small, oval frame, and an everyday dress. The last, she wanted for the sole reason that she could hold the material to her face and smell her mother's fragrance, an odd but comforting mixture of rose water, perspiration, and baked bread.

The dress had long ago lost Anna's scent, but it continued to sit in its own coveted drawer in their rented Warsaw apartment. Ira had chosen Poland's capital because it contained the largest population of Jews in all of Europe. As the Nazi Party rose to prominence in neighboring Germany, he was confident that they were protected here, though Agata had begun to notice signs that should have had them all alarmed.

Still, she had seen her father flourish over the years. He had a heavy, defeated air about him on the train out of Germany. His shoulders had been hunched, his eyes perpetually reddened, and he had little appetite for food or companionship. Agata had been left alone with the shock of her mother's death and the new little girl that was suddenly her responsibility.

Things had changed once they settled into Warsaw. Ira had obtained a job at a school there teaching mathematics, and his old vibrancy had emerged. He was respected there for his knowledge and his personality, and there had been no shortage of women who thought him a suitable partner, even with two little girls. He began to smile again, though his kind, brown eyes occasionally took on a melancholy.

They managed to find a wet nurse quickly, which allowed Agata to attend school. The bullying she had experienced in Germany vanished, and she developed a confidence she didn't know she had. Yet, her thoughts frequently turned to Elsa as she sat in her classroom. She fretted over every little thing, from the tiniest cough to the fact that she always seemed to be underweight. Agata felt the responsibility of the growing little girl grow heavy on her, but it was also one she relished.

She couldn't imagine where Elsa got her capacity for love. From that first time she'd laid eyes on her in the hospital, Agata had felt her compassion. It had only grown since. She felt empathy for the smallest of creatures, insisting on carrying out spiders she found in their apartment, or stepping around ants crossing a sidewalk. Every time she had begged Ira for a pet, Agata could see his angst at having to reject the notion, because the apartment building did not allow pets.

It was that apartment that Agata now rushed to, as the Polish Defensive War had begun.

It had only been one week prior that the Nazis had signed an agreement with the Soviet Union to invade and conquer Poland. Their plan had been hatched and signed openly. The goal was to remove Poland's sovereignty as an independent nation and eradicate its citizens so Nazi Germany and the Soviet Union could divide its fertile land between them for their own people.

Most Poles scoffed at the idea. The Polish Warsaw Army had seen its ranks swell since World War I, as had forces across Poland. They were confident that they were ready to repel an invasion.

Yet, as Agata worked at her first job as a typist on the other side of the city, a growing group of coworkers had gathered around the radio for news of the Nazi invasion. The initial reports were dire. The Germans appeared unstoppable.

For the first time in history, the world witnessed *blitzkrieg*, a highly coordinated attack from the air and land. The results were devastating. As many as 1.5

million German soldiers were invading Poland along more than 1,700 miles of shared border, amounting to nearly 900 invaders per linear mile. One village after the next was falling into their hands. Buildings were obliterated, and the number of killed and wounded grew with the continued reports. Additionally, warships were off their coast, pummeling Westerplatte, a port city that guarded the coastal mouth of the Baltic Sea.

A commotion outside the offices had drawn everyone to the windows. While Warsaw was far enough away from the German border, its citizens had been listening to the same news as Agata and her coworkers. As they watched, the streets grew frenetic with honking horns, people were so crowded on the streetcars that they were leaning out the windows, bicycles whizzed past, and everywhere, everywhere, people were running.

Agata grabbed her handbag and rushed out the door and into the cacophony of shouts and cries. People were headed in every direction at once, and she found herself pummeled along as she tried to make her way toward Elsa's school. She managed to push and scramble her way onto a streetcar and then another as they traveled this way and that, and in between, she ran the streets of Warsaw, zigzagging from one neighborhood to the next, until she arrived breathless at the school.

Others had begun arriving to whisk their children to safety, though many teachers, including Ira, tried to convince them that the school was their safest place. It was larger than most buildings, built of sturdy brick and concrete, and contained enough room for the children and their families.

Agata paused at the bottom of the steps to hear her father encourage the parents to join them there.

"Go home," he was saying, "and gather all the food you can carry. Bring clothes, blankets. We will have a place for you here. It will only be temporary," he continued as he raised his voice to be heard over the bedlam, "the Polish Warsaw Army will keep us safe!"

A parent pushed past him at the top of the steps, rushing for the broad doors, calling for his children. Then another and another rushed past him until Ira appeared almost like a whirling dervish as he begged them not to panic.

Agata shoved her way past the others and squeezed close to Ira. "Where is Elsa?"

It took a moment for Ira to catch his breath. As another person propelled past them, they knocked his glasses, and he hurried to straighten the wire rims before he lost them completely. "She is fine," he managed to say. "She is in her classroom."

"I am taking her," Agata said forcefully.

Ira managed to drag her away from the double doors, where fewer people knocked them about. "Agata, listen carefully. Go home. Get food, clothes, blankets, and pillows."

"I am taking Elsa."

"Elsa will be safe here." He placed his hands on her shoulders. "I know how much you love her, Agata. We both do. I must keep her here where she is safe. You should be here, also. Gather the things I told you, and return here. I promise we will be safe here."

"We will not be safe here," Agata retorted hotly. Her father was so mild-mannered that she rarely argued with him, and his eyes widened in surprise as she continued. "I have heard reports of the Nazi's hatred of Jews. We all have," she added as he shook his head. "We can no longer deny it. They will kill us."

"There are over half a million soldiers in the Polish Warsaw Army," Ira insisted. "The Germans will never take Warsaw."

Agata managed to push past him as she rushed into the school. It was sheer chaos. Women and children were crying as they ran toward the exits. Men shouted for their children. The floor was littered with possessions dropped in the commotion; a handkerchief here, a small shoe there, papers rumpled by scurrying feet.

She knew where Elsa's classroom was located at the end of the corridor, but she called out to her long before she reached the door. She was astonished when, huffing and puffing, she reached the doorway to find her eleven-year-old sister sitting calmly at her desk, reading.

"Elsa," Agata breathed as she rushed to her, "we must leave now."

Ira was on her heels. "No, Agata, she is safer here."

"Where do you want to be?" Agata asked her.

Elsa looked up from her book with enormous, doe-like brown eyes. "We have protectors, Agata," she said calmly.

"What protectors?" Agata waved her arms as if to say there were none there.

"Where would you go, Agata?" Ira asked. "Where would you go that is safer than it is here?"

Agata took Elsa's hand. She hadn't realized until that moment how much her own trembled. Her senses seemed heightened far beyond anything a human should endure, and yet there was something in her soul that told her this was only the beginning.

In contrast, Elsa's hand was warm and steady. She squeezed her older sister's hand to reassure her. "We will be safe here. The Army will repel them."

"Our apartment is no safer than we are here," Ira continued. "Less so."

Agata took a deep breath. "Daddy, I want to leave this community."

He took a half-step back. "This community?" he repeated, puzzled.

"We will be safer on the other side of town."

"The non-Jewish side," Ira said flatly.

"But God is here," Elsa said.

"God is there, too," Agata insisted. "But the Nazis, should they break through our defenses, will come with a vengeance for the Jews."

Ira shook his head.

"We have all heard the reports," she continued. "We know what they are doing to the Jews in Germany."

"They will see," Ira said firmly but gently, "that we are a peaceful people here. They will see that we are educated. We are enterprising. We work hard. We are vital members of the community."

"They will mark us," Agata insisted. "They will force us to identify ourselves, just as they have in Germany—"

"I will proudly wear the Star of David." Ira's voice took on a determined quality that overrode his gentle disposition.

"Wear it, and they will know you by your difference."

"My difference? We are all human beings—"

"Not in their eyes. In their eyes, we are animals. We have seen their papers. We have seen how they portray us. We have seen them morph our bodies into overweight, filthy, grotesque caricatures that are half-man and half-ape."

"Agata, please," Elsa said, squeezing her hand.

"Elsa and I can pass for Gentiles. Let us go, Daddy. Let us go to the other side of town. We will find a school there, I promise."

"You would leave Daddy?" Elsa's lip quivered. She slowly came to her feet and moved toward Ira, dropping Agata's hand. "I love you, Agata. I love you as my mother and sister. But I love Daddy, too."

"Daddy can come," Agata hastened. "If he will."

Ira stared at her. After a long moment, he said quietly, "I will remain right here. People will gather here, as we have instructed them. I am needed here. And I beg you, Agata, I implore you. Stay here with us. Forget about going home for food and clothing. I will go later, once you are settled here. Don't leave. We can stay right here in this room."

"Please, Agata," Elsa pleaded. "Stay here with us. Please."

Agata walked slowly to the windows. The crowds were gathering outside; some were returning with pillowcases and suitcases filled with those things they believed they would need. Others still called for their children as they hurried up the sidewalk to the great double doors. Still others whisked their children away from the school, disappearing into the throngs that filled the streets, amid shouts and cries and the clatter of streetcar bells as they tried to move through the crushing crowds.

Agata could feel the emotions of both Ira and Elsa. Elsa was perfectly calm as she had been in her arms the day she was born. She was like a serene statue amidst the chaos. She believed. Somehow, in her short life, she held onto a faith that Agata had never managed to possess. Elsa knew she was safe. She knew that God protected her despite the centuries of Jewish history and persecution. She loved everyone, and she believed that her love would conquer any hatred anyone harbored against her, just as she had softened Agata's heart all those years before. Agata found herself wishing that, for once, she carried even a fraction of that same faith within her own soul.

Agata's heightened senses also felt Ira's conflicting emotions. He was wounded, as he had been since Anna had died. His smile had returned; so had his good nature, his laughter, and his purpose. But his soul was still devastated by Anna's loss, and now he looked upon Agata with mourning and distress, believing he was losing Agata forever, too.

He could order her to remain, she realized. Just as other parents were grasping their children and leading them away like sheep, he could do the same with her. But, he wouldn't. From the moment her aunt had placed Elsa in her lap, he had treated her as an adult. He had known she was merely a child herself, and yet, he had no capacity to raise two little girls. His soul had been crushed, and every day was a battle to place one foot in front of the other. He had come to depend upon Agata; she knew that now, as she had known it then.

She crossed the room and grasped each of their hands in hers. "I will go, but I will be back for you."

"Where?" Ira gasped. "Where could you possibly go?"

Agata swallowed. "I will find an apartment on the other side of town. I can afford it. I have a good job; you know that, Daddy. If nothing else, it will give us another place to go, should we ever need it."

"Please, don't go," Elsa said. Her eyes welled with tears. "Please, Agata."

"She needs you," Ira added. "Get an apartment tomorrow, if you need to. I will go with you. But stay here, just for tonight. Just until this chaos is over."

It would have been so easy to stay. With one decision, she could have stopped Elsa's tears and erased the haunted expression from her father's face. She could have remained with Elsa while Ira went back to their apartment for supplies, or she could have used the adrenaline pumping through her veins to gather the supplies for them. She could have assisted the scores of families lined up on the sidewalk outside the school as they filed into assigned rooms and duties.

But her soul knew she could not stay.

"I will be back tomorrow," she said, wiping away Elsa's tears with her finger. She turned to her father. "I promise, I will be back. Let me do this. Let me find a safe place for us."

Agata did not hear her father's objections as she turned her back on them. His voice carried down the corridor amidst Elsa's cries for her to return. She wiped her own tears from her cheeks as she pushed open the doors to rejoin the mayhem.

The throngs pushed her this way and that, so she felt like she was attempting to run through thick mud. She made slow progress, and yet, something inside her propelled her forward. She reached the end of the block to find cars racing past, ignoring intersection rules, and she hesitated to get her breath. Someone from behind pushed her to the ground, stomping over her dress as she lay prone, scores of feet scuffling over her while she tried vainly to rise.

A hand reached through the crowd. Amidst the shouting, his words were louder and deeper than the others. "Get back!" he shouted as he grasped her by the waist and hauled her to her feet. "Get back!"

As the mob stepped back and then rushed forward in another direction, the man pulled her away from the others. It was easy to see why the crowd had obliged him and given her space. He was a soldier in the Polish Army, his cropped, sandy hair almost hidden beneath a crisp cap bearing the Polish White Eagle. His trim figure was clothed in an olive uniform, and he wore a wide black belt and knee-length black boots.

"Are you alright?" he asked.

"Fine, thank you." Agata wiped her hair off her forehead and was surprised to find pebbles from the ground in her hair.

"Where were you going?" he asked.

"I—" She hesitated. "I don't know."

"The school—"

"No. I need to leave the Jewish sector. I need to be across town."

"Is that where you live?"

Agata looked around her in impatience. "I am wasting time here. Thank you for assisting me to my feet, but I must go. The Germans—"

"The Germans are coming," he finished. "And we are digging in. You will be safe if you remain in Warsaw, Jewish sector or no."

"Then, thank you, and good-bye." She turned to run, but he held out his hand and stopped her.

"Do you have an address where you are going? I have a motorbike. I can get you there faster than you can run."

"Shouldn't you be somewhere right now? Like, fighting the Germans?"

He laughed so unexpectedly that Agata was shocked. "There will be time enough for that, don't you worry. My name is Piotr. Come. My motorbike is over there, on the opposite corner."

As Agata rushed across the busy street with him and settled behind him on the motorbike, she took a long look at the school down the street. It was difficult to know what was happening as people rushed in all directions at once. Her eyes fell on the top step, at two figures holding one another so tightly they appeared as if they might be one. A tear rolled down her cheek as the motorbike zoomed to life, and she held onto Piotr as they took off. Soon, the people blended behind them while the memory of Ira and Elsa on the step seared into her mind. "I will be back tomorrow," she thought. "I will be back, just as I promised."

8

Hank, Festungsfront Oder-Warthe-Bogen, September 1, 1939

Hank lay prone on the rough ground as he peered over the hill at the ground below. The sun's path and the forest's density had cast him in shadow all morning, but that would soon change. He aimed his shroud-covered camera at the unfolding scene, so only the lens was visible.

He was located along the easternmost edge of the Festungsfront Oder-Warthe-Bogen, or the Fortified Front of Oder, Warthe, and Bogen, in far western Poland, his sights set on the border with Germany. Rumored to be the Nazi's most highly fortified underground network, it consisted of roughly one hundred pillboxes and defense structures, all interconnected underground in tunnels purported to be 25 miles long and up to 130 feet deep.

The Germans had begun constructing the military defense line in 1934. Oddly, they had claimed it to be a crucial defense against a possible Polish attack. As Panzers rolled over the uneven ground between the pillboxes from Germany into Poland, he'd watched countless men emerge from the fortifications on foot before forming loose infantry lines that continued their invasion into Poland. He was not one to overestimate, but he knew he was observing well over a hundred thousand men in his position alone. His report, which he would write this afternoon wherever he and Rafe found a suitable hideaway, would mean even more with these photographs.

The invasion had not been totally unexpected, though he was certain that the scale would take everyone by surprise. Earlier in the year, the Nazis had swept through Czechoslovakia, which the Germans called the Sudetenland, and Austria. Although parts of Europe had protested with fiery speeches in parliamentary halls, Hitler had not received so much as a slap on the wrist. There had been rumors for months about a Polish or French invasion, with the buildup along the Germany-Poland border partly obscured by the expansive underground tunnels and facilities.

As German fighter planes flew overhead in massive formations, Rafe slipped up beside him. "We have to go," he whispered hoarsely.

"I know. I just want to finish this roll."

"No," Rafe said. "We have to go. *Now.*"

Hank pulled his camera back and peered at Rafe. "What's happened?"

"We have a visitor."

Hank jerked around to look beyond them but saw no one. Still, he'd heard that tone in Rafe's voice too many times to count. They'd become adept at covert photography and following leads into dangerous situations during the Spanish Civil War, but neither of them had ever seen anything on this scale.

"This way," Rafe said, staying low to the ground and half-crawling behind the hill to the other side. He stopped as Hank joined him behind a particularly dense thicket of fallen trees and underbrush. He nodded, and Hank moved around him to peer around the edge. "Careful," Rafe warned.

"How many are there?"

"Only one. He arrived a few moments ago."

"You stopped me for only one?"

"Take a look where he's at."

Hank studied a young man standing along the dirt path, a lane so narrow that it was a minor miracle either of their vehicles could traverse it, as it seemed more suited for livestock. They'd left theirs as close to the trees as Rafe could manage, obscuring it between the rolling terrain and forest. He used his camera's telephoto lens to snap a few pictures. The soldier wore a well-fitting German uniform, but appeared to be a private, especially with his field helmet. "He's separated from the others," Hank murmured.

"Maybe he needed a piss?"

"Whatever he's doing," Hank said as he watched him lean into their open vehicle, "we've gotta get rid of him. Do you have the key?"

"Of course, I do," Rafe answered. "And our gear."

They crept closer in a labyrinth manner, both sets of eyes on the German soldier. The man moved into the tree line, where they could only observe his back. "Told you," Rafe whispered. He picked up a few hefty rocks and pulled his slingshot out of his back pocket. As the man emerged from the woods, he returned to his vehicle. Then, as if he'd thought of something, he went back to the one Hank and Rafe were using. "One more step," Rafe said as he aimed. "Revelation 12," he said calmly. "And there was war in heaven… And Satan prevailed not." There was a high-pitched sound and then a sturdy thud as the heavy rock found its target in the middle of the soldier's neck. "But I paraphrase," Rafe added as the young man hit the ground.

Hank and Rafe scrambled down the rest of the hill and raced for the vehicle, only to discover their exit was blocked by the German truck. "Hurry!" Hank said as he dashed to the truck. He threw himself into the front seat as Rafe clambered into the driver's seat, tossing the gear to Hank. Within a split second, he turned the ignition and began speeding along the road in reverse.

The soldier appeared to make a feeble effort to rise to his knees, but he went down again.

"I hope you didn't—" Hank began.

"He's okay. Just knocked a little loopy. I've never killed anyone with a slingshot—yet." He reached an opening that didn't appear large enough to back into, yet Rafe expertly navigated the truck until he was heading along the road they'd traveled only a few hours before. It turned toward a sloping hill and open fields still brilliant green from summer. The marching men and tanks appeared surreal in the picturesque setting.

"Fuck," Rafe said. He managed to cut a fresh path through the lumbering underbrush that shielded them from the approaching Germans. "You realize we're not safe anywhere, right?"

Hank glanced into the back of the vehicle. "There are weapons back there and maybe another uniform."

"The uniform might come in handy. The weapons won't. There are too many of them."

"Turn south," Hank said, pulling a map out of his duffel bag. "They're probably heading due east. They won't turn south for several miles."

"Confident of that, are you?"

"I'm counting on this being the advance guard. More will come, but it will take days before they truly fan out."

"I don't think so," Rafe said. "There are too many of them, and they're moving fast."

"Then we have to move faster," Hank said as he glanced behind them.

~~~~~

Artillery shells and small arms fire lit up the horizon. Hank looked up from his seat on a bale of hay to catch Rafe standing in the barn's open pedestrian doorway, silently watching the action. It was unusual for fighting to continue after dark, but the sun had set long ago, and the Germans kept advancing.

"Soldiers need rest, wouldn't you think?" Rafe asked as if reading Hank's mind.

"They always have before," Hank answered. He removed the film from his camera, popped it into a small canister, and shoved it into the steel toe of his boot. Then he slid his foot into the boot and tied it.

"Doesn't that bruise your toes?"
~~~~~

"Not usually. The boots are two sizes too big. It only bothers me if I have to walk long distances. Besides, if we're ever searched, nobody thinks of looking in my boots."

"That's because they figure you'd be crazy to shove something that big in there."

Hank smiled wryly. "Maybe I am crazy. Crazy to be here, anyway. Where do you suppose we are, anyway?"

Rafe closed the door, but it did nothing to deaden the noise. The barn was cast into gloom as only slivers of light pierced between aged wood panels. Where usually a full moon might cast blue or white beams across the floor, tonight they were muted red from the fighting, which pooled like blood on the straw-covered ground. It evoked unwelcome memories of the Great War. During that war, the occasional night fight was illuminated by white flares to more easily spot enemy positions, often turning night into daylight. Newer technology had determined that red light provided better night vision, but it seemed surreal, as if they were in a perpetual state of blazing sunset.

Hank watched as Rafe's dark shape moved across the room to join him at the bales of hay as a horse nickered in a nearby stall. While Rafe retrieved his maps from his rucksack, Hank reread the letter he'd written a few minutes earlier. It read:

Dearest Dottie,

How are you and the kids? I miss so much about North Carolina. I miss watching the stars with you over open fields, sitting in the porch swing, and I especially miss your cooking. There's no cornbread or fried catfish in these parts, and most especially, no banana pudding!

I am sorry I missed Mary's 19th birthday celebration! Time is slipping by, lovey. Next year, our oldest can bid those teenage years goodbye! Is she still dating Buck? He seems like a nice young man.

Have Susanna's grades improved? Only one more year after this one, and once she has her high school diploma, she can get secretarial training and that good job she wants. She's always had an independent streak. If she applies herself to her studies, she can go far, I betcha.

I must admit, Dottie, I am relieved that Ray is only now turning thirteen. I've seen so many young men killed or disabled from the Great War, the Spanish Civil War, and now the Germans have invaded other countries. I would hate to see him at an age where he would want to enlist.

I miss all the kids, but I mostly miss you, lovey. It's been twenty-three years now since we married in front of that Justice of the Peace. Do you remember the gift waiting for us from the Welcome Wagon? A box of necessities, like toilet tissue and feminine pads! We laughed for days.

Can you believe how fast time has flown? I remember it like it was yesterday. I shipped out one week later to fight in Europe, and I still have our wedding picture, such as it was, in my wallet. I look at it every night before I fall asleep, as I pray that the Good Lord will watch over you and the kids, and even Rufus, that lovable mongrel.

I'm going to ask the magazine if I can do a few domestic pieces soon, Dottie, just like we talked about. I love photojournalism, but it's tough not seeing you and the kids. I'll be back home in less than a month, and we can all go somewhere nice for a few days, maybe rent a place at Rodanthe and enjoy the beach. I could do with some swimming and flying kites like we did when the kids were small.

Please give my love to the kids and a hug to Rufus.

I love you, lovey, and hope to see you soon,
Hank

He carefully folded the letter and placed it neatly into an envelope. Before he could seal and address it, Rafe turned on a small flashlight and focused it on the map he'd laid out across the floor. "We should be right about here," he said, pointing with his free hand.

Hank set the envelope on the hay stack as he slipped to the floor to lean over the map.

"We should be near Będzin," Rafe said. "Judging by the size of it on the map, we should be able to locate a phone there."

"Good. I finished the article for the magazine; I can dictate it over the phone. I need a dark room to process the film and a postal service. With luck, the photos can arrive within three weeks."

"I wouldn't bet on it," Rafe said. "We need to get someplace where they won't be intercepted."

The wide barn doors swung open so abruptly that it startled both men. Before Hank could fully react, a man shouted in Polish, *"Ręce w górze! Ręce w górze!"*

As Rafe placed his hands in the air, he shouted in Spanish, *"Somos guerrilleros!"*

"We're resistance fighters now?" Hank asked, raising his hands.

"Fuckin' Affirmative," Rafe replied.

Two soldiers descended upon them as a third picked up Hank's letter and the nearby article he'd recently completed.

"¿Dónde están tus papeles?" one asked gruffly. Rafe pointed at his jacket pocket, and the man wrestled the papers out. He shone a hefty flashlight onto the paperwork. *"¿Eres español? ¿Qué estás haciendo aquí?"*

"What the hell?" Hank said as he presented his papers.

"He wants to know if I'm Spanish and why I'm here."

Before Hank could respond, the man peered at him curiously. *"¿Por qué hay un americano aquí?"*

"He wants to know why an American is here."

"Tell him we're journalists."

Rafe replied to the man. His response was lengthy, and as Hank listened, he noticed the uniforms were Polish. The barn had begun filling up with other men, and through the open door, there appeared to be several hundred heading their way on foot and in light tanks. "Tell him we want the Americans to know that Germany is an aggressor in Poland."

As Rafe complied, the conversation went back and forth. The officer was obviously intrigued by their unexpected presence. The soldier who had picked up the letter and article carried them to his commanding officer, and they conferred in whispered tones. After an interesting back-and-forth, the soldier who had removed their identification was called over.

"Can they speak any other languages?" Hank whispered.

"If they could speak English, they would be."

"Tell them I also speak—"

"You speak one word of German or Russian, and I'll fucking slit your throat myself."

"Dammit."

"My guess is they can't read English, either, so they don't know what they just took off you. It could be German military plans, for all they know."

The senior officer returned to them and spoke to Rafe in halting Spanish. After a moment of nodding and Rafe pointing at their gear, he turned to Hank. "They're taking us to Będzin."

"Wonderful!" Hank beamed. "They're giving us a ride?"

"Not so fast, Shirley Temple." As the soldiers patted down Hank and Rafe and inspected their bags, he continued, "They're taking us to a command post. I suspect they will try to find someone there who can read English. If your writing checks out, they might let us go."

"What do you mean, 'checks out'?"

"If they don't suspect we're German spies."

9

Max, Będzin, Poland

Max sat at a desk barely large enough for the paperwork he'd been handed. His chair was even smaller, reminding him of the child-size chairs in primary school. About the only thing you could say about it was that it rolled, which was nice when he didn't feel like getting up. But it was metal, uncomfortable, and so short that his knees were awkwardly bent.

He shared the office with five females. Most of the time, he felt like he was witness to a typing pool of gossipy girls, though he couldn't type and he wasn't part of their gossip circle. They didn't have a window because they were located in an area between the hallway and the mayor's office, but if he sat just right, he could see through to the mayor's window and view the sky. That was all he could see, as the second-floor office was too high to observe the busy sidewalks below.

"Max," the mayor said, stepping into the doorway.

"Sir?" He stood.

"Get me a couple of rugelach, will you? From that Jewish bakery, what is it?"

"The Mond-Weiss Bakery?"

"That's the one. Tell her to bill my office."

"Yes, sir." Max grabbed his coat and hat and hurried out the door. He dressed nicely these days. With his new paycheck, he could afford a couple of suits he rotated, a pair of dress shoes he kept shined to perfection, a wool overcoat, and a matching hat with a nice brim. Between the footwear and the hat, he figured it added a couple of inches to his height, and he tried to stand tall as he walked, as if he were someone important. He was, after all, an assistant to the mayor.

When he entered the bakery, several women were waiting in line, and Max inwardly groaned at the delay. However, Mrs. Weiss spotted him immediately, waved her arm in his direction, and called for him to come forward. As he stepped in front of the others, she said in a breathless voice, "Max works for the mayor."

Max tilted his chin upward as she announced his importance.

"Celina, would you help the next in line, please?"

As Celina made her way from stocking shelves to the counter, she glanced in Max's direction. She seemed a little older somehow, her brown eyes perpetually smiling, her shoulder-length bob silky. But she was a Jew, and she wasn't Stella, Max reminded himself. He returned her smile begrudgingly. Something must have been off about it, because her own smile faded.

"Would you like something special today, Max?" Mrs. Weiss asked.

"Several rugelach," he answered smoothly. "Please put it on the mayor's tab."

"Of course, of course." Though there were several rugelach in the display case, she leaned forward and whispered, "I'll get them from the back. I have a fresher batch." She disappeared through a door and emerged a moment later with a neatly folded paper bag. "Is half a dozen alright?"

"Perfect," Max answered. He bowed his head slightly before turning toward the door. As Mrs. Weiss began assisting the next customer, he made his way out of the open door and onto the sidewalk. Polish troops had started marching down the middle of the street, with tanks and other vehicles interspersed among them, and civilians had stopped to watch and cheer them on.

It startled Max. He had heard a rumbling in the mayor's office about Germans invading from the west and Soviets from the east, but anything that didn't affect him directly was meaningless to him. With the troops entering Będzin, the invasion was taking on new significance.

He dipped his hand into the bag, pulled out a rugelach, and ate it leisurely as he watched. The German border was much further to their west, so these troops must simply be passing through, he surmised. Yet, as he continued to observe them, he decided he could elevate his standing by rushing into the mayor's office and announcing the arrivals. He licked his fingers, crushed the bag closed again, and hurried along the sidewalk, dodging in and around onlookers.

By the time he arrived at the administration building, there was a line of tanks stopped alongside the promenade, and as he rushed into the building, he was stymied by soldiers milling around in the hallway. They grew more numerous the closer he got to the mayor's office, and as he started through the door into the outer office, one soldier stepped in front of him and placed his hand on his chest.

"Your business here?" the soldier asked.

"I work here!" Max impatiently pulled his coat open to reveal his name tag, neatly pinned to his suit jacket.

The soldier stepped aside without apologizing, and Max rushed in. He plopped the bag onto his desk, started to remove his hat and coat, and turned to the women, who had all stopped their work to observe with wide eyes.

"What's happening?" he whispered hoarsely to the closest clerk.

She shook her head. Tatiana was a matronly woman. Her hair was always pulled into a tight bun at the nape of her neck, the hair slick and neat. She was normally unflappable, her mouth permanently pursed and ready to cluck disapproval, her sharp eyes taking in every detail.

"You must know something," Max pressed. "You must."

"The Nazis are moving quickly," she hissed. "Too quickly."

"What does that mean, 'too quickly'?"

"Across the border. They are overrunning our troops, but fighting is fierce. The mayor is pleading with the Polish Army not to allow the city to be destroyed.

They must not fight here." An uncharacteristic tear showed briefly in the corner of her eye before she batted it away.

An officer stepped to the doorway, but he was half-turned toward the mayor.

"All our offices are yours," the mayor was saying from deeper in his office. "We will clear things out for you. Our staff is at your disposal."

A soldier arrived from the hallway and rushed in toward the officer. "Excuse me, sir," he said. As the officer turned toward him, he whispered something in his ear.

The officer recoiled. "Are you sure?"

"Quite sure, sir. Quite sure. But no one can speak his language."

A hubbub grew in the hallway. Max strained to listen to the conversation between the officer and the soldier, but he couldn't make out the words. Then the mayor's voice rose above the commotion. "I'm afraid not."

"No one?" The officer and soldier moved into the office and stopped directly in front of Max's desk as the mayor stepped to his doorway.

"No one," the mayor said. "No one speaks English here."

"I do!" Max almost shouted the words.

Everyone's eyes turned toward him. He could feel their shock and confusion as the room became silent. Będzin suddenly felt very small, as they stared at him in disbelief. After all, he had spent his entire lifetime in this one neighborhood. They thought they knew him. They thought they knew all about him. But they were about to learn that they didn't know him at all.

"I speak English proficiently," he said in English. "I wish you all a good day. The air is warm. The sun is strong. Love live Poland."

They stared at him in stunned disbelief.

Then, the officer pointed at him. "You're coming with us."

10

Hank, Będzin, Poland

Będzin was a vibrant city. Even with the Polish Army spilling into every available street, the city's culture and economic vibrancy were on full display. As the soldiers drove them into the city, Hank soaked up the city's essence as only a seasoned international journalist could. He quickly learned that Będzin had a diverse range of industries, including metals manufacturing, chemical factories, and the garment industry. The soldiers debated the population figures, and, with Hank's limited understanding of Polish, he concluded that Będzin had around 50,000 citizens, over half of whom were Jewish. Many of the Jews' ancestors had lived in the area since the 13th century.

He tried to relate their ancestry to his own. He didn't even know where his ancestors were in the 1200s. He'd been told they arrived in America in the mid-1800s, but he had no idea where they had lived before his grandfather settled in rural North Carolina around 1880. That meant, he deduced, his family had roots in North

Carolina for a mere 59 years—barely a lifetime—while the Będzin Jews had been deeply rooted there for 700 years.

The imposing Będzin Castle and the equally impressive Jewish synagogue were in proximity, towering over part of the city and the busy Czarna Przemsza River, where shipments of manufactured goods were still being loaded despite the Nazi invasion.

Hank noted that the streets were surprisingly much broader than those in his hometown, and the architecture was awe-inspiring, with the relatively new Będzin Power Station, schools, multi-level office buildings, theaters, art centers, and a bustling rail station. It also boasted fortified medieval town walls. In addition to the original castle, there was the Mieroszewski Palace, which appeared larger than America's White House.

They passed trams and vehicles on the busy streets, which were intermingled with a growing number of military vehicles and tanks, until they arrived at a dignified administration building with columned terraces on two floors. What struck Hank as they were directed out of the vehicle was the sheer number of people on the overflowing sidewalks.

Hank and Rafe were taken across an expansive courtyard, through the marbled foyer, and up a set of wide stairs to the second floor. An attractive woman with deep brown hair and vivid blue eyes greeted them from behind a sturdy typewriter on a spacious oak desk. The soldiers conferred with her for a moment as she glanced several times in their direction. One of the soldiers handed her Hank's duffel and Rafe's rucksack, along with the letter to Dottie and the magazine article.

Leaving the bags on her desk, the woman motioned for Hank and Rafe to follow her. They entered a room where several women were busily typing and filing, then went to another office where a stout woman with short hair was on the phone. She eyed them with interest while she spoke, and when she hung up the phone, she conferred with the receptionist in hushed whispers as she was handed the papers.

As the receptionist returned to her desk, the other woman stood and pointed to the chairs against the wall. *"Czy mówisz po Polsku?"*

Hank recognized the word *Polsku,* and he assumed she had asked if they spoke Polish. Both shook their heads and responded with a list of languages they spoke between them.

"Siadać, siadać," she said, beckoning again to the chairs.

As they sat, Hank said, "Obviously, we're gonna need a Polish language book."

"Ya think?" Rafe asked.

The woman disappeared through an office door near her desk. Hank leaned forward and caught a glimpse of expansive windows and a man in uniform. He stood as the woman handed him the papers, glancing up to briefly meet Hank's eyes. As the woman returned to her desk, the man followed her.

"Jakie języki mówisz?" He asked when he reached them. At their blank expressions, he repeated, *"Język?"*

"Oh, holy shit," Rafe breathed.

"American," Hank said as they both stood. "Spanish," he added as he gestured toward Rafe.

"Amerykański?"

"Si, Amerykański," Hank answered, butchering the word as he repeated it.

To his surprise, the man laughed.

"Si is Spanish, you imbecile," Rafe said.

"Well, how do I know what *'yes'* is in Polish?"

"Siadać, siadać," he answered, pointing to the chairs.

As they sat back down, Hank said, "Well, now we know that *siadać* means sit."

"Do we?" Rafe responded.

The man spoke to his secretary in rapid-fire Polish, and she immediately picked up a large black phone and dialed a number. After talking for a moment, she said to her boss, *"On jest w drodze."*

At that, the man disappeared down the labyrinth of offices.

"He said the word *jest*. Does he think we're a joke?"

"I have no fucking clue," Rafe answered.

They sat in silence for what seemed to be a very long time. When the man returned, another man accompanied him. The second man had an eager air about him, as though he were somehow excited at their appearance there. He was dressed smartly in a business suit, his hair cropped short. Both of them eyed Hank and Rafe for a long moment before the second man spoke in halting English with a hint of a British accent. "Which is the American?"

"I am," Hank said, standing. He half-waved his hand at Rafe. "We both speak English."

"Max Kursell." He shook both their hands as they introduced themselves. "Major Ludwik Adamik. Come into the major's office, please."

"Boy, are we happy to meet someone here who speaks English," Hank said as they followed the men into the major's office. At Max's direction, they sat in sturdy wood chairs with leather upholstery in front of Ludwik's desk as the major handed Hank's letter to Max.

Max read through it, a small smile crossing his face. Then, he turned to Ludwik and appeared to translate the letter into Polish. Ludwik nodded and directed the letter back to Hank.

"I hope you didn't say anything sexy in that letter," Rafe said.

"Not a chance," Hank said, returning it to his pocket. "She lets the kids read them."

Max had already turned his attention to the magazine article. He read this one more slowly. When he was finished, he walked around Ludwik's desk and placed it in front of him. They conferred for quite a while as Max appeared to translate the information and then discuss its contents. After a time in which Hank and Rafe became increasingly anxious, Max turned to them. "You are journalists?" he asked.

They both answered affirmatively. Hank added the magazine's name.

"Yes, yes, but why are you in Poland?"

"That's a loaded question," Rafe answered.

By the time Hank and Rafe finished explaining their work during the Spanish Civil War and their coverage of Nazi Germany, the four men had moved to a couple of sofas in the corner of the office. The secretary, whose name they learned was Zofia, had brought in a tray of tea and appetizers, which they all devoured.

"So, you see," Hank said as he finished his explanation, "we want the world to know that Germany has invaded Poland. We want Americans to know of the Nazi threat."

Max and Ludwik conferred for a moment. Ludwik nodded, and Max began to speak. "I am a civilian," he began. "I am the *starosta*." He waved his hand as if trying to think of a word. "It is equal to assistant mayor. I manage parts of the government."

"You speak excellent English," Hank said.

"I graduated from Oxford." He adjusted his tie as if he were pleased with himself. "We are very excited that you are here. I will help you to submit this," he half-waved the magazine article. "And we want you to write more. We want people around the world to know what is happening here."

"You'll help us submit it?" Hank repeated incredulously.

Max pointed at the phone. "I assume that you telephone someone?"

"Yes, and dictate the article."

"Film taker in bag?"

"A camera? Yes. You didn't remove the film?"

"Remove," he repeated slowly.

Hank sighed. "It was empty. A new roll."

"New. You have used?"

Hank hesitated.

"We will find them. Share them willingly, and we will help you contact your magazine."

"You also want to see what we've seen," Rafe interjected.

"*Tak.* Yes."

Hank and Rafe exchanged glances. Then Hank removed his shoes and extracted a film canister from each. The men watched, puzzled.

"Good idea hiding it there," Rafe said wryly. "A bit puzzled why you disclosed your hiding place so quickly."

"You keep—?" Max asked, motioning toward his shoes.

Hank nodded. "We're on the same side," he said to Rafe loud enough for Max to hear.

"Are we?" Rafe muttered under his breath.

Max shook his head as if he didn't understand.

"The shoe size is purposely too big," Hank said sheepishly.

Max and Ludwik conferred briefly. "Good to know we are on the same side," Max said, turning back to them.

"I can process the film," Hank said. "All I need is a dark room. I have the supplies in my bag."

Max adjusted his collar and cleared his throat. His chin was elevated as he spoke. "Here is our offer, Hank and Rafe," Max said. His tone was amicable, but his words were slow, and red flags began to pop up in Hank's mind. "You will remain here in Będzin until the Nazis have gone. There is heavy fighting, and we have every reason to believe we will be victorious. We may repel them as early as tomorrow. We want your photographs—" he struggled with the right word, "and pencil reports. We will use them and also allow you to send them to your magazine. I will allow you to use the phone, and I will listen. Once the enemy is out, you will be free to go. Until then, you are our guests."

"Lodging?" Rafe asked.

"Lodging?" Max repeated.

"Sleep. Roof. Room."

"Ah. It will be provided." He slightly slurred the last word. "And you will have plenty to eat. You will be stationed with our soldiers."

"As prisoners?"

He moved his hand as if in dismissal. "Of course not. You are my guests. You may freely walk the city with a military escort. You will receive the same food and sleep as our soldiers."

Hank and Rafe exchanged glances.

"Where else are we gonna go?" Rafe asked Hank.

"We're as safe here as anywhere."

"Safer, I'd say." Rafe stood and shook Max's hand. "It is our pleasure to remain as your guests."

A few minutes later, a soldier was escorting them down a hallway to a corner office. In the distance, they could hear the sounds of bombardment, the constant cannon fire causing the floor to tremble as if in a minor earthquake.

Rafe glanced behind them. "Do you believe he went to Oxford?" he whispered.

"Not a chance," Hank said. "I don't know what it is about him, but I don't trust him. But, I'm not quite ready to bite the hand that feeds us."

"Do me a favor, okay? Give me a heads up before you do that."

"What, so you can outrun a trained soldier?"

"Nope. So I can outrun you."

11

Agata, Warsaw, Poland

Agata had not returned the next day, as she had promised Elsa. Nor the day after that or the day after that. As the city grew more chaotic, she found herself confined in one sector as her family was restricted to another.

Most of Poland fell within days as the largest and most intimidating army ever seen bulldozed through the country. The Nazi system of war began with indiscriminate aerial bombardment that destroyed block after block of infrastructure, resulting in so many simultaneous fires that the populace could not fight them all. Hospitals, schools, private homes, and daycare centers were set ablaze as casualties mounted. Women and children were as apt to be targeted as Polish soldiers. By the time the ground forces arrived, there was little left of the towns and villages except rubble and ash.

Rumors abounded. Those who fled into Warsaw reported that the Germans were not the supermen they had been portrayed to be; rather, they were drugged. Speed was a priority in the Nazi advance, which meant there was no time for sleep. Instead, there were stations set up in advance of the troops that handed out methamphetamines like one would offer water to marathon runners. The troops never even stopped as they popped stimulants. The result seemed to be men disconnected from reality, their eyes crazed or dazed. The drugs removed any empathy they might have had for those they conquered, leaving behind men so spurred by drugs and hatred that tales of atrocities spread like wildfire.

Polish forces attempted to halt or slow their progress, but Nazi air superiority left them at a woeful disadvantage. The rumor was that over 160,000 Polish troops had surrendered in the first days.

The Germans reached the southwestern suburbs of Warsaw on September 8. Though the Polish Warsaw Army prevented them from overtaking the city, they had it nearly surrounded. So many air-raid alarms went off that no one paid attention to them anymore; it was a constant, never-ending siren, day or night. Wandering the city meant navigating bombs that were impossible to dodge, as it seemed to be a divine decision whether one was hit or spared. Death was no longer the most feared outcome. It was becoming gravely wounded, with nowhere to go to relieve the suffering. Remaining indoors offered no better refuge as one building after another was bombarded. The entire city of more than one million people was engulfed in flames, with smoke plumes rising so high that everyone had to shield their faces to avoid choking.

Agata lay on a hard floor with only a thin blanket she'd quickly packed a week earlier to keep her warm. A few feet away was her suitcase filled with hastily tossed clothing and an extra pair of shoes. Piotr had deposited her on the doorstep with instructions to hide in the stock room, as the Gentile owner was sympathetic to the Jews. At the thought of him, she heard a noise in the corridor and sat up to find him standing there in the shadows.

"Agata!" he breathed, rushing across the room. Before she could come to her feet, he was down on his knees, encircling her with his arms. "You're still here!"

She held him tightly, not wishing to let go. As long as she was in his arms, there was no war outside those doors. When at last, he reluctantly pulled away from her, she was startled to discover that his face had become haggard and streaked with soot and grime.

He leaned back on his haunches and pulled a package from his rucksack. "I brought you a few things. Are you finding food?" His eyes met hers with concern.

"A little, here and there," she answered.

"This may help." He passed a canteen to her. "It's filled with water, but it'll come in handy if you can find places to refill it."

"This alone is like gold to me." She glanced at the rectangular vessel. "You aren't giving me yours, though, are you?"

He shook his head. "It's from a comrade who died." His eyes were downcast as he grabbed two more packages from his rucksack. Each was small, perhaps no larger than her hand, and wrapped in coarse cloth. "This is squirrel," he said, passing it to her.

She recoiled. "Squirrel?"

He reached out to grab her hand with his own. "I promise you, it is safe to eat. Warsaw is in a dire situation, and regular meat is…" He hesitated. "…nonexistent."

She managed a smile. "Of course. You're not going to tell me it tastes like chicken, are you?"

"More like rabbit," he chuckled. "And nuts." He handed her the last package. "Boiled potatoes."

She held the packages to her breast. "Thank you for remembering me."

"Remembering you?" he asked incredulously. "You're all I think about."

She set the items on the floor beside her and reached for his hands. They were grimy like his face, the nails embedded with dirt, and they were rough as he tightened his grip on her. "What is it like out there?"

"We're getting reinforcements regularly," he began in a forced, cheery voice. Then he sobered. "I am not going to lie to you, Agata. We're getting reinforcements because the Nazis are overrunning the region. They are retreating here, to Warsaw, for a last stand." At her concerned expression, he added, "We will defeat them. We must. This is our land, our country. We can't allow anyone to march in and declare it to be theirs."

"Where are you fighting?"

"The line shifts for me each day. I don't know when I will be able to see you again. They are sending me to the north of the city."

"Will you be closer to the Jewish sector?"

"Perhaps." He raced his fingers along her cheek. "If I am, I will check on Ira and Elsa."

"Do you promise?"

"I promise." He urged her closer, pulling her into him. "You mustn't give up hope."

"It is all I have left," she answered. Her voice was low and caught as she spoke. "After this is over, I want to see you again. The thought of it keeps me going."

"We will see one another—while this is ongoing and after. You have my word."

"Be careful," she chided softly. "I gave my word to my father and sister, and I have been unable to keep it. It haunts me."

As he leaned into her, she placed her hand against his neck, her fingers teasing his hair at the nape of his neck. It was longer than she remembered as she curled her fingers around the locks. When he kissed her, she felt as if she were melting into his arms. His kiss was deep and passionate, urgent and almost desperate. When he pulled away, he did so with a loud sigh.

"I don't want to leave you," he said. Before she could respond, he hastily added, "But I must. I have already been gone too long."

They both rose. He bent down to pick up his helmet. He held it awkwardly as he gazed at her. "I will be back. I promise. Never give up on me or Poland."

"I won't," she whispered.

12

Max

The skies were bluer here and the clouds fluffier. As Max settled into his new corner office with large windows on two sides, he had difficulty deciding which view he enjoyed more. On one side, he had a neatly manicured courtyard with hedges sporting hats of snow, sporadic winter pansies struggling to emerge from beneath the white stuff, and the pathways past them fastidiously shoveled. On the other side, he had more action as he peered into the street below and watched the pedestrians, soldiers, and various vehicles sharing the broad avenue.

The city had come alive in a way he could not have imagined just twenty-four hours ago. There was an excitement in the air, a sizzling combination of fear that the Germans were nearing the city and pride in the Polish army, which was poised to defeat them. On every block, citizen debates raged over the best defensive positions or whether to mount an assault; everyone was suddenly an expert on military strategy. He could hear it all from his open window, the constant buzz that had not been there the day before.

On the distant horizon, he could clearly see the dingy, wretched smoke of cannon fire, the plumes in stark contrast to the powder-blue winter skies. Even the clouds appeared to be moving more quickly, as if attempting to escape the acrid smoke. A row of tanks rumbled past the building, the unexpected tonnage rattling the window glass as though an earthquake had begun.

Max longed to watch the onslaught, his loyalties torn. This was a dream come true for the *Jungdeutsche Partei,* and he wondered where the other members were and, specifically, what Stella was doing. If the Nazis won, they could don their armbands and take positions in the newly formed government. However, if the Poles successfully prevented them from entering the city, he may still have an important position. That is, if the American and the Spaniard remained.

He turned back to his newly assigned desk and frowned as he held up the magazine article that had yet to be submitted. He recognized a few words here and there, and now, as he studied it more closely, he realized that the vast majority of his translation for the major had been completely fabricated. Beads of sweat popped out across his brow. He turned around in his swivel chair and looked out the windows again. This office was his for only one reason: they thought he spoke fluent English. Sooner or later, they were bound to discover someone else who actually knew it, and then what would he do?

He stared at the paper again. The handwriting, though printed, was uneven, and the letters blurred. He had only guessed that they were journalists based on the article's formatting, the presence of a camera, and the excessive amount of film an individual would rarely have. Even worse than the writing was speaking to Hank and Rafe. They spoke more quickly than the radio programs in which he'd learned English, and both had different accents and pronunciations. He was barely able to catch a word here and there.

And now Major Adamik wanted the article translated into Polish.

Max folded the note and shoved it into a pocket as he crossed the room. There was just one thing to do: go home and get his English-to-Polish dictionary.

~~~~~

Max was unprepared for the pandemonium as he stepped outside the building. He supposed it made sense as he could hear the voices from his office even if he hadn't been able to make out the words. Still, it was jarring to see people who would normally walk with controlled purpose now rushing this way and that, as though the sky were falling. It made him hasten his steps, his heartbeat quickening as he joined the throngs. Many stopped along the way to cheer on the passing army vehicles, but he dodged around them, eager to get his book and get back to work. He didn't want the soldiers to give his office to anyone else in his absence.

"Max! Max!"

At the sound of his name, he almost hid, thinking his ruse was discovered, but he quickly realized the voice was female. His eyes darted around
~~~~~

the crowded faces. After a moment, the horde parted, and Stella rushed through to him.

"They're on our doorstep!" she shouted excitedly. Her face was aglow, and he wanted nothing more than to scoop her into his arms and kiss her.

But, as others glanced their way, he grabbed her hand and led her to a quieter area. "Stop smiling," he directed, swinging her around to face him.

"Why?" she demanded.

"They are not here yet. Do you want the Polish Army to pick you up?"

"Why would they? I have done nothing wrong."

"Oh? Now that they are here and we are locked in a battle with them, you and I are collaborators."

"Huh! That is not true."

"Isn't it?"

"It is not. We knew nothing of their plans to invade. We only know that we like their system of government."

"And you don't think they are here to change our system of government to their own?"

"Isn't it exciting?"

"Stop it, I say. Stop it!" Max wiped his forehead. "What are you doing here, anyway?"

"The shop where I worked closed."

"Closed? Why?"

Stella shrugged. "Excitement. Fear. Maybe a little of both." She peered at him, her eyes narrowing. "Why are you here and not in the mayor's office? I would have thought you'd be very busy there."

"I am very busy." He pulled at his suit jacket as if straightening it. "I have been promoted."

"Promoted! To what?"

"I am now a liaison to the military."

"The Polish military?"

"Do you see another here?" He waved his hand toward the tanks passing by them.

"What are you doing for them?" she breathed, her brow furrowing.

"English translation."

"You don't speak English!"

"How do you know that? I do, actually. And I am on a mission, and you are delaying me."

"Be that way, then." She pouted briefly before adding, "What will you do when the Nazis arrive in Będzin?"

"How do you know that they will?"

She shrugged. "I am hedging my bets."

"For right this moment, today, I am a military liaison. That is all I know for now." He waved as though pushing her away. "Now, go."

As she started to leave him, he pulled her back into an embrace and kissed her. Startled, he thought she might pull away, but she didn't. She leaned into him, her tongue flicking inside his mouth and her body pressing against him. She smelled of flowers and musk, and he held her more tightly as he inhaled her essence. Then she abruptly stepped back. "Call on me later," she said, "when you are no longer working your military liaison shift."

Then she was gone, as if she had never been there; her petite figure disappeared among the taller men and women crowding the sidewalk. He stared in the direction she'd gone, but when he didn't spot her among the cluster of people, he turned back in the direction of home.

He ran the few blocks to his house, passing by Mrs. Weiss's bakery and several neighbors, who stopped to stare at his flailing arms and uneven gait. By the time he reached the apartment building, he was out of breath. He paused in the stairwell, his hand over his chest, gulping for air, before he felt that he could climb the stairs without passing out. His mind was churning—he kissed her! And she'd kissed him back!

Max reached the second floor and opened the apartment door. He had spent his life in that apartment. He knew every inch like the back of his hand. Yet, as soon as the door had opened fully, he knew something was off.

It was a tiny apartment. The door opened onto a room that served as both living and dining, separated not by a wall but by two worn rugs that marked the boundaries of each space. The dining table was overflowing on one side with a hodgepodge of patterned material ready to be transformed into clothing. On the opposite side were neatly folded finished pieces, and separating the two piles was his mother's sewing machine.

Near one end of the dining table was the entrance to a galley-style kitchen that was too small for both of them to fit in at once. Between the dark cabinets and a dangling yellow bulb that provided the only light, he was always eager to minimize his time there.

He stood in the doorway, but his mother was not in the kitchen or at her sewing table.

He heard the sound of drawers banging shut, and he rushed through the living area to one of two minuscule bedrooms. He expected to find his mother in her bedroom, but her single bed was neatly made; the dingy, homemade quilt was wrinkle-free and tucked in as if it were worth a fortune, with a flat pillow at its head. A compact dresser rested against a wall, its round, tarnished mirror reflecting his face, his eyes wide, his face pale.

Another banging drawer caught his attention, and he whirled around to the second bedroom door, where he discovered Felka hunched over his nightstand with something in her hand.

"What are you doing?" he shouted, his voice cracking as though he were in puberty.

Felka whirled around. "What is this?" she screamed back, shaking her fist.

He recognized the black and red colors of the material she held balled in her hand, and he felt his face grow chilled. It took him a split second to close the gap between them as he yanked the armband out of her hand.

"You're a Nazi now?" she screamed.

"Shut up, old woman," he hissed, inches from her face.

She swung her open palm at his face, but he ducked back and missed the blow.

"Do you want all our neighbors to hear you?" he asked, his voice distorted and tense.

"Do you want all our neighbors to know you are an enemy Nazi?" she retorted. When he didn't respond, she wailed, "I did not raise a Nazi!"

"Stop it!" he yelled. He tried to slap her, but it was her turn to avoid the blow. "Stop it!" He went after her, cornering her in the bathroom. "Do you want to get us both arrested?"

"Why would they arrest me? I have done nothing!"

"Neither have I!"

"Then, what is this?" She pointed to the armband with the distinctive swastika. "You are a traitor, traitor!"

"Stop it!" He placed his hands on the doorframe, his slender body filling the narrow doorway and preventing her escape. "If I were a traitor, would the mayor have promoted me today?" At her surprised expression, he continued, "That's right! I am a military liaison—the Polish military, in case you're too stupid to guess! I now control all of the media in and out of the city!"

"I do not believe you."

"Believe me or don't believe me, I don't care." He left the doorway and returned to his bedroom. He found his English translation book tossed onto the bed. As he rifled through his drawers in the nightstand and chest, he found his underwear, shirts, socks, and slacks in disarray. He turned around to find Felka standing in the doorway, watching him. As he shoved the armband into his pants pocket, he spat at her. "I pay part of the rent here now," he said menacingly. "If you ever—and I mean, *ever*—walk across that threshold into my room again, I will have you evicted."

"Ha!" she said, though her voice was less than convincing. "You think Mrs. Weiss would ever evict me, after decades here?"

"Mrs. Weiss will not have a choice. *I* will." He grasped the book firmly in his hand, and as he made his way to the door, Felka remained just out of his reach. He turned in the doorway. "You had better be quiet, old lady, or—"

"Or you'll what?" She planted both hands on her hips.

He turned without answering to discover their neighbor, Miss Chmiel, standing in her open doorway staring in their direction. She had been ancient when he was merely a child, and yet she hung on like a wrinkled immortal year after year. She had never been married and had never appeared to have had employment, though the rumor was she had been a schoolteacher before he was born. Now he stared back at her, his eyes taking in her thin, gray hair, pulled into a severe bun, her pale blue, red-rimmed eyes wide and unblinking, her figure hunched and shrunken. "What are you staring at?" he demanded.

She made a gurgled noise with a sudden intake of breath and stepped backward into her apartment, closing the door. He heard the sound of her chain being drawn into the chain holder, as if that could keep him out. He did not look back at his mother, but wheeled around and took the stairs two at a time. There was no time for this nonsense now. He had to get back to his office and translate that article before they gave his new office to someone else.

13

Hank

Będzin fell less than four days after the Nazis crossed into Poland.

Hank and Rafe made their way to the roof of an office building as the Nazi soldiers rolled into town in tanks and vehicles. The procession began on September 4th and continued through the next day, the sheer volume of soldiers that streamed in reminding Hank of an ant farm.

The Polish Army had pulled out hours before the town surrendered, with some of the citizenry attempting to follow them. The result was a ragtag line of wheelbarrows, carts, bicycles, and pedestrians. Reports filtered back into town of some Polish soldiers scattering or surrendering in the face of the Nazi onslaught, with figures reaching over a hundred thousand. A pipeline of journalists reported that Polish forces were fiercely fighting elsewhere.

The mood was one of shock and despair.

The door onto the roof opened suddenly. Hank and Rafe jerked their heads in tandem, expecting to see German soldiers flooding the roof terrace. Instead, they were met by a half dozen journalists.

"Mind if we join you?" one asked as the others hesitated.

Hank motioned to the area beside them. "Not at all. Stay down." They introduced themselves and their magazine.

"Jerry Winston," said one man as he knelt beside them. "*Life* Magazine."

"The States?" Hank asked.

He nodded. "You're American, too?"

"North Carolina."

"New York."

"Where'd you come from, just now?" Rafe asked.

"Been roaming the countryside, trying to find a safe place. They're everywhere. They have Będzin surrounded. Nazi aircraft are strafing the refugees on the only road out of town."

"Strafing civilians?" Hank and Rafe asked in unison.

Jerry nodded solemnly as Hank peered over the guardrail, using his telephoto lens to zoom in on the action below. Many of the citizens who had remained had come outside their homes and offices to stand on the sidewalk and solemnly watch the German procession through town. The infantry had joined the armored division, but instead of marching in formation down the street, many left their ranks to harass the onlookers.

A woman stood near the corner of a general store with a swaddled baby in her arms. Hank began to snap pictures as a soldier left the march to approach the woman. His strides were long and purposeful. As others scattered in front of him, he continued as if his sights were narrowly focused on her. As he reached her, he snatched the baby from her arms and slung it against the wall behind her.

"Fuck!" Rafe started to scramble up.

"Don't," Hank barked as he continued photographing.

"I want to—"

"I know. I do, too. But look down there. If you can even find the right guy by the time you get there, you'll have a hundred Nazis on you. We can be of more use by documenting what happens."

Rafe bit his lip as he settled back down beside Hank. The woman had begun screaming as she tore the swaddling from the baby. Even from this height, they could see that the blood was spattered across the building and sidewalk. The soldier hurled the woman to the ground and began kicking her in the head.

As men nearby rushed to her aid, they were surrounded by Nazi soldiers. Soon, it appeared as though the Nazis were rioting. Civilians dispersed in all directions as panic gripped the street.

"Revelation 12, verses seven to nine," Rafe said. "'And when Satan was cast out of Heaven, he was sent to Earth and his angels with him.' There they are, my friend." He jabbed his finger in their direction. "There is Satan's army."

A shout began on the other side of the building, and Hank and Rafe crouched down as they rushed across the roof. Several journalists were busily snapping pictures, and one had a bulky video camera that he was attempting to conceal with strips of material.

"I have never seen anything like this in all my years of covering wars," Hank breathed as he photographed an onslaught of brutality continuing to unfold before him.

"Covered a lot of wars, have you?" Jerry asked.

"Decades' worth. Nothing like this. Ever. Not even close."

Jerry swung around to remove a roll of film and insert another. "We're leaving Będzin after this. Want to join us?"

"Where are you going?" Rafe asked.

"Romania."

"Have they been invaded?"

"No. That's why we're going there."

Hank paused his photography. "Aren't you supposed to run toward the action?"

Jerry smiled wryly. "In case you haven't heard, the Nazis have declared war on journalists. If they catch any of us, we'll be hanged."

"Surely a court—"

"There are no courts. What you're seeing down there is their form of justice. It happens on the street in full view. We've witnessed them snatching people off the street—mothers, children, old men. Sometimes, they commit outright murder. Other times, the people disappear. Nobody knows where they've been taken."

"Do you know a safe passage?" Rafe asked.

"If we leave today and get to the border as quickly as possible, we have a chance. The Nazis are moving into Poland's interior. They aren't as concerned with the southern borders—yet."

"Where are their leaders?" Hank mused.

Jerry chuckled wryly. "Their leaders are just as bad, if not worse. So, you coming?"

Hank and Rafe exchanged a long look. They had been together for so long that Hank often felt more comfortable with Rafe than Dottie. They'd been like brothers through bloody conflicts and heightened emotions, but something felt ominously different about this invasion.

"I'm okay with staying," Rafe said.

"We're going to take the chance," Hank said. "Somebody has to be here to document this."

"If they find those pictures, you're dead men," Jerry warned.

Hank hesitated. "Can you take a few rolls with you? If you think—"

"Sure. We don't intend to be captured," Jerry added with a slight raise of his brow. "It'll be safer in the country than here."

Hank opened his camera and extracted the roll, popping it into a canister. Then he removed his shoes to retrieve two more rolls. As he handed them to Jerry, he said, "I've been taking photographs of the brutality here ever since they entered Będzin."

Jerry removed his hat and slipped the film into a pocket under the label. He called out to the others in a stage whisper. Without questioning him, they immediately halted their work and made their way to the roof door, remaining low. "I'd get off the roof if I were you," he said, shaking Hank's and Rafe's hands. "They'll be up here soon."

"Good luck to you," Hank said.

"And to you." He tapped his hat before joining the others at the door.

As Hank watched them disappear, an explosion rocked the area, and they hurled around to watch a plume of smoke rise in the distance. Even with his best friend beside him, he felt utterly alone. Smoke from fires and vehicle exhaust began to fill the air, blotting out the sun. As he peered past the guardrail, he watched as the other journalists raced out of the building, scattering down a series of alleyways.

"Do you think we made the right decision?" Hank asked quietly.

"Fuck if I know," Rafe answered. His voice was uncharacteristically hushed. "Let's get out of here."

"Where do we go?"

Rafe peered over the side as Hank threaded another roll into his camera. He took two shots of the German army marching down the street, with men interspersed among the tanks.

"Hey," Rafe said. "Is that Max? What the fuck is he doing?"

Hank stared into the street below. Max stood on the sidewalk between two uniformed officers as the tanks rolled past, his arm raised high in a Sieg Heil salute.

~~~~~

The door opened with so much force that it banged against the wall.

"I got the car," Rafe announced as he strode into the room. "Don't ask where it came from."
~~~~~

Hank tossed a rucksack to his friend.

"Is that it?"

"That's it," Hank said as he slung a duffel over his shoulder. "Let's get out of here." He brushed past Rafe and headed to an open vehicle that looked like it might have been abandoned years ago. He heaved the duffel into the back as Rafe's rucksack joined it. He was already in the passenger seat before Rafe hopped in behind the wheel and started the engine.

A Kübelwagen careened off a cross street and screeched to a halt in front of their vehicle. Instinctively, Rafe shoved the gear shift into reverse, but a similar vehicle raced into the alleyway behind them, blocking their escape.

Two men stepped out of the Kübelwagen wearing the typical German uniforms that struck fear in the Polish population. One wore a rifle slung over his shoulder, and the other walked with the confidence of his superior.

"Hände in die Luft," the rifleman instructed.

"He said to put our hands in the air," Rafe said as he complied, and Hank followed suit.

"Aus dem Fahrzeug!"

"He wants us out of the vehicle."

"How are we supposed to do that with our hands in the air?" Hank asked.

"Fucking carefully."

They slowly exited the vehicle while the rifleman motioned for them to stand by the wall. Hank felt his heart sink. The faces of Dottie and their children lodged inside his mind's eye, almost obscuring the scene unfolding in front of him. It occurred to him that Dottie may never know what happened to him. He began wondering what day it was and how many days he had left on this assignment before he was due to depart for home. With events unfolding as quickly as they were, he had lost track.

The senior officer casually moved in front of them. He eyed Hank carefully before turning to Rafe. *"Sprechen Sie Deutsch?"*

"Ja, ich spreche Deutsch," Rafe replied. He nodded toward Hank. *"Er tut es nicht. Ich bin sein Dolmetscher."* Without taking his focus off the German, he said, "He wants to know if I speak German. I told him that I did, but you do not, and I am your interpreter."

Hank could only nod, his throat so parched that any words he might have spoken would have sounded like a croak.

The German observed Hank for a long moment before saying, *"Steig in den Truck ein."*

"He wants us in the truck," Rafe said as he started to step forward.

"They're not going to kill us?" Hank asked, eyeing the rifleman.

"Not here," Rafe answered.

The officer issued instructions to the men who had blocked their truck from behind. It didn't take Rafe's interpretation for Hank to understand that they had been ordered to search their flat. As they moved inside through the door still open from Rafe's and Hank's rapid departure, the rifleman slung his rifle over his back and reached into the truck to retrieve their belongings. They had barely settled into the back seat of the Kübelwagen before they took off, barreling through the center of town.

~~~~~

Hank was only slightly relieved when the vehicle came to a stop in front of the administration offices. They were led upstairs and down the hall toward Max's office. It felt both familiar and foreign, as the faces he'd become accustomed to seeing were replaced with scores of men in German uniforms. The air was filled with their brusque accents, punctuated by the occasional female voice. As they passed by one office, Hank glanced through the open door to find the secretarial pool of women being lined up against an inner wall. Certainly, they would not have driven them here just to kill them, he thought. He found some solace in the fact that no one was screaming or begging for their lives, and no shots were fired.

When they stepped into Max's office, they discovered Max standing behind a disheveled desk. At the sight of the officer, he assumed the Nazi salute. "Heil Hitler!" he announced. The officer responded in kind and stood between Max, Rafe, and Hank, forming a loose circle.

"I see you have met *Oberführer* Wilhelm Keller," Max said. His voice contained a nervous timbre, and Hank wondered if the salute was a ruse for self-preservation. He invited the men to sit. While Rafe and Hank complied, the officer remained standing, his eyes riveted on them.

"I have told *Oberführer* Keller that you are Spanish and American journalists and can be very helpful to their cause," Max continued.

"Do you mean propaganda?" Rafe asked.
~~~~~

Max cleared his throat. "You will continue writing your articles as you have. You will continue to submit them to me, and I, in turn, will provide them to the *Oberführer*. As in the past, anything that is deemed unacceptable will be destroyed. Otherwise, you are free to phone in your reports as you have been."

Rafe and Hank exchanged glances as Max repeated the information to Keller.

"What's the catch?" Hank asked.

"The catch? There is no catch," Max answered. "Of course, the reports will be focused on the facts."

"The facts?" Hank repeated.

"No more fictitious reports," Max said. "The Polish Army put up a brave fight, but in the end, they scattered like little girls. They were no match for the Germans, who are a superior race, nearly superhuman."

"You're fucking kidding me," Rafe said.

"You do not wish for me to translate that," Max said.

"The fuck I don't."

Keller stepped forward. "Some English I know," he said haltingly.

The men stared at one another for a long moment before Hank broke the silence. "What kind of 'reports' are you expecting from us? We witnessed atrocities against unarmed civilians. Can we report that?"

"No," Max said, shaking his head. "You are mistaken. The civilians were armed and putting up resistance. The Germans only used necessary force to disarm them and place Będzin under their control. The city has surrendered," he added.

A soldier entered the room, saluted Keller, and handed him the duffel and rucksack. They conferred in hushed voices as Rafe tried to listen. At one point, the soldier pulled out Hank's camera.

Max turned to Hank. "You took photographs of the Germans entering Będzin."

The memory of the woman with her infant flashed through Hank's mind. He knew he would be eternally grateful to have removed that film and given it to Jerry. He wondered whether the other crew had managed to escape Będzin, and he hoped they had reached safety. "I did," he answered.

"They were good photographs," Max said. "You are to take similar photographs. The world must know of German superiority."

"You removed the film?" Hank asked. "That was a new roll. You ruined the whole thing if you removed it."

Max shrugged. "You will be supplied with plenty of film. The *Führer* wants to see these things."

"The *Führer*? You want us to take pictures for Hitler?" Hank said, his voice rising.

"Oh, fuck no," Rafe said. "And I translate," he added, turning to Keller. *"Oh, fuck, nein."*

Hank grabbed Rafe's arm. "We'll do it. You have a deal."

"What the fuck?" Rafe bellowed.

"We'll do it," Hank repeated, his eyes locked with Rafe's.

"Good," Max answered coolly, though beads of sweat had popped onto his forehead. "You will be assigned a driver, a Nazi soldier, of course. He will take you to the desired locations. When you return, you will hand in your camera. Their men—*our* men—will develop the film and return the camera to you with fresh film. You will live in the barracks with junior officers. This means," he added, "you will have semi-private accommodations. You will be watched. Do you understand?"

"Semi-private?" Rafe asked. "You mean the shitter's private, right?"

Hank spoke over him. "We understand."

Max spoke to Keller in German. Keller then spoke to the soldier, who returned the bags to the two men. "He will get you settled in," Max said to them. As they started to depart, he added, "Do not do anything foolish. You must understand that to do anything foolish is suicide."

Rafe and Hank silently followed the soldier into the hallway. They allowed a few feet to get between them and their escort before Rafe whispered, "What the fuck, you fucker?"

"You're welcome," Hank answered.

"I refuse to be a mouthpiece for Hitler's propaganda."

"Listen," Hank whispered, his eyes riveted on the soldier's back in front of them. "This will buy us some time. We need to figure out how to establish a second pipeline."

"How are we gonna do that when we'll be watched like children in a playpen?" Rafe growled.

"We've done it before," Hank answered. "And we'll do it again."

14

Agata

A thin strip of light made its way from a window near the tall ceiling of the warehouse, and Agata reluctantly opened her eyes. Two other figures sleepily met her gaze.

Janina was around the same age as Agata. She was slender with pockmarked skin and hazel eyes. She'd arrived with her friend, Irena, who lay beside her now. Irena was slightly older and more robust.

The windows were tall and wide, as most warehouses tended to have here. As Agata rolled over to stare at them, the skies were dark, and she realized the light had been from the full moon. She was just about to roll back over to catch a few more minutes of sleep when she heard a key in a door they had never used.

Before any of the girls could react, the door swung open to reveal a well-dressed woman in black, chunky heels, and a wool coat. Her eyes widened as she discovered their hasty movement in the shadows.

Rather than rushing away in fright, she descended upon them like a one-woman storm.

"How many of you are there?" she demanded.

As Agata came to her feet, she answered before she had time to think. "Three, *Pani*," she said, using the respectful term for a woman.

"Three." The woman waved her arm toward a row of boxes. "Stand there, the three of you, so I can see you."

Agata, Irena, and Janina complied, each attempting to straighten their attire and hair to varying degrees.

"Is there no one else here?" the woman demanded. Her voice was commanding; it was that of a woman who expected to be heard and respected.

"No one, *Pani*," Janina mumbled, looking at her feet.

"How long have you been here?"

Agata's eyes met the others before she answered. "I have been here a week, *Pani*. Janina and Irena have been here, perhaps five days."

"Which one is Janina?"

"I am Janina."

"Then you are Irena?"

Irena nodded silently.

The woman turned to Agata. "And you?"

"Agata."

"You three have taken bread from my bakery."

"Yes, *Pani*," Agata said, "but we left you money for it."

"Yes," the woman said. "You did."

It occurred to Agata that this was why the woman had arrived earlier than usual, before they could arise, hide their belongings, and leave for the day ahead. It had been silly of her to sleep and eat in the same place; she must be savvier in the future if she were to survive.

"Move over here, under the windows," the woman said. "Let me have a good look at you." As they complied, she studied them carefully. "You," she said, pointing at Agata, "why are you here?"

Agata swallowed. "I lived in the city center. I thought this would be safer."

"The city center?" The woman repeated. "The Jewish quarter?"

Agata nodded.

"I lived there with my father and sister, but I left when—"

"And where are they now, your father and sister?"

"Still in the city center."

The woman nodded, her eyes narrowing. "I recognize you." When Agata did not respond, she continued, "You work at the textile plant. Don't deny it," she continued firmly, "I have seen you enter through the employee entrance."

"Yes, *Pani*. I do."

"What do you do there?"

"I am a clerk."

"Do they know that you are Jewish?"

The question took Agata off guard. "My mother was Gentile."

"What was her name?" she asked as though she knew everyone in Poland.

"Anna Heinrich."

"Heinrich," she repeated. "And what is your surname?"

"Goldberg," Agata swallowed.

"Your father is Jewish."

She nodded.

"Then, you are Jewish." Before Agata could respond, the woman turned to the others. "And why are you here? Did you arrive together or separately?"

As she quizzed the others, Agata's mind began to race. It was well known how the Germans felt about the Jews, as many German Jews had immigrated to Poland and Warsaw in particular over the past decade. They brought with them stories of cruelty, subhuman treatment, and discrimination.

Poland had been referred to as a Jewish Paradise, or *Paradisus Judaeorum*, centuries ago, but antisemitism had ebbed and flowed. While some Poles, including her employer, did not care about her religious beliefs, others wanted to purge them from their communities. As Agata struggled to listen to Janina and Irena, she learned they had escaped in advance of the Germans, walking with other refugees until they reached the relative safety of Warsaw.

"Then, you are all three Jews," the woman said, clasping her hands in front of her.

"We will leave," Agata offered, "and cause you no further inconvenience."

"Nonsense." The word was snapped and firm. She turned to Agata. "Does your employer know you have been staying here?"

"No, *Pani*."

"Does anyone know?"

She shook her head.

"Do not bring anyone else here, do you understand? Not your father or your sister. For the time you remain here, you are to leave before daybreak and not return until after dark. Never approach this building or anyone who works here during the day. Do you understand?"

"Yes, *Pani*."

"Do you?" She turned to the others, who also agreed to comply with her orders.

"Never practice your religion where anyone else can see or hear you. Is that understood?"

All three nodded.

"No lights in this warehouse. Is that understood? Not even a candle." As she rattled off additional restrictions, they all agreed. Agata's mind continued to race. She had intended to remain there only until she could find a suitable room to rent, but the woman's demands led her to believe she would be staying for the long term. She was befuddled. The Polish Warsaw Army would push back the Germans within days, and she would be reunited with Ira, Elsa, and Piotr.

"I will return this evening. It will be long after the bakery has closed. There is no need for you to take another loaf of bread. I will deliver food to you."

Surprised, they each profusely thanked her, but she waved their words away. "My name is Helen. You do not need to know more." With that, she was gone.

~~~~~

The guilt threatened to consume her. Though she tried to push thoughts of Elsa and Ira from her mind while she worked, the images of them at the school kept invading her mind. Her soul would not allow her to
~~~~~

forget that she had promised to be back the following day, but she had been unable to keep that promise. She kept seeing Elsa's trusting brown eyes in her mind's eye. Sometimes, she was a small child, calling her *Siostra Mamo*, meaning "Sister Mama." Other times, her dreams were invaded by an older Elsa; still a child, her eyes had taken on the characteristics of an old soul, deep and knowing, penetrating and with an understanding that contradicted her age.

Aerial bombing continued relentlessly day and night. There were scattered bomb shelters around the city, but they were crowded and often inconveniently located. Frequently, bombs fell at the entrances, burying people within. Despite the bombardment, scores of people took to the streets to clear the shelter entrances, moving one rock or handful of debris at a time, passing them along makeshift lines. Others fought against raging fires that consumed Warsaw, block by block.

Although Agata continued to show up for work each day, the amount of time she actually worked on the job varied from day to day. Coworkers were trembling, concentration was nearly impossible, and a collective trauma had set in.

Agata returned to the bakery warehouse long after dark, though the continued fires and bombing lit the area in a surreal red swath. She'd spent another frustrating and increasingly dangerous evening attempting to reach the city center, where Ira and Elsa might still remain. The streetcars were no longer running, their tracks cratered. Many streetcars, buses, and cars littered the streets, some still smoldering. Explosions were common among vehicles as flames reached their fuel tanks.

If there were safe havens in Warsaw, she did not know where they might be. The entire city was in flames. She prayed constantly, her body trembling, asking God to protect her father and sister. Her thoughts were a jumble of contradictions. At times, she was convinced she'd made a mistake and that they should have remained together at the school. Other times, she was persuaded that they should have come with her; perhaps they could have left Warsaw together. But, she countered, where could they have gone? The Nazis were everywhere. With that realization, she fought against an ever-present feeling of hopelessness and powerlessness. A voice rose inside her, urging her to place her faith in Piotr and the rest of the Warsaw Polish Army, but just as quickly faded away.

She slipped inside the warehouse and slid the door closed behind her. It was the same door Piotr had led her to on her first night there, through a narrow alley filled with trash from the manufacturing plants. She had to step past rats and roaches, but once inside, she was grateful to have a roof over her head. Times had certainly changed from their neat little apartment and the bedroom she'd shared with Elsa. The bed seemed luxurious now as she thought of it.

The long corridor was dark and windowless, a good place to sit or sleep to escape the worst of the booms. She wandered to the end to retrieve her blanket from the stash she'd hidden behind heavily laden shelving. Agata paused at the entrance to the large room, where shelving that had once been piled high with inventory had dwindled alarmingly. No supplies were getting into Warsaw, and food was running low.

The tall windows revealed a constant flicker of red flames against a heavy smoke, the stench seeping into every crevice. A streetlamp was struck, spraying glass and emitting a glimmering blue light before being swallowed by the darkness. Then the flames returned like an immortal monster.

Through the light, she spotted a small pile on a chair in the middle of the room, and she made her way toward it. It was about a third of a loaf of bread wrapped in cheesecloth and three chunks of cheese. She broke off a piece of the bread and left the rest for Janina and Irena, though they had not yet returned, and selected a piece of cheese. As she returned the bread to the chair, she spotted an envelope on the seat.

She moved under one of the windows, hoping the light would help her see more clearly. Opening the envelope, she poured out the contents: three sets of identification. Puzzled, she opened each one in turn until she found one marked Agata Heinrich. The birthdate and place of birth were the same as those on the identification she normally carried, and she paused to consider how anyone could have obtained her old identification. They would have had to have taken it from her handbag, which she always kept with her. Almost always, she realized. Each morning, she left her handbag behind as she made her way down another hallway to the bathroom, where she attempted to clean up and dress for the day ahead.

The same photograph was on this identification. She tried to retrieve her original paperwork, but it was no longer there. With its absence, she felt her identity as Agata Goldberg slip away as well. She studied the new identification again, her birthplace in Germany jumping out at her. With the Germans on Warsaw's doorstep, she hoped her birthplace would not become a liability among the Poles.

She tucked the paperwork inside her lingerie, admonishing herself for having left the original unattended. If she had to sew a pocket in her undergarments, she swore this one would never leave her side.

Agata studied the other identifications before placing them back in the envelope and returning it to the chair underneath the bread and cheese.

A newspaper had also been placed on the chair, and she retrieved it, bringing it back to the window, where she attempted to find enough light to read the small print. It was an old paper, creased and crumpled, as though it had passed through a multitude of hands before it found its way to her. The United Kingdom and France had declared war on Germany on September 3, less than 48 hours after the invasion of Poland had begun. There was a glimmer of hope that they would come to their aid and repel the Nazis, returning Poland to its status as a sovereign, independent nation.

Then she sat on the floor with her back against the wall and cried as the bombs pummeled the city.

15

Agata

Warsaw surrendered to Nazi Germany on September 27. One hundred and forty thousand Polish troops were rumored to have relinquished their arms. They were paraded through the city, purportedly on their way to prison camps. They appeared gaunt, grimy, and exhausted, their faces smeared with smoke and ash, their eyes reflecting trauma and bewilderment at their country's fate. Some limped along as they nursed wounds, their comrades attempting to keep them on their feet, while others showed clear signs of abuse.

Agata stood on the sidewalk, watching the men march by, searching for Piotr. When she did not spot him, her mind went into overdrive. He was there, but she had missed him. He had been in another column in another part of the city. He had escaped and was hiding somewhere in Warsaw, or he'd been able to flee the city. She could not bring herself to consider that he had been killed in action.

In contrast, the German soldiers were robust in uniforms that had been spared the worst of the fighting. With the Germans controlling the skies, it almost felt as though they had simply waltzed into Warsaw after the aerial bombardment had crippled the city. As much as 90% of the city was damaged or destroyed, from simple homes to ancient castles, all denominations of places of worship, nearly all of Warsaw's cultural heritage, including museums, theaters, and galleries. What they did not destroy, they looted, sending priceless artifacts on trains bound for Berlin.

By December, all Jews were required to wear the Star of David. Although armbands were preferred, some individuals also sewed them onto their clothing, often placing them on their chests above their hearts or on their backs. One could spot the white star easily from half a block away. It may as well have been a bull's-eye. A population that had been vibrant only months earlier was now rendered as less than human, inviting Germans and Polish Gentiles to abuse them without restraint or retribution.

Everyone was required to carry identification. Jews had theirs marked, further separating them from the rest of society.

That December, as Agata huddled in the frigid warehouse night after night, the last vestiges of her old identity slipped from her. She did not wear the Star of David, nor did she submit to the long lines of Jews required to queue at government offices for new identification.

Everywhere, massive Nazi flags hung from the buildings, the garish red background appearing to represent the blood that was spilled everywhere they went. It was impossible to go anywhere without seeing them. At the end of every block was a checkpoint, usually containing vehicles blocking the way with soldiers on either side. Agata had been stopped each time she ventured out, always by a different set of soldiers. She held her head high as they studied her identification papers. They usually commented on her birthplace, inquiring why she was now in Warsaw. She always answered that she had come to visit her aunts before the invasion, but she knew she needed a different story.

Simply being stopped was a monumental risk. She retained enough of the German language from her younger years, but she feared her sentences were halting. And there were eyes everywhere. If one was friendly with the soldiers to carry on their business, the Polish community judged that person as a collaborator. Not being friendly could draw the soldiers' ire. It was a thin line, and neither side was a winning one.

Her job was gone, the building now a towering mound of rubble in the middle of a city block that she no longer recognized. Helen did not always leave food for her, and Irena and Janina had never returned. She needed to leave, but she did not know where to go. Rumors abounded about atrocities in and out of the city.

Returning to the city center was not an option. Agata told herself that someday, this would all be over, and she would be reunited with Elsa and Ira. But, to go to the Jewish sector now would place her in too much danger. Something deep within her soul urged her not to risk being labeled a Jew.

She tried not to think of little Elsa and how frightened she must be. She attempted to console herself with the knowledge that she was with their father, and he would protect her at all costs. He would ensure she had food and everything she needed to survive. Yet, even as she told herself these things, she wondered how that could be possible under Nazi rule.

By the following October, all Jews throughout the city were required to relocate to a designated area. Rumors abounded about the overcrowding and lack of food and water. Shortly after, the Nazis erected concrete barricades in the middle of city blocks to separate those Jews within from the Gentiles that lived outside. At the few gates into the Jewish sector, Nazi soldiers were positioned with strict orders on who could go inside.

It was now impossible for Agata to reach her sister or father.

16

Hank, 1943

Everything happened gradually until it happened all at once.

Będzin, along with the surrounding area, was annexed into Germany only a month after the Nazi invasion. The rails that once served as a vital supply route for civilian goods were now repurposed to transport infantry and supply the German Armed Forces. Będzin had become an essential cog in the Nazi war machine, its vast manufacturing capabilities pumping out goods around the clock.

As soon as Będzin became a part of Germany, all Jews over the age of ten were ordered to wear white armbands with a vivid blue Star of David. As they were now easily identified, they became vulnerable targets. It began with a constant barrage of hate speech on Nazi-run radio stations, the only stations citizens of any faith were permitted to listen to. They blared in restaurants and public places. Hitler's speeches were particularly popular, drawing citizens to gather around large television sets strategically erected in businesses. He blamed the Jews for the loss of World War I, and the low status of some Germans, attributing their lack of work or money to Jews robbing them. After these broadcasts, assaults were commonplace against anyone wearing the Star of David.

Hank suspected that Max had become a puppet or useful idiot for the Nazi regime. To supposedly protect the Jews, he implemented a system of segregation under the Nazis' watchful eyes and direction. All Jews were being systematically moved into one area of the city, their previous possessions now the property of Nazi Germany. Artwork, jewelry, and other valuable items were confiscated and sent by rail to Berlin. Their businesses, real estate, and bank accounts were seized. Sometimes, their companies were shut down completely, while in other instances, they were awarded to non-Jews. It all depended upon the needs of the Third Reich. The money traveled by train to Berlin under the protection of heavily armed soldiers.

Jews were no longer permitted to hold jobs without written Nazi authorization, and the only opportunities provided to them were as the lowest-level workers, regardless of their previous occupations. The Będzin Power Station cut off electricity to the Jewish quarter, and food and water began to run short.

To complicate matters and as if invading several countries was not enough for Hitler, he had invaded the Soviet Union in June 1941, transforming his ally into his enemy, and catching Stalin completely by surprise. The Soviets had begun to invade eastern Poland as part of the Axis powers, but now a line had been drawn that separated them from the Nazis. The Soviets had given the Nazis their first major defeat and shown the world that these superhumans could, in fact, be defeated. In turn, Nazi Germany ramped up the war effort throughout Poland, as more of everything was sorely needed, including uniforms, ammunition, tanks, aircraft, and other types of weaponry.

By 1943, the structures throughout the Jewish quarter were overflowing as Jews from rural areas were brought to Będzin for the war effort. Homes built for one family were expected to house seven or eight. While Jews had been encouraged to emigrate to other continents before the war voluntarily, they were now prohibited from leaving. They were prisoners within Będzin, guarded by scores of Nazis, used as slave labor in the factories.

Hank was a prisoner, too, though his and Rafe's circumstances were far more humane than those of the Jewish inhabitants. He had not received any correspondence from Dottie, and he didn't know if any of his letters had reached her. He kept himself busy during the day, between Max's assignments for them and an underground media pipeline that Rafe had tapped into. As long as he was kept busy, thoughts of home were pushed into the dark recesses of his soul.

In the dark of night, however, they reared their heads. He dreamt of Dottie, Mary, Susanna, and Ray. He had nightmares that they were attending a funeral service, and when he peered at the tombstone, he discovered it was his. He dreamt that one or all of them needed him desperately, but he couldn't reach them. He dreamt that the magazine had stopped his paychecks, and without them, his family became homeless, and America had been turned into one huge dustbowl.

Only rumors about the world outside Poland reached him, and he never knew whether to trust them. Max informed them rather arrogantly that Germany had declared war on America after Japan destroyed or damaged almost all of the American battleships at Pearl Harbor. After that, he dreamt of Nazis invading North Carolina and his family being subjected to inhumane conditions, conditions from which he could not protect them.

Hank learned through his German sources that additional factories were being built between Będzin and a small village to their north called Oświęcim. While the area had been industrialized previously, the war effort had significantly accelerated its growth. And while the Jews were not allowed to leave their Będzin zone on their own, the Germans had begun calling for volunteers for the additional factories. Overcrowded and underfed, many volunteers hoped that the new location would provide ample accommodations. They were transported on repurposed cattle cars, with trains departing several times a week. Rumors flew that Jews from Oświęcim, Kraków, and as far away as Warsaw were also transported to the new facilities. As a result, it was rumored that the new location, formerly a small internment for Russian prisoners of war, had grown larger than Będzin and Oświęcim combined. Its name, Hank learned, was Auschwitz-Birkenau.

For the past few years, Hank and Rafe had played an elaborate game of cat-and-mouse with their journalism. Each day, they dutifully covered the day's stories provided by their German handlers, usually Max. Assignments often consisted of covering German soldiers receiving commendations and promotions, of carefully choreographed scenes from Będzin factories showing the happiness of the workers, which Rafe called "pure propaganda shit," or Polish people playing ball games, dining at sidewalk cafes, or other activities to show the normalcy—and supposed complacency—of Germany's newly acquired land. All of this was sent to Berlin, where it would be used to prove the superiority of the Nazi machine.

Then there were the real stories.

And Otto.

Hank sat in the abbreviated back seat as he glanced at the back of Otto's head while he drove through the streets of Będzin on the way to the Jewish sector. Rafe sat up front, a position he sometimes exchanged with Hank, as Otto dutifully transported them from one job to the next.

Private Otto Schubert, or the generic Obersoldat, was twenty-one years old. He'd spent his seventeenth birthday running out of a pillbox and crossing the Polish border, having spent the previous ten years in training as a Hitler Youth to serve the Third Reich. He had been assigned as Hank's full-time driver and escort, an assignment that could stretch into the overnight hours or go for weeks without a day off. He slept in the same facility, ate his meals with them, and, as Rafe was fond of saying, did everything but shit with them.

Now Otto had the shakes, and he had them bad.

Otto pulled in front of the gate closest to the chemical factory. The soldiers called out their greeting to him as Hank hopped out of the back seat. As Rafe joined him, he leaned into the vehicle to retrieve two large boxes. *"Ich werde in fünf Minuten zurück sein,"* Hank said.

"Someday," Rafe said as he carried one of the boxes past the guard, "you'll say that without an American accent."

"If I don't remember anything else once I leave this place, I will remember how to say 'back in five minutes' in German," Hank said under his breath.

They passed by a block of squalor on their way to the chemical factory as citizens hungrily eyed their boxes. Hank tried not to look at them; if he did, he felt a wave of guilt sweep over him. Besides, his eyes were needed to survey the ground in front of him, as it was uneven and often covered in debris. Furniture, crates, and used building supplies were stacked against the structures as if every day were moving day.

Two young girls stopped in the street to watch them, and Hank quickly snapped his camera several times, hoping that the surrounding squalor would frame their images. Too young to wear the Star of David, their hair was neatly combed, their clothing neat but soiled, their shoes worn and dusty. The smallest reminded Hank of Susanna when she was little.

They reached the back door of the chemical factory, a large concrete brick structure whose drab gray exterior nearly blended into its surroundings. The metal door locked automatically upon closing, but today it was propped open with a single brick.

They made their way inside, stopping momentarily to adjust to the dim light cast by grimy windows high up near the two-story ceilings, locations that were not meant for people to peer through, but rather for natural light to replace nonexistent bulbs.

"There you are!" a burly man exclaimed in German as he made his way toward them. These regular encounters, along with their constant escort, had allowed Hank and Rafe to learn conversational German. They exchanged pleasantries as if they were old friends while they made their way to a corner office. Once there, the man closed the door and lowered the blinds across the broad, cloudy windows overlooking the factory floor.

"What do you have for me today?" he asked as they placed the boxes on the desk.

"A little of this and that," Rafe answered as he held up a bottle of beer in one hand and schnapps in the other.

"Gut! Gut!" he exclaimed with delight. He combed through the boxes, discovered more alcohol in the form of gin and even a small bottle of cognac, before finding various food items. *"Gut! Gut!"* he repeated appreciatively. Then abruptly, he placed everything back in their boxes and retrieved a key from his pocket, which he used to open his center desk drawer. He retrieved several boxes of Pervitin. As he handed them to Hank and Rafe, they quickly stuffed their shirts with the thin pill boxes.

They were out the door in under three minutes, making their way across the slum to the gate, where the soldiers were still conversing with Otto. Their laughter and casualness were a stark contrast to the rifles slung over their shoulders and the grim mood inside the gate.

Reaching the light truck, the two men hopped back inside. Rafe had already pulled a box of Pervitin out of his shirt. As he handed it over to the guards, Otto was quick to pull away. They hadn't gone half a block before he held out his hand. *"Eins,"* he said, indicating one.

Rafe opened another box, extracted a single pill, and plopped it into Otto's open palm. As the young man swallowed it dry, Rafe slipped the opened box into Otto's jacket pocket. "That ought to hold you for a while," he said in halting German.

Hank watched the interaction with the same guilt he felt every time. Before the war, Pervitin was a commonly available over-the-counter medicine, much like aspirin in the United States. Unlike aspirin, which targeted pain, Pervitin made a person more alert. It could be used by students studying all night, long-distance drivers, shift workers, or even doctors performing lengthy operations. It was so popular and reliable that it soon caught the attention of top military brass.

The problem with soldiers was that they needed rest. A man could only march so far before his body grew tired, and even forced marches required breaks to keep the men from passing out. They also needed sleep. And when a soldier was sleeping, it meant he wasn't marching.

All that could—and did—change with Pervitin and a similar product, Isophan. Both made soldiers so alert that their minds failed to register the need for breaks or sleep. As a result, they could advance deep into enemy territory without the need to sleep for as much as seven days. The pills ensured *Blitzkrieg*, a rapid advance by air, vehicles, and infantry, could overwhelm the enemy forces with such speed that the enemy was woefully unprepared for the advance. It created the myth that the Nazi army was filled with a superior Aryan race of superhumans.

One pill could cause alertness. Several taken over time could create feelings of superiority and grandiosity. As the soldiers continued to take them, it resulted in escalating forms of aggression.

The problem, Hank quickly observed, is that some soldiers became addicts because the active ingredients in Pervitin and Isophan were methamphetamines.

And no matter how quickly the factories churned out the pills, they could not keep up with demand. The chemical factory in Będzin's Jewish quarter had been a possible solution; by converting the original purpose from processing metals to generating pills, the transportation issues from Berlin, which often resulted in lag times and shortages, were resolved through manufacturing on-site. Every day, thousands of the little pills were manufactured and boxed in the facility that Hank had just left, but the vast majority of those pills did not remain in Będzin but were disbursed throughout the immediate area.

As Otto barreled through Będzin and citizens scattered in advance of his careening vehicle, Hank tried not to think about the drug supply chain he and Rafe had created. Each week, they bribed the commissary staff with drugs to get alcohol and food, which they brought to the factory in exchange for more drugs. They then bribed the guards at the gate, Otto, and numerous others for access to areas officially deemed off-limits, to process film in clandestine locations, and to convey the real, unaltered stories to the Allies through underground networks.

Otto stopped the vehicle in front of a bar, which was lively despite the noon hour. With his shakes gone and a newfound confidence, he was ready to party. While all three entered the establishment, Rafe and Hank would soon find their way out the back door. They weren't giving Otto the slip, as the drugs also seemed to provide the soldiers with superhuman senses. It had all been prearranged. Within the hour, the two would return and be on their way to an official gig.

As Hank and Rafe exited through the back door, Hank said, "Are you sure we're doing the right thing?"

"First John, verse 5:19," Rafe answered. "The whole world lies in the power of the evil one. And I paraphrase." He glanced at Hank as they made their way down the alley. "We are fighting Satan, my friend."

"I know. That's what you always say. But, if we fight like this, are we any better?"

"What would you prefer to do? Stand around with niceties? Bake them a cake, or sing for them? The only way to fight against brutality, heartlessness, and evil is to fight on their terms. They don't understand anything else."

They entered the back door of an office building and made their way up the stairwell to the roof. It was empty, as it always was. With the Jews confined to their own sector, the population of the rest of the city had dwindled. Offices were vacant, and the army had seized most of the landlords' rental homes for their soldiers.

They crouched down and made their way to the side of the roof that provided an unhindered view of the Jewish sector. Hank snapped several photographs. A bread line snaked for several blocks, as it always did at this time of day; the people appeared noticeably thinner, their clothing hanging as if it were all oversized. Several of the buildings appeared burned out, and one was still smoldering; Hank would have to dig to find out what had occurred there overnight. A soldier walking beside the bread line suddenly stopped and struck a young woman in the back of her head with the butt of his rifle. He continued walking as several people in line attempted to help the woman off the street where she had fallen. Hank hoped he had captured it all on film. As he snapped, he dictated observations to Rafe, who dutifully wrote them down.

There was so much more to photograph, and so much he wanted to write, but time was of paramount importance. He slid away from the barrier along the edge and removed the film, placing it into a canister. He handed it to Rafe, who quickly made his way to the door and down the steps. Hank knew he would bribe his point of contact to use the phone to call in a story to the magazine and to have another person smuggle the film out. The bribes, like the others, consisted of boxes of Pervitin.

As Hank slipped a new roll of film into the camera, he couldn't help but question his role as a drug dealer. Bribing the factory manager was akin to buying drugs on the black market, and bribing others along the chain was clearly the distribution of drugs, even if they had been over the counter in Germany. They were addictive. Maybe, he thought, it was no worse than bribing alcoholics with alcohol. But when he thought of Otto and compared him to his son, Ray, his heart knew what he was doing was wrong.

Ray had joined the military after the attack on Pearl Harbor. Barely sixteen and too young for service, a flawed system had allowed him to join. Letters from home had finally begun to trickle through, and they were agonizingly slow to reach Hank; he suspected that numerous Nazis read them before they ever reached him. Dottie had to know this, and Ray would certainly know and understand the government's policy of "loose lips sink ships," so Hank received vague information, only that Ray was somewhere in the Pacific fighting the Japanese.

Hank made his way back down the stairwell and along the alley to the bar, where he joined Otto. Hank ordered a drink as he always did, which caused Otto to order another. As he leisurely raised the glass to his lips, he knew this would keep Otto in place for the additional minutes Rafe would need to get their information out.

Maybe Rafe was right. Perhaps they had to fight differently. The soldiers could have murdered them when they were first discovered, and they'd had ample opportunities to knock them off since. It was their usefulness in their propaganda machine that kept them alive. He only hoped the film and underground reports would be helpful to the Allies and those back home. After all, he thought as he raised his glass again, if he were going to compromise his morals and ethics, it had better be worth it.

17

Max

In Germany, the process to exclude Jews, political dissidents, and others the Nazis deemed undesirable took years. It was a gradual undertaking, often with baby steps, so the general populace wasn't alarmed by a sudden cultural change. Max learned immediately, however, that such would not be the case in Poland.

Much of the city's medieval architecture was saved through a hasty deal and total surrender. The Polish Army either fled or surrendered before the Nazis were on their doorstep, leaving a void that the newcomers quickly filled. With the language now officially German and Rafe speaking passable German, Max realized his position as an interpreter was on tenuous ground. With troops running roughshod through the city, he went through great efforts to discover who was in charge and then track him down for a deal.

His point of contact would be *Oberführer* Wilhelm Keller. With his Nazi armband and newly appointed corner office as proof of his esteemed stature, he positioned himself as a liaison to journalists for propaganda that Berlin would surely want, as well as an insider who could identify threats to the Nazi regime.

The Jews were an easy target, as they were more easily identified. The Nazis began by burning or confiscating their homes, businesses, and synagogues, and soldiers were often given free rein to confiscate any of their less valuable possessions for their own personal use, while those items of considerable value were sent to Berlin. An area of the city was established to corral the people, and barbed wire was erected faster than Max could have imagined possible.

As Jews were rounded up and sorted, Max accompanied Wilhelm to the block where Mrs. Weiss owned much of the property, including the apartment where his mother lived and the bakery that he so often frequented. Max witnessed the sorting with dizzying speed, as if the process had been repeated countless times and was so well-oiled that there was hardly any thought given to it. Able-bodied men were placed in one group and able-bodied women in another, as they would be used for slave labor. They were immediately marched through the city under guard to the Jewish sector.

The elderly and the invalid were shot on the spot, their bodies left where they fell. Children suffered the worst atrocities, as they were separated from their parents, and those too young to work were killed in ways too violent for Max to watch, but he could not avoid their screams. His nerves were rattled so severely that he was certain someone would notice him shaking.

He remained close to Wilhelm, afraid that soldiers would mistake him for an undesirable, and barked orders whenever possible to further cement his status.

They were thankfully getting ready to leave the neighborhood when Mrs. Weiss was hauled out of her bakery with her daughter, Celina. Max was so close that he witnessed the recognition and relief in Mrs. Weiss's eyes when she spotted him, but when his eyes rolled from her to Celina, he found the younger woman's face growing pale as she stared at his armband. For the briefest of moments, he wanted to tear the armband off and run out of sight, but he forced himself to assume a noble stature.

"That woman and her daughter," he said to Wilhelm in German, "are hard workers. I suggest that you send them to the Jewish sector."

"Max!" Mrs. Weiss shouted. "Max!"

Max glanced again in her direction. Soldiers were manhandling her, knocking her kerchief askew, and Celina had been pushed against the brick wall.

"You know them?" Wilhelm asked slyly.

"I do. They have performed work for my family in the past," he answered smoothly. "That is how I know that they work hard."

Wilhelm called out to a soldier nearby. "Tell them to move those two women to the Jewish sector," he ordered. As the soldier left to carry out his order, others began to converge on the bakery with torches in hand.

"Must you do that?" Max asked Wilhelm.

"Of course. Are you a Jew lover?"

"Absolutely not. But if your soldiers are hungry, the bakery is always filled with pastries they might not have experienced since they left home. And the bakery connects to apartments where non-Jews live."

As the soldier returned, Wilhelm ordered him to stop the fire. The young man rushed back just as the plate-glass windows shattered.

Max pointed to a beautiful home across a side street from the bakery. From the front, it appeared to be one story, but he knew from his mother's deliveries of clothing to Mrs. Weiss that there was a full wine cellar. A portico rested in the center, supported by four columns that underscored its importance amid the surrounding apartment buildings and businesses. It was smaller than a standard manor house, but impressive nonetheless. It was painted an immaculate white and set off by multi-colored pansies in giant planters, the blooms stubbornly visible despite the snow. "That is my house," Max said, tilting his chin upward. "Of course, you are welcome to stay there, if you'd like."

Wilhelm glanced at the house appreciatively. "Thank you, but the mayor has offered me accommodations at the edge of town."

"Ah. I know the home. It sits along a rise with a beautiful view. Does it not? Rows of chestnut trees frame it, and a beautiful oval garden just beyond the front door."

"Yes, that's the one. How did you know?"

"It is the most desirable one, of course, befitting someone of your importance."

As the soldiers approached the home, Wilhelm gave an order to protect it, and they quickly began seeking out other targets.

The mayhem grew around them, the stench of smoke mingling with the sounds of shattered glass, children crying, and women screaming. As Max peered down the street toward the apartment he shared with his mother, he was horrified to see the building next door to them on fire, the flames licking at the outside walls as they shot through the broken windows.

"If you could excuse me," Max said, taking a few steps away from Wilhelm.

"Wait, wait."

Max reluctantly stopped, his heart pounding.

Wilhelm reached into his jacket pocket and extracted a pad of paper. He wrote quickly on a piece of paper, tore it off, and handed it to Max. "You must have this paper with you wherever you go." As Max began to read it, Wilhelm added, "It says you are assigned to my office. You will not be bothered."

"Thank you," he breathed appreciatively. "Thank you! I won't be but a moment." As he hurried off, he glanced back to see that a soldier had garnered Wilhelm's attention. With his back to him now, he ran along the sidewalk until he reached his apartment entrance. He bolted through the door but immediately came to an abrupt halt.

The narrow, open stairwell was filled with soldiers, most of whom carried items they thought had value but couldn't possibly use—silver candlesticks, paintings, fine porcelain, furs—one even took a rolled-up Oriental rug. Max had lived in this building his entire life, and he never knew that people who had lived hand-to-mouth for decades owned items like these. As one soldier brushed past him, he caught sight of his double-armed loot, and he knew these were family heirlooms.

He heard women shouting upstairs and pushed past soldiers as he rushed up. One grabbed his sleeve as he tried to blow past him, and he turned and spat, "I work with *Oberführer* Wilhelm Keller. Do not dare touch me again!"

As that soldier quickly turned and ran down the stairs, others gave Max a wide berth. As he reached the top of the stairs, he found the door to Miss Chmiel's apartment open. The air was filled with the weak, reedy protests of an old woman, and he longed to hold his hands against his ears to block out the sound. Another set of screams soon joined hers in a voice Max knew all too well.

He burst into Miss Chmiel's apartment to find his mother trying to argue with the soldiers, unsuccessfully attempting to place her body between the Nazis and their neighbor. Max strode up to her and grabbed her by the elbow. "You! The *Oberführer* wants you!" he shouted in German.

She stared at him wide-eyed.

For the first time in your life, shut up! Max wanted to shout. Instead, he hauled her out of the apartment, unceremoniously pulling her past their apartment door.

"Wait! My things! They will take them!" His mother's voice was a mixture of pleading and stubbornness.

"Shut up!" he said, striking her across her face.

Her hand went instinctively to her cheek, where her pale skin had already begun to turn beet red.

"Come with me, old woman!" he shouted in German for all to hear. "The *Oberführer* awaits!" As his voice thundered through the staircase, it seemed that the soldiers had suddenly disappeared. Perhaps concerned he would stop the plundering, they ducked into open doorways or fled outside to other unprotected structures.

A shot rang out above them. Max instinctively stopped in his tracks and stared up the stairs. Miss Chmiel's constant wailing was gone, the air replaced with the pungent odor of gun smoke. A moment later, he heard heavy footsteps and the sound of breaking glass. "Come on," he hissed, increasing his hold on his mother.

Once outside, he nearly dragged his mother a few paces from the building before pulling her into an alley.

"Who are you?" she demanded.

"Are you crazy?" Max hissed.

"My son would never have struck his mother," she said as tears filled her eyes. She held one hand against the red welt forming on her cheek. "He would never have spoken to me as you have. I don't know you anymore!"

"Stop your wailing and listen to me." He blocked her body with his, so that any onlookers rushing along the sidewalk would see his suit and Nazi armband and, hopefully, keep moving. "I just saved your life back there, you idiot."

"I am not—"

"I am important now. I am not some stupid little Polish boy any longer. I am a man, and I have chosen sides." He jabbed his finger at his armband. "You see this? This will keep us safe. This will keep you from ending up in the Jewish sector." He grabbed her arm and began to exit the alley.

"Where are you taking me?" Felka struggled to break free of his grip.

He swung back around, his open palm outstretched. "You are coming with me. You will not fight against me. You will go willingly, like someone who has good sense. You will not look at anyone we pass, do you understand? You will hear things that will give you nightmares, but you will not look. Do you understand?"

Felka began to whimper.

"Do you understand?" Max shouted as he shook her.

"I understand," she managed to gasp.

"If you do not obey me, I will leave you on the street. The Nazis will do to you what they want, and nobody—nobody—will come to your aid. This is the only chance you will ever get, old woman." With that, he grabbed her arm again and strode purposefully into the street. This time, Felka did not struggle against him. As he made his way toward Mrs. Weiss's home, he felt her clinging to him as the chaos grew around them. Everywhere, there was smoke, flames, breaking glass, and children and women screaming and crying. It felt like the end of the world, and to many, it was.

~~~~~

They reached Mrs. Weiss's home, marching straight up the path to the front door. Max opened it and pushed Felka inside.

"Where is Mrs. Weiss?" Felka asked. Her voice had grown reedy and thin.

Max shut the door behind them. Although they could still hear the pandemonium, it was now muffled. He moved down the hallway, glancing into various
~~~~~

rooms. The further they went into the interior, the less he heard the sounds outside. This would work well. Very well, indeed.

The wallpapered walls were adorned with paintings in gilded frames, illuminated by gold-colored light bars. As Max stepped toward one, he realized they were all originals. The wallpaper in the parlor was burgundy with a gold pattern in damask baroque, but as he moved from one room to the next, every room was a different color—emerald green, sapphire blue, and amethyst. The bedlam outside faded completely as he became mesmerized by the opulence.

The furniture was beyond anything he had ever witnessed. Unlike his simple, small furniture with straight lines, this furniture was intricately carved with elaborate claw feet, and the sofas and chairs were upholstered in crushed velvet, every inch of wood shining as if it had just been polished. He moved into the kitchen to find every countertop spotless. The refrigerator was full of food, and in the center of the table was a bowl of fresh fruit. He picked up a red, flawless apple and bit into it.

"Where is Mrs. Weiss?" Felka repeated. She stood in the doorway, her body looking frail and smaller than she had appeared only a few moments earlier, as if she were visibly shrinking.

Max set the apple on the table and pushed past her into the hallway. He marched to the staircase, pausing momentarily to admire the detailed carving on the mahogany newel posts before climbing the stairs. Though the house appeared to be one story from the front, there were bedrooms at each end of the upstairs hall and one in the center. All had windows overlooking a courtyard behind the house. It was easy to identify which had belonged to Mrs. Weiss. The bed was covered in a gold satin spread, not the aged quilts he had grown up using. Perfume decanters were meticulously arranged on a dressing table beside an ornate hand mirror and a matching brush.

"This is my bedroom," he announced.

"But, where is Mrs. Weiss?" Felka asked.

"Where is Mrs. Weiss? Where is Mrs. Weiss?" Max mocked. "Will you shut up with that? I don't want to hear that again. Mrs. Weiss is gone. She isn't coming back. This is our home now."

"But this isn't my home!" Felka's lower lip trembled. "I want to go back to my apartment!"

Max waved his hand to encompass all that he saw. "You would rather go back to that dark, damp cell than stay here?"

"Yes!" she cried out.

"For God's sake, why, woman?"

"Because it's my home!"

Momentarily shocked, he simply stared at her.

"I have work to do," she continued, seizing his silence as a sign to continue. "I have clothing to make. My customers are waiting for it."

"Your customers?" He took a step back. "Your customers are gone, you silly woman. You will never sew again."

"But I like sewing!"

"I don't care what you like." He pushed past her and moved into the bedroom in the center of the hall. "This is your bedroom."

"Why?"

"Because I said so, that's why." Max glanced around. Being in the center of the house, there were no side windows overlooking the streets below; only one window offered a view of the courtyard at the back. "Listen to me. Are you listening?"

"I am listening."

"You are not to leave this house without me. Do you understand?"

"Why not?"

"Because you will be raped and killed, that's why not. And you are not to go to any window except this one, do you understand?"

She nodded silently.

"Do you understand?"

"I understand."

"Say it louder!"

"I understand!" she sniveled.

"Stop your crying. You get on my nerves." He grabbed her arm. "Your world is gone. Your jobs—both of them—are gone. Your apartment is gone. It is probably in flames as I speak." Felka gasped, but he continued. "The Polish military is gone, Mama. They abandoned us to the wolves. But this—this—is our lair. I will get a soldier—a *German* soldier—to guard it. You will be safe here. You have plenty of food, enough for a whole army! You will sleep in a better bed than any you've ever experienced. You will live like a rich woman!"

Max dropped her arm, walked back down the hall, and hurried down the staircase. He had been gone too long. He stopped at the front door, his hand on the knob. "Close all the drapes and keep them closed. And—one more thing." He studied her closely as he spoke. "You are no longer my mama, do you understand? You are Felka, the cleaning woman. You are to act like a servant whenever I bring a Nazi into this home, and they will all be Nazis. Do you understand?"

Felka stood with her mouth agape.

"Do you understand?" he bellowed.

"Yes," she said, her spine straightening. "I understand."

He pointed his finger at her. "Do not do anything stupid, and anything you do outside this house is stupid."

"I am a prisoner now, am I?"

"Yes. You are a prisoner. Be thankful you are here." He opened the door. Instantly, the tumult was almost overpowering. "And not out there," he added. He stepped through the door, closing it firmly behind him. As he walked down the path to the street, he called out to a young private. "You! You, there!"

The young man stopped and stared at him.

"Do you not know who I am?" Max bellowed. "This is my house. Guard the front door. Do not leave until I give the order. Call out to the first soldier you see passing, and post him at the back door. If anything is disturbed within, you both will be executed!"

As the soldier hurried to his new post, Max turned on his heel. The administration building was only a few short blocks away, but it felt as though it took him forever to push past the throngs of people yelling, shouting, crying, and screaming. By the time he reached the beautiful gardens he had overlooked only recently, he no longer heard them. It was all just noise, like the hum of bees.

"Max! Max!"

He felt a yank on his sleeve, and he whirled around, but at the sight of Stella, his face softened. "What are you doing here?"

"Isn't it wonderful?" she said excitedly.

"Isn't *what* wonderful?"

She threw both arms in the air. "This! It is our dream, Max!"

"Where is your home? Is it still standing?"

"I don't care about my home anymore, Max. I am going to be a Nazi soldier!"

"You cannot. That is not for a woman."

"Then, I will find a special purpose. I am no longer Polish," she declared. "I am Aryan!"

Max grabbed her and pulled her to him. He didn't care about the commotion erupting around them. He didn't care about Mrs. Weiss or the scores of Jews who would never see their homes or businesses again. He didn't care that the whole city lay under a canopy of oppressive smoke or that Nazi soldiers had abandoned whatever discipline they once had to loot and rape the population. All he cared about was having this beautiful, golden-haired woman in his arms. He was Max Kursell, and in this moment, he was beginning a powerful new phase of his life.

As he leaned on his toes to reach upward to her and his lips found hers, he felt the young, spindly boy of his youth slip away. In its place was a dynamic, influential Nazi leader. It didn't matter that he'd come upon his corner office under the veil of a lie; that, also, was behind him. He no longer had to translate English texts. He could command that Rafe and Hank write the articles in German. After all, German was the new official language. It hadn't yet been declared, but it would soon enough.

He took Stella as though she had always belonged to him, and damn any soldier that dared to interrupt them. He didn't know why *Oberführer* Wilhelm Keller trusted him, or maybe he didn't. All Max knew was that at this moment, he carried with him a piece of paper that made him off-limits to everyone else. On this day, he had moved from a pathetic apartment filled with trashy furniture and a dining table covered in material to Mrs. Weiss's opulent home. And it was all his.

And so, he thought, was Stella. She gave herself to him, pressing against his thin chest, and her lips passionately parting for him. She knew he was powerful. And she wanted this as much as he did.

18

Agata, Warsaw, 1943

The world had turned upside down and inside out.

It was impossible to recall what everyday life had been four years earlier. It was as though Orson Welles's *War of the Worlds* had leaped from the radio into Poland, the aliens from outer space replaced by Nazi soldiers. However, the goal was the same, as the Germans made it clear they wanted Poland for German citizens, and Poles were expected to disappear, either voluntarily or through force.

Ten years earlier, more than half of German voters had been quick to point out that the majority had not voted for Adolf Hitler. The Nazi Party had received 43.91% of the popular vote, leaving 56.09% to claim that they had been against Hitler. The vote had been enough, though, to give the Nazis a majority, with the remaining ballots divided among six other parties.

Agata didn't know where those dissenters had gone. They had either climbed aboard the Nazi bus or gone deep underground.

In Warsaw, in place of local police departments comprised of residents, Nazi soldiers reigned supreme. Autocratic rule had replaced the courts, with their judges, bailiffs, prosecutors, and defenders. Due process disappeared, along with the opportunity to defend oneself. A person could be accused on the street and executed on the spot; their body left for the populace to haul away.

Meanwhile, Polish dissenters, also known as political prisoners, disappeared off the streets. Jews, Roma, who were also called Gypsies, so-called criminals, and others deemed asocial disappeared as well. Agata could see the same face in the neighborhood day after day, until one day that person had vanished without a trace. It happened too many times to count. Scores of families searched for their loved ones, not knowing whether they had been transported to another country, jailed inside Poland, or executed. Often, children were left without any adults in their family; every block was filled with a child crying for their mother, digging in the dirt for food they'd never find, or becoming fodder for bored Nazi soldiers.

Intellectuals were targeted. Hitler declared that Polish educators, doctors, writers, lawyers, scientists, economists, journalists, and even librarians were enemies of the Third Reich. The Nazis needed an uneducated population so they could feed them the same propaganda that the Germans had received for more than a decade. Those who disagreed were targeted.

There had been a steady stream of refugees at the beginning, but now they were no longer permitted to travel. The uneducated, thugs, and thieves now reigned supreme.

Hatred grew and festered unfettered. The Poles had lost the war within weeks of the German invasion. It had been as though there was a war between good and evil, and evil had won. Once it took hold, it metastasized into hatred of everything and everyone that was not German Aryan and a zealous supporter of Adolf Hitler.

Agata's life had changed dramatically, and she feared it could never be the same as it had been before the invasion.

She was twenty-one years old now, and Elsa would be fifteen if she were still alive. Agata had long ago given up on trying to reach her sister and father, and the decision had devastated her. It had become too dangerous for her to leave her hiding place for anything other than food or water. The hospitals were gone, bombed beyond recognition, as were the shops, bakeries, fishmongers, and butchers. To eat, one had to become resourceful. Food became the overwhelming driving force in her daily existence.

If there had been a silver lining, it was that Germany turned on its ally and invaded the Soviet Union in 1941. Then, in December of 1941, Germany declared war against the United States just four days after the Japanese bombed Pearl Harbor. This meant that the United Kingdom had been joined by the Soviets and Americans against the Germans, allowing some Poles to dream of liberation. Meanwhile, the German expansion had conquered Belgium, Finland, France, Austria, Hungary, and the Sudetenland, among others.

Helen turned out to be Piotr's aunt, so it was no surprise to Agata that he had led her here. Shortly after the surrender of Polish troops, Agata received a note from Piotr via Helen's underground resistance network. He was alive, and he had not been captured. He had fled with thousands of others to undisclosed locations, and they were plotting their overthrow of the Nazi-installed regime. The letters continued to arrive sporadically, each saved in a growing bundle tied with an old hair ribbon. She wrote back on scraps of paper, and in those moments, she felt a connection to Piotr, despite the miles and circumstances that separated them.

Supply chains were in turmoil, leading to the closure of Helen's bakery. Only a small portion of the warehouse now remained intact; indiscriminate bombs had obliterated the rest. The door that Agata once used was blocked by rubble, and to anyone performing a cursory inspection, it may have appeared as if there was no entry to the building wreckage. But Helen and Agata were imaginative, and they had carefully constructed a wall of debris that hid an entry into the warehouse. They were forced to crouch to squeeze through the entrance, and afterward, they tossed fresh dirt and debris to hide their tracks. The windows had been painted with a mixture of any colors they could find.

An underground network had emerged for those desperate to escape Warsaw. Agata never knew how Helen had ingratiated herself into it; the woman refused to tell her, only advising her that the less she knew, the safer she would be. Piotr's letters never mentioned specifics in case they were intercepted, but Agata wondered if he was somehow involved.

Almost every night as the skies grew black, a tiny group of people was led to their haven. They often traveled with only the clothes on their backs and perhaps a little bit of money in their pockets, which Helen refused to accept. Sometimes, it was a woman escaping alone; other times, there were small children with grimy faces and hungry expressions. Occasionally, a man would be among them, usually an elderly relative.

And with each group that appeared, Agata asked if they knew Elsa or Ira Goldberg. Night after night, month after month, the travelers shook their heads. Each group left before dawn that night or the next, never remaining for more than a day and a half. With each departure, Helen pleaded for Agata to join them. Some said they were traveling east now that the Soviets were the Germans' enemies. Others believed that if they could reach Northern Europe, they would be safer than in Poland. Still others set their sights on Eurasia.

Agata might have taken the chance, had she been all alone in the world. But something deep in her soul urged her to remain in Warsaw until she knew her sister's and father's fates.

It was a frigid night with heavy clouds that brought Piotr to her. After a man, a woman, and a child had emerged through their secret passageway, Piotr appeared, and the energy completely shifted for Agata. She rushed to him, nearly knocking him off his feet, her arms around him. He held her in an embrace that was so tight, she could feel his ribs and shoulder blades. He was haggard, his face drawn, and dark circles had emerged under his eyes. His clothes were threadbare, his shoe soles nearly worn through. But the smile that lit up his face revealed that his spirit was still there.

They were not alone just yet, as the young family was to share their tiny quarters for the night. The man was even worse for wear than Piotr. He was dressed in a ragged coat that seemed too thin for the season, his shoes sporting holes filled with old newspaper. His hair was long and unkempt, and even in the gloom of the warehouse, Agata could detect large, dark circles under his eyes. His wire-rimmed glasses were askew, and one lens had a crack across it. He carried the child in his arms, wrapped in a blanket that was unraveling. The child was unnaturally quiet, and Agata wondered if it had died, for it did not move despite the crawl into the warehouse.

While Piotr spoke to the man, Agata moved closer to the woman, whose face was cast in shadow by a tattered shawl. She shivered in the freezing temperatures, and Agata could provide nothing that might have warmed her, for she, too, suffered from shivers that she feared would not subside until spring had arrived.

The woman gathered the threadbare shawl around her, her eyes darting to her clothing as though she were ashamed. "They take our water and call us dogs when we drink from puddles," she said. Though her voice was barely over a whisper, Agata could feel the resentment. Before she could respond, the woman continued, "They take our food and laugh when we dig through the dirt to find a morsel."

Her husband joined in. "They take our clothing, so we must wear the clothes of dead people so that we do not freeze."

"And your child?" Agata asked, nodding toward the baby.

The man shook his head. "Her heart beats, but I fear she is unconscious."

Agata asked to hold her. Reluctantly, the man relinquished her to Agata as Piotr peered over her shoulder. She pulled back the worn fabric to find a wrinkled little body, sparse hair, and nearly blue skin. She placed her hand over the child's heart and barely perceived a faint heartbeat. "Is she a newborn?"

The woman let out a sob. "She is three."

"When was the last time she has eaten?"

The parents shook their heads. "Maybe two days ago," the man answered. "Maybe three. It was the last time for all of us."

Agata gathered her shawl around the child, holding her close to warm her. She wished she had milk to keep the child alive, but as she gazed at the tiny face, she realized the child was probably beyond the ability to swallow.

"Do you know Ira Goldberg?" she asked them as she rocked the child. She turned her attention to Piotr. "Have you heard anything?"

Piotr and the woman shook their heads without meeting Agata's eyes. Piotr appeared particularly distressed.

Helen moved closer to them. "Give us your names," she whispered, "or write them on the wall there." She nodded toward a wall that was already filled with penciled names of those who had passed through. "If anyone looks for you, they will know you were here. Add the date after your names."

The man nodded to the woman, and she made her way to the far wall, careful to remain under the windowsill. As she began to write their names, he leaned toward Agata. "Is that—Agata, is that you?" he asked incredulously.

"Yes!" she answered.

Before she could say more, his words spilled out. "I worked with your father at school. Caleb. Caleb Kotler. I thought I recognized you."

Agata tried to picture him, but she was unable to recall the faces of Ira and Elsa, what the school had looked like, or the people they had known. "I'm sorry," she said. "I don't remember you. It has been a difficult time."

"Of course. Yes. And we have changed."

"All of us have," she answered. "Do you know if they are alive? My father and sister?"

"They were taken only a week ago."

"I wanted to tell you," Piotr said, leaning in. "In private," he added.

"What do you know? Where were they taken? By whom?"

Caleb shook his head. "It has been happening…" His voice faded.

"Just the two of them?"

"No. The Nazis have been relocating people from the Jewish sector. How long has it been since you were there?"

"Years," Agata answered, her voice revealing her agony.

"They brought in so many people… They turned our community into a ghetto; almost half a million people were crammed into the area."

"Half a million!" Agata exclaimed. "How is that possible? The area is—what—perhaps a square mile?"

Piotr wrapped an arm around Agata, and she turned to face him. "People have been disappearing," he said sadly. "Members of the Warsaw resistance say that Jews are being told that they would be transported to the south, where they would have their own community. Some have even gone willingly. The beautiful, vibrant community that you knew and loved, Agata," his voice choked as he continued, "is now like living in hell. There is no food left in the city center; people are starving. Some are eating—well, whatever they can find." He placed a thin hand against her cheek as if ready to wipe away her tears, but she felt numb inside as though shock had long ago taken over her body.

"Of course," Agata said softly. "The goal is to survive. Is it not? Tell me, did my family go willingly?"

Piotr nodded toward Caleb, and the older man responded. "They did not wish to leave. But once they were tapped, they had no choice. They had nothing to take with them."

"But our home—"

Caleb shook his head sadly. "Your home has been gone for a long time, Agata. It was bombed, and what wasn't destroyed was ransacked early on. The Germans took all they wanted and burned the rest."

"Did they harm my sister? Father?"

"The less you know, the better," Piotr interjected sadly.

"Don't tell me that!"

Caleb continued in a low voice. "They got in the vehicle on their own two feet. Your father is not as healthy as he once was. They are both thin, very thin."

Agata gazed at the little girl in her lap. When she looked back at Caleb, she realized that he, too, was nothing but bones obscured by the oversized clothing. "But alive."

"Yes. They were both alive."

"And they are taking them south, you said? Where?"

"We don't know for certain," Piotr said. "None of us knows."

As Agata's face fell, Caleb added, "Some have said the vehicles take them to the train station. If you follow the tracks…"

"Follow the tracks?" Agata breathed incredulously. "Poland has extensive rail lines. You must know that."

"Not any more. Most have been bombed or otherwise destroyed," Caleb said quietly. "If not by the Nazis, then by the *Armia Krajowa*."

"The *Armia Krajowa*?" Agata repeated.

"Poland's Home Army," Piotr said. "It is, perhaps, the largest resistance force in Poland, though it's difficult to tell. Everyone is underground."

"Then, how do I find them?" Agata asked, anguished.

Caleb spoke first, drowning out Piotr's objections. "Follow the rail lines south out of the city if you can."

"You have no idea where they might be heading?"

Caleb shook his head. He appeared exhausted, and he leaned against a pile of boxes.

"You can't leave," Piotr said, pulling Agata closer to him. "You are safe here, as safe as one can be under these hellish circumstances. If you leave, you are likely to be picked up before you can find them."

Agata glanced over her shoulder at Caleb. "Where are you going when you leave here?"

"We don't know," he said sadly. He tilted his head back and closed his eyes.

"They will be moved from one haven to the next," Piotr added in a tense whisper. "They won't know whether they will be sent to the north, south, east, or west. It all depends on where the Germans are. And they are everywhere."

"If it is safe enough for them, it will be safe enough for me."

"No, Agata, it won't. There is a huge difference."

Caleb's wife held out her arms for her child, and Agata reluctantly handed her back. She doubted the child would live until dawn, and perhaps, that was better than existing in this hell. She tried to console her own guilt at not having food to keep the child alive by telling herself that God was waiting on the other side of the veil to love and nurture this innocent little girl.

She turned back to Piotr. "How is it different?"

He pulled her into an alcove. "They are escaping, Agata, wherever and however they can. They are not searching for anyone. It is like searching for needles in a haystack, yet with bombs all around. It would be ludicrous for you to try it."

Helen sat in the shadows, nearly undetectable in the gloom of the warehouse. "He is right, Agata. People are disappearing every day. You could travel south along the rail lines, only to discover when this is all over, that they were taken north. None of us knows for sure."

"But I must find my sister," Agata insisted. "I promised her that I would return, and—" She stopped as she fought back tears of pain and frustration.

"Your sister understands why you never came back," Piotr said sadly, pulling Agata against his chest. "This, I know."

"You don't understand, Piotr. Perhaps, no one does. On that day when you found me, I was only going to secure a place in a safer part of the city. I was coming back for them the next day. They expected me to return for them."

Helen rose and patted Piotr on the shoulder. "I will stay the night. I'll be in that far corner, over there."

Piotr nodded and pulled Agata down to the floor, where they made a makeshift bed from shawls and clothing.

As he held her, Agata pleaded, "Tell me what you know. And do not tell me it is best that I not know."

Piotr's eyes were kind but veiled. He had aged substantially since the invasion. He took a deep breath. "Treblinka is a camp located north of the city. It is rumored that people are killed if they enter Treblinka. If they are sent to Majdanek, near Lublin in the east, they are put to work in Nazi factories." He grimaced. "The Nazis have a war machine. They are woefully behind the Americans' production, and they are using slave labor as they attempt to catch up."

"And the south, as Caleb said? Where would they have sent them?"

"Due south is Kraków."

"That is almost two hundred miles from here."

Piotr nodded. "Yes. But they would travel by train. It is only a few hours by train."

"Tell me about these people who leave here," Agata said, nodding toward Caleb and his family, now bedding down together.

"Are you sure?"

"I will do this with or without your help."

"Then you must understand what you are getting yourself into." He took a shaky breath. "Men and women in the underground resistance arrive before dawn and gather up the refugees. They will break into three groups, three distinctly different directions."

"And is anyone going south?"

He shrugged. "One will head south if it is clear. If you do this, he or she will take you out of the city to a place such as this. From there, I cannot tell you who will help you on your journey."

"Someone will take me there?"

Piotr shook his head sorrowfully. "No, sweetheart. You will be on your own once you leave Warsaw. Sometimes, they will be able to tell you how to reach the next safe place, and perhaps the next. Everything is fluid, Agata. You must understand that. What was safe yesterday is teeming with Nazis tomorrow." He held her against his chest as his eyes closed.

"When do you leave?" Agata whispered.

"Dawn," Piotr said before his breathing began to change to a fitful slumber.

~~~~~

Agata was ready as Piotr, Caleb, and Caleb's family prepared to leave. His wife still held the tiny child in her arms, and Agata could not bring herself to
~~~~~

look under the wrapped shawl to see if she still lived. There was an emptiness in both Caleb's and her eyes, and she understood that they must know, and perhaps, they were prepared to bury her once they had escaped.

Three men and a woman arrived before dawn, when the skies were at their blackest and grim clouds obscured the moon's light. They collected a packet of notes from Helen and secured them inside their layered clothing.

"Do you know one another?" The question came from a burly man.

"Yes," Agata and Piotr answered simultaneously.

"Then, say your goodbyes to one another now. Once we leave here, there will be no talking. None. Any sound can give us away and endanger us all. Do you understand?" They all murmured their understanding, and he continued, "When it comes time to separate, there will be no farewells. None. Every second counts. Every delay puts us all in danger. Is that understood?"

Agata cast a sideways glance at Piotr as they all answered.

"You will not be given food for the journey. You may or may not receive food and drink at your first stop. Do not ask how long it will take. We don't know. Everything depends on rapidly changing conditions. Do you understand?" Again, they all murmured their agreement, and he continued as if he'd recited these words hundreds of times. "Do not ask for breaks. We will give you a break when we decide it is safe to do so. The length of the break depends on conditions."

Helen stepped forward with a small cheesecloth bag for each of them. "It is cheese and bread," she said quietly.

As they began to thank her, the burly man said, "Say your goodbyes. You will have one minute and one minute only. The longer we delay, the more likely we are to be caught." He turned to Caleb. "Is that your baby?"

"Yes, but—"

"Do whatever you can to keep it quiet. Any noise, especially a crying baby, could bring the Nazis down on all of us."

He nodded his head as his wife wiped away a tear.

"Good-bye, Agata," Piotr said, wrapping his arms around her and kissing her.

"Where are you going?" she asked.

"I must rejoin the *Armia Krajowa.* I don't know where I will end up, Agata, but I will find you. One way or another, I will find you." He kissed her again on the forehead. "I will be with you for a little while, until we are out of the city. As you travel south, listen for my sister's name, Matylda Wiśniewska. She will help you."

Agata repeated the name.

He nodded. "She is a nurse. She was assigned to the Polish Warsaw Army, and she escaped before the siege. She is part of the *Armia Krajowa* now, just like me."

The guides were already standing at the door, motioning for each of them to move into the alley. Before Agata ducked her head to move through the exit, she looked back to wave goodbye to Helen, but the older woman was moving slowly away from them as she dabbed at her eyes. She almost called out to her, but then realized they must remain silent, so she slipped through to the alley as the darkness and mists of morning surrounded them. A sickening feeling overcame her. This had been her home in the worst of times, and she knew she would always associate the place with her life being uprooted. Yet, it had also been a place of comfort and relative safety, and she had no idea what might lie ahead.

19

Max

Max slowly replaced the phone receiver in its cradle. His hands were trembling, but his mind felt numb. Wilhelm had instructed him to act immediately, but he stared out his office window without truly seeing the activity outside. Wilhelm's office was directly across the hall from Max's in a larger corner office with a dedicated meeting room, and he would undoubtedly witness him leaving his office to perform his assignment.

He slowly stood on unsteady legs. Wilhelm always stepped across the hall to give him instructions, as the distance between their desks didn't take a full minute to traverse. He phoned him, Max decided, because he did not wish to look him in the face.

He grabbed his hat and coat, stepped into the hallway, and then stopped in front of Wilhelm's door. "Heil Hitler!" he said, saluting with an outstretched arm. Wilhelm did not respond. His back was to the door; his head bent over a mound of papers.

Max waited a long moment before returning his arm to his side and making his way down the hallway and stairs to the first floor. As he started through the lobby, he ran headlong into Stella.

"What are you doing here?" Max asked. The woman had an uncanny ability to be present every time he left the building.

"What are you talking about?" she answered. She was dressed in fancy heels and a red dress, her hair in an updo under a stylish hat with dyed red feathers. He suspected the entire ensemble came from Mrs. Weiss's or her daughter's closet. She pointed to the picnic basket that dangled from one arm. "We always have lunch at this time of day, *kochanie,*" she continued, using the Polish endearment for love.

Max groaned. "I can't do it today, Stella. I was just given a mission."

"So, I'll wait. How long can it take?"

"Possibly hours. No, don't wait. Tell you what, can you deliver it to Wilhelm? He is in his office, and I think he always eats at his desk."

She took a small step backward, her brows knit. "Give this to Wilhelm? I have a bottle of wine here and meat."

"I know. But I can't see you today. Will you do that for me? Please?"

"Alright, Max. I will do it for you," she said, but her eyes were veiled and her lips downturned. "What are you doing, anyway?"

"It is classified."

"Classified," she repeated, cocking her head. "I can't wait to hear all about it."

"You'll be waiting a long time, Stella. And I am running late." He shifted his eyes upward as if Wilhelm could see them conversing in the lobby. He would certainly be able to see him leave the building. He leaned forward and kissed Stella on the cheek. "I will make it up to you this evening. I promise." Stella had moved into Mrs. Weiss's old home with them. Although she claimed the room at the opposite end of the hall from Max, she rarely spent the night there, preferring instead to sleep in Max's arms.

"I will hold you to it. Oh, I almost forgot to tell you. Your mother is wandering the streets again."

"What? I've told her repeatedly to stay inside." Max thought of the beautiful home she could explore to her heart's content, but it seemed that every chance she got, she was attempting to return to her old apartment. It was infuriating.

"I know. I tried to stop her. She can be very willful."

Max wiped his forehead of perspiration. "I'll try to find her when I'm finished."

"I'll do it, *kochanie.* You have much on your mind." With that, she continued through the lobby. He watched her ascend the stairs, his stomach in a knot, before pushing through the double doors at the front of the building.

There were always military vehicles parked in front of the administration building, as if waiting to give a ride to an important official. However, as Max donned his coat and hat, he decided to walk. It would give him ample time to think.

This would be his first time seeing the Jewish sector. He'd directed multiple missions in which he carried out Wilhelm's orders, missions in which he led the military to known Jewish neighborhoods so they could remove them. He occasionally led them to known enemies of the Nazi ideology, providing names, home addresses, and places of business. Sometimes, he didn't know their loyalties, but he ordered raids on people he simply didn't like, such as bullying boys who had grown into silent men who gave him sideways glances as he passed them in the street. He kept lengthy lists and submitted them weekly to show his loyalty and service.

Yet, in the past, he had directed from afar. He had rounded up the necessary troops and officers, provided them with the orders, and then left without verifying that they were being carried out. Sometimes, he could view the neighborhoods from his office windows, and he would watch as the vehicles arrived. But when they began to pull people out of the buildings and pandemonium ensued, he would turn from the windows and turn on his radio to play static-filled classical music to drown out the shouting.

This time, Wilhelm specifically ordered him to go to the Jewish sector in person.

Perhaps, Max thought as he hurried along, this was a test. Possibly, Wilhelm was watching him now as he rushed along sidewalks that had been bustling before the invasion but were now as silent and empty as a ghost town.

He arrived at the main gate, breathless and his heart thumping. He presented his papers at the gate and told them his purpose. He requested a dozen soldiers to assist him and waited for them to arrive, his back to the people inside the concrete barricades and barbed wire.

An officer approached him, and he nervously lit a cigarette. As the officer drew closer, Max offered the pack to him. While he extracted a cigarette, Max leaned forward to light it for him. He noticed the officer eyeing his armband.

"Max Kursell," he said, extending his hand.

"Ah, so you are the famous Max Kursell," he answered with a smile. "*Bereitschaftsleiter* Klaus Braun."

"*Bereitschaftsleiter*," Max repeated. "You are just the man I needed to see. I need at least fifty soldiers to escort a group of Jews outside the city."

Klaus peered through the barbed wire at several privates who were pointing toward Max. "Which group?"

"I am to assemble it. I have requested a dozen soldiers to assist me in lining them up." Max followed Klaus's gaze. "They are getting the soldiers together now."

"And you will select the Jews?"

Max nodded. "*Oberführer* Wilhelm Keller sent me. My understanding is the orders came from higher up."

"And he sent a civilian to do this?"

"I would wish nothing more than to hand this operation over to you," Max said, his expression veiled. "And I certainly will, once I have chosen the Jews."

"How many are you to assemble?"

"At least two hundred."

"Any particular ones? Perhaps I can help."

"Those who are a burden on the system, I assume. The weaker women, any elderly, children too young to work." Max puffed on his cigarette as he leaned back on his heels.

"Ah. I understand. I know exactly the type."

"Then, you know what you will do with these filthy Jews once they are out of the city."

Klaus turned to look him in the eye. "I need the order to be given."

Max removed a pencil and a pad of paper from his coat's inner pocket and wrote the orders, signing his name at the bottom, *im Namen von,* and *Oberführer* Wilhelm Keller. If there were questions later, there would be no doubt that he acted on Wilhelm's behalf. He ended with today's date.

Klaus studied the orders before folding them neatly and placing them in his pocket. "I understand." He nodded toward the returning soldiers. "I will round up the fifty men to escort them."

"Thank you." Max lifted his chin as he passed through the gate. As the men surrounded him for instructions, he noticed out of the corner of his eye that Jews who had begun to watch them out of curiosity abruptly disappeared. By the time he had informed the soldiers to round up at least two hundred of the weakest or least productive Jews they could find, and they had disbursed, the street was empty.

~~~~~

It took a surprisingly short time for the soldiers to assemble two hundred Jews, and as Max walked the line, he felt a tremendous sense of accomplishment. The troops had handled it exactly as he'd instructed them, so he had a cooperative, even eager, group of people lined up, some with suitcases and others with clothing in their arms. He kept his gaze from the throng's faces,
~~~~~

something he had learned to do early in the German occupation. It was best never to make eye contact; it was too easy for their emotions to shine through, and it could haunt him later.

"Everyone, listen closely," he said now with a megaphone provided by a soldier. As he spoke in his native Polish, the crowd quieted and turned toward him. "You are going to a new factory. This is very easy work, which is why you have been selected. It is only a short walk away, an easy walk. You will be provided with living quarters and more food than you have here." An appreciative buzz passed through the crowd. "Thank you for your continued cooperation. We will begin soon."

His eyes fell on a woman who appeared far along in pregnancy, and he called a soldier to him. He turned away from the line as he spoke to him. "Why did someone add a pregnant woman to the line?"

The soldier's eyes wandered through the crowd, rested on the woman in question, and turned back to Max. "Because she is bringing another filthy Jew into the world. We are trying to get rid of them, not create more of them."

Max nodded and waved his hand in dismissal. It had never occurred to him that a pregnant woman could exist in the Jewish sector. It was a ghetto the likes of which he could only imagine in hell. For anyone to find comfort in another's arms was beyond comprehension. Of course, the soldier was correct. This was not a breeding ground for more Jews.

As he continued to stride along the line, he heard someone calling his name. He turned to find Mrs. Weiss and her daughter, Celina, hurrying to catch up with him.

"Please, Max," Mrs. Weiss began before she'd even reached him, "let us go, too."

He shook his head. "No. It is not possible."

"Why not? We are good workers; you know that. We will work twice as hard as any of these people in line."

"It is not that," he said as he tried to turn away from her. "You are needed for more strenuous work. This is very light work, work for old people and invalids."

"Max," she pleaded, grabbing onto his sleeve, "please let us go. We have nothing here. We have no electricity, no fresh water. We drink out of puddles in the road. We have no food. We are starving here."

Max glanced up to find several soldiers eyeing the exchange as if ready to attack her for touching him. He shook his head at them, but they continued to observe them. "It is not possible."

"Max, please," Mrs. Weiss continued. "I always took care of you and your mother. You know that. When you had nothing to eat, I fed you. When you did not have rent, I looked the other way."

He carefully and deliberately extracted her hand from his sleeve. "You do not have your things packed," he said lamely.

She laughed wryly. "Things? What things? We were dragged out of the bakery. We had no time to pack. I don't even know if my home still exists."

Max hesitated. Further down the line, he caught sight of Otto pulling up in front of the gates. Hank and Rafe hopped out, Hank's camera glaringly large. He felt sick to his stomach. He had to leave before they attempted to take pictures of him. The last thing he needed was to be associated with this farce.

"Max, please—" Mrs. Weiss's voice was rising, and Hank turned to look in their direction.

"Fine," he said curtly. He motioned for a nearby soldier. "Add these two women to your list." He gestured toward Mrs. Weiss and Celina. In doing so, his eyes locked on hers. It was the briefest of moments, but it was startling to see the dark circles under her eyes and how much larger they appeared, as if her face had shrunken. Her silky hair had been shaved down with what appeared to have been an uneven blade, the tresses mere spikes. Had he encountered her in that state at the bakery, he would have insisted that she see a doctor at once. Now, she stared back at him with an expression that he knew he would never forget. It was overwhelming sadness and disappointment, and he couldn't help but understand that these emotions were directed at him personally.

"Thank you, Max," Mrs. Weiss called as they were led away. "God will reward you."

He whirled on his heels to begin the short walk toward the front gate when he was caught short by a man who appeared much taller than he was. Dressed all in black, he sported a black hat that effectively hid his face. "Yes," he said in a voice so deep that it did not sound human, "God will not forget this day, and you will never be able to hide from it."

"Privat!" he called out to the nearest soldier.

"Yes, sir!" The soldier hurried toward him.

Max waved his hand in the direction of the strange man, but when he turned to point him out, he was gone. His eyes roamed the crowd, but the line was neatly formed, and he was nowhere in sight. Neither was he elsewhere in the barren road, as those not rounded up by the soldiers had long disappeared from view. He swallowed. "Have you seen *Bereitschaftsleiter* Braun?"

"Yes, sir. I saw him a short while ago. He was outside the gate."

"Excellent." Max set out with long, quick strides toward the gate. There was nothing else for him to do here, and the sooner he got out of there, the better. He found Klaus on a portable radio in his vehicle, ordering additional troops to converge at the front gate as soon as possible. Max waited patiently until he finished, then thanked him for his help. "I have work waiting for me," he said, though he knew immediately that he did not owe this man an explanation. "Are you all set here?"

"We are. We will have a sufficient number of troops here within the next five or ten minutes."

"And then, you will begin the march?"

"We will. Is there anything else? Any particular place you want us to stop?"

"I will leave that to your discretion."

Klaus clicked his heels and saluted, and Max returned the gesture.

"Carry on," Max said. A soldier approached Klaus, and as he turned to address him, Max hurried away from the gate, past Otto's inquiring, haunted stare, and down a side road. When he was convinced that he was out of sight of both the Jewish sector and Wilhelm's windows, he found a grassy area beside a building and retched.

20

Hank

Something strange was in the air. Hank could feel it long before they reached the gate to the Jewish sector. It was energetic but ominous, like the electric energy of an approaching thunderstorm. The gate was busier than usual, and as Hank caught sight of a uniformed officer a block away, he said to Otto as Rafe interpreted, "Keep driving. We have to come back later."

"I can't, man, I need it. I need it bad."

Observing Otto's severe shakes, Rafe said, "Okay, then let's get in and get out." He hopped out of the vehicle before it had barely come to a stop.

Hank moved Otto's extra uniform out of the way and handed Rafe one box of food and alcohol. With one eye on the officer heading their way, he bounded over the low side, grabbed the second box, and hurried to catch up to Rafe. The area was buzzing like a beehive, as soldiers he didn't recognize shouted orders to a gathering line of Jews just inside the gate. As one soldier moved to stop them from entering, another, familiar with their routine, stepped in and waved them through.

Hank could feel the eyes of the soldiers and citizens boring into his back. They quickened their step, reaching the alley leading to the factory's back door in record time. Before they reached their destination, Hank's heart sank. Machinery was piled up in the alley, propped against the wall, and spilling onto the ground. The back door was closed and locked.

"Leave the boxes," Hank said hoarsely.

They briskly tucked the boxes behind some machinery and hurried around to the main doors, where new equipment was being delivered. Finding an opening, they scurried past the movers, only to be halted by a soldier with a surly expression.

"Where is the manager?" Rafe asked in German.

"He is gone. Sent away," the soldier answered.

"Sent away where?"

"What is it to you?" he spat.

Hank stepped in. "Tell him we were sent to take pictures of the new setup."

As Rafe complied, the soldier eyed Hank's camera suspiciously. He appeared to recognize Max's name, but the younger man continued to stand in their way.

"Ask him why they are changing the equipment."

Rafe interpreted and then said to Hank, "They are switching out chemical manufacturing for ammunition."

"They're going to make ammunition here? Where will they make the Pervitin?"

Rafe again translated, then turned to Hank. "They're not."

"What do you mean, 'they're not'?"

The soldier shouted suddenly. Both men instinctively jumped, then eased when they realized he was bellowing orders to the movers. Then he turned to them and said something in German.

Rafe grabbed Hank's arm. *"Danke,"* he said as he began pulling him away.

Hank quickly moved outside with Rafe. "What's going on?"

"He said for us to come back later when the equipment is installed. I thanked him and got the fuck out of there."

Hank opened his mouth but shut it abruptly. Through the gate, he observed the officer he'd seen earlier. He was leaning in to speak to Otto. "Do you see what I'm seeing?"

"Fucking Affirmative."

"We're not going back for those boxes."

"You think?"

They acknowledged the soldiers at the gate, but their eyes were riveted on the officer. There would be questions, as the regular guards would expect their pills, but everyone seemed to understand that there was entirely too much activity. As they neared the vehicle, they heard the officer speaking sternly to Otto.

Otto spotted Hank and Rafe and pointed in their direction, answering the officer as if attempting to protest. Before Hank could ask for a translation, Rafe said something in German as he motioned toward the camera hanging around Hank's neck.

The officer then responded in rapid fire, motioning for them to follow him back through the gate.

"What's going on?" Hank whispered.

"Holy fuck, he wants us to take pictures of the Jews. Get your camera up and start snapping."

"Jeder lächelt, lächeln," he said to the group.

"He's telling them to smile," Rafe muttered as Hank began taking pictures. "They're at the gates of hell, and he wants them to smile."

The officer began again in rapid fire, motioning toward the people in line.

"He wants pictures of smiling faces and their suitcases, the little girl holding her doll." As they looked into the faces of those in line, they were met with haunting and forced Cheshire grins. "Holy fuck," he repeated.

"Gut, gut," he said finally. He motioned toward Otto, leading the way as they followed. When he reached the vehicle, he said something to Otto, pointed briefly to them, and then strode back inside the gates.

"Get in," Rafe said as he jumped in beside Otto.

As Hank climbed into the back, Otto and Rafe spoke as they pulled away. Although he could not understand the language completely, he picked up familiar words here and there, and he could feel the tension. He could clearly view Otto's profile from his seat. The man was breaking out in sweat, despite the crisp air, and his hands were shaking. He was surprised he hadn't asked Rafe for his customary pill.

Rafe turned in his seat, and Hank leaned in. "The officer ordered Otto to follow the line of vehicles leaving Będzin. The Jews are following; other soldiers are marching them out."

"Where are they going?"

"I don't know. To another factory?"

"That makes no sense. Why wouldn't they put them on a train?"

"Beats the hell out of me. Look, when we stop, the brass back there wants you to take pictures of the people walking happily out of Będzin."

"Did you say, 'walking happily out'?"

"That's exactly what he said."

"Holy fuck," Hank said.

~~~~~

The wait was extensive, and the longer they sat in the vehicle, the more nervous Otto became. Rafe explained to Otto that the pill factory had been closed down and would be replaced by an ammunition manufacturing facility. Otto was clearly upset and began rocking back and forth.

"I told him to cut it out," Rafe said finally. "Just look around us. We've got Nazis in front and Nazis behind. He can't lose control now."

"What do you think is going on?" Hank spotted the first in line as they rounded the far bend, and he climbed out of the vehicle. Rafe joined him in the middle of the road as Hank snapped a couple of pictures. "They're too far. I've gotta wait for them to get closer."

Rafe peered up and down the road. "There's got to be hundreds of soldiers here. Do you see those transports?"

As if on cue, someone blew a whistle and shouted an order, which was passed down the line. The soldiers scrambled out as if they were preparing for
~~~~~

battle. As they formed crisp, orderly lines, Hank turned and snapped photographs. He caught one of Otto as he joined their ranks. The young man appeared as though he might double over and puke. His skin was as pale as a ghost, and even from this distance, he could see sweat pouring out from under his helmet. He stood at attention, his rifle over his shoulder, his hands shaking so hard that his shoulders shuddered.

It was another half an hour before the first in line came into clearer view, and Hank and Rafe moved to the shoulder, snapping pictures as they passed. There were a few men who struck Hank as odd, because men were more valuable in factories and as manual labor. Most of the procession consisted of women and their children. Several women carried infants, and one waddling pregnant woman appeared ready to give birth at any moment. They were eerily silent. For a moment, Hank recalled the women and children in his North Carolina town, gathering for church or the occasional parade. The North Carolinians would chat, seemingly nonstop, as laughter filled the air. Their children would also run and play; even if they'd been instructed to remain close, the mothers couldn't keep them from games of tag. In contrast, these children marched in complete silence, their eyes on the ground.

As the procession reached the front of the line of vehicles, an officer called out an order for them to halt. Hank continued snapping pictures of those directly in front of him. An elderly man stared back at him, and he lowered the camera and looked down the line.

A sickness swept over him. He felt sweat breaking out across his brow, and the scene in front of him began to waver like a watercolor painting.

An order was given, and the soldiers began marching the civilians into a thickly wooded area on the other side of the road. As the crowd cleared, Hank took a step forward to follow them, but a vehicle sped up, cutting off his movement.

Rafe was at his side in an instant. Hank recognized the officer as the one who had ordered Otto to participate in this detail. Now he reached his hand out, pointing to Hank's camera. His message was clear, even though Hank did not fully understand his words. He barely heard Rafe's translation as he opened the camera and extracted the film. He handed it to the officer as if in a trance.

"We are not to take any more photographs here," Rafe translated.

"Verstehen?" the officer asked.

"I understand," Hank responded without Rafe's translation. *"Verstehen."*

"He says if we attempt to enter the woods, we will be shot," Rafe said.

"I figured as much." Hank's eyes were locked on the officer's eyes. His eyes might have been hazel, but they were almost too dark to tell. It wasn't the color, Hank realized. They were veiled. As a journalist, he had a lifetime of reading people, sensing when they were lying, and detecting their motives. He could not read this officer at all.

The vehicle moved forward and parked on the shoulder with the others. The officer remained in his car. After a moment, Hank and Rafe moved to the opposite side of the road, furthest from the others. A lone bird cawed, and he instinctively glanced up. He was surprised to discover that it was a beautiful day. The skies were a serene azure, dotted with a few scattered, fluffy clouds —the kind he liked to watch roll past when he was a child, lying on his back in an open field, his arms folded beneath his head. For a moment, he was transported back to that time and place, when the air was so thick it blew the scent of salty ocean air inland, when the white clover bloomed, and butterflies of every color flitted past on lazy afternoons.

A gunshot rang out, jerking him from his memories as flocks of birds took to the skies from both sides of the road. Without thinking, he ducked behind a vehicle and met Rafe's eyes as he found him crouched beside him. Another shot popped, and then the air was filled with screams and the rolling thunder of too many gunshots to count. A little girl's voice rose above the din, screaming for her mother.

As Hank peered around the corner of the vehicle, he spotted the officer's vehicle turning around in the road. He passed them on his drive back toward Będzin, his face immobile, his eyes focused on the road ahead.

As soon as he had disappeared around the distant bend, Hank rushed across the street with Rafe on his heels. They stopped at the tree line as Hank fumbled to load another roll of film, his hands trembling so hard that he had trouble threading it. He had been through numerous battles before, particularly during the Spanish Civil War, and had a reputation for steel nerves. This was different. This was not two armed forces facing off against one another, each with a commanding officer and trained soldiers. These were children, women, and elderly men, unarmed and helpless.

He got the roll in, snapped the cover shut, and began taking pictures from the cover of a wide tree. Smoke filled the air, causing him to cough, and he didn't take the time to aim; instead, he snapped continuously.

He felt Rafe yanking at his arm, but he felt frozen in place until the man nearly dragged him away. "They're leaving," Rafe said hoarsely.

Hank nodded. He knew they could not risk being misidentified as one of the civilians. Adrenaline would run high with these soldiers, and all it took was one to spot them, take aim, and plant bullets in their heads. They raced across the street, located Otto's vehicle, and hunched down beside it, facing the opposite direction.

One by one, the roar of engines starting reached their ears. One by one, they rolled past them in the direction of Będzin. Transport vehicles loaded silent soldiers while intermittent shots resounded, the remaining soldiers finishing off those that weren't yet dead.

Otto was one of the last to step away from the tree line. He moved as if he were not a man but a machine, with one foot precisely in front of the other while he stared straight ahead. When he reached their vehicle, he did not stop but continued past it. Only when he found a tree stump along the opposite woods did he hesitate. He stood for a very long moment beside it. Hank quietly pulled out his camera and snapped his picture, a lone olive figure, featureless in his issued helmet and unadorned uniform, staring into the woods opposite from where he'd come, his rifle still held against his shoulder as though he was in formation, his shakes oddly gone.

He was still standing there when the last of the men departed. As Hank and Rafe joined him, he removed his helmet and sank to the tree stump, allowing his rifle to slide down beside him. Hank moved to take it from him, but it was hot, and Otto held onto the barrel as though oblivious of its heat.

"I shot her mother in front of her," he said flatly.

Hank and Rafe stared at his profile as Otto kept his gaze straight ahead.

"She was screaming for her mother even after she fell." He turned slightly toward them. His eyes were wide and incredulous. "And then I shot the child. She fell with her doll in her arms."

After a moment of stunned silence, Rafe's voice sounded crude in the stillness. "We've got to get out of here." Without waiting, he began a purposeful stride back to the lone vehicle. "Hank!" he shouted.

Hank pulled at Otto's uniform. "Come on," he said.

Otto grasped Hank's hand with surprising force and pushed it from him.

"Hank!" Rafe shouted. "Otto!"

Hank reluctantly moved away from Otto. Rafe was right. The officer could return at any moment, and he needed to get the film into his shoe. He didn't know what he might have, but if he had captured anything at all, both of them could wind up beside those in the woods. He clambered into the back seat, removed the film and his boot, and managed to get the roll into his usual hiding place. He was retying his boot as Rafe continued to shout for Otto.

Hank turned around to peer behind them. Otto sat motionless on the stump, his eyes still riveted on the woodland. Then, as they both watched, he grabbed his pistol from his belt. With one smooth movement, he lifted the gun, placed it against the side of his head, and pulled the trigger.

Hank jumped out of the car as Rafe scrambled across the seat to the driver's side and started the engine. "Hank!" Rafe shouted. "Hank, get back in the car!"

He stood as if paralyzed, his eyes riveted on Otto's body. He had fallen off the trunk and now lay beside it, the blood pooling on the ground. He turned back to Rafe. "There could be someone alive in the woods. Maybe they're wounded but not dead."

"Get in the car, Hank!"

Hank took a step toward the area where the civilians had been taken.

"Get in the fucking car, Hank!" Rafe roared. "I'll fucking leave you behind!"

Hank reluctantly climbed into the passenger seat, his body acting mechanically. He had barely settled before the vehicle jumped into gear, and Rafe floored it. Hank grasped the grab handle on the door as they barreled along the road, heading away from Będzin.

21

Max

Max sat slumped on the park bench. He had never felt so sick in his entire life.

The sun had long ago dipped beyond the horizon, and the temperature had plunged. He shivered, his arms wrapped around his body, the ice and snow feeling as though it was attempting to close in around him. He stared upward at the skies, perhaps hoping to catch a glimpse of cheery stars and moonlight, but dark clouds had descended, effectively cutting off all light, as if it were attempting to mirror his soul.

He had sat there for hours. He should have returned to his office, if for no other reason than to tidy up his desk and close and lock his door. But he could not. His feet had grown heavier with every step, and a crushing pain in his chest left him feeling as if he might crumble right there on the sidewalk.

He had listened to the troops march the Jews out of the city. Someone played a drum at the start of the line, which he found absurd. He sat on a side street and watched the procession from a block away as it passed between two city blocks. No one appeared to glance his way. All seemed to be focused on what was ahead of them. Soldiers were undoubtedly considering where they had been ordered to stop, while the civilians might have been imagining a new place with more food and less turmoil. He could not think of Mrs. Weiss and Celina. His mind would not allow him to go there.

He didn't know whether the soldiers were aware of the full orders, and he suspected they weren't. He had recognized *Bereitschaftsleiter* Braun sitting in the back seat of an open vehicle, his personal driver at the helm. They had been in the last car as if they were grand marshals in a holiday parade. In front of him were at least twenty more vehicles. Roughly two hundred Jews walked in between them. The elderly, women, and children considered too weak or useless to remain alive were forced to walk several miles through the city to its outskirts.

When he closed his eyes, he envisioned the road they would travel. There were agricultural fields they would have to pass before reaching a heavily wooded area. He thought he was far removed from it now, but when the first shots rang out, they sounded as if they were only a short distance away. The constant barrage reverberated like the height of battle, a heavily engaged conflict between two superpowers. Yet, he knew the shots came only from the German soldiers. The Jews would have been completely vulnerable and defenseless; their screams intertwined with the bullets.

Max was not prepared for how long it seemed to continue. When he thought it was finished, another shot rang out and then another in a haphazard fashion. He imagined soldiers rummaging through the bodies, dealing a final shot to those still fighting to survive.

When the massacre was over, he was surprised to hear more screaming. He turned his head to discover the commotion came from the Jewish sector. The mayhem had continued for hours. Even now, under the dark clouds and in the frosty air, he continued to hear the shouts, cries, and screams from the other side of the city. It was surreal that he could listen to it, and he supposed it was due to the silence in the non-Jewish part of town. The streets were now deserted, with citizens inside, perhaps discussing what they thought had occurred. The Polish Underground Resistance would no doubt find the site during the night, and word would spread throughout Poland.

And he had ordered it.

He took a deep breath. But he had not actually murdered anyone. He had simply been following orders, and those orders were to instruct the *Bereitschaftsleiter* in the Jewish sector to round up approximately two hundred Jews. Yes, he had passed along the instructions to lead them out of the city, take them into a wooded area, and kill them. But he hadn't fired the weapons. No, the murders were on the soldiers' heads and consciences.

A dark shape moved between the trees, and he stood, startled. "Who's there?" he called out.

No one answered, and he remained motionless. The figure had been tall, much taller than himself. And it had been a human form. No, it couldn't have been human. It was too tall for that.

After a moment of panning the area that surrounded him, he looked in the direction of his office.

Wilhelm was testing him. He was sure of it. Wilhelm had only to pick up his phone to reach the *Bereitschaftsleiter*'s office. He could have informed him directly what he wanted done. Alternatively, he could have sent a messenger with the orders in a sealed envelope, as was their usual practice. Not even the messenger would have known he was delivering the death sentences of so many civilians.

He turned away from his office and in the direction of his home. Wilhelm had tested him, and he had delivered. He would have to watch his own back now.

~~~~~

Stella met him at the door to Mrs. Weiss's home, and he knew immediately that something was wrong. She was still dressed in her fancy, bright red dress, which struck him as odd. It certainly hadn't been only a few hours since he'd seen her with her picnic basket. Her facial expression was what concerned him most; her eyes conveyed a mix of panic and anxiety.

"Darling!" she called out in an unnaturally loud voice. She'd opened the door before he had started up the path to the door, and now he abruptly halted. She raced down the path and hugged him. "*Oberführer* Keller is in the parlor. I can't find your mother."

His eyes moved to the house. The draperies in the parlor window, usually closed, were wide open. The lamp was lit on a round table, casting a muted golden glow over a darkened figure sitting in the wingback chair beside it. The fainter glow of a cigarette moved
~~~~~

smoothly from the chair's arm to the figure and back. "How long has he been here?"

"At least an hour. Where have you been?"

"What does he want?" Max asked, ignoring her question as they made their way up the path to the door.

"I don't know," Stella whispered as they moved into the foyer.

"Wilhelm!" Max called out jovially, striding into the front parlor. "What a pleasant surprise!"

Wilhelm rose and greeted him briefly, one hand holding a cordial while the other had a cigarette.

"Have you eaten?" Max asked. His eyes dropped to the table, where a platter filled with meats, cheeses, and bread appeared to have been picked over.

"Fräulein Kowalska has been a gracious hostess."

"Stella, please," Stella interjected.

"You must stay for supper," Max said, pouring a double shot of dopplekorn. He turned his back as he poured, concerned that Wilhelm would notice his trembling hands. He downed half of his drink in one gulp, the rye and wheat-based alcohol burning his throat as it slipped down his esophagus. He wiped his mouth with the back of his hand and turned around.

"I explained that it's your cook's day off," Stella said nervously, "but I am happy to—"

"Do you even know how to cook?" Max asked pointedly.

She paused to stare at him. "Obviously, not as well as your cook, but—"

"I won't bother you," Wilhelm said. He returned to the wingback chair and motioned for Max to join him.

Max sat on the other side of the table. "I am here on business."

"Oh. If you need anything, please…" Stella began. Her voice faded as silence grew between the two men. She quickly moved to the parlor window, where she drew the heavy drapes before slipping out of the room and closing the door behind her.

"I hope you weren't waiting for me very long," Max said. "I was... was…"

"…making certain my orders were followed, I'm sure," Wilhelm finished. He glanced around the room. "Do you know where your cook is today?"

Max hesitated. "I must admit," he said finally, "that I do not. It is her day off, as Stella said." When Wilhelm did not respond, he added, "Is there something that I should know?"

"Is there?" It was Max's turn to remain silent. After a moment, Wilhelm continued, "I understand all went smoothly today with the assignment."

"Yes." Max downed the rest of his dopplekorn and swirled the glass in his hand to give himself something to focus on.

"I spoke with Klaus Braun. He was impressed with how easily you persuaded people to volunteer for their" he paused, "final mission."

Max nodded. "I am afraid it won't work as well the next time."

"I suspect not. They were too close to the city; the shots heard too easily."

"Oh—" Max looked up, startled.

Wilhelm waved off his concern. "It was not your fault. It was Klaus's. He should have instructed them to move further away."

"With all due respect, I believe the shots would have been heard regardless."

"Perhaps. But, they might have been muffled." Wilhelm rose and poured himself another drink. "I drove to the site to inspect their work."

Max's heart sank, and he felt ill. "Should I have—?"

"Yes. You should have."

A silence fell between them, and Max's hand gripped the glass more tightly.

"The filth was exterminated," Wilhelm continued casually, as though he were speaking of cockroaches in the kitchen. "But what was a bit concerning, I might say, is the death of one of our own men."

"What?" Max breathed. "Surely, no one had the means to fight back—"

"It was *Obersoldat* Otto Schubert."

"Otto?" Max's mind raced.

"He had been shot in the head. And your journalists—Hank Mullins, I believe his name was—"

"Was?" Max breathed.

"—and his sidekick, Rafe. I can't seem to recall his last name offhand. Cabrera, is it?"

"Surely, Hank and Rafe would not have murdered Otto—"

"And they stole Otto's vehicle."

"They're gone?"

"They're gone, but they will be found."

Max waited for him to continue. When he didn't, he asked, "Who is searching for them?"

"Does it matter? Of course, it doesn't," Wilhelm answered himself. "All that is important is that they will be found and executed for their driver's murder."

"Of course. As they should be."

Wilhelm swirled the golden liquid in his glass before taking a hefty sip. "You have grown quite pale, Max."

Max rose and poured another double. He felt Wilhelm's eyes on his back, and he intentionally turned back around before partaking of the liquid courage he so desperately needed. "I am concerned," he said carefully, "that they have taken photographs of the event. And I am troubled they will fall into the wrong hands."

"As am I. That is why soldiers are now combing the countryside and the city for them. They can't have gone far. They will find them, and the film."

Max nodded. "They were in the Jewish sector as I was rounding them up. They might have photographs of me lining them up."

"And you did not confiscate their camera?"

He shrugged. "I thought perhaps you had ordered it. In any event," he hastily added, "the ones in line were happy. They thought they were going to a better location. I thought it would be good for the Reich Ministry of Public Enlightenment and Propaganda."

"And who allowed the journalists to accompany them?"

Max felt a chill racing up his spine. He knew without looking that Wilhelm always carried a pistol; he had never seen him without it, even in his own office. He could pull it out now, shoot him dead in Mrs. Weiss's front parlor, and perhaps Max's mother would find him.

Stella would flee; it is what he would do in similar circumstances. She could, perhaps, find her way underground. "I don't know," Max answered, realizing that Wilhelm was waiting for his answer. "When I left the Jewish quarter, I did not see them. I thought they had already left."

"Your job was to supervise them."

"My job, sir, was to assemble two hundred Jews and fifty soldiers."

Wilhelm placed his glass on the table and slowly clapped twice. "Which you did. Bravo."

Max remained standing, his feet rooted to the floor, his drink held firmly in his sweating palm.

"What do you know of the young woman living in your home?"

"Stella?"

"Stella Kowalska. She is Polish."

Max hesitated. "Yes," he said after a long moment. "She is of Polish birth. However, she is a founding member of Będzin's *Jungdeutsche Partei*. I met her before the German invasion, when we all had to meet underground, lest the Polish Army kill us."

"Do you know that she also meets with the *Armia Krajowa*?"

"Poland's Home Guard?" Max placed a hand over his chest, seeking to quiet his erratic heartbeat. "If she does, I am sure it is as a spy—a spy for Hitler. She is quite" he paused as he thought of the right word "zealous about the Nazi cause."

Wilhelm casually reached for a cube of cheese and placed it in his mouth. He chewed for a moment before answering. "The problem with that theory, dear

Max, is that she doesn't pass along information to our spy network."

"Surely, she has meant to—"

Wilhelm took another cube. "It is of no consequence." He locked eyes with Max as he thoughtfully chewed. "You must know that we must maintain tight control."

"Yes, of course." Max attempted to calm his trembling hands.

"You see," Wilhelm continued casually, "while we have been chatting, my guards have apprehended her."

"Where will she be taken?" Max breathed.

"She will not be taken anywhere," Wilhelm answered. He waited a moment before continuing. "My guards had orders to slit her throat on your front lawn and leave her there."

The room began to spin, and Max tried to force himself not to drop his drink or faint. Surely, the man was jesting. Yet, as he stared into Wilhelm's cold gray eyes, he knew he was not. Men like Wilhelm did not pull pranks. "Then, I suppose you will kill me next." His voice was hoarse, and the words forced.

A long silence enveloped them. "On the contrary," Wilhelm said, finishing his drink. "You have been watched, Max, as we all are. You see, we live in a fishbowl in the Third Reich. Every move we make is observed, recorded, and analyzed, as it should be. Our commitment is not to the individual. It is for the collective cause."

"Yes. Of course it is."

"That is why we all must be willing to make sacrifices."

"Of course. It is for the greater good." His words came automatically, as though his brain had ceased to reason.

"Your actions have been what I would have expected from you," Wilhelm was saying.

"I didn't have a lot of training—"

"Excuses are not necessary, and they hurt your cause. Rather, you have performed every task asked of you. Your shortcoming lies in who you trust."

"Who I trust?"

"Your girlfriend, as an example. The journalists, as another."

"I did not provide any information to any of them. You can end my life tonight, but know that I never passed along information of any kind."

"I know that already, Max," Wilhelm answered smoothly. "That is why you are being given a new assignment."

Max's mind reeled as he grappled with the idea.

"Your shortcoming, as I said, is who you place trust in. So, you will be sent away from Będzin."

To the camp, Max thought, or perhaps to the woods where he would be executed far from the place where he had spent his life.

"Are you familiar with Oświęcim?"

"Oświęcim? Of course, I am. It is not far from here."

"That is correct. It is not far, and yet, it is worlds away."

"What do you mean?"

"Only Germans live there now, Max. And soon, only Germans will live in Będzin."

Max tried to swallow, but it stuck in his throat.

"There is a series of camps around the factories at the edge of Oświęcim. It has grown quite large, actually." He took a deep breath, his eyes riveted on Max's reaction. "Initially, the labor camps were administered by men. However, more men are needed at the front. Therefore, we have been ordered to replace the men with female guards. They must be German, not of Polish descent. Of course, they must be loyal to the Third Reich. They must be willing to die for Hitler, if it comes to it."

A silence fell on them. Max waited for Wilhelm to continue. When he did not, he asked, "I understand, but what does that have to do with me? Am I being sent to the front?"

"No, Max. You are being sent to Oświęcim to hire women for the camp."

Max almost laughed. "To hire women?"

"It is an important job. The women must be tough. They must have a fighting spirit. They cannot be soft or easily misled by manipulative prisoners."

"Prisoners," Max said. "You mean, laborers?"

"Prisoners, Max. Forced labor. Let's call it what it is."

"Of course. But, wouldn't Berlin send us guards?"

"Berlin has its hands full." Wilhelm stood. "A driver is outside waiting for you. Pack a suitcase, but don't waste time. You will be driven to Oświęcim tonight. Tomorrow at precisely seven o'clock, you will report to the administrative offices in the center of town. You will begin interviewing. You will have a quota, and every applicant must be properly vetted for bloodline and loyalty. Do you have any questions? You should have none."

Max rose and saluted. "There are no questions, my friend. I will report to Oświęcim, and I will perform the job to the satisfaction of the *Führer* and all of Germany."

A tiny smile tugged at the corner of Wilhelm's mouth. "Of course you will." With that, he picked up his cap, placed it on his head, and made his way out the door, leaving it open. As Max followed him to close the door, he realized that Wilhelm had left it open in full view of Stella's body, crumpled and bloodied along the path.

22

Agata

Agata had dozed off when the light truck abruptly stopped, nearly catapulting her off the rudimentary bench. When she heard the driver rap on his door several times, she quickly moved to the back of the vehicle and slid out from under the rigid tarp that served as the transport's roof. The sky was filled with ominous clouds that had effectively obscured the moon, and the truck blended seamlessly into an ever-present mist. She turned toward the driver as she attempted to orient herself.

The driver's window was down, and now he pointed toward a ditch along the side of the road. "*Mitternacht, mitternacht,*" he said in a stage whisper.

"*Danke,*" Agata answered, but he was already speeding into the deepening mists. She quickly crouched as she wandered into the ditch among the reeds, tamping the plants underneath her feet to prevent her shoes from getting sucked into the muck. It had been so dark under the tarp that she could barely see her hand in front of her face. Even with the mist, the night air was preferable.

She raised her head to peer around her. On the other side of the ditch behind her was a wooded area so shadowy that someone could have been hiding a few yards from her, and she doubted she would have been able to spot them. To her left and right for as far as she could see, the rain ditch ran alongside an unpaved road, weeds and reeds intermingling to obscure the ditch's depth. She could barely make out the retreating truck's taillights as it sped along the road, occasionally jostling as it hit bumps or potholes. Across the road, on the other side of an identical ditch, was a recently plowed, flat field that offered no cover.

It had been over a week since she left Warsaw. Every day brought new surprises and experiences that caused her to constantly question her decision to leave the relative safety of the bakery warehouse. Yet, she knew that she'd had no other choice than to find Elsa. Better that she died searching for her than live with the knowledge that she hadn't tried.

She'd spent time in isolated barn lofts, a building half-filled with animal feed, a pigsty, and even an abattoir that threatened such waves of nausea that she thought she would have to strike out alone. Often, there was no food, and the only source of water was the troughs for the livestock. Occasionally, there would be a crust of bread or a slice of cheese stuffed in a cleft the animals couldn't reach. On those occasions, she would savor every ounce, for she knew not when she might eat again.

The drivers usually arrived long after dark. They didn't speak beyond an instructional word or two, did not look her in the face, and often deposited her somewhere else in a matter of minutes. It made the journey agonizingly protracted. The days were spent in hiding. Sleep was elusive as every sound jolted her awake and wide-eyed, and an increasing paranoia overtook her.

The last driver had been a German soldier. She'd been so astonished that she nearly didn't go with him, convinced he would take advantage of her helplessness in horrific ways. It was only her understanding of the German language that made her realize he meant to take her to the next mysterious stop. Whether he had been paid handsomely for a ride he might have taken otherwise, or he operated out of benevolence, she would never know.

His instruction, *mitternacht,* as she exited his vehicle, was the German word for midnight. As she stood in the ditch with reeds up to her chest, she knew she could not spend an entire day hiding alongside the road as she waited for midnight to arrive. Agata rolled her eyes toward the skies to find the slightest sliver of sunrise peeking through the mist. It was only a matter of time before the sun rose high enough to illuminate the terrain and reveal her position.

The only recourse was to hide in the woods. She scrambled up the far side of the ditch, her dress soaking up the mud as she fought against sliding back into it. She had long ago lost her possessions, what little she'd had on the night she'd left Warsaw, due to too many abrupt departures.

A set of headlights sliced through the mists in the distance, hastening her desire to reach the wood line. She'd barely reached a sizable tree and slid around on the far side of the trunk before a truck similar to the one she'd just left bounced along the road as men's voices filled the air. She recognized the language and the accents. The Nazis commanded these parts. The knowledge filled her with dread and a strange sense of foreboding.

"You'll be safer over there."

Though the voice was soft and calm, Agata nearly jumped out of her skin as she whirled around. "Where are you?" she asked in a hoarse whisper.

"Over here," the voice answered. "Ahead and to your right."

"How many of you?" Agata asked as she squinted into the murky shadows.

"Only the one."

It was a woman's voice, and if Agata had to guess, she was young, perhaps no older than herself. As she started to move toward the voice, the woman added, "Stay low."

Agata crouched and moved from one tree to another until she discovered a woman sitting calmly on a log as though it were broad daylight and peacetime. As she squinted to see more clearly, she determined that the woman wore a simple gray dress under a dark shawl that covered her head and upper torso. Though her feet were in the shadows, she appeared to be wearing the same clunky black shoes as Agata.

"What is your name?" Agata asked.

"Celeste," the woman answered genially. "And you are—?"

"Agata."

"Agata," Celeste repeated. "You are traveling alone."

"Yes."

"Where are you going?"

Agata hesitated. No one had asked her for a destination. She had only made it known that she wanted to travel south, and somehow that directive had been passed along from driver to driver. The woman had not spoken German but Polish, with a flawless West Slavic accent. Her eyes roamed beyond Celeste, but she did not detect another's presence. Still, she reasoned, it could be a trap. In a world turned upside down, no one was above suspicion.

"You were traveling south," Celeste said, breaking the silence.

"Yes."

Celeste nodded toward the road. "This is the road to Kraków."

"Yes."

"These days, no one travels to Kraków on their own volition."

"Perhaps not."

Celeste reached into a dress pocket and retrieved a small package. She held it out to Agata, opening her palm so she could see it more clearly. "You look hungry."

Agata started to reach for it, but stopped. "You'd better keep it. You never know when you might find more food."

"Ah. But I have had my fill, and there is more where this came from." She waved her hand as if to cajole Agata into taking it.

The gnawing sensation that had been a constant source of discomfort got the better of Agata as she accepted the package. She sat on the ground against a wide oak tree and opened the cheesecloth to find several hardened pieces of crust, assorted berries, and a wedge of cheese. "Thank you," she managed to say before she plunged the first piece of crust into her mouth. She groaned with the pleasure of food and forced herself to suck on it to make it last longer.

"You are searching for someone," Celeste said.

"How did you know?"

Celeste turned her head toward the road, revealing the slightest bit of white hair beneath the shawl. It surprised Agata, as the woman's voice was so youthful. With a sinking feeling, she realized they all had aged disproportionately since the start of the war. "It is the only excuse for a woman to be traveling alone on the road to Kraków."

"But I wasn't alone," Agata hastened to correct her.

"You were," Celeste said with a smile, "and you weren't."

"And what of you?" Agata asked, eager to turn the focus away from herself. "Why are you sitting in the woods all by yourself?" She swiveled her head to peer around them. "Or are there others?"

"There are just the two of us this night," Celeste said. "Tomorrow, there will be others."

"How do you know?"

"Citizens are on the move." She sighed, and the first sign of weariness crept into her voice. "Some move to the south against their will. Others attempt an escape to the north."

"Why north?"

"Why not?"

"North is Warsaw. I just came from there. Whatever I find in Kraków cannot be worse than Warsaw."

"Can't it, though?"

"What do you know?" Agata forced herself to wrap up the remaining bits of food. She stuffed the package into her pocket before guiltily turning her face to Celeste.

"It's alright," Celeste said. "It is yours to keep." She rearranged her skirt. "As for your other question, it is obvious that you have not witnessed the daylight hours in some time."

Agata pondered her statement before answering. "I suppose you're right. I've been in hiding every day."

"Between Warsaw and Kraków, you will find death and destruction. It will only become more intense as you reach Kraków."

"Were you there? What do you know?"

"I know that you must be very determined to find your loved one if you are risking your own life to travel there."

Agata sighed.

"You are searching for one you love, are you not?"

After a long moment, Agata replied. Her voice caught in her throat, and she cleared it self-consciously. "My father and my sister."

"Ah."

"I learned shortly after I left Warsaw that they had been separated. The men were placed on a train toward the outskirts of Warsaw. The women were ordered onto one heading south, presumably to Kraków."

"And you are here, on a longer journey to Kraków than the outskirts of Warsaw."

Agata swallowed. "I had to decide. I love my father very much. My mother died when I was young, and for so long, I felt it was just the two of us against the world, as my sister was so little. In fact, I cannot imagine a world without him in it." She hesitated before continuing, "I knew I could not follow both. I had to imagine what my father would have wanted me to do."

"And your father would have wanted you to follow your sister." Celeste's voice was gentle and without judgment.

Agata nodded. "He would have told me that he could take care of himself, but my sister… Elsa has always relied on me."

As the sun rose and the mists parted, that simple statement began a long-winded explanation that lasted well into the morning hours, as Agata told this stranger in the woods of her mother's passing, her sister's birth, and the dual role she'd acquired of both sister and mother to Elsa. She wiped away tears as she recounted her resentment of Elsa in the moment when she wanted her mother to return to life, her growing love for her little sister, and the moment she left Elsa and Ira with a promise to return, a promise she had never been able to keep.

When she finished, she dabbed at tears escaping down her cheeks. "I feel a tremendous amount of guilt," she admitted.

It was a moment before Celeste replied. "Guilt is when you wish you had made a different choice."

"I suppose it is," Agata said quietly.

The sound of trucks along the road had grown steadily louder as daylight emerged. Agata glanced around the trunk she'd leaned against to peer in that direction. A berm prevented a view of the road, but she still felt exposed. She was also extremely fatigued and didn't recall the last time she had a decent sleep. She ducked to a bit of lower ground, spread apart some leaves, and lay on the bare earth. Then she covered up her body as much as possible. "Are you going to rest?" she asked.

"I am rested enough for now," Celeste answered.

Agata closed her eyes. She tried to relax, knowing that another was close by and could sound an alarm, but something deep inside her gut urged her not to let down her guard.

"You speak German," Celeste said.

"Yes," Agata responded, supposing that Celeste heard the curt exchange with the soldier who had dropped her off.

"Fluently?"

"Yes." She opened her eyes to squint at Celeste, who hadn't moved from the log.

"Yet you are traveling like a refugee."

Daylight pierced through the tree branches overhead. "Your point?"

Celeste shrugged. "You seem independent. Resourceful."

"A lot of good that's done me."

"What would your mother do if she were here right now?"

Agata thought for a moment. "I'll tell you what she wouldn't do," she said. "She wouldn't hide under a stack of leaves." She hesitated as she attempted to recall memories of her. "She always appeared to be in charge… until she wasn't." She rolled onto her side so she could view Celeste better, but the reposition meant she had to cover herself up again. "Anyway, I doubt if she could have been in charge of anything, with the world imploding as it is."

Celeste didn't answer, and Agata closed her eyes. She was drifting off when Celeste spoke. "You know," she said, "beyond the trees is an open area. Mostly agricultural, a bit hilly. There hasn't been any activity there since the invasion."

Agata opened her eyes and waited for her to continue.

She nodded toward an area farthest from the road. "On the other side of it is a small village. There is an abandoned factory at the edge of the village. They once made clothes."

Agata fought to keep her eyes open as she wondered why Celeste was telling her these things. She had no idea what time it was, but darkness would come eventually, and she was to be picked up at midnight.

"Do not travel south through the woods," Celeste continued.

"Why not?" Agata asked sleepily.

"That is where you will find the villagers."

~~~~~

When Agata awakened, Celeste was gone, and the moon had risen. She felt a moment of panic as she
~~~~~

tried to survey her surroundings. She felt an ache deep inside as she wondered which direction Celeste had chosen to travel, and whether a driver had arrived to transport her to another hiding place. She would have liked to have had someone with her on this journey, as the loneliness and vulnerability had set in with a vengeance. She thought of Piotr and wondered where he was and what he might be doing. Had she been alone in this world, she might have joined the resistance.

She brushed off the leaves and debris and made her way to the tree line closest to the road. As the moon rose ever higher, she slipped across to the ditch, burrowing down in the reeds to await her transport.

As dawn broke, it found her in the same position. She had dozed off and on throughout the fitful night between bouts of panic and worry over the absence of help. Every errant thought attempted to cross her mind. Perhaps the driver had been detained. Maybe someone had discovered those willing to risk everything to help others. The route might no longer be safe—and neither was she.

As the sun rose, she made her way into the trees but remained on the edge closer to the road during an unbearably long day. She waited with bated breath every time a vehicle passed by, whether it was one with an engine or a cart pulled by tired-looking donkeys. Though she waited for them to stop and glance her way, none ever did. The adrenaline saved for rushing out of the trees and through the ditch evaporated.

The following night arrived. Once again, she made her way into the ditch. It rained that night, filling the trench with rainwater. She removed her shoes and held them level with her waist to keep them from getting sucked into the mud. As the moon rose ever higher and remained partly obscured by purple-colored clouds, she began to shiver uncontrollably.

The first vestiges of dawn found her in the same spot as the day before. She climbed out of the ditch and, shaking with the cold and dampness, made her way back into the woods. She'd had hours to think of her next moves as it became apparent that she could wait forever for a transport that might never arrive.

Agata made her way to the opposite side of the woods. She was unable to see the village from this vantage point. A small rolling hill curved past unkempt fields, blocking her view. It was open terrain, just as Celeste had said. She imagined herself walking across the field as a vehicle appeared in the distance. There would be no place to hide.

Instead, she wandered south through the woods, keeping an eye on the terrain, until she eventually spotted an opening in the undulating landscape. If she could reach that opening, the gentle hills would provide some cover until she came out the other side.

She sat against a broad trunk and removed the package of food Celeste had shared with her. The berries provided much-needed hydration, and she tried to close her eyes and suck on one at a time for as long as possible. She had attempted to catch rainwater the night before with her outstretched palms, but no matter how hard she tried, she could not manage to quench her thirst.

As she opened her eyes, she noticed something yellow lying on the ground, perhaps fifty feet from where she sat. She squinted as she attempted to identify it. It wasn't a pile of autumn leaves, and as she stared harder, a strange sensation began to rise within her.

Finally, she rose on shaky, fatigued legs and made her way toward it. As she approached, other colors and shapes caught her attention, scattered across the woods as if a strong storm had picked them up and carried them to be deposited in random, chaotic patterns among the trees.

The bit of yellow that had caught her eye was a doll with mud-caked hair and a dirty yellow dress. She wiped off the debris and held the doll to her chest as she continued. Suitcases were scattered about, their contents strewn across the forest floor. Clothing, shoes, and bars of soap were interspersed with photographs. She stopped to pick one up to find it inscribed on the back. "To Polly," it read, "I will love you forever." As she turned it back around and wiped off the debris, she found herself staring into the sepia eyes of a young man in a World War I uniform.

She grew oblivious of her surroundings as she continued, her eyes focused on the ground. The effects extended so far that she began to realize they had to belong to a large group of people. Agata made her way back to the tree line. She could see between the gentle hills at this vantage point, though the path meandered, so she could not see through to the other side. Her eyes followed the path, a dirt road wide enough for a vehicle or horse-drawn cart. It veered off before reaching the woods, presumably to meet up with the road that had brought her to this area some two days prior.

As she stared at the surroundings, clutching the doll and a mix of photographs, she realized the sky had darkened as a large flock of vultures gathered. As she stared, the flock multiplied, almost as if the birds possessed a silent language that carried for miles. Their broad wingspans glided gracefully on the wind as they neared the woods.

Agata stepped back, her heart pounding. Like someone who did not want to watch a train wreck but could not help but keep her eyes riveted on it, she continued making her way toward the south, where the vultures converged.

She heard the sounds and encountered the stench before she saw the carnage.

There was an infernal buzzing in the air like thousands of flies were clustering. The vultures swooped into the open area before waddling into the woods. As they gathered around too many bodies to count, they made raspy hissing sounds and grunted like pigs at a feed trough.

Agata covered her nose and mouth and turned away, but not before the images had burned into her consciousness. These were the villagers Celeste had warned about.

She moved behind a tree to block her view of the massacre behind her and stared toward the dirt road. She had no way of knowing whether any villagers had survived. Her gut warned against going there, as she had no idea who or what she might encounter. Celeste had not mentioned the size of the village, though it had been large enough to sustain a clothing factory, and it was likely that the villagers had also worked these fields. Her eyes narrowed as she attempted to identify what had been cultivated there. The fields were overgrown, indicating that they had been left untended for at least one season, if not more.

Even as the warning grew inside her, she stepped out from the woods as if her feet had a mind of their own. Her clothing and hair were in various stages of dampness, but the rain had stopped.

She made a mad dash for the road and the opportunity to become obscured between the hills, but the distance was greater than it had appeared from the woods. Sharp pains began just under her ribcage as she gasped for air. With each step she took, she peered at the waterlogged ground ahead in a vain attempt to find tall weeds in which to hide, but there was nothing. As unkempt as the fields had become, nothing was tall enough to conceal her.

By the time she reached the road, she was heaving. Doubled over by the pain in her sides and with her shoes coated in mud that was determined to slow her progress, she forced herself to continue. Somewhere behind her, she heard the sound of an engine, and she prayed that it was not turning onto this same road of dirt and muck where she sought refuge. Eventually unable to go any further, she sank to the ground as she vomited the berries she'd consumed earlier.

23

Agata

It might have been a bustling village in its day as roads from four directions converged into a traffic circle in the center of town. Rather than facing due north, south, east, or west, as near as Agata could determine, they pointed northwest, northeast, southwest, and southeast, leading her to believe they were constructed to face specific towns. Not far from the circle was a squat, flat-roofed factory whose roofline was interrupted by two dormant smoke stacks. The concrete-and-brick structure was punctuated by uncovered windows so clear and clean that they might have been washed only that morning. Had Celeste not mentioned its existence, and Agata had not discovered the bodies in the woods, she might never have approached it.

She found a door creaking on its hinges as the wind blew through, forcing it open. She took a couple of steps inside to see an expansive room filled with dozens of tables piled high with material, a sewing machine at each end. She lingered at each as she made her way to the opposite end of the room, noting the fans still spinning against each wall. She couldn't remember the last time she had encountered electricity, and she was surprised to find it here.

A set of offices was located at one end of the room, each consisting of a desk and chair, and some contained typewriters or fans. The desks were covered with paperwork in various stages of organization; some were neatly contained in metal organizers, while others were far more haphazard.

She discovered a metal lunch pail on one desk with a bowl and spoon beside it. Without hesitation, Agata sat in the creaking metal chair and devoured the bowl of bean and yellow turnip soup. In earlier days, she might have considered it meager and unsatisfying, but today she felt like a queen. She found a biscuit inside the pail; it was about half the size of a pack of cards and made with a type of flour she didn't recognize, but she forced it down with the half-full glass of water beside it. With the glee of someone finding gold in a mine, she also located three nuts at the bottom of the pail.

As she finished eating, she considered the food and the abandoned village. The soup had been cold and partly congealed, the biscuit hard. She would have heard the villagers had they been marched into the woods the morning she'd been dropped off. Besides, she reminded herself, Celeste had already discovered them. They must have been killed the day before she met Celeste, their factory work interrupted as the manager was eating his lunch.

It didn't make sense. She made her way back to the factory floor and picked up a finished shirt. It was sturdy and stiff. The threads were a mismatch of brown and olive, but the work was good. While it was impossible to tell if they were meant for Germans or Poles, she quickly determined that, due to the occupation of Poland, the factory had been making German uniforms. Why, then, would the workers have been slaughtered?

A feeling of dread crept up her spine. She had to reach Elsa quickly, before it was too late.

She tracked down a duffel bag, carefully selected several long-sleeved shirts, and placed them inside. Skirts were harder to find, but she eventually found a corner of the factory with skirts that fell just below her knees. She closed the bag with care.

Agata made her way to a window and peered into the center of the village. Other than a stray dog wandering at the far end, it appeared completely deserted. With a prayer for protection on her lips, she rushed from the factory into the nearest open structure, an end unit in a block of connected homes. It was dark inside, the heavy curtains falling across the small windows. She made her way upstairs to find ladies' clothing, which rounded out her new wardrobe. The lady of the house had larger feet than her own, but she stuffed the shoes to keep her feet from sliding inside them.

She hesitated at a bathroom door to stare at the clawfoot bathtub. Unable to resist, she turned the faucet. As the pipes creaked and moaned, brown water spewed into the tub, followed by water that was a bit clearer. She quickly stripped, filled the tub, and climbed in. A sliver of soap made her feel luxurious as she removed weeks of grime from her body, face, and hair.

Although the water was only tepid, she did not want to leave the tub. The water made her feel cradled in its embrace. She lay back and considered her plan. If she were to survive and find Elsa, she would have to be resourceful, cunning, and shrewd. She couldn't question whether it might be possible for her to rise to a level of survival she'd never had to experience before. Her life depended upon it. Perhaps Elsa's life did, too.

~~~~~

As the sun traversed the sky to the other side, indicating that darkness would soon arrive, Agata knew it was time to leave. She would not take the road from which she'd arrived, but a different road that led toward the southwest and Kraków.

As she left the home, carefully closing the door behind her, she was dressed in a new shirt and skirt with an aged, dark coat over one arm and the duffle bag in her hand. The shoes felt strange as she walked down the empty street toward the far edge of town, and she hoped she could break them in easily. She had miles to walk.

As Agata came to the last cross-street before leaving the village, she was startled to discover a banged-up vehicle parked along the edge of the road. She hesitated, listening for signs of life. Hearing none, she moved to the side of the vehicle. There was no roof, leaving open two bucket seats in the front and a narrow bench in the back. The doors were missing, the tires had dangerously smooth tread, and its serviceability was questionable. But as Agata leaned in further to peer inside, the gleam of a key in the ignition caught her eye.
~~~~~

At that moment, a sound caused her to bolt upright.

In the doorway of a building on the opposite side of the vehicle was a man who appeared as startled to see her as she was of him. Even from the distance that separated them, Agata could see his eyes scanning from her to the vehicle, and she could have sworn she saw the recognition on his face as he realized the key was still in the ignition.

She moved, and he quickly held out both hands with his palms out. "No, no," he said, shaking his hands. "No, no, no."

Agata froze. He was dressed similarly to her, in a mixture of olive and brown, though his clothing showed signs of age and wear. His boots were covered in layers of dirt and muck, unacceptable in the German army unless the men were marching. His head was bare of the customary German helmet or field cap, and she could see no insignia. As he stepped toward her, she instinctively stepped backward by the same degree, though her eyes raced to the key and ignition.

The man asked something in a language she did not understand. She looked back at his face, the concern in his voice still lingering in the air. When she did not reply, he asked, *"Polsku?"*

Agata continued to stare at him. He was so close to her that she could see his widened eyes and the anxiety etched on his face.

"Deutsche?"

As her silence continued, another man appeared beside him. He was younger and dressed more sharply in an obvious German uniform, a cap in his hand, though the uniform was ill-fitting. Her first impulse was to run. Her mind raced ahead of her, picturing her running out of the village as they effortlessly caught up with her in their vehicle. Just as rapidly, she envisioned an attempt to lose them in the village in one of the many deserted structures.

The younger man asked in German, "Do you speak Polish or German?"

She hesitated. The wrong answer could endanger her.

He repeated his question in Polish. "Which is it?" he asked when she did not reply.

She looked to the older man. For the first time, she noticed a camera hanging from one shoulder, its massive lens protruding as if it had just shifted into position behind him. His hands were still outstretched as if imploring her. "Either," she answered. "Both."

The two men appeared to relax slightly, though the younger one took a step toward the vehicle. The older man said something, which the younger translated into German. "Are you a villager here?"

She shook her head.

Once again, the older one spoke, and the younger one translated. "Do you know what happened here?"

She hesitated and looked away.

The younger one took the opportunity to move swiftly to the vehicle and extract the key. He was dark with olive skin that appeared almost swarthy. His hair was black, and from this distance, his eyes seemed alluring. It was unusual to see someone with his coloring in Eastern Europe, and she wondered if he was Italian or Spanish. Agata felt her heart sink as he placed the key into his pocket, though she knew she could not have escaped in their vehicle. Perhaps if the men had not appeared when they did, she might have been miles down the road in it already.

With the translator between them, the older man said, "My name is Hank. What is your name?"

"Agata."

"Agata," he repeated.

The younger man added, "I am Rafe."

Agata frowned. "Hank. Rafe. What nationalities are you?"

"We could ask the same of you," Rafe replied. They conferred between themselves before Rafe added, "Hank is American. I am Spanish."

"American?" Agata seized on the word as her eyes became riveted on Hank. "Are the Americans here? The Americans are in Poland?"

At the sight of her face suddenly aglow, they both relaxed. Hank reached into his shirt pocket and extracted a pack of cigarettes. She took one offered to her and stepped closer so he could light it.

"Just Hank," Rafe said. He smiled briefly at Hank. "We are still awaiting American soldiers."

"Are they coming?"

His smile faded. "The Americans are busy in North Africa at the moment."

"And the English?"

"The same."

Agata's face fell.

"Do you know what happened here?" Hank asked through his translator.

Agata nodded toward his camera.

"I am a photojournalist. I am here to document the war."

"I see."

"Are you Polish?"

"Yes," she answered, adding, "But I prefer to speak German. I need the practice."

Hank laughed before Rafe had translated entirely, leading her to believe he understood a bit more than he had let on. "We all do," he answered.

"I am not from the village," she answered. "I was told there was a clothing factory here." She held up her duffel bag.

"It is unusual to find an unescorted woman in these parts," Hank said through Rafe's translation. "It is also extremely dangerous."

"Yes. I know."

"Where are you going?"

"South."

"Toward Kraków?"

She nodded.

They exchanged worried expressions before speaking at once. "You can't go there."

"You don't know what is happening there."

Agata swallowed. "My sister is there."

"On her own accord?"

She shook her head.

"Where was she taken from?"

"Warsaw."

Again, they exchanged telling looks.

Agata looked toward the sky. It was beginning to darken, and she needed to get moving. "I go to Kraków now."

As she started to take a step, Hank moved to stop her. "Wait," he said. As Rafe translated, he continued, "We can take you with us. You can ride, not walk."

"To Kraków?"

"To the east."

"Into Soviet territory?"

Hank and Rafe nodded reluctantly.

"No, thank you."

"The Soviets are fighting on the side of the Americans now."

Agata chuckled wryly. "The Soviets fight on the side of the Soviets. Always. They are as bad as the Germans."

"Yes," Rafe said. "But we travel to Allied territory, away from the Germans."

"My sister is not there."

"And you travel to reach your sister," Hank added.

"How do you propose getting past the Germans?"

Agata pointed at Rafe's clothing. "How did you?"

The men chuckled. "Point well taken," Rafe responded as he pointed at her outfit. "I take it this clothing was not yours? That is why you wanted to reach the clothing factory?"

Agata nodded as she looked again to the skies. It looked like a cloudy night, and she silently prayed that there would be no more rain.

"If you insist on trying to find your sister," Hank said, "then get to the west of Kraków. You are more likely to find your sister at Oświęcim. Are you familiar with it?"

Agata shook her head. "Only the name. It is small, yes?"

"Yes. That is where the trains go from Warsaw, from Kraków, also."

Hank locked eyes with Agata's. His eyes were wide, soft, and sad, somehow a mixture of compassion and having seen too much. "You must understand that you are unlikely to find your sister."

"Perhaps," she answered, tilting her chin upward. "But I must die trying, if that is my fate."

"The Nazis are taking anyone who isn't German. It no longer matters if they are Jewish, political dissidents, or what they call undesirables. You must be German to get through." He hesitated before adding, "A woman is in particular danger."

As Rafe translated, Agata prepared to leave. "Perhaps," she said. "But, again, I must try."

"Can I get your name and your picture?" Hank asked.

Agata hesitated.

"If your family searches for you later, it could be helpful," Rafe said.

"And if the Germans find your camera and your notes?"

"We will only have a picture on the camera and a name and date on a pad."

"Not the location?" Agata asked.

"No."

"And if you are tortured?"

"To give up information on you?" Rafe smiled. "Are you a spy they are after?"

"No. Not a spy. Agata Heinrich."

Hank held up the camera. "Your picture?"

She nodded. The cigarette had long ago burned down, but she still held the stub in her hand. She stared directly into the lens without blinking, her expression immobile. It was an odd feeling to have her photograph captured here in this peculiar village, and a strange feeling to know it might be seen around the world: a lone young woman wandering between Warsaw and Kraków, searching for her sister. Perhaps, Elsa might see it.

Hank and Rafe shook her hand and offered again to take her east with them. She declined and turned to go. Then, abruptly, she turned back around.

"You asked earlier if I knew what happened here."

"Yes," both men said in unison.

She pointed toward the traffic circle in the middle of the village. "Take the road to the northwest. You'll see woods about a mile beyond the village. They slaughtered them there."

"Who?"

She shrugged. "I suppose it was the Nazis. Who else could it be?"

"Why?"

"Why?" she repeated. "If you were a Nazi, why not?"

As she turned her back on them and began to walk, she heard activity behind her. A moment later, their vehicle's engine sputtered to life. The sound of the engine grew fainter as they sped away from her, and she realized that she had never felt so alone in her entire life.

24

Hank

An onslaught of emotions threatened to derail Hank, and only his years of experience kept him from falling apart. Journalists relied on objectivity and on keeping their feelings and personal beliefs at arm's length to cover a story impartially. But as Hank took photographs and Rafe counted the bodies and made notes, it was increasingly difficult to hang on.

The stench was overwhelming, with some of the bodies in various degrees of post-mortem edema and others turning black, their faces and limbs contorted. Wild creatures, including vultures, had further violated many. They had to drive off the latter to investigate the scene; it hadn't been difficult, since vultures are easily spooked, but it had left a haunting impression. The dead consisted of children, women, and men of all ages. For the first time, Hank witnessed able-bodied men who might have served the Third Reich as slave labor, gunned down instead. Retaliation, he thought.

The woods were littered with toys, suitcases, clothing, and other personal belongings, leading him to speculate that the villagers had been duped into believing that they were being relocated. One infant still had a pacifier in his mouth, the back of his head blown off, and several children clutched their dolls or wooden toy trucks.

"I didn't get an exact count," Rafe said, joining him. He had a bandana tied around his face to prevent the smell from permeating his nostrils. "I estimate close to five hundred."

"Five hundred! How is that possible?" Hank peered through the woods, where barely any ground had been left uncovered. "How many soldiers would have been needed for that?"

"Maybe only a handful. They had weapons; these people were unarmed. Some were scattered as if they were running, trying to escape."

Hank clenched his jaw. "I don't even have words for this."

"I do," Rafe said. "'Hell is empty, and all the devils are here.'"

"Revelation?"

"Shakespeare. Now do you believe me?"

"About what?"

"Revelation 12, verses seven to nine."

"Oh, please."

He continued undeterred. "And I paraphrase: when Satan was cast out of heaven, he and his angels were hurled to the earth. Not hell, Hank. Earth. The battle between good and evil continues here, with us."

"Fine. I'm beginning to believe you."

"Only beginning to?"

Hank moved toward the tree line, where he could attempt to breathe fresher air. "If you're right, then it's obvious who is winning."

"First John, chapter 5, verse 19—"

"And you paraphrase," Hank interjected.

"The whole world is under the control of the evil one," Rafe said as he joined him at the edge of the woods.

"Well, that's helpful."

"However, the Bible goes on to say in the Book of John, chapter 12, verse 31: the ruler of this world will be cast out."

"So, the Jews we saw assembled and marched out of Będzin were not an anomaly," Hank murmured as if he hadn't been listening.

"I'd say it is standard operating procedure," Rafe said as he lit a cigarette. He offered Hank one, then rocked back on his heels. "The orders came from higher up. Berlin, probably. I'd bet anything on it."

Hank strolled to the vehicle, his feet feeling heavy and his movements slow. When he reached it, he leaned against it and puffed on his cigarette. "I don't understand it. How many countries has Hitler invaded now; how many does he have complete control over?"

Rafe removed his bandana from his face but left it dangling around his neck. "Poland, obviously. Czechoslovakia, or what they refer to as the Sudetenland." He held up one finger and then two.

"Austria. Denmark. Norway," Hank added. Both men now held up five fingers.

"Belgium. Holland. France," Rafe said.

"Two more are in play now. The Soviet Union,"

"And Italy, now that the Italians ousted Mussolini, and Hitler reinstated him in the north as his puppet government."

"Don't forget Britain's Channel Islands."

"I'm out of fingers." They stood side by side, leaning against the vehicle and facing away from the woods, smoking. "The Nazis' entire ideology is based on hatred of other groups," Rafe added.

"We've seen firsthand the brutality. I have never before witnessed a total lack of empathy, of humility, of a moral or ethical compass." Hank dabbed at his eye. "I'll never get this out of my memory. I never believed human beings were capable of this."

Rafe jabbed his thumb toward the woods. "We are too far from Będzin for this to be the work of the same group."

Hank paused. "It's just as you said. Berlin had to have issued a widespread order. Multiple groups of soldiers have carried out—and may continue to carry out—indiscriminate slaughter."

"We have to get these pictures to the west. The world has to know what is happening here. This is your calling, Hank. This is why you're here."

"We shouldn't have let that girl go," Hank murmured. "We knew what they did to those civilians, and now, these."

"She had a purpose." Rafe kicked mud off the bottom of his boots as he spoke.

"She was heading south. There is an evil hovering over southern Poland."

"Yes. She was walking through the gates of hell. And she was doing it to find her sister."

Hank stared down the road as if he could see her. "She can't have gotten far. I say we go after her and take her with us."

"The more we have with us, the more dangerous it becomes for all of us."

"Self-preservation, my friend?" Hank continued without waiting for his reply. "Anyway, she'd just be one more. And, what if it was Dottie out there? I'd want someone to rescue her."

"But what if it was Dottie attempting to save Susanna or Mary? And what if some stranger yanked her off the road and took her in the opposite direction? That girl's sister might depend on her reaching her."

"Agata's life might depend on whether you and I get to her before the Nazis do." When Rafe didn't respond, Hank added, "You know what they will do to her."

Rafe brushed nonexistent lint from his Nazi uniform. "She and I had the same idea about our clothing."

"It's a good idea, too, to dress like them."

"Good thing Otto and I wore a similar size, and he hadn't yet taken this to be cleaned."

"But it isn't exactly a Roman shield, is it? All it does—for you and for her—is prevent someone from afar from suspecting you enough to warrant getting closer." He put out his cigarette. "I say we go get her."

"I say we continue on our way and allow her to continue on hers."

"I don't know if I can forgive myself if I don't try."

"We already tried. And you may never forgive yourself if you force her to go with us and we find out later that her sister died because of it. Besides, we can't go back in that direction. They have to know we're gone. They've likely discovered Otto and know his vehicle has disappeared with us. In fact, Little Orphan Annie, we're wasting time here." As if to prove his point, Rafe climbed into the driver's seat. "You coming?"

Hank reluctantly joined him. "Where to? What's the plan?"

~~~~~

Rafe settled onto the floor of the church belfry and opened a tablecloth to reveal an assortment of food, including cheese, a few eggs of dubious age, hard bread, carrots, and turnips.

"Not bad," Hank said appreciatively as he settled in next to him. He opened his piece of cloth.

"What the hell is that?" Rafe asked.

"Crawdads."

"They're fucking insects."

"People eat them. They're kind of like lobster. They had them in Spain, don't you remember?"

"They're fucking insects," he repeated. "Only poor people ate them and only when completely desperate."

"What do you think we are now?" Hank pointed to other items. "I also found lots of pecans. Must be a pecan grove near here. And look. A potato."

"Too bad we left those boxes at the drug factory."

"At the former drug factory. What do you think all those soldiers are going to do when their drug supplies run out?"
~~~~~

"And they're all facing withdrawal? They'll blame the Jews, of course."

"Okay, so what do we eat now, and what do we save for later?"

Rafe moved the nuts, cheese, and bread to one side. "These will last the longest."

"The crawdads and egg will need boiling. Too risky to do it here," Hank added.

"And we already decided to spend the night at the highest point in the village."

"That leaves the carrot, turnip, and potato."

They eyed the sorry-looking vegetables.

"They'd be better in a soup," Rafe said.

"A seafood soup." Hank removed a half-empty cigarette pack from his pocket. "I think I'll have a cigarette."

"Fuck," Rafe said. "I'll have one, too. But tomorrow, for breakfast, before we head out, we'll get in somebody's kitchen—not like they're coming back—and cook up soup. But I'll tell you right now, I'm not eating fucking insects. You'd better not adulterate my fucking soup."

Hank kept his cigarette low as he peered over the wall. "I don't think we should be here when the sun comes up."

"Yeah," Rafe said. "I suppose."

It hadn't been challenging to decide where they should remain while they charted their course. The Catholic Church was situated near the center of the village, where all roads converged. It was a small building, as churches go, and plain. At least, Hank thought, it looked like it had been unpretentious before it was burned and looted. The roof was gone, the stained windows in shards, and several walls were missing. The pews were charred, indicating a massive fire. Yet, it appeared to have been burned long before the villagers had been marched into the woods. In the beginning, it was well-known that Catholic parishioners played a significant role in resisting the Nazis and assisting Jews who needed to hide or escape. As the Nazis conquered parts of Poland, they burned the Catholic churches along with Jewish synagogues in attempts to prevent groups of people from congregating and to erase Polish culture.

A few of the Będzin churches had been saved and converted to Positive Christianity, a religion unique to Nazis. Although Hank and Rafe had never attended a service, their religious beliefs were prominently displayed. As the Nazi Party rose in Germany, they issued a pamphlet outlining their ideologies, which included a statement regarding freedom of religion. As it turned out, it meant they were free to follow *their* religion; as they gained power, all other religions were systematically wiped out.

Positive Christianity was unlike any form of Christianity that Hank had ever known. It was based on the intolerance of people who did not fall neatly into the Nazi ideal. This included Jews, Catholics, Hindus, Muslims, and even other forms of Christianity.

Hank had concluded long ago that Positive Christianity bore no likeness to Christ's teachings. They certainly did not open their arms to strangers, practice compassion or acceptance of others, or exhibit high morals or ethics. It had also been reported that Positive Christianity could border on occultism, though Hank had no firsthand knowledge of it. He did, however, have firsthand knowledge of the atrocities they committed in the name of Christ.

"I think you're right," Hank said quietly.

"About what?" Rafe had leaned back against the wall, his cigarette extinguished, his face in shadows as he dozed. He kept his eyes closed as Hank responded.

"It is a battle of good versus evil. It's been harder to recognize because the evil ones come cloaked as Christ's followers."

"I'm not even going to ask where the fuck that came from."

There was a moment of silence as Hank gazed out of the charred belfry, the stone walls and stairs saving the tower from complete ruin. The roads in all directions were pitch-black, and he wondered where Agata was sleeping tonight. He got his bearings and considered their options, because once Rafe had dozed for an hour or two, he planned for them to hit the road. They could travel at night with their headlights off. Their soup would have to wait. Daylight would bring more traffic and more opportunities to be discovered. Besides, Nazi checkpoints were often lit up at night, allowing them to identify them in sufficient time to get onto an alternate route.

Hank ruled out travel to the southwest, which led to Kraków, Oświęcim, and Będzin. To the southeast lay Romania, which the Iron Guard ran in collaboration with Nazi Germany; their behavior rivaled the Nazis' atrocities, so that was not an option. He surmised that Romania, with its vast reserves of troops, equipment, and oil, currently played a crucial role in the fight against the Soviets. After all, they purportedly controlled the fourth-largest Axis force in the world after Germany, Italy, and Japan.

North was just as bad, as the Germans also controlled Poland in that direction. Even if they were able to cross the country and live to tell the tale, Lithuania met them on the other side, and they had shown fealty to Germany.

To the west was almost an entire continent under Nazi control. There was a smattering of neutral countries, such as Switzerland or Sweden, but they were too distant from their current location.

That left the east. Had it been 1939, the Soviets would have controlled eastern Poland as a result of the Molotov-Ribbentrop Pact, an agreement between Nazi Germany and the Soviet Union that divided the country between them. Once the Soviets completed their invasion of the territory agreed upon by Hitler and Stalin, it was renamed the Polish Soviet Socialist Republic, and the citizens went to the polls to elect their leader. What they found on the ballot was one name: Joseph Stalin. Their stint as a Soviet territory had flown out the window when Germany turned against their ally, invaded eastern Poland, and then the Soviet Union in 1941 in Operation Barbarossa. However, Soviet pushback was earnest, resulting in constantly shifting lines. For Rafe and Hank to attempt to flee to the east, they would meet more Nazis before reaching the Soviets, and God only knew whether the Soviets would welcome them.

Holy shit, Hank thought as he pondered their situation. They were surrounded.

25

Max, Oświęcim, Poland

The bar was long and narrow, the dark wood and low lighting casting most of the room into shadows. Earlier in the evening, those shadows had moved and morphed, but as the night wore on, they had dissipated, one by one. The owner-bartender had flipped the sign in the window from "open" to "closed" and was busy cleaning up behind the counter, while an older woman wiped down all the tables and set the chairs on top of them in preparation for cleaning the floors.

In the furthest corner, Max sat alone, his back against the wall, a cigarette in one hand and a drink in the other. He watched the employees without really registering their actions, his mind moving between the stupor of drunkenness and intrusive thoughts he fought to keep at bay.

"Can I get you another, Max?" the woman asked. She held a worn cleaning rag in a hand covered in age spots, and her nails were worn down. She must have been attractive when she was younger, Max thought. Her face was pleasant but rounded with age, and her neck was slack. Her eyes were clear blue, the kind the Aryans particularly prized. Her hair must have been the color of wheat back in the day; he could detect strands of it now, intermingled with white. She smiled pleasantly as she slipped into a chair across from him.

"No," he said.

"Is it time for you to head back home?"

It was a question she asked every night when the bar had long been closed, and they were nearing the time when the employees, too, would go home. The woman lived alone; they had chatted before. She was German, brought to Oświęcim to serve the employees of the nearby camp, who filled the bar every evening after work. Her husband had been killed during World War I, and her two sons were now fighting at the front.

"Yes, Katarina. Do you know of any women searching for employment?"

"You are still looking?"

"I am always looking."

"Ah. I suppose you are."

"What about you? I can triple the pay you receive here."

"I wouldn't last at the camp, and you know it."

"I can arrange an easy job."

"That's not what I mean."

His eyes tried to lock onto hers, but he had difficulty focusing. "What do you mean?"

"We've had this conversation before, Max. I like being a barmaid. And if I leave, Hinrich would have to find someone to replace me."

Max turned his attention to the man at the bar. He appeared to be middle-aged, somewhere in between

Max's age and Katarina's. He was trim, his movements efficient as he worked behind the bar, his energy apparent even at this late hour. "Hinrich can get his wife to work here."

"Not since you hired her in the camp." Katarina smiled sadly.

He looked back at her, his lids beginning to droop. "Don't you have a roommate?"

"There are others in the house. I wouldn't call them roommates. We simply rent beds."

"What about that young woman, the one with the long, brown hair?"

"What about her?"

"Can she work in the camp?"

Katarina shook her head. "You know she is Polish. She wears the letter "P" ordered by the Germans. I suppose one day soon, she will be sent the way of the Jews."

"Ah, that's right. Only Germans are allowed to work in the camp. What work does she do now?"

"You know what she does, Max." Her voice was firm but gentle. "She works in the fields, growing vegetables for the camp."

"What is her name again?"

Katarina leaned back in her chair. "You know her name, Max."

"I have forgotten it."

"It is Bogdanka."

"Bogdanka what?"

"Max."

"I am serious; tell me."

"Bogdanka Laska." Katarina rose. She barely suppressed a groan as she straightened her back.

Max rose unsteadily to his feet. He remained behind the table for a moment as he tried to right himself as if he stood on a teetering boat. After a moment, he stepped around the table, bumping into it and spilling the remainder of his drink.

"Don't worry about that. I'll get it," Katarina said, making a move to right the glass.

"I am not worried about it."

"No," she said. "I don't suppose you are."

He made his way to the front of the bar, wobbling enough to grasp the edge of the bar at intervals.

"Good night, Max," Hinrich said amicably. He moved ahead of Max and opened the door into the city center.

A blast of cold air hit Max full in the face as he stepped outside. For a moment, he wondered if he'd left his coat in the bar before realizing that Katarina would have given it to him. He vaguely remembered walking over at noon in a great hurry, not bothering to put on his hat or his coat. Now, he couldn't remember why he'd been so harried.

He recognized a soldier moving across the courtyard, and he waved him over. The young man saluted him as he approached, and Max sloppily returned it. "Do you know Bogdanka Laska?" he asked him.

"No, sir," the soldier replied. "I'm afraid I do not."

"Find her," Max answered. He waved his arm in the direction of the camp. "She lives in one of the boarding houses along the edge of town."

"Yes, sir. And would you like me to bring her to you?"

"No," Max answered. "Take her to the camp."

"To work, sir?"

"As a prisoner."

"Yes, sir."

"That is all."

The soldier saluted again. "I'll get right on it, sir."

"See that you do." Max returned the salute, and as the soldier hurried off in the direction of the boarding houses, he stumbled his way along the street toward his apartment. He struggled to put his key in the lock, his hands trembling from a mixture of frayed nerves and stout alcohol. When he managed to get it open, he hesitated as he stared at the long, narrow staircase leading to his apartment, unsure if he should attempt it or sleep on the stairs as he sometimes did. He decided after a moment that he wanted the comfort of his bedcovers, as the night air had made him cold if not sober. A gust that pushed the door against him solidified this thought, and he wrestled to extract his key, closed the door, and tottered up the stairs with each hand outstretched to the walls to secure him.

The door at the top of the stairs did not require a key and opened into a large room with hardwood floors in an intricate pattern, gold-patterned wallpaper against a creamy white background, gold fixtures, and high ceilings. A row of windows with wispy white curtains stretched nearly from the floor to the ceiling and overlooked the square below. Max paused at the round table, unsteadily dumping out his keys and pocket contents onto the freshly starched doily, before moving further into the interior.

The grand fireplace was roaring, its warmth inviting, no doubt stoked to perfection by his housekeeper. He almost plopped into one of the oversized off-white chairs where a cozy, homemade throw rested over the arm. He would be warm here. He knew that because he'd spent previous nights in that chair, sleeping off a stupor.

Instead, he began to loosen his tie as he moved into his bedroom. Another fire roared invitingly, effectively banishing the cold. He plopped down onto the bed and pulled the bedcovers around him so only his shoes poked out from underneath the covers. As he began to close his eyes, they hesitated on the chandelier above the bed, set into an intricate inlaid design.

Everything was right there in the square for him. His office was on one side, and his apartment on the other. He could order his housekeeper to cook for him, or he could pop into any of three restaurants. He was always seated promptly, even if it meant evicting someone from a table to do so. He was an important man here who could hire a person to work in the camp or, with a wave of his hand, banish them there as a prisoner, as he had just done with Katarina's roommate, whose name he had already forgotten.

The apartment had come fully furnished, as all of them did in Oświęcim. He didn't know if his had belonged to a Jew or a Polish Gentile, and he didn't care. All the photographs and personalized mementos had been removed before his arrival, in a process they called sanitizing.

Katarina was one of only a few who dared to call him by his first name. To everyone else, he was Herr Kursell. He had been methodical about disclosing his background, which included German and Aryan descent, with important Germanic peoples sprinkled in to make an extra impression. Gone was the skinny little kid who was bullied in Będzin, and whose mother sewed for wealthy Jews and worked nights in a factory. Gone was the boy who begged Mrs. Weiss for more time for his mother to pay the rent and accepted scraps of her donated food to stay alive.

Now, he was Herr Kursell, the son of a man who died at the front fighting for Germany while his wealthy mother lived in Berlin and partied with Hitler. He was not Polish, and he had not grown up in Będzin. No one here knew him. As he drifted off to sleep fully clothed, he knew Wilhelm must have investigated him, but they undoubtedly needed every German man at the front. It was why he was scraping the bottom to find women to work in the camp, which had a depressingly high turnover rate, and why he had been chosen for the job.

A flash of self-doubt tried to horn its way into his mind, that indeed, there must have been men too old to fight who they could have sent here, but he pushed the thought out of his mind as he succumbed to an alcohol-induced sleep.

26

Agata

When Agata was younger, she read about people who had accomplished heroic or nearly superhuman deeds, such as climbing Mount Everest, discovering the North or South Poles, or pushing their bodies to extremes in other ways. Yet, as the days melted into one another so that she no longer knew how many days had transpired since she left Warsaw, she realized that every human being had more strength inside themselves than they had ever acknowledged.

She didn't know how many miles she had traveled each day or how many were still ahead of her. She knew she'd dropped a considerable amount of weight, as her primary source of food was through foraging. She drank from puddles or ditches, and often she didn't feel as though she could continue to put one foot in front of the other. Yet, somehow, she did.

Along her travels, she encountered scores of people along the roads, especially as she approached the outskirts of Kraków. Most were refugees. They consisted of the elderly, invalids, women, children, and infants. Some walked, while others were carried or pushed in makeshift strollers; the most infirm were often transported in wheelbarrows. Most no longer acknowledged anyone else on the road, keeping their eyes fixed on a distant, nonexistent object. Agata came to think of their blank expressions as death stares. Their consciousness had somehow checked out, yet they continued to place one foot in front of the other, mile after mile, through the hot sun, torrential rains, or freezing nights, just as she did.

No one walked in Agata's direction. Occasionally, she would discover someone peering at her in curiosity as she made her way past the exodus. The words of Celeste, Hank, and Rafe haunted her. More than once, she had to pass trenches alongside the road that were filled with bodies bloated beyond recognition, their bloodied corpses evidence of atrocities that were beyond her comprehension. Despite her best efforts to remain positive that she would reunite with Elsa, she fought against near-constant despair, her thoughts often turning to how a hatred once associated only with Satan could ever have gained control of an entire culture.

She saw her depression mirrored in others' faces. She often wondered if this was the end of humanity. While the Nazis believed in the annihilation of anyone not wholly descended from the Aryans, Agata wondered what kind of creature would be left who thought it necessary to murder others who were unlike them. It was not a race that she wanted to be part of.

Yet, here she was, speaking German when she encountered checkpoints, channeling her mother's and aunts' accents and characteristics to blend in with the enemy.

She sighed when she spotted another checkpoint ahead. They had become more prevalent as she neared the Kraków suburbs. She shifted her bag to access the identification she kept on her.

"Going the wrong way?" The soldier joked as though he thought himself very witty, but it was the same greeting she had heard for days.

"Going to Oświęcim," she answered, handing over her papers.

"Why? Looking for a job there?"

Something sparked inside Agata. "Are they still hiring there?" she asked casually.

He handed her back her papers. "As far as I know. There's a shortage of men to work in the camps. They've opened it up to women now."

"Where do I apply?"

He shrugged. "There are posters displayed in Oświęcim. That's all I know."

"Thank you. Am I free to continue?"

He took a half-step back and waved his hand, indicating she could pass. He was a young man, perhaps no older than eighteen, Agata realized with a start. He might have been working at an ice cream counter, delivering papers, or attending a university, had he not been part of this war.

As she began to walk past him, he added, "It's a long walk to Oświęcim. It could take you days, a week, or even longer. I could drive you there."

Agata hesitated and turned back to face him. There was a hunger in his eyes as if she had suddenly become prey. "Thank you, but I shouldn't. My father would be outraged if he discovered me alone with a man without a chaperone."

His laugh was too sinister, and his smile fell just short of a snarl. "And walking the roads alone is safer?"

Agata took a few steps backward. "You know how fathers are!"

As she passed another young man who had been within range of their conversation, he said, "Herr Kursell is in charge of the camps."

"Herr Kursell?" Agata repeated.

"Max Kursell. He is interviewing all the applicants, if you know what I mean." His eyes raked over Agata as he spoke.

"Thank you," she answered as she continued to walk.

Something deep within her soul began as a whisper and grew into a shout that she could no longer ignore. It was as if someone else were walking beside her, and they were urging her to get off the main road. Despite her attempts to ignore the feeling, it persisted, growing so loud and obnoxious that she could no longer brush it aside.

Eventually, she discovered a footpath off the main road that was too narrow for a vehicle to traverse. As she made her way along it, she was soon obscured by giant reeds. She discovered a creek on one side of the path and grazing land on the other. She fought against buzzing insects, and as the number of bites began to add up, she questioned her decision.

Then, the sound of an engine started in the distance and grew louder. She hesitated as she listened. As it drew closer to the path she had taken, she heard the laughter and banter of young men. She pressed her back against a tree to steady herself.

After a moment, the engine grew faint again as though it had passed the footpath. As she forced herself to continue her journey, she sensed that there was no way she could know for sure whether it was the young men she'd just encountered. Yet, as she continued on her way, she envisioned the two of them driving into the sunset, believing they would both have a chance with her this evening. She wondered how many other women had fallen prey to them, and whether, when or if this hellish existence was over, they would revisit their deeds under a brighter, harsher light.

~~~~~

Oświęcim was a town with a storied history. It was founded in the 12th century and quickly became a hub for east-west commerce due to its proximity to major rivers. Later, a network of railways was established, and the town expanded as multiple industries developed, including chemicals. Although Agata knew the town as Oświęcim, a name it had held since the 11th century, though in various spellings, she quickly learned that the Germans had renamed it Auschwitz.

The Nazis seized control of the town in 1939, annexing it to Germany. Since then, the size had burgeoned with construction. Another chemical plant had been built, huge subdivisions to house Nazi soldiers and camp personnel, and a set of camps had been expanded from the original Army barracks.
~~~~~

Agata quickly discovered that the Polish population had been expelled from the area, and eight surrounding villages had been destroyed as the Germans created a 15-square-mile buffer zone around the area. Despite the less-than-honorable sources, Agata believed that only her stated quest for a job and her paperwork identifying her as German allowed her to reach the village a week later.

Posters advertising the positions directed applicants to Max Kursell's office in the Market Square. There was no other information, so Agata didn't know whether they might require a typist, a bookkeeper, a cook, or something else entirely.

Taking a deep breath and offering a quick prayer for protection, she made her way to the Market Square. Every building she passed had huge Nazi flags draped from the tops of the buildings, and those surrounding the Market Square were no exception. As she moved deeper into the center of town, she sensed a change in the energy. It felt like the still air before the onslaught of a monstrous storm. The energy didn't match the bustle of activity, as every street seemed crammed with military vehicles. She slowed her gait and realized that no one looked into anyone else's faces nor met their eyes. Instead, they stared ahead, just as the Polish refugees had done, though they were dressed well and appeared to be well-fed.

Agata became self-conscious of her own emaciated figure. She was grateful for the structured clothing she'd discovered, as she knew her own clothing would have draped like a tent over her as the months in hiding and then the weeks on the road had reduced her to nothing more than skin and bones.

She found the building easily. The two-story structure dominated the square, featuring no less than seventeen windows on the top floor and nearly as many on the ground floor, broken only by hefty double doors flanked by two columns. Agata was relieved to discover a ladies' room off the expansive lobby, and she quickly made her way there to change into fresh clothes, wash her face and hands, and comb her hair.

A few minutes later, she emerged. Standing tall with her chin high, she climbed to the second floor on a wide marble staircase. Then she wandered the hall until she came to a corner office with an opaque window marked Herr Max Kursell, Camp Administration. She hesitated with her hand just shy of the door handle. It felt as though a black cloud was descending over her, and she almost sensed that if she touched the handle, it would burn her hand. She shook off the feeling of dread and foreboding, took a deep though shaky breath, and opened the door.

Four women of varying ages sat behind sturdy, dark desks, engaged in various frenetic activities. Two did not look up from their typing. A third glanced up with a scowl. The fourth let out an exasperated sigh as though Agata had rudely interrupted them. She was tempted to leave and might have, had she not been so determined to find her sister there, but the eldest of the women stood abruptly.

"What is your business here?" she demanded. Her eyes raked over Agata's clothing.

"I was told you were hiring, and I was to see Herr Kursell."

The woman's narrowed eyes moved briefly to another door that was marked with his name. Then she grabbed a clipboard containing a stack of papers and shoved it toward Agata. As Agata stepped forward to receive it, the woman said, "Fill out the top application and give it to me when you're finished."

"Thank you," Agata said. Thankfully, she noticed a pencil slipped into the clip. She backed away from the desks to a chair against the wall by the door. Setting down her bag, she settled into the chair and began completing the application. She wrote that Fürstenwalde, Germany, was both her birthplace and her last place of employment. Under "Skills," she selected administrative duties, such as typing.

She hesitated when she saw a question regarding the ability to speak other languages. To answer incorrectly could be catastrophic. She was acutely aware of the elderly woman watching her, as if suspicious of her presence, and said a quick prayer for guidance. Then she wrote that she could speak Polish.

When she was finished, Agata handed the clipboard to the woman. She began skimming it with a scowl before she abruptly stopped and looked up at Agata. "Stay here," she said.

The woman knocked on Herr Kursell's door. A male voice instructed her to enter, and she slipped inside. Agata could hear their voices but, try though she might, could not make out their words. A moment later, the woman opened the door wider and beckoned to Agata.

Agata picked up her bag and entered the room. It was smaller than she might have envisioned. A monstrously large, dark desk dominated the room with a disheveled, overflowing bookcase against one wall. Two large windows, one positioned behind the desk and the other beside it, appeared to dwarf the room. There were two chairs in front of the desk, and to Agata's relief, she sensed that the door behind her had been left open.

Behind the desk sat a man who did not rise to greet her but was instead reading her application. His face was narrow and angular, his light hair cropped short. He stiffly held his mouth just short of pursed. When he looked up at Agata, his eyes were dark and veiled.

"Why do you speak Polish?" he demanded without first greeting her.

Agata answered without hesitation. "I am from Fürstenwalde. It is close to the Polish border—what was the border before the war—and a major commerce center. We frequently had merchants from Poland as well as other countries."

"Your name is Heinrich. Who is your father?"

"Henri Heinrich," she answered promptly, using her uncle's first name and her mother's last.

"Your mother?"

"Herta." As she mentioned her aunt's name, she envisioned her cousin, who was five years her senior. Agata knew nothing of Max Kursell. As she held his gaze with her own, she hoped he had not been from the Fürstenwalde area and had not known her mother's family.

After a moment, he asked, "What are you doing so far from home?"

"Looking for work," she said.

"There is no work in Fürstenwalde?"

She shrugged. "Not as much as we once had. Commerce has been affected by the war." As she said this, she wondered if the war effort had expanded, rather than contracted.

He did not seem to notice her discomfort. He looked back at her application. "What do you know of the camps?"

"Very little, I'm afraid," she answered. "I assume they house soldiers. I can type and—"

"We need translators," he said abruptly.

"Yes," she answered. She started to say more, but stopped herself. It was better to say too little than too much.

He stood, placed the clipboard on his desk, and clasped his hands behind his back. He was shorter than she'd expected as she realized he had to look up to meet her eyes. "The camp is an extensive complex. It consists of more than forty buildings, including a labor camp for the factory," he began as if he had memorized a monologue. "There is also a prisoner-of-war camp housed there. Of course, there are kitchens, medical facilities, logistics, and supply…"

She continued to stand in front of his desk with her bag held neatly in front of her. "My skills are flexible. I can work in any area in which I am needed."

His eyes raked her from bottom to top, and she was again grateful for the door having remained ajar. Then he reached for a piece of paper and wrote something in large, sweeping cursive. As he handed it to Agata, he said, "You will report to the camp entrance at precisely seven o'clock tomorrow morning. You will be provided instructions and your assignment."

"Thank you, Herr Kursell," Agata replied. She glanced at the paper. Beneath her name, he had written "Polish Translator" and "Women's Camp."

He had not tested her ability to speak Polish, nor had he questioned her education, work experience, or skills. An odd sensation began in the pit of her stomach, and for the briefest of moments, she felt a dark and sinister cloud around Max Kursell.

"Do you know—?" she began.

He waved her toward the door. "They'll answer your questions." With that, he sat down and picked up a piece of paper.

Dismissed, she stepped into the other office and closed the door behind her. The elder woman cynically raised one eyebrow.

"Can you tell me where this camp is?" Agata asked.

27

Hank

Hank cried out and bolted upright, jerking himself awake. He sat motionless for a moment while he got his bearings before slinging his legs over the side of the cot. He had a nightmare about the people in the woods again, the shots echoing in his mind. As he replayed Otto committing suicide, he wished he'd never left his side. Had he remained, he might have been able to stop him. He also wondered for the umpteenth time whether he could have done anything to stop the slaughter of the innocent civilians. Though logic told him he could not, his soul chastised him.

As his eyes adjusted to the murkiness of the cellar, he ticked off the items in his mind as if to do so would reassure him that he was safe. The smattering of tiny windows was taped over with layers of newspaper, not to keep the sunlight out but to prevent the woefully underpowered cellar bulbs from being spotted from the outside. Overgrown bushes further shielded the windows, casting the room into constant darkness.

His cot was pushed against one wall, and he could barely make out Rafe's figure on a separate cot against the opposite wall. Rafe appeared to be facing the wall, unaware of Hank's dream anxiety or perhaps choosing to ignore it. He certainly should be used to it by now, and he had his own to deal with.

Hank's duffel and Rafe's rucksack were tucked under their respective beds, the only personal items that they possessed. He wished he were home right now. He should have been back in North Carolina years ago, waking up next to Dottie in a warm, cozy, and light-filled home instead of trapped behind enemy lines. He wondered if the nightmares would cease once he'd left this country, or if he would carry the images with him through the rest of his days. He suspected the latter despite his yearning to forget them.

To say that he was eager to leave was the understatement of all time. The German occupation wore on, day after grueling day, and with each one that passed, he wondered why the Allied forces hadn't come to their rescue, despite knowing the Soviets were busy fighting the Nazi invasion near Stalingrad and the Caucasus.

But it certainly wasn't as if the Poles were waiting for the Soviets to rescue them. They viewed the Soviets and the Nazis with the same loathing. Both had committed atrocities against the Poles, dating back centuries and stretching into recent times. Neither was welcome in Poland. They wished for the Americans or Brits to rescue them, as they had more faith that the Americans and Brits would leave afterward, rather than becoming another dictatorial occupier.

Hank's eyes picked out the bulky equipment on the other side of the musty cellar. It reeked of pungent ink and paper, a scent that permeated everything.

Like clockwork with the first rays of light, he would hear furniture being moved above them, and then the small trap door would be opened. It was usually Matylda crouching down to peer inside and announce her presence. Sometimes, she would continue down makeshift steps that were halfway between stairs and a ladder, scooched to avoid the low ceiling. Other times, Rafe or Hank would meet her at the opening to take the food tray from her.

Boxes filled with paper and ink would soon follow, along with notepaper upon which bits and pieces of stories were written. They were impossible to corroborate, and Hank never knew how much was fact and how much was propaganda. His job was to take the bits and pieces and weave stories from them, and print a newspaper, if one could call it that. Matylda and Piotr, her brother, members of the Home Army, served as translators and also collected the papers in the late evenings. Rafe and Hank would listen from below as scores of people stopped by, presumably to take stacks of newspapers and covertly distribute them.

Rafe and Hank were confined to the cellar during the day, but they learned from conversations with their hosts and visitors that most Poles remained indoors, except to obtain necessary food items. During the day, the Nazis were ever-present. One never knew if they would be stopped or taken in for interrogation.

The real activity, at least in this part of eastern Poland, occurred between midnight and dawn, with most citizens safely tucked into their beds before the sun rose. The Home Army, or the *Armia Krajowa,* was rumored to be somewhere between a quarter and a half a million strong. A vast underground network provided the Allies with intelligence on Nazi troop movements and numbers, giving Hank hope that the Allies would soon arrive to defeat the German forces. He was able to write letters to Dottie and articles for his magazine back home, and he was told they were smuggled nightly to the Allied spies. He could only hope they eventually found their way to the intended recipients, as he rarely received a response from either and had no way of knowing whether letters were being passed along the underground network and on their way back to him.

It was the *Armia Krajowa* and their members that benefited from Hank's paper, or so he was told. He was not allowed to know where the papers were distributed, by whom, or to whom. If anyone was captured, the less they knew about the overall operations, the better. It wouldn't prevent the Nazis from torturing or imprisoning them, but it protected the network from further compromise.

Through the sources, Hank learned that the facilities located south of Kraków had been converted to extermination camps. It was a callous progression of efficiency; to shoot thousands of people required thousands of bullets, and Hitler's hubris had spread the war into so many directions at once that ammunition was desperately needed on the front lines. Instead, the sources reported that gas ovens had been installed, capable of gassing thousands with increasing effectiveness. The level of cruel ingenuity was sickening and appalling to him.

In fact, the concept was challenging to grasp and accept, as if something inside him could not fathom such evil human beings, despite Rafe's Bible recitations. Hank wrestled with it as he wrote his articles. *Armia Krajowa* spies were located in Oświęcim, the town closest to the camps known as Auschwitz and Birkenau. Only once had he been able to make out a name that someone along the line attempted to strike out: Katarina. These spies reported that most people living in Oświęcim were associated with the camps in one way or another, working there as guards or in administrative positions, or supplying the camps with agricultural products, goods, and services. There were several bars where they would gather in the evenings, down a few drinks, and soon, loose lips would divulge bits and pieces of information. Strung together, cohesive stories began to emerge.

Hank rose from his bed, ran his hand through his hair, and stretched. The clock on the makeshift stand showed a quarter past five. It was frigid in the cellar, the constant temperature resulting in consistent sniffles and sore throats. It was too late for him to leave, which he sometimes did to satisfy his journalist curiosity, and too early for Matylda to arrive with their breakfast, which usually consisted of beets and imitation eggs they called Halszka's scrambled eggs.

Rafe stirred in his bed, pulling the covers higher around his neck, while Hank began his daily stretches. It was rather like a dark, dank prison. Every time they left the safety of the cellar, they ran the risk of capture, and it was increasingly more evident to them that Hank's nationality and his camera combined to make him appear like an Allied spy. He supposed that he'd become one.

The men had begun an exercise routine they could perform in their room to maintain sufficient physical shape, holding out hope that the Germans would soon be defeated. And the Nazis were being defeated in small ways, Hank reminded himself as he stretched. In addition to performing intelligence services, the *Armia Krajowa* was also involved in sabotage and guerrilla warfare. As the Germans swept across Poland and into the Soviet Union, the saboteurs dismantled or destroyed sections of train tracks carrying supplies to the troops. It was a nuisance, at best, as the Nazis then had to stop the trains, bring up rail supplies, and repair the tracks, which sometimes took days. They also disrupted the rails transporting prisoners to the camps that were now spread across Poland. The latter was more problematic, as the Germans didn't care how long the Poles remained in the cattle cars without food, water, or sufficient air, so additional measures had to be taken to draw them away from the trains long enough to open the boxcars.

It was a living nightmare, Hank realized. And, as the war dragged on, the nightmares of his dreams were beginning to pale in comparison.

28

Matylda

Matylda Wiśniewska scrambled the eggs in a large metal bowl while she kept one eye on the back door. Today, she had only three eggs for four people; three were men, and due to rationing and shortages, she knew today's breakfast was going to feel woefully inadequate. She set the bowl on the wooden table and began to chop a small kielbasa into miniature cubes. She carefully added a bit of minced onion, since one onion had to last all week, and minced a soft and wizened green pepper. While a pat of butter melted in the pan, she added a touch of water and whisked vigorously until foam formed along the top. The act of making breakfast was comforting to her, perhaps because, for those few fleeting minutes, it made her life seem normal again when it was anything but.

As she added the mixture to the pan and continued alternately scrambling and heaping the food, she felt her heart sink. She would give anything to have Aleksy there with her. They had been married for only a month when the Germans invaded. Aleksy was a captain and was immediately dispatched to the western border. It was then that Matylda had lost track of him. Events had unfolded so rapidly that within days, the Nazis were claiming large swaths of Poland. The Polish troops that were not captured were deployed elsewhere in an elaborate chess game.

The last rumor she'd had of his company was in Warsaw, where her brother Piotr was also desperately fighting to defend the city from the invading army.

Matylda had been in Warsaw during the siege. Despite having high hopes of being reunited with Aleksy, her days had been long and exhausting. She was a trained nurse and accustomed to treating war wounds from the Polish-Soviet War, which had begun in 1919 when she was finishing her schooling. She'd served until its end in 1921. In nearly twenty years between that war and the Nazi invasion, she was proud to work with the *Armia Krajowa*. The goal of most Poles was to maintain an independent Poland, free from the equally aggressive, communist Soviets and the nationalist Nazis.

However, she had never seen anything like the German invasion and the start of World War II. The Nazis were a juggernaut, seemingly unstoppable, and the unthinkable—that the Poles would be overrun so quickly—was now a bleak and stinging reality.

Matylda left Warsaw days before it fell. She'd been in a convoy sneaking between enemy lines, hunched in the back of a tented truck with wounded men lying around her in various stages of pain and distress. She'd busied herself caring for them, her raw nerves set aside while she focused on their needs, despite the constant barrage of cannon and gunfire that surrounded them.

She didn't know if they would reach a safe location. None of them knew. Each made their pact with God, she supposed, because death was as inevitable as life. They couldn't see the date it would come calling for them, but calling it would.

She'd made her way to her childhood home, a farm southeast of Warsaw in rural Poland. Nowhere was safe, but it was far from the main roads. Piotr had arrived sometime later, a source of comfort in a world gone mad.

The eggs were finished, and she lifted the pan off the stove as the back door opened, allowing a frigid blast of air to swirl through the kitchen. She turned to watch Piotr stamp the snow off his boots before he made his way inside.

He laid bundles of ink and paper on the table and then extracted a pile of notes from inside his bulky jacket. As he hung his coat on a peg by the door and then sat at the table to pull off his boots, Matylda divided the breakfast onto four plates. She added chunks of bread and cheese beside them and poured small glasses of goat's milk for the men in the cellar.

"I've got a letter here for Hank," Piotr said with a broad smile. She remembered when a smile could light up his entire face, but these days, it stopped short of reaching his eyes, which always appeared exhausted. "I think I'm as excited as he is when they arrive."

She set the pan beside the sink and rifled through the notes. "He's looked every day for a letter from home. This should make him happy."

Piotr nodded and squeezed her shoulder. "No word from Aleksy, Maty. I'm sorry."

"No news is good news, isn't that what they say?" she asked, swallowing her disappointment. He reached his hand out to grab hers, and she clasped it. Piotr was nearly twenty years younger than she, the product of her father's younger second wife after Matylda's own mother passed away from tuberculosis. "I'd best bring this down while the food is still hot." She balanced a tray while Piotr moved the table and chairs out of the way and pulled up a worn rug to reveal the trap door. "Eat yours before it gets cold, Piotr."

"I will, Maty. Do you need help carrying that down?"

"No, but thanks. Hank and Rafe always help me."

As the trap door was pulled back, the light from the dingy kitchen windows cast a wintry glow into the basement. She called out to them as she turned around and began to descend along the sturdy makeshift stairs. "I'm coming down with breakfast, gentlemen. Cover yourselves up!"

Rafe appeared from the darkness, his hair disheveled and his clothes wrinkled. He cast a wide, welcoming grin at her as she passed the tray to him before climbing down the rest of the way.

Matylda was self-conscious of her figure in front of Rafe, though she didn't know why. Her work with the resistance placed her in contact with men nearly every day, yet she didn't feel her heart flutter the way she did with Rafe. Perhaps it was his Spanish good looks, his dark, soulful eyes, or his sleek black hair. He was slender, as everyone except Nazis were these days, but she was rail-thin, her ribs prominent when she glanced at herself in the mirror. Her coloring contrasted with Rafe's; she sported shoulder-length, straight blond hair, and her eyes were blue. She walked with an embarrassing slight limp, which served as a grim reminder of a Gestapo interrogation. She had been picked up in a massive countryside raid and held for two weeks, during which time the Nazis broke her leg below the knee in an attempt to force her to identify members of the Home Army. And that had been only the beginning.

Her spirit had somehow survived despite the torture, although she was prone to nightmares. Her father and stepmother had also been picked up in separate raids shortly after, and they'd been missing ever since. Unable to work the farm alone, she'd considered fleeing, but where could she go? The farm was as safe as anywhere, she'd decided. And it was fate that she'd remained, as Piotr had been able to find her there.

She shook off the melancholy that was ever-present as she turned to Rafe and Hank. "The *Armia Krajowa* has assassinated Franz Kutschera, the Nazi Chief of Police in Warsaw," she announced with obvious satisfaction.

"The Butcher of Warsaw?" Hank breathed.

"I would not want to be him right now," Rafe said. He set the tray on a stack of boxes that served as a table.

"What do you mean?"

"He is being led through the Gates of Hell at this very moment." Rafe shook his head. "How many times have we written about him? How many hundreds or thousands of Poles appeared on his daily execution lists?"

Hank turned to Matylda. "He was tried in absentia last year by the Polish underground, was he not?"

"He was. He was convicted and sentenced to death. A mission for his execution was given to a group of twelve in Kedyw, called the *Pegaz*. They gunned him down in front of the SS Headquarters in Warsaw." She handed Hank and Rafe a stack of notes. "You'll find it all in here. This must be highly publicized. This is a major victory for us."

"What of the twelve? If they killed him in front of the SS Headquarters—"

"All are alive as we speak, though several were wounded. All got away. The SS will be after them, we're sure."

"Were there other German casualties?" Hank watched Rafe rifle through the notes. It was interesting how much Polish they'd both picked up since spending time with Matylda and Piotr, and occasionally with others in the underground.

"Five killed, nine wounded," Matylda answered. "They killed the Butcher's chauffeur, two soldiers, a police officer as they sped away, as well as the Butcher himself."

"This will be one of the most important issues we'll publish," Rafe said.

"We'll get on it right away." Hank hesitated. "How far and wide will the Nazis look for the executioners?"

Matylda shrugged and avoided his eyes so her concern would not be evident. It was something they all tended to do. Giving in to concern or fear only brought them down a spiral from which they'd have to climb back out sooner or later. It was best not to go there at all. "We all must be diligent. In the end, it won't matter who pulled the triggers. They will attempt to make us all suffer." She smiled, but it was forced. "But this is proof that we can resist. We can decapitate them. And we must. Poland must be made free again." As Rafe and Hank agreed, she reached for her skirt pocket. "I have a very important letter for you, Hank."

Hank reached for the envelope, which appeared to have been opened numerous times, the paper crumpled, and the ink smeared.

"And you, Rafe." She handed him a similar envelope. Their hands lingered for just a moment as the envelope passed from one to the other. "I will be back soon. Oh, and I have another piece of information to share with you. The Allies appear to be planning an invasion of France."

"What?" Rafe and Hank said simultaneously.

Matylda nodded. "At Pas de Calais. Your general, George Patton, is leading it. Intelligence says he has as many as fifty assault divisions. The Nazis are massing in France in preparation for an invasion."

"When?" Hank breathed.

"The sooner, the better, I say. Though Pas de Calais is a long way from us," she chuckled, "just the knowledge that Americans have landed in mainland Europe will bolster our spirits." She stepped onto the bottom step.

"Don't go," Rafe said.

Matylda hesitated, glancing from Rafe to Hank.

"He's right," Hank said. "We get so few visitors," he added with a half-smile.

"Piotr!" Matylda called up. "Could you hand me my plate, please?"

"Well, hell," he said as he handed it to her, "I may as well come down there, too. It might be warmer, and I won't have to eat alone." A moment later, he climbed down the steps with his half-eaten food. They arranged themselves around the room, wherever they found a place to sit.

Hank sat on his cot. Ignoring his food for the moment, he opened the envelope.

"Is it from Dottie?" Rafe asked.

"It is," he breathed, his voice catching in his throat. "It was written over a month ago."

"That is fast in these times," Matylda said as she ate her eggs. The additional food, though meager, had gone a long way in making three eggs into a meal for four. "I am a bit surprised that you got it at all."

"Read it to us," Rafe urged, "unless it is too personal—"

"No, I'll read it," Hank said. He took a breath and read,

"Dearest Hank,

We all hope and pray that this letter finds you well and safe. All the churches here have joined in a prayer chain, so God receives prayers every day about you and Ray from people you don't even know. Some have written pen pal letters, but since I never know if or when you might receive mine, we have hesitated in sending the others.

Mary and Buck married at the county courthouse. When you get home, they plan to have a proper church wedding. Mary says you must give her away. They married, my darling, because Buck is leaving for military service. He'd been exempted because of his work in the munitions factory, but now the women can handle that. They call all the women Rosie the Riveter! They are all proud to do their parts.

Susanna now works at a hospital in Raleigh. She rents a room in a boarding house. She went to Raleigh with several of her high school friends, so she is not alone. There are so many soldiers returning…"

Hank hesitated. "The rest of the sentence is blacked out," he said.

"Perhaps," Matylda offered, "we can try to read it under better light."

"Perhaps," Hank agreed before continuing,

"There's been no news from Ray. All we know is he is somewhere in the Pacific. He is so young, and I wish he hadn't gone, but there was just no stopping that boy. He is stubborn, like someone else I know.

I am fine, my darling, but I miss you terribly. I know how much you enjoy your work, but after this war, we're looking forward to you spending some time with us. Your momma has angina, and the doctor thinks she gets stressed too easily. He says there's nothing that can be done but for her to calm down. I know she will when she sees you again.

Please give our best to Rafe. You two need to stay safe for the women who love you.

Love always,

Your Dottie"

Hank grew silent, his expression darkening as though a heavy weight had descended on his heart. Matylda stepped forward and squeezed his arm through layers of clothing. "You'll be home soon," she whispered.

"Yes," he said, his voice melancholy, "when this war is over, I'm going home. I need my family even more than they need me. I know that now."

"And the war could be over soon," she said, her voice quickening. "Imagine! George Patton is leading the invasion!"

"I have a nagging thought," Piotr said. He had finished his meal and was making his way to the steps, peering up as though he expected someone to come through the door.

"What is it?" Rafe asked.

Piotr turned toward them. "The Nazis know of the Allied plans. They're amassing across the English Channel in Nazi-held Pas de Calais in northern France, though the French coast is probably another thirty miles to the west. It's the closest coastline to England, perhaps a mere thirty miles from Dover."

"So, they see Patton assembling the Americans there," Hank finished.

"Certainly," Matylda said, "the Americans would not be so foolhardy to assemble an assault in clear view of the Nazis."

"Untold numbers will die," Hank said sadly.

"It must be the price every man, woman, and child is prepared to pay for freedom from this evil institution," Piotr said. "We must be ready."

"Yes," Hank said. "Rafe is right. He always says that Satan's army had been banished to earth, not hell."

"And Satan's army is the Nazis?" Matylda asked.

All eyes turned to Rafe, but he seemed oblivious to their conversation. He sat on his cot, his food untouched and growing cold, his letter held quietly in his hands.

Matylda made her way to him as a lone tear dropped off his cheek onto the paper. "What is it?"

Rafe shook his head.

"Rafe?" Hank added, joining her.

Rafe stood and folded the paper before carefully placing it in his rucksack. "The Vichy government," he said finally, his voice choking. "They have executed my father."

29

Max

Max completed the hiring form and briefly looked it over. He would hand it to the office manager, who would assign it to a typist. Afterward, it would be sent via teletype or mail to Berlin, where a thorough background investigation would be conducted. Earlier in the war, it might have taken weeks or months to receive approval, but he was under pressure to provide more employees for the rapidly expanding camp, which had now evolved into multiple camps, each with its own unique identity. It wasn't his duty to assign Agata to a specific area; that was the camp commandant's responsibility. His job was to keep the pipeline full, and of late, he hadn't met his quotas.

He set down his pencil and gazed out the window without truly seeing what was beyond the glass. He didn't know why there was such extensive employee turnover there, and the information was vague. He was usually told that an individual did not work out because they were too soft, spoke cordially to the prisoners, or broke the rules by assisting the prisoners in obtaining food or supplies. Yes, he thought, they were now known as prisoners. There was no sense in sugarcoating it. Those fit enough to survive were the most valuable in slave labor. They had their own turnover rate, as most lasted only weeks or months. The trains arrived daily with a fresh supply of prisoners, and the pressure on him to fill the growing number of employee positions only increased.

He rose, grabbed his hat and coat, and on his way past his desk, he picked up the paper. He dropped it in the office manager's inbox on his way out the door. He didn't owe anyone there an explanation of where he was going, so he didn't provide one.

Max paused outside the administration building to light a cigarette. The stench was foul today. It varied depending on the direction of the wind. It was something he didn't have to contend with in Będzin, but the outer edge of Oświęcim was only a mile from the camps. It was worse, he thought, than living next door to a chicken farm. He peered at the skies. If he tried long enough, he might be able to make out the slightest tinge of blue amidst the ever-increasing black clouds created by the giant smokestacks. The smoke traveled the way of the stink, and today, it was directly overhead.

Stepping out quickly, Max was relieved that all his business was conducted close by, avoiding the need to remain outside for extended periods. He walked briskly, passing various shops that were only sparsely attended.

"There you are, Max!"

He turned in the direction of the voice. "Katarina," he said in greeting.

She fell in beside him, and his pace eased. "Max, do you know anything about Bogdanka Laska?"

"Who?"

Katarina repeated the name more slowly.

"Why should I know who that is?" he asked, his eyes focused on the restaurant ahead.

"You asked me about her the other day. You asked if she could apply for a position in the camps."

"Did she apply? I don't remember her."

"I told you that she didn't qualify."

"Is she a Jew?"

Katarina shook her head. "Catholic. But a Pole."

"Oh. No need to apply, then. Only Germans are hired there."

"Max, stop." She tugged on his arm, and he dutifully paused. He didn't know why he obeyed her. Perhaps she reminded him too much of his mother. Rather than being annoyed at this, he felt strangely comforted by it. Her eyes were earnest as she said, "The Gestapo picked up Bogdanka on the night we talked about her."

"What did she do? No. Don't tell me. I don't want to know. It's none of my concern."

"Don't you think it's rather odd that she lived here all this time and was never bothered, and on the night you asked about her, she was picked up?"

"Pure coincidence. I had nothing to do with it." He raised a brow. "Is that all?"

"Do you know where she is, Max?"

Max allowed his eyes to roam from Katarina's intense expression toward his destination. On the horizon and visible above the restaurant, plumes of fresh smoke billowed from the camp chimneys. He turned back to Katarina. "Perhaps," he said, "she went up the chimney."

He did not wait to register her expression. He stepped out promptly, his strides long. He was vaguely aware that she remained behind him and did not attempt to walk alongside him. The conversation was over. Perhaps, it should never have occurred. He stopped at the restaurant door and turned back slightly as he opened it, but Katarina was gone.

The atmosphere was thick with cigarette and cooking smoke inside, a pungent mix of tobacco, kraut, and sausages. The walls were darkly paneled, and the dining rooms a collection of small, intimate spaces, as though someone's home had been converted years before into a public restaurant.

"Herr Kursell," the maître d' said as he hurried to greet him. The man had thin, graying hair, the long locks slicked back from his forehead to form a dovetail in the back as if the length could compensate for the scarcity. He was impeccably dressed in a dark blue suit and white shirt. He took Max's hat and coat from his hands, and it was only then that Max realized he'd never donned them. "Fräulein Sauer is already here, sir."

"Where did you seat her?"

"At the bar, sir, to await your arrival."

"Very good. Take me to my seat—discreetly."

"Of course, sir."

The maître d' led Max down a corridor off the foyer. It was not one that patrons commonly used; instead, it skirted the perimeter of the rooms to reach the one at the rear. That room was empty and cooler than the others. While the cooking aroma persisted, the air was less clogged with smoke. The maître d' pulled back the table so that Max could sit on an upholstered bench against the wall, providing him with a full view of the room and the hallway beyond it.

"Your usual, sir?"

"Yes. And wait a few minutes before escorting the Fräulein."

"Of course, sir." He had no sooner disappeared than a waiter appeared in his stead, sporting a tray with a cocktail known as Göring-Schnaps. With a flourish, he placed it in front of Max.

"Keep them coming," Max directed.

"Certainly, sir. And would you care for a menu today?" He held the tray behind him, revealing his starched white uniform as he dutifully awaited Max's answer. When Max shook his head, he continued, "And would you care to order now, sir, or—"

"I'll signal you."

With that, the waiter stepped backwards until he had reached the door. Then, he turned on his heels and disappeared down the hall.

A few moments later, the maître d' led a young woman toward him. Max swirled his drink in the glass before taking a sip, his eyes riveted on her. At a time when many women wore the same generic German uniform identifying them as camp employees, Gretchen Sauer was dressed in a shockingly sunny yellow, form-fitting suit, signifying her status as a member of the elite. Her hair was past her shoulders and perfectly coiffed, the rose-blond strands shining. She removed a pristine white glove as she approached, her eyes locked on Max's as the maître d' held out a chair for her. Once situated, she said, "Thank you, Günther."

"Of course, Fräulein Sauer."

As he stepped back, the waiter stepped forward, again bearing a tray. This time, he deposited a Fanta Klassik in a tall crystal glass in front of her. Max was vaguely aware that the waiter's eyes were upon him, perhaps waiting for a signal, but Max ignored him. "What is that?" he asked Gretchen, pointing to the glass.

"It is a new concoction," she answered, "and all the rage throughout Germany. It was created by Coca-Cola expressly for Nazi Germany."

Max took a careful sip of his drink. "What is in it?"

"That's the beauty of it," she answered. Her voice was smooth, and she kept her chin slightly elevated, as though she had a lifetime of culture behind her. "It is made from apple fibers and whey."

Max grimaced. "I imagine it tastes like garbage."

"It is garbage, I suppose." She chuckled softly. "But it tastes rather like lemonade."

"What is the alcohol in it?"

"There is none."

"Ah. That is why I have never heard of it."

"So, dear Max, are we to chit-chat about Coca-Cola, or get on to more pressing matters?"

Max caught the waiter's eye and raised two fingers. The waiter nodded and immediately disappeared toward the kitchen.

"And what are we having today?" Gretchen asked.

"Ölsoldaten."

"Seriously? Fried sardines on bread?"

Max shrugged. "Or, you can use your rations for something else."

Gretchen sighed. "I will be relieved when food production picks up."

"It is not the production that is a problem. It is the winter snow. It is worse this year, I believe."

"Winter snow is not responsible for my coffee disappearing."

"Ah. The Royal Navy blockade."

"I am so tired of drinking malt coffee and pretending it is real coffee." She tapped her fingers on the table. "I am considering leaving for North Africa."

"You're insane."

She raised her glass to ruby-red lips. "Perhaps."

"Why not ski? There are many excursions—"

"The ski slopes are not where my position takes me."

"And what is your position, precisely?"

"You always ask, dear Max, and I always tell you that I cannot tell you."

The food arrived and was placed in front of them with an exaggerated flourish. "Will there be anything else, sir?"

Max shook his head and gestured for him to leave. He did not make a move to eat, and neither did Gretchen. After a long moment, he asked, "Do you have anything you can share with me?"

"I do, actually."

Max's eyes shifted. As he surveyed the rest of the room, he knew they were utterly alone, and yet, he didn't feel alone. There were always eyes and ears in Nazi Germany and its occupied territories. One never knew where a listening device was planted.

"The papers," Gretchen began, her voice silky and low, "report a change in fortune."

"For who?"

She shrugged. "We have abandoned parts of North Africa."

"And yet, you want to go there."

"Perhaps what I want has nothing to do with it."

"Go on."

"General Paulus surrendered at Stalingrad. He is now a prisoner of war in the Soviet Union, along with his surviving troops."

"Hitler cannot be happy with that."

"Paulus should wish to die in enemy territory. Returning to Germany, he will fare worse. There is a back-and-forth between Germany and the Red Army, taking and retaking towns."

"And here in Poland?"

"Eastern Poland is under strain. The lines are fluid."

"And yet, you go to North Africa."

"That is where I may be needed."

"Have you no other news for me? No good news?"

"What of you, Max? Have you nothing for me?"

He finished his drink. As if by magic, the waiter appeared with another one. There are eyes and ears everywhere, he reminded himself. "It is boring here in Oświęcim. All I do is look to hire German women who already work for the Nazi cause. Why would a woman come here to work for Germany?" he mused. "There must be plentiful jobs in Berlin."

"Yes," Gretchen said. "There are plenty of jobs." She finished her drink but waved off another one. "They find milkmaids, illiterate young women living on rural farms, with no prospect of a life beyond pulling a cow's teat, and dangle money in front of them. Those are the women you see here, Max, who are willing to work in the camps."

"They are hard, most of them."

"They have to be." She looked pointedly at the glove she had left on the table. "Keep it for me. It is a sign that I will return." She rose but again waved off the waiter's assistance. With her food left untouched, she hesitated only briefly. "Take care, Herr Kursell." With that, she quickly exited the room.

The waiter was there in a flash, but as he reached for Gretchen's meal, Max said, "Leave it."

"Yes, sir."

"That is all."

"Yes, sir."

He took a large bite of his sandwich and chewed thoughtfully as he watched the waiter move down the hall to provide him with some semblance of privacy. He waited a long moment, took another hefty bite, and then reached for the glove. He slipped it into his lap as he ran his hand over it. There was something hard inside, as he had suspected. He peered around him, took another bite, and when he felt it was safe, he extracted the tiny piece of paper. On it were only a few words.

Felka exported to camp, sewing unit.

30

Agata

The walk from the edge of town to the camp might have taken only half an hour had it not been for the constant checkpoints. The paper provided by Herr Kursell got her waved past each guard, only to have to stop and show it to another. As she walked, military vehicles passed her on the road, quickly traversing the road between open fields. At the same time, Agata was grateful for the walk and the opportunity to assess her new surroundings.

Another village must have once existed between the town and the camp. It was razed now, perhaps burned to the ground. Oddly, the chimneys remained. As Agata walked past, she marveled at the ability of the slender brick chimneys to remain in a row like so many sentinels, while everything around them was obliterated.

An agricultural field appeared on the opposite side of the road, but she couldn't identify the crops from their leaves. About midway, however, she stumbled across an apple orchard. A lone man toiled in the orchard, and a basket lay at his feet as he picked fruit that should have been harvested months ago. She made a mental reminder to stop there, perhaps on her way home, and inquire about the cost.

She thought of her new home and her good fortune at finding something so quickly. She had discovered rental advertisements posted on a board in the square and had made her way toward the edge of town closest to the camp. A stout, stern woman rented her a bed in her home, which had been converted into a boarding house. She shared a bathroom with seven others and a bedroom with three young women. The room itself consisted of single bunks with barely enough room between them to walk, but Agata was grateful to sleep on a mattress after so many weeks on the road. It was out of the elements, safe from unexpected visitors, and she was able to get a tepid, albeit expeditious, bath. Although Agata had no money, once the hostel owner saw Herr Kursell's note, she agreed to collect the week's rent when she was paid, along with the rent for the upcoming week. Apparently, his signature was enough to open doors throughout the town.

As Agata neared the camp, she was astonished at its size. She had expected a work camp adjacent to the chemical plant, along with a few administration buildings or barracks. What she saw instead was a city that dwarfed Oświęcim. There were too many buildings to count, though she slowed her walk so she could absorb her new surroundings. At one end of the camp were several black stacks spewing inky smoke into the air, which lingered over the camp like dense fog. It emitted a strange smell, and Agata wondered what type of chemicals were produced in the factory. As she drew closer, the stench reminded her of the bodies in the woods and those she later found deceased in trenches.

The checkpoint guards became burlier and gruffer as she neared. Finally, she reached the final checkpoint beside a gate that proclaimed in German, *"Arbeit macht frei,"* or "Work sets you free." She thought it was odd, as she'd never considered that any work she'd performed would set her free.

The last guard was different from the others. While the others she'd encountered did not look her in the face or eyes, he did. He was young with only tiny patches of scattered stubble, thin, and wiry. He wore his uniform as the others did, with an erect stature as though he must always be at attention. He greeted her, as the others did, with the Sieg Heil salute, which she returned.

"So," he said as he looked at her paperwork from Herr Kursell, "you are new here."

"My first day," Agata said a bit nervously.

"You won't make it," he said curtly.

"Pardon?"

He handed the paper back to her. "Lose your expression if you want to keep your job."

"My expression? I wasn't aware—"

"Look angry. Act angry. Those who don't are quickly fired."

Agata folded the paper and returned it to her pocket.

He pointed at a nearby building. "Go there. You'll receive further instruction."

"Thank you."

He swore under his breath. "Don't thank anybody here, got it?" He shouted the last two words in a voice that sounded so hostile, she thought he was going to strike her.

A quick glance told her that a line was forming behind her and that people were staring at her curiously. She avoided his eyes as she left the guardhouse and made her way to the nearest building. She wandered past scores of uniformed men, careful not to make direct eye contact with any. She was also shocked to see scores of people so thin that she didn't know how they survived, though she tried not to stare. Their clothing was in varying stages of neglect and was obviously too thin for the climate, and many were barefoot, though the hard ground was covered in frost. They parted as she walked past and maintained their distance.

Inside, she found a classroom with three other new hires. She selected a desk among them and sat. When she looked at the others, she found them staring straight ahead. A growing unease began to take hold of her, seemingly taunting her naivete. This was not an ordinary work camp for the chemical factory. A sinister cloud hung over the air as though she had walked into a lion's den, and the lion was circling.

The morning was filled with stern lectures. No materials were given to reinforce the lessons, and they were forbidden from taking notes. The instructor wore an SS uniform. He appeared aged in a way that Agata could not quite put her finger on. He spoke in a brusque manner; his eyes remained fixed on the wall behind them, and his face did not have natural expressions. He announced early in his lecture that there would be no questions.

She struggled to remember everything she was told. She ticked off information in her head: the camp was constructed on forty acres. Three train tracks converged there, which brought new prisoners every day. It was the first time she heard them referred to as prisoners, and her heart began to sink when she thought of Elsa.

There were thirty warehouses filled with supplies, where one of the newly hired young men was assigned to work. A crematorium and chambers were located in one area, but the instructor did not elaborate on what took place there, as none of the new hires would be assigned to that area. It was apparently a place to aspire to. The chemical factory was located in another area. Then there were communal buildings, such as toilets, showers, a cafeteria of sorts, medical facilities, administrative offices, and completely separate buildings for guards. Her title, like those of the other females, was *SS-Aufseherin,* which meant female SS overseer.

As the morning crept on, another instructor took over for the first. This one was older and carried a constant smirk. Before he spoke, he turned his attention to Agata, the only woman in the room. He announced that there were thousands of male guards at the camp and only a few hundred women. Women were expressly forbidden from entering the male areas for any reason and were always to defer to male guards, regardless of the circumstances.

There were also male regions, including a prisoner-of-war camp divided by nationalities and faith.

Women were also forbidden to enter this area. Agata tamped down the thought of Piotr in such an area and offered a brief prayer that he was still free.

The number of guards was growing as the camp expected to double in size, and they were all Germans. No other nationality was permitted to work in the camp.

As the hours turned to afternoon, a train appeared just outside the windows, and a whistle blew throughout the camp. The instructor ordered the students to rise and stand at the windows to watch. The train consisted of cattle cars. Uniformed soldiers moved from one to the other, sliding open the doors. From that point onward, it was ordered chaos.

"Expect the trains three times a day for now," the instructor said as they watched. "The number will increase. The soldiers will order the people out of the cars. They are to remove any bags or possessions and pile them in designated areas." His face seemed to warp into a sinister smile. "That is where the confusion begins. Everyone wants to tell us how important their bags are and how they cannot be parted from them. The soldiers will make them understand that there are no exceptions." He looked directly at Agata. "None."

Agata nodded in understanding, though she did not fully comprehend what was happening.

The instructor continued. "The prisoners are lined up. Do you see the men standing there, with the batons?" As we all nodded, he turned to one of the other new hires. "You, there. You are assigned as a bookkeeper. You will stand beside those men at each incoming transport." The young man nodded but appeared perplexed. "They are doctors. As people arrive, they determine where they go. Those too weak, too old, or otherwise infirm will be taken directly to the chambers—anyone who cannot work. You will receive additional instructions, but you will log in their money and possessions. The possessions will go to the warehouses, and you will send the money to Berlin."

Agata tried to let this information sink in. She wondered if the chambers were a medical facility, given that the doctors had selected them to go there. Still, she didn't understand why their money and possessions were confiscated. She tried not to allow her mind to wander to Elsa, but she couldn't help but wonder and worry whether all that Elsa owned, regardless of its use or sentimental value, had been taken from her here.

"During the same sorting," the instructor continued, "men are separated from the women. Men go to one set of camps and women to another." He pointed at the arriving prisoners and the hysteria that was forming as couples were separated from one another. The soldiers became brutal, beating the arrivals when they would not willingly separate.

What had transpired thus far had been nothing compared to what they witnessed next. As the men were separated from their wives and children, the children were then separated from their mothers. Nearly every mother clung to her child, arguing an exception should be made, appealing to the soldiers, or becoming furious or hysterical in turn. Children screamed and cried for their mothers as soldiers led the older ones away and carried the smaller ones. Doctors then separated the children into two distinct groups.

The instructor turned to Agata and the man standing next to her. She kept her eyes trained on something in the distance—she didn't know what, because her brain was no longer fully registering what she was witnessing. She did not wish to look into the instructor's face, afraid her eyes would betray her horror.

"You, girl," he snarled. "You speak Polish?"

"I do," she answered in German.

"You will meet every transport. You will translate the doctors' and soldiers' orders for those arriving from Poland." He half-turned toward the last new hire. "I am told you speak Hungarian?"

"I do," the man answered quietly.

"You will translate for those arriving from Hungary." He paused as he looked back into the courtyard. "Do you see the lines that have formed? You two translators will then lead your assigned lines through the camp to their barracks—or the chambers."

As the chaos continued, they were ordered back to their seats. "You will work six days a week, eleven hours a day. Until we hire more people, you will frequently be required to work longer hours or on a seventh day. You men may be sent to the front lines; when you are, women will take your positions. You will be paid weekly; you'll learn your pay then. Your meals are also provided. There is plenty of food and a canteen where you can get more." He smiled, though his eyes remained veiled and his expression felt sinister. "You will also find a cinema, sports clubs, and entertainment. Do your jobs as assigned, and you will be taken care of—handsomely."

When the class was finally dismissed, they were led to a building where they received new uniforms, including coats, shoes, and boots. Then they were brought to a third building where they were allowed to eat their fill.

Agata was acutely aware of a group of female guards at one end of the cafeteria, while the males dominated the rest of the room. She juggled her pile of clothing with a tray of soup and sausage and made her way toward the women, but set her tray on a separate table. As she seated herself, she could feel their stares boring into her, perhaps assessing her. After a moment, they stood and left without speaking.

Agata should have been famished, as she could not recall the last time she had eaten. But as she swallowed the broth containing a few sparse vegetables, she wondered how she would ever find her sister—or, if Elsa was even there.

31

Hank

The invasion took place not at Pas de Calais but nearly 200 miles to the south, at Normandy. Through the extensive Polish spy network, Hank learned that it hadn't been the Americans acting alone, but in coordination with the British and Canadians, among others. It hadn't been led by General Patton but by General Dwight D. Eisenhower. The troop buildup further north had been an elaborate ruse that effectively fooled Hitler and routed the Nazi soldiers to the wrong area entirely.

The French Resistance had played a key role, and it was the French underground that now routed information to the *Armia Krajowa.* It was rumored that Adolph Hitler now made all military decisions, both strategic and tactical, and he had been asleep in Berchtesgaden in the Bavarian Alps during the invasion. With no one willing to awaken him, he'd slept until noon. Unwilling to believe the invasion had begun two hundred miles further south at Normandy, he did not react until nearly four o'clock, and then, he deployed only two Panzer divisions.

This gave the invasion a tremendous advantage. The figures were so massive that Hank repeatedly questioned them, unwilling to put wild overestimations in print. He was assured by numerous sources that they were correct: close to 160,000 Allied troops were now in France. It included 4,000 landing crafts and 1,200 warships, over 23,000 parachutists, and more than 800 aircraft.

And this was just the beginning.

The information lagged behind, although Morse code enabled faster communication than traditional ground-based spies. With the successful Allied invasion, estimates indicated that nearly a million Allied troops were joining the fight on European soil, with more on the way.

The Polish Underground was abuzz with competing beehives.

Before the war began, Poland had been a hotbed of clashing politics. On one side were the communists. It might have seemed logical that Poland could join the Soviet Union, as they shared a border, but the Poles had suffered tremendously at the hands of the Soviets. Before World War II began, the Soviets had enacted genocide on the Poles with a concerted effort to exterminate Poles based solely on their race. When the Germans invaded, it simply shifted the genocidal efforts from communism to Nazi nationalism.

Hank found himself in increasingly complex struggles. His newspaper was fact-based but part of a greater effort to steer political views toward a country free of both the Soviets and the Nazis. Yet the Soviet

Union was now aligned with the Allies, including America and the United Kingdom, while the Polish government remained in exile. The Soviets were approaching from the east while the Americans attacked from the west, and if both sides were successful, the Nazis would be squeezed between them and perhaps annihilated or captured.

Some Poles pinned their hopes on the Americans reaching them first, which gave them a chance at Western-style democracy. Others supported the Soviets and communism. And there still remained supporters of Nazi-style nationalism.

Working as a journalist while simultaneously supporting the *Armia Krajowa* faction that wished to expel both the Soviets and the Germans was increasingly fraught with danger. The trusted circle became smaller, with Hank and Rafe receiving their information almost exclusively from Matylda and Piotr. Though Rafe argued that they were trustworthy and verified the facts as they received them, Hank wasn't completely convinced. His steady catchline, "Trust but verify," was now impossible.

~~~~~

There was a new moon, a type of night when the moon seems turned away from the sun, blending seamlessly into the darkness, like an angel too overcome with grief to watch the continued earthly confrontations. There was also a steady drizzle that reminded Hank of tears and sufficient lapis clouds to conceal any light from distant stars. It was impossible to see the terrain, as it appeared as though there was no
~~~~~

delineation between the sky and the ground. It caused Hank some anxiety, as he was accustomed to observing things with his camera, but he knew the night was chosen precisely for its murkiness.

The silence was broken by Rafe's voice next to him, his words spoken in a raspy whisper. "Fucking Vichy fuckers."

Hank didn't respond, and neither did Matylda nor Piotr on the other side of him. At the mention of Vichy France, Hank's mind wandered even though he fought to remain focused on the present moment.

Less than a year after Germany invaded Poland, the Nazis used the same Blitzkrieg type of assault to invade and occupy France. By June 1940, France had negotiated an armistice with Germany, which divided the country into territory occupied by the Nazis and other territory in the south of France that, on paper, was to be governed by the French. In reality, Vichy France, so named for the new French capital of Vichy, was a puppet government. The Nazis gave directives to the French leaders, who then carried out those directives. These included turning over all Jews to German forces and the establishment of the Vichy Secret Police, the equivalent of Germany's Gestapo, whose primary mission was to destroy the French Resistance that had sprung up, similar to Poland's Home Guard.

"My Mamá and Papá," Rafe continued, "fled Spain for Southern France. They thought they would be safe there."

"There is no place safe in all of Europe," Matylda said quietly, "nor in Africa."

"Still," Rafe said, "I must find my mother. I must get her out of France."

"How would you get there?" The anxiety in Matylda's voice was palpable. "You cannot expect to get through the German lines. There are hundreds of miles between you and your mother."

"I must try." Though Rafe's face was cast in shadows, Hank felt him turning toward him. "Do you remember that girl we saw a while back? The one who was literally walking through the German lines to reach her sister?"

"Agata," Hank answered. He focused his eyes on what he thought might be the distant horizon, though it was nearly impossible to tell. "She was German-born, as I recall, and I think that she planned to pass as German. You, my friend, could not hope to impersonate a German, even with your language skills and pseudo-uniform."

"Agata?" Piotr said. "Do you know the last name?"

"Agata…" Hank paused. "Heinrich. She was going south to—"

"—to find her sister, Elsa," Piotr finished.

"Do you know her?" Hank angled so he could see Piotr's face. In the shadows, he could only see his eyes, wide and unblinking.

"I met her in Warsaw on the day the Germans started their bombardment. She stayed at my aunt's warehouse for a time. We heard that her sister and father had been rounded up and put on trains. She was determined to reach her sister."

"Where was her sister being taken?" Matylda asked.

"Toward Kraków," Hank answered.

"Ah. Where the trains go, now from all over Europe," Matylda said.

"Was she well?" Piotr pressed.

"Yes," Hank said. "She was well enough to insist on walking to Kraków. I advised her to move around it, not through it, to Oświęcim."

"She didn't even know for certain that's where her sister was going," Rafe said, "or whether her sister was still alive. Yet," he added, "if she could brave the German lines in Poland, then I must brave them to reach and rescue my mother."

"Quiet," Piotr said suddenly.

As they all ceased their conversation and looked in the direction Piotr pointed, a light flashed twice and stopped in the far distance to the south. It was so faint that Hank wondered whether he had seen anything at all. Then, another light flashed twice to the east. Piotr flashed his light twice in response before springing up.

Hank, Rafe, and Matylda each scrambled to their feet and grabbed a reel of wire. Though they could not see the others in the distance, they had to assume each group performed as directed. Hank focused on his reel, racing to what he thought would constitute a mile inside the train tracks, while Matylda and Rafe ran in the opposite direction.

When the line ran out, Hank tucked it inside the tracks and ran back to where the wire began. Piotr was already attaching the timed detonator. Hank attempted to watch, mesmerized by how the man could perform such delicate work in pitch-blackness, but Piotr hoarsely ordered him to get out of there.

Hank didn't have to be told twice. He raced to the west, stumbling over the uneven ground, away from

Piotr, Matylda, and Rafe. He stopped along a ridge to catch his breath and look over his shoulder. Two figures raced along the same path he had taken. One was shorter than the other, and the taller one appeared to be supporting the first one by its elbow. This, he thought, had to be Rafe and Matylda. When they disappeared into a ravine, Hank turned back to the west and continued his escape.

When the first explosion detonated, the ground shook as though an earthquake had struck, causing Hank to tumble off his feet. He instinctively covered his ears to stop the ringing as the skies lit up in a fireball of red, orange, and yellow. Strong winds carried the heavy smoke, so it appeared as though a thick fog had settled across the landscape.

He lay still for a moment, stunned by the magnitude of the blast. It had happened like clockwork. He had laid the wire; another man, whom he would never know, had attached it to the explosives, and Piotr had installed the timed detonator.

Shouting began in the distance, and he hunkered down in an attempt to identify their location. Then he spotted lights in the distant east, watching until he realized he was staring at a long line of headlights heading toward him. He was unable to see Rafe, Matylda, or Piotr's positions.

He had just begun to stand when a second explosion rocked him, and he tumbled back down. This one was smaller in comparison, but only due to its proximity to him. As he stared toward the east, the headlights seemed to lift off the ground and become airborne, enveloped in the fire and smoke amid men's screams.

More headlights came from the north and south when a third bomb detonated. This one, he knew, was the one Rafe had set, as it was located in the opposite direction from his own. Then, the fourth and fifth explosions rocked, this time to the south.

"What the fuck?" Rafe yelled as he came over a rise. "Run, dammit it!"

Hank bolted up and raced after Rafe, who was half-dragging Matylda in an effort to keep her moving swiftly. They had nearly reached the edge of the farm property when the sixth and last explosion detonated. He glanced back but could see no sign of Piotr.

They burst into the farmhouse and raced to the trapdoor leading into the cellar. Rafe quickly pulled back the rug underneath the hefty dining table, held open the door, and waited for Hank and Matylda to scramble down the steps. Hank watched as Rafe fumbled with the rug, attempting to place the heavy material underneath a table leg as he lowered the door.

"I know I left a crease," Rafe said. "I know I did."

He made for the steps to climb back up, but Hank stopped him. "Listen."

The sound of footsteps outside the house reached them as they held their breaths, boot heels clicking on the bricks. Then, the door opened and shut quickly. They heard the rug being tamped down and the table legs slamming back down.

"He's staying up there," Matylda said in horror.

They stared toward the door, though they could not make out its outline in the pitch-blackness.

Then Matylda moved toward the steps. "I should be up there. He should be here."

"No," Rafe said, pulling her back.

Hank moved around them to grasp the makeshift stairs and move them to the darkest part of the cellar. "Here," he whispered.

They had no sooner joined him in the corner than the area outside the house lit up as though it were daylight. Streams of light found the most minor chinks in the foundation wood and cast white ribbons across the floor, over the printing equipment, and across the beds.

Rafe held his hand over Matylda's mouth as men burst into the farmhouse. They heard Piotr's voice, muffled and calm, while the others shouted over one another with conflicting orders and demands for answers. Hank stood as still as a statue, his back pressed against the wall, as he waited for the table to be moved and the Gestapo to order them out.

Yet, the door was never opened.

They listened to the sounds of other doors opening, of contents being thrown about, and of furniture being overturned. The sounds grew fainter as they moved to the top floor. Through the murky light cast by the headlights outside, Hank saw Rafe with Matylda pulled in front of him, his arms enveloping her, his hand across her mouth, while tears streamed down her face and over his hand. Rafe rested his head on her shoulder and closed his eyes.

Then Piotr's voice rose above the others as he was led outside, proclaiming his innocence.

Within minutes, the headlights pulled away, and they were left in utter darkness.

They waited for an unbearably long time before placing the steps back in place and climbing up, then wrestling with the door, which Piotr had effectively blocked. When they finally emerged, they discovered the house had been ransacked. The table had been turned on its side, with its heavy top against the door, and chairs were strewn around it. In their fury, the Nazis had inadvertently hidden the trap door even more.

Hank looked up to see Matylda staring out the window at the red skies filled with fire and smoke. "They took Piotr," she said in a stunned, quiet voice.

"They didn't kill him," Rafe said as he hastily moved to her side. "There's still hope we can get him back."

She turned to them both. "It might have been more merciful, had they taken him out and shot him."

Hank gasped.

"Why?" Rafe breathed. "How could you say that?"

"They will take him now to their torture cells. They will try to force him to identify his co-conspirators. And they will kill him anyway."

A jolt went through Hank's body, and when he spoke, it surprised him how authoritative he sounded. "Then, we have to get out of here. If they find Matylda, they will have all the leverage they need to get Piotr to talk."

"He's right," Rafe said. He started back toward the cellar. "I'm grabbing our bags. We'll fill them with as much food as we can. Matylda—Matylda—" he stopped as she turned back to the window.

"I can't leave," she said quietly. "Not as long as there is a chance…" Her voice faded into a sob.

Rafe and Hank exchanged a tortured look. "I'll get a third bag," Hank said finally. "Go, Rafe. Get our stuff."

Hank found another duffel upstairs and filled it with handfuls of clothing from Matylda's bedroom, which were now strewn across the floor. He had just descended the stairs and had begun filling a burlap bag with food when the distinct stench of petrol reached his nostrils. Rafe scrambled up the steps before pushing them further into the cellar.

"Come on," Rafe said, grabbing Matylda. "Hank, get her out of here. I'll be right behind you."

Surprisingly, Matylda did not protest. Her face was filled with pain and resignation as Hank brought her outside. "Which direction?" Hank demanded.

She nodded toward the edge of the field as she wiped the tears from her cheeks. "That way. There is a tunnel about five kilometers from us."

Rafe joined them outside. "Hurry!" he said as he grabbed Matylda's hand.

As they raced across the field, another plume of smoke ascended behind them, consuming the printing equipment, the cots, and finally, the entire house.

32

Max

Perhaps the best thing about having sex with a former milkmaid is that they definitely knew how to use their hands.

Max was propped up against the headboard, his head and shoulders on his pillow, as he watched Anke Bauer dress. She was not an attractive woman; her long, dishwater blond hair was too severely pinned into a bun that was tighter than a schoolmarm's, and her figure was too squat and chunky, her breasts too flat, the difference in measurement between her hips and waist too scant. But it was her facial expression that most concerned him.

Her eyes were dark green and tended to appear almost black in inadequate light. They were soulless and as hard as ice. Her lips were, too; he'd never seen her smile or laugh, but as the years had crept past, they grew thinner and tighter with deep lines etched permanently around them as if she constantly pursed them. The lines around her eyes were deeper today, too, and she had dark bags beneath them.

She was not the type of woman that a man grew to love. Although she passed herself around a circle of officers in and out of camp, Max had never seen her on the arm of a man on the way out to dinner or the theater or casually walking about town. Anke Bauer did not move casually in that way that women did, swaying her hips and smiling coquettishly. She walked with a hand on her hip pistol as if she might need it at any moment, and even those she had been intimate with were greeted with suspicion.

He supposed that others used her just as he did because of those hands.

Anke leaned toward a piece of paper on the dresser. "What is this?" she asked pertinently.

Max surprised himself at how quickly he could jump out of bed and retrieve the paperwork, berating himself for leaving it there. "There is a guard in Auschwitz, a woman called Agata Heinrich. I am told she works for you." Max said, casually sliding the paperwork into his sock drawer.

She had abruptly stopped pinning her hair when he approached, and now she took turns eying him and the closed drawer with equal suspicion. "You cannot be asking me about another woman." Her eyes narrowed, and her cheeks grew flushed with anger.

"Don't be ridiculous," Max said, his voice rising. "It is purely business."

"Ha!" She placed her hands on her hips. "Then tell me, and I will take care of her. Follow proper channels."

Max leaned against the bedpost. "You're an idiot. You are only her superior inside the camp."

"I am—"

"Don't fuck with me. I am not in the mood for it. Besides, I am following orders from Berlin."

There was a flash of light in her eyes, and she moved closer to the bed. She smiled for the first time Max could remember, but it was a mirthless, sinister smile. Her eyes narrowed further, and her lips tightened. "Is she in trouble?"

"You would love that, wouldn't you? It turns out, she is very valuable to Berlin, so tread softly."

He detected her expression turn to disappointment before she turned back to the mirror. "Then, why ask me about her?"

"When you return to camp this afternoon, tell her to come to my office after her shift today."

"You can't be serious." She turned back around. "Go to the camp and fetch her yourself."

"No wonder they call you the Ausch-Bitch. You forget that I hired you, and I have the power to fire you."

"You forget that I have connections in high places."

"No, Anke. You have connections in low places. I could fire you, forbid you to leave the city, and you could do what you do best every day and every night. I doubt anyone would pay you after getting it free all this time." When she did not respond, he reiterated, "Instruct the woman to come to my office at the end of her shift today."

Anke stood for a long moment, her face impassive as she stared at Max.

"Did I make myself clear?" he asked.

"You did." She gathered her fur-trimmed coat and a matching hat. It was too good for the camp, and Max knew she only wore it when she was about town. He wondered about this, as she was the type to flaunt it in front of its former owner. Without another word, she walked out of the bedroom. He heard her footsteps, heavy with her chunky heels, as she made her way through the living area and down the steps. He waited until the door closed behind her before he made his way to the window to catch a glimpse of her as she clomped across the courtyard like a farmer in a field.

He had never paid her, and to his knowledge, no one else did, either. He wondered about her motivation. If she had wanted a high camp position, she could have targeted one or two. Instead, she was a joke.

But she was a dangerous joke.

~~~~~

Max stood in the shadows, the glimmer from his cigarette the only sign that he was there. The air had grown chilly; the wind was brisk as it swirled through the courtyard, seeking a way out. He pulled his collar higher around his chin and watched as Agata made her way down a side street toward the courtyard.

He could not see details in the waning light, but when her figure moved beneath each amber streetlight, his eyes moved appreciatively over her. Her thick coat hid her curves, but he allowed his mind to envision what she might look like under it. Soon enough, he would have that coat off her. Her camp uniform should fit her snugly, as was the regulation.
~~~~~

As she walked, he realized there was a great deal of difference between the gait of an upper-class lady and that of the lower classes. The latter strode with the urgency of work that needed to be done, their gait flat-footed even when wearing heels. Their arms tended to swing as Anke's had, and their hips remained fixed as if stationary under their spines.

An upper-class lady could be spotted in the distance. They didn't tend to hurry, but when they did, they glided. Their legs, accustomed to slender heels, moved differently. Their hips swayed, and they didn't swing their arms; instead, they held them close to their bodies, often folded in front of them. When an arm did manage to move outward from the body, it did so with a sensuous, fluid motion.

Agata reached the courtyard and paused for a moment as if attempting to identify which building was the office she had approached so long ago. He should have known then that there was something odd about her desire to work in the camp. But then, he thought as he dropped his cigarette butt onto the ground, he'd had a quota to meet. And that quota had only risen.

He moved beyond the shadows. He knew he'd caught her attention because her head swung in his direction. Her face was in shadows, and he wondered if she was attempting to identify him. They both began walking at the same time; her movements were quickened, while his were measured.

He reached her before she had come close to his office. Instead, she was tantalizingly close to his apartment.

"Fräulein Heinrich," he stated. He knew she had heard his voice, though he'd intentionally kept it low.

She slowed her gait but did not stop.

He fell in beside her. "I believe you are here to see me. Herr Max Kursell." He stepped in front of her, effectively cutting off her path. Her eyes displayed recognition, though she hesitated, and he held out his arm toward his apartment door. "This way." He placed his hand firmly on her outer arm, which had the effect of wrapping his arm around her from behind as he led her to his door. It was already unlocked, as he had carefully planned his movements while he awaited her arrival.

As she dutifully stepped inside, she halted. "This is not your office."

"Your German has become much better," he said. He switched to Polish. "Or, shall we drop the charade and speak in your native language?"

Her eyes flitted from one side of the narrow stairwell to the other before landing on the door. He turned and locked it and then made a point of tantalizing her by holding up the key. He then motioned to the stairs. "This way, please," he continued in Polish.

He thought for a moment that she was going to attempt to bolt. He remained positioned in the doorway, but the frosted glass did not provide them with the privacy he needed. It could also be easily broken if she wished to clash with him there. "Please," he repeated cordially.

After a moment, she made her way slowly up the stairs. He remained a few steps behind. He felt more than saw her head turn slightly, as if she were striving to ascertain his position.

When she reached the apartment, she stepped just inside before stopping and turning to him.

"Fräulein Bauer told me you wanted to see me." She said the name as if emphasizing that someone knew where she was, which was not lost on Max.

"Yes," Max said. "Please. Sit." He strode further into the room and gestured toward the off-white, wing-backed chairs. "May I take your coat?"

Before she could respond, the housekeeper walked swiftly into the room and then stopped abruptly. "I beg your pardon, Herr Kursell," she said. "I didn't know you were home."

"Fräulein Heinrich was just taking off her hat and coat," he said, slipping easily into German. "Can you take them from her, please?" His voice was smooth. "Frau Rökk, you have done an efficient job with the fireplace, as usual."

"Thank you, sir." She crossed the room. Without asking, she began to assist Agata with her coat. Perhaps because the older woman was present, Agata appeared to relax a bit. She removed her hat and handed it to the housekeeper. "May I get you something to drink?"

Agata's eyes moved to Max.

"*Volksgetränk*," Max said.

"Yes, sir." Frau Rökk bowed slightly as she moved to the coat closet and carefully hung up Agata's coat and hat before returning to take Max's coat. As she did, he gestured to one of the upholstered chairs.

"Please. Sit." He sat in the opposite chair before waiting for her to take her seat.

Agata slowly sat in the chair closest to the fireplace, her attention on the flames. It was unusual for a fireplace to be maintained with high flames, as rationing was a way of life. But he was Max Kursell, and the rules did not apply to him. He watched as her eyes roamed from one picture to another before settling on one in particular.

"You like that one?" he asked.

"It reminds me of one I used to see when I was young."

"Ah. Yes. Young and in—what was it?"

"Fürstenwalde," she said.

"Of course. Where you were born."

Frau Rökk returned, bearing a large silver tray laden with a pitcher of beer and two glasses. She meticulously placed the glasses on the table between Agata and Max and poured the beer. Then, she moved plates of potato biscuits from the tray onto the table beside the glasses. Straightening, she asked, "Would you like me to stay and serve supper?"

Max shook his head. "No, you go home to your family, Frau Rökk. Thank you."

"Yes, sir. The food is ready for you in the kitchen, sir."

Max nodded. He watched Agata tense as the older woman retrieved her outer garments and moved into the stairwell, the sound of her shoes against the steps growing fainter as she neared the door. There was a moment's hesitation, and Max nearly came to his feet and tossed the key down to her, but he heard the door opening as she used her own key. He leaned forward and retrieved a biscuit from his plate. "Eat. Please," he said as he took a bite.

He watched as Agata made no move to eat. After he finished the biscuit, he raised his drink to his lips. He drank it slowly, observing her. She avoided looking at him, instead feigning interest in the room. He returned his glass and wiped his mouth with the back of his hand.

"So," he said, returning to Polish, "why don't you tell me why a young Polish lady of obvious breeding would risk her life to get into Auschwitz, when every other Pole is willing to risk their lives to get out of it?"

Her eyes moved back to him. They were methodical and calm. "I don't know what you are talking about."

"Ah. But I think you do." He paused for effect. "Let us begin with your father."

"Henri Heinrich." The name rolled off her tongue.

"Ah. But Henri is your uncle, isn't he? But his name is not Heinrich. And his wife—"

"My mother. Herta."

"Herta is not your mother. She is your aunt. Your own mother, Anna Heinrich, died in Fürstenwalde. And that is when you left for Warsaw."

A glint of recognition passed through her eyes, though her hands remained still in her lap. A moment later, the veil returned.

"And your father is—or *was*—Ira Goldberg."

As he emphasized the past tense, Agata's spine straightened noticeably. "Do you plan to kill me?" she asked calmly.

He studied her for a long moment without answering, reveling in the heightened tension between them. Her eyes met his with an unwavering gaze. A woman who was not afraid of death intrigued him. "Not today," he replied.

She appeared to process this for a moment.

"Rather," he said, "I will keep your little secret—for now—but I want something from you."

Her chin rose slightly, and her eyes remained locked on his. "I can only imagine."

"No," he said. "I don't think you can." He rose and strode to the fireplace, where he rested his hand on the mantel. After a moment, he turned around to find her watching him intently. "You must understand that if you tell anyone what is asked of you, you will die the same death as the condemned Jews."

"And that is supposed to frighten me?"

"I don't care if it frightens you. It will happen whether you are frightened or not. Do you understand?"

Agata nodded.

"I want you to tell me whether you understand and what you understand."

"I understand you will require me to do something. And if I speak of it to anyone else, I will be murdered."

"Ah. And you put it so eloquently." He stared at her for another long moment. The risk he was taking was beyond anything he had ever attempted. He returned to his seat, but rather than lean back as he had before, he leaned forward and steepled his hands in front of him. "There is a woman in the camp that I wish for you to find."

Agata's eyes widened; she clearly had not expected this. "But you have records of everyone in the camp already."

"No," he corrected her. "I do not." He waved his hand dismissively. "Oh, I have records of every employee—every guard, secretary, nurse… I do not have records of the prisoners. Those are kept inside the camp."

Agata's face paled. "The SS maintains the death books."

"I am not asking you to look through the death books."

"Then—what? A prisoner? You want me to locate a prisoner?" Agata almost laughed. She had been searching for her own sister in vain, and now he thinks she can locate someone else with a snap of the fingers? She turned her head to the side. He never mentioned Elsa, only her mother and father. He doesn't know. She turned back to face him.

"Her name is Felka," he said.

"Does she have a last name?"

"I do not know it."

"Then how will I know I have located the right one?"

"She worked in the sewing unit about a year ago."

"A year ago? Prisoners rarely last—"

"If anyone could survive, it would be her." When Agata did not respond, he continued, "You are not to approach her. You are not to ask anyone about her. You are simply to discover anyone named Felka and bring their descriptions back to me."

"Is this a young woman?" Agata said quietly.

"No. It is nothing like that. She is—I don't know, middle-aged—but she may appear much older. You may know her by her eyes. They were piercing blue eyes, the last I saw her."

Blue, like yours.

She hadn't said it, but Max knew she had thought it. He knew by the way she stared into his eyes as if she were searching for an answer there. Perhaps he should kill her. Only Anke would know that they had been together, and an investigation would not be launched on her word alone.

"I will do it," Agata said. "Is there anything else? Hair color, height?"

"Gray hair," he said. "She is about your height, perhaps shorter. She might be stooped. Her weight—"

"Her weight would have changed. Is she Jewish?"

"Is she—?" Max felt the blood drain from his face.

"I ask only because the Jews are separated from the rest of the population. It will allow me to search in the right areas."

"No," he answered. "She is not Jewish. She is a Christian. A Pole."

"Then I will find her." A long moment lapsed. "Am I free to go now?"

Max stood. "Would you like some food? I don't know what Frau Rökk prepared, but—"

"Thank you. No." Agata also rose. "There is food waiting for me at my boarding house."

"Rationed food?" Max almost snickered.

"Yes. Rationed food."

He grew somber. "Then, take something with you. I have fresh fruit, a rarity these days."

"Thank you, but no. I am fine." She made her way to the coat closet and retrieved her coat and hat. Unlike Anke's, her coat was made of plain wool with no adornments, and her hat was simple, as if it were designed to keep her head warm rather than make a fashion statement. Max dutifully assisted her in donning the coat and stood back to watch her as she glanced in the mirror while positioning her hat. She must have been beautiful before the camp had hardened her. Even the guards changed once they entered it. Yet, she didn't have the hardness around her eyes and mouth the way that Anke did.

He couldn't imagine asking Anke to find Felka. The woman would have located her, questioned her, blackmailed him, and killed her anyway. "Remember," he said as he followed her down the steps, "do not tell anyone of this, especially not Anke Bauer."

She reached the landing and turned back to him. "I will not tell anyone."

He retrieved his key, reached around her, and unlocked the door.

"You can trust me," she whispered as she opened the door.

Anything he might have said would have been lost in the wind. He stepped outside and watched her walk away. She moved with purpose yet fluidly, her head held high with confidence. I hope I can trust you, he thought. I don't want to kill you. But I will.

33

Agata

The days turned into weeks and the weeks into months. With the camp complex as large as a city, Agata despaired of ever finding Elsa, if she had ever been there at all. Guards, or attendants, as the females were commonly called, were forbidden from speaking to prisoners except to give orders, and paranoia ran rampant. Still, she managed to ask dozens of prisoners if they knew her, each day in a hoarse, clandestine whisper, but the response was always the same: eyes averted, chin tilted downward, a soft, nearly imperceptible shake of the head.

As the true purpose of the camp came into focus, she realized she had not ventured into the mouth of the lion but rather, descended into hell.

The war had turned the world upside down and inside out. The prisoners were not a threat to Agata, either physically or psychologically. The employees, however, demonstrated varying degrees of depravity that she often could not imagine a human being inflicting on another. The moral and ethical compass in most guards was dysfunctional at best or obliterated at their worst.

Three times a day and often four, she hurried to the courtyard when the whistle heralded the arrival of a new train. The chaos, heartbreak, terror, and abuse were so rampant and overwhelming that a shell formed around her psyche, causing her to go numb to it all. With each set of arrivals, she led a group of women to a set of barracks, often emptied only that morning, or to a holding place where another attendant received them.

It hadn't taken long for her to comprehend what was happening.

The doctors determined the fate of each new arrival within seconds. The older, infirm, ill, weak, or otherwise appearing unable to work were led directly to the holding area. Other guards, often male, led them into gas chambers after they undressed. Prisoners then disposed of the bodies in a process that was ever-changing as they instituted "efficiencies." Their clothing and possessions were sent to the warehouses, where other prisoners sorted them. The guards laughed and called the warehouses "Canada" because of the perception that Canada was a wealthy, abundant nation. Often, the trains that brought new prisoners were later filled with warehouse "supplies," as they were called, before departing to parts unknown to Agata.

Those that the doctors chose to survive would be worked unmercifully until they regularly dropped dead. They arrived believing they would begin a new life, though it was forced upon them. Within a short time, they realized this was where their lives were intended to end.

The largest nationality was currently Hungarian, followed by Poles. A smaller but still significant population came from France, the Netherlands, Greece, Bohemia, and Moravia. They even came from as far away as Norway. It was apparent now why so many were surprised when Agata told them she was traveling from Warsaw to the Kraków region. This was the pit of hell that anyone not gleefully carrying out Satan's work wanted desperately to escape.

At first, she looked at every new arrival, expecting to find Elsa among them. Between arrivals, she was tasked with inspecting the Polish barracks and providing translation services as needed. She was rarely asked to translate, as the guards' batons and pistols seemed to be the only interpreters they preferred.

Agata was standing in her usual spot, directing the arriving women into separate lines, when a surreal sensation came over her. She turned around slowly, her eyes wandering past the women as she continued to point to the lines. On the other side of the doctors, similar lines were being formed with arriving men, who were the first to be separated from their wives and loved ones. She scanned the men, though she knew it was improbable that her father would be among them. Instead, her eyes fell upon a young, fit man with tousled, sandy hair. He had been directed to a line comprised of younger, more athletic-looking men than was typical on the trains. Some were in uniform.

She stepped forward and narrowed her eyes in an attempt to see him more clearly. Agata had no doubt it was Piotr. Her initial impulse was to rush to him, fling her arms around him, and tell him that she would figure out a way to get him out of the camp. But that was foolishness and would only get them both killed. As the line was instructed to march further away from her, she knew they were going to the prisoner-of-war area. She didn't know exactly where it was located, only that it was beyond the civilian men's subcamps.

As she watched him walk away from her, he tilted his head and began to look behind him, as though he could sense her watching him. A guard instantly pounced on him, striking him with the butt of a rifle. He stumbled forward from the blow and immediately lowered his head toward the ground before regaining his balance and continuing with the rest of the men. It was a stance they were all to require of the prisoners: head lowered in submission, eyes on the ground.

A woman screamed behind Agata, and she turned to see Anke whipping a newly arrived prisoner with glee in her eyes. Then Anke abruptly shoved her face into Agata's.

"What are you doing?" Anke yelled. Her eyes were crazed, and flecks of saliva flew from her mouth. "Get these *Schwanz* to their designated location. Stop staring at the men, or I'll use this whip on you!"

Agata briskly stepped around her and began issuing orders to the women in their native Polish. Then, she made her way to the front of the line to escort them further into the depths of hell.

34

Matylda

The *Armia Krajowa* network was strained, yet miraculously, it managed to remain active and defiant. Along with Hank and Rafe, Matylda rarely spent more than one night at a single location. They left under the cover of darkness, often with a destination in mind that changed upon sighting a tank or soldiers in their desired direction. The result reminded her of chased rabbits, zigzagging this way and that, often circling back to a spot where they'd hidden days earlier.

In each encounter with others in the Home Guard, someone inevitably had been injured and required medical assistance. She tried to do what she could with her dwindling supplies to clean and stitch wounds or fashion a makeshift splint. Fevers were more difficult because she had nothing to give them, and sometimes, with a gentle shake of her head as she left, she conveyed to the others that the person was likely doomed.

They exchanged the latest news with everyone they met, building a mental picture of the shifting Axis and Allied lines. Later, Hank, Rafe, and Matylda would discuss how their current position fit into the rapidly changing map. They joined in with sabotage efforts, which frequently consisted of destroying train tracks, disrupting supplies from reaching the Germans, and leading Nazi units on goose chases to prevent them from fighting a larger battle against Polish soldiers. Their allegiance was not to the Allies or the approaching Soviet Army, but to the Polish Underground State, led by the Polish government in exile in London. Their ranks were still rumored to be somewhere between a quarter and a half a million, with some estimates even higher.

Matylda kept low to the ground as a train was derailed yet again. In earlier days of the war, the trains were guarded by Nazi soldiers, so they were forced to escape as soon as the explosives were planted. As the war dragged on, however, they discovered the trains were often manned only by the conductor and his assistants, as the soldiers were needed at the front, the war having devolved into one of attrition.

One member of the *Armia Krajowa* raised his rifle into the air, signaling that only two civilians manned the train. Hank, Rafe, and Matylda sprang forward, racing down the sloping terrain to the tracks to fling open the doors and recover boxes. They were only three among a hundred people raiding the train. None of them wasted time determining the contents. They fanned out to separate train cars, each likely to have different supplies than the others, and carried what they could to the spot where they had watched the derailment.

As they joined one another and redistributed their loot, two gunshots rang out and echoed in the still night air. Sometimes the conductor and assistants were German, and other times, Polish. Their nationality did not matter. If they were driving a train for the Nazis, they were the enemy, and the enemy was always killed. As they lugged their boxes to a prearranged hiding place, they knew there were two fewer enemies to drive those trains.

It took the better part of an hour to locate their hideout, a tunnel hidden deep in rugged underbrush. Unlike the Riese tunnel complex in southwestern Poland, which was so extensive that military leaders and perhaps Hitler himself were rumored to use it as a command center, this one was relatively short, having collapsed about a hundred feet inside. They would not have found it on their own, but were given the coordinates by other members of the Home Guard. Inside, they had found candles, blankets, cauldrons for cooking, and a hodgepodge of paraphernalia to help them survive.

They opened the boxes with the glee of children on Christmas morning. One box held rifles; after food, it was their most valuable asset, as it would be distributed throughout the Home Guard. Another box contained gifts from family members to Nazi soldiers serving in Poland. This would require opening every box individually. However, it was always worth the effort, as they always contained homemade food or delicacies. The third box included first aid supplies, which were routed to Matylda, and the fourth held rations. The larger portions of each box would remain in the tunnel for future Home Guard refugees and eventually make their way across Poland.

Conferring amongst themselves, they decided to open a few of the gift packages and make a meal of them, as they usually did not require cooking. They were happily opening the packages when a figure appeared in the tunnel entrance.

All three grabbed rifles from their stash.

"What the fuck?" Rafe shouted.

"I am a friend. I have a message for Matylda."

"Matylda who?" Hank answered.

"Wiśniewska."

"State your name," Rafe shouted.

"Ira, but she doesn't know me. If she is here, I will leave the message at the entrance and be on my way."

"We'll make sure she gets it," Hank answered. "How did you know to come here?"

"You raided a train this evening," Ira answered. "Someone there recognized her." The figure knelt briefly. When he rose, they saw the outline of a rifle carried across his back and the glint of the moon on wire-rimmed glasses. As abruptly as he appeared, he was gone.

They waited a few moments before Rafe ventured forward. He knelt to retrieve a message left on the floor, ironically, written in the margin of a newspaper that Hank and Rafe had printed.

"Never thought I'd see this paper again," Rafe said as he rejoined them.

"Is the message legitimate?" Hank asked.

Matylda took the paper. "It's too dark."

A moment later, Hank lit his cigarette lighter.

"Matylda Wiśniewska," she read, "we regret to inform you—" Her voice faltered. "I can't read it."

Rafe took the note from her and continued reading. "We regret to inform you that your husband, Aleksy Wiśniewsky, was killed in action on the Eastern Front by a Soviet sniper." He looked up to meet Hank's eyes. "That's all it says. No date. Nothing more specific."

Both men turned to Matylda. She stared at them for a long moment as if she hadn't heard Rafe. She stared as if stunned, her eyes growing larger. As her knees buckled, Rafe sprang forward and caught her in his arms, the paper drifting to the floor. Hank bent to retrieve it, reread the short note, and made his way to the entrance to the tunnel. When he returned, he found Matylda crumpled on the floor, her body wracked with sobs, while Rafe held her.

Hank shook his head. "The messenger is well over the next hill," he said. "I couldn't risk calling out to him."

"He probably didn't know any more than what was in the message," Rafe answered.

"It isn't possible," Matylda sobbed. "It must be a mistake. Why would the Soviets kill him?"

"It might have been friendly fire," Hank answered, joining them. "The sniper saw a movement, didn't know it was an ally, and…" His voice faded.

"The fucking Soviets," Matylda said.

"She's been hanging around you too long," Hank said to Rafe with a slight smile before becoming somber once more.

"You two don't understand," Matylda said, wiping the tears from her face. Her movement was in vain, as more tears swept down her cheeks. "The Poles have always been sandwiched between the Russians or Soviets or whatever the fuck they want to call themselves—and the Germans. Neither one is our friend. Neither is our ally. They are both our enemy."

Rafe squeezed her hand.

"We had plans," she continued. "When the war was over, we were going to buy a farm. We were going to plant rye and potatoes. It was Aleksy's dream. He was a farmer. He never wanted to be a soldier." She leaned against the stone wall. "My chest—" she gasped.

"What do you need?" Rafe sprang forward to soften her body against his.

She shook her head.

"Are you having a heart attack?"

"No. God would not be that virtuous." She continued sobbing. "Oh, that I could die and be reunited with Aleksy right now."

"You need a drink," Hank offered. He disappeared into a stash of boxes and returned with an open bottle of Jägermeister. He held it out to her.

She shook her head.

"You must," Rafe said gently. He took the bottle from Hank and held it to her lips. "Drink. It will make you feel better."

"Feel better?" Matylda asked. "Or go numb?"

"Isn't it the same these days?" he responded.

As Rafe coaxed her into downing the alcohol, Hank said, "I'll find some food for us."

When Hank returned only a few moments later with a gift package filled with homemade delicacies, he found Matylda nodding off in Rafe's arms, and Rafe asleep in hers.

35

Agata

As Agata's roommates slept in their small, shared room, she lay awake, praying, planning, and plotting. There were scant, if any, records kept of the prisoners led directly to the gas chambers. If Elsa had been taken directly there, Agata might never know of her fate. But, she debated, Elsa had been fit when she last saw her. She was not old or infirm, and she could work. She redoubled her efforts to watch those arriving or departing their jobs. Yet, despite her prayers, none looked like Elsa. She was sure that if her sister recognized her, she would have attempted to reach her.

Her hopes had gradually dissipated, replaced with the black clouds and stench that permeated every inch of the camp. She stopped looking into others' faces, her expression becoming like those she'd encountered on her travels, her eyes riveted on a nonexistent object somewhere in the distance. It was counter to all her plans to find her sister.

She could quit. She was an employee, not a prisoner, and she was so well-paid that she had managed to put aside quite a bit of money, even after paying for her room and board. Her uniforms were provided, and the guards had plenty of food, even as the prisoners starved.

Reluctantly, Agata made the excruciating decision to leave the camp by the end of the month. The bigger question was where to go. Countries under Nazi occupation surrounded Poland. She had wandered the country between Warsaw and Oświęcim, and she did not wish to sleep in trenches or under trees again, nor wonder when her next morsel would come. Many of the guards had left menial jobs, such as milkmaids, tramcar conductresses, or janitorial staff, for the far more lucrative pay in the camp. Agata also had to consider the Nazi occupation itself. She was in a protected class as long as she was employed at Auschwitz. Once that protection ceased, she could easily find herself on the other side of the equation, a prisoner herself.

Agata was considering her options as she led yet another group to a building that had been vacated only an hour earlier. With her clipboard in hand, she walked through the door at one end, marched the length of the barracks, and then instructed the women on their new living situation. She had already brought them through the never-ending line for their only set of clothing and a bowl they would use for both eating and bathroom matters. Now, she introduced them to the concrete and brick communal cell that had been initially built for Soviet prisoners during a previous war.

There were 117 bunks on either side of a center hall, arranged in three tiers. There were supposed to be multiple straw mattresses in each tier, since each prisoner was initially assigned a mattress. However, as Agata counted the number of prisoners she escorted, she knew each would have less space than a coffin, as more than 1,000 women would share a facility built for less than half that number.

As the women began to protest, other attendants entered the room. Agata felt a switch inside her as her voice became louder, deeper, and nastier. She had been counseled twice for being too polite and her voice too soft; once more, and she would be dismissed. Though it was only a matter of time before she left, she wanted it to be on her own terms.

~~~~~

After a few minutes, Agata left with the other attendants. They would remain outside to catch anyone who dared leave the barracks before they were properly escorted, but the new arrivals could argue and debate among themselves all they wanted. Eventually, the others disbursed, but Agata remained, idly waiting until the next train arrival. The temperatures were mild, and there was no rain, which would have turned the camp into shifting muck. It might have been a beautiful day, had it not been for the plumes of black smoke from the stacks and an odor that permeated everything.

Several women were marched along the path from one of the warehouses to the barracks in what was called a work column, their shift having ended. They must have been long-termers, as they were called, because the attendant turned back before they reached
~~~~~

their destination, allowing them to continue without an escort. They moved in a single, silent file.

As they began to pass in front of Agata, they dutifully lowered their heads, all but one with their eyes on the ground.

"Do you know Elsa Goldberg?" Agata asked. Most shook their heads, their eyes still averted. The one who glanced sideways at Agata, a movement that could have elicited a beating from the other guards, widened her eyes before averting them and shaking her head.

"You know her," Agata whispered hoarsely.

The woman kept her gaze averted and shook her head again. They all attempted to quicken their shuffled steps.

Agata knew she could order them to stop and interrogate them, but that would draw unwanted attention from the other attendants. Instead, she watched them continue to a building just beyond the one she had just left.

She waited until they had passed through the doors, the woman who had glanced at her peeping again in her direction before disappearing inside. Agata allowed a moment to pass as she surveyed her surroundings. When she knew the other attendants were occupied elsewhere, she quickly made her way to the building.

It was much smaller than the one with the new arrivals, another sign that the prisoners were long-term workers deemed valuable to one of the missions there. Agata heard the hubbub inside as she cracked open the door, but when she entered, the room went completely silent, sentences half-finished.

"Line up," she said in Polish, her voice brusque.

They immediately complied. It took only seconds for those in the bunks to slide onto the ground and assume positions as though they were soldiers. They had been trained through abuse and knew any who dawdled could risk a beating or worse. From the number of bunks, it appeared this structure was built to house around 40 prisoners or soldiers, depending on its use. However, as the number of trains increased, a hundred might have been assigned there. Only fifteen were currently present.

Agata walked slowly down one side, stopping to stare into each woman's face. They did not return her gaze but kept their eyes on the ground in front of them. She asked periodically if anyone knew Elsa Goldberg, but all shook their heads in unison.

When she finished with one side, she walked back on the opposite side, stopping longer at the woman who had just passed her. Again, she asked if anyone knew Elsa, and again she was met with mute shakes of the head.

Agata returned to the woman who had glanced in her direction. "You know Elsa Goldberg," she accused her.

The woman shook her head vehemently, her eyes on the ground. "No," she insisted.

Agata studied the women in line. One side stood at attention, silent and still. As she watched, several women on the opposite side inched closer together, their shoulders touching. She marched down the aisle to them. "Move," she ordered.

They glanced at one another fearfully before putting a mere inch between them.

"Move!" Agata shouted. "Over there!"

The expressions were horrified and fearful as the women moved to the other side of the room, and Agata could feel the rising tension. Her eyes landed on a tiny figure lying in a fetal position on the lower bunk. It appeared as though a small child was hidden there, and at first, she wondered if one of the women had given birth and somehow managed to conceal it. She shook her head. That was impossible. She dropped to her knees and reached inside the bunk as several women gasped behind her.

Turning, she asked, "Who is the leader here?", referring to the person the prisoners elected in each barracks to provide a semblance of hierarchy and order.

"I am." A rawboned woman with gray hair stepped forward.

"Your name?"

"Felka."

"Felka?" Startled, Agata blurted, "What is your surname?"

"Kursell. I am Felka Kursell."

It took Agata a moment to compose herself and continue. "Felka, assign some women to watch the doors and windows. If anyone approaches, you are to tell me immediately."

As Felka ordered several women to each end, they assumed positions they were no doubt familiar with, having watched the movements in the camp many times over.

Agata turned her attention back to the form. She placed her hand on the body. It was cold, stiff, and lifeless, the figure not responding to her touch. She thought the person was dead and wondered why the others had gone to such lengths to hide her. Then, she placed both hands on the shoulder and turned the body toward her. A barely audible moan, almost akin to a death rattle, escaped the young woman.

Agata fought for breath. This could not be her sister.

"Elsa!" she cried out. She sensed the women moving closer, forming a semi-circle around her. "Elsa!" She shook the woman's shoulders as tears began to stream down her cheeks. "Elsa, it's me, Agata! I'm here, Elsa!"

"You're Agata?" a woman whispered hoarsely.

Agata looked up to find incredulous expressions surrounding her. Their eyes appeared enormous within sunken, ashen faces. She nodded. She could feel their confusion as they took in her clothing and processed her position in the camp. "No one must know. Do you understand?"

A wave of relief swept over them. The woman who had repeated her name said, "She has been calling for you in her delirium."

Agata squeezed away more tears and turned back to her sister. "What is wrong with her? How long has she been this way?"

The women deferred to Felka. "She is suffering from starvation and exhaustion," she said. She waved her hand. "We all are, to some extent."

"When was the last time she ate?"

"This morning," said another. "At least, I tried to get some broth in her."

"Broth?" Agata repeated. "Hot water, you mean?"

The woman nodded.

Agata turned back to her sister. "Elsa, listen to me. I am here, and I am going to get you food. You must survive, Elsa. You must survive. That is all God asks of you today. Survive, and I promise I will get you out of here."

Elsa's body remained drawn into a fetal position. Her face was shrunken, her eyes closed. Her lips were cracked, and as they parted, Agata could feel her sister wince with the effort. When she spoke, her voice was so faint that Agata had to lean close to hear her words. "*Siostra Mamo.*"

"Yes," Agata said, tears again streaming down her cheeks. *"Siostra Mamo,"* she repeated the term Elsa used for her since she was little, which meant Sister Mama. "I am here, Elsa."

"Someone is coming," one of the sentries called.

Agata came to her feet and quickly wiped her tears. The women again formed a semi-circle around her, but this time, they faced outward toward the door. Several moved in to conceal Elsa.

By the time the door opened, the sentries had joined the rest of the women, who had fanned out to form a line.

"Let that be a lesson to you all!" Agata shouted in her nastiest, loudest voice. Her eyes passed over the attendant at the door, who froze at the sound of Agata's voice. Agata waved her baton threateningly. "She will not do that again. None of you will, or all of you will suffer the punishment!"

The women stood with their eyes downcast.

Agata marched to the door and scowled at the attendant, who backed out the door before Agata.

"This barrack is assigned to me," the attendant said in German once they were outside. She might have been a young woman, but her scowl made her appear much older. Unlike the prisoners, her hair was shiny and carefully coifed, and her uniform impeccable. As she stared into Agata's face, her eyes exuded an evil death stare. "What did they do? I will take care of it."

Agata stared her down with the same intense stare, her adrenaline coursing through her. "Did you hear what I told them? I took care of it."

"What did you say? I don't speak Polish."

"I threatened all of them with their lives if a single one disobeyed me. You will not say or do anything further. Do you understand me? You will not undermine me!" Agata towered over the other woman with squared shoulders and feet wide apart, as she channeled every bit of anger through her voice.

The woman stepped back. "Of course not," she answered.

And that was the way it was, Agata thought. They could be monsters with helpless prisoners unable to fight back. But they were cowards inside. "Get out of my way," Agata growled. As the woman stepped back further, she added, "And stay out of my way." She glared at her until the attendant began to walk away. Once out of sight, Agata turned in the opposite direction. At least now she knew which attendant was assigned to Elsa's barracks.

~~~~~

Getting food to Elsa was a challenge that was just short of impossible. Providing any food to prisoners was
~~~~~

strictly forbidden. At the least, it would result in immediate dismissal; at the most, she could end up a prisoner like her sister. If the infraction was bad enough, she could be executed.

Yet, she was determined to keep her alive. Her sister's fate was now in Agata's hands. Just as she had stepped up to the task of caring for her as both sister and mother after their mother's passing, she would step in again. God surely would not let Elsa die now that they were reunited.

Food was plentiful for the guards and attendants. The cafeteria was open all the time, allowing employees to grab their meals at their convenience. But as Agata ate her meal with new eyes, she realized very little of it could be transported. Soup was challenging to carry, and even if she managed with the bowl on a tray, there were eyes everywhere. She could be spotted by prisoners or staff, and either one could be catastrophic for both Elsa and Agata. She prayed as she sat there, slowly eating; she prayed as she hadn't done since learning of Elsa's transport out of Warsaw.

Another attendant set her tray down on the table near Agata. They greeted one another curtly, though neither knew the other's name. It was the way of things there. Those whose names were well known tended to be the most vicious, such as Irmgard Grese, Johanna Bormann, or Elisabeth Volkenrath, all of whom had been rumored to have killed female prisoners.

Agata's eyes absent-mindedly scanned the other woman's tray and landed on a whole carrot, a bell pepper, and an onion that sat beside a tin of fish.

The attendant, noticing her gaze, chuckled. "For my family," she said. "It makes a decent soup."

"We can do that here?" Agata asked without thinking. Before she could think of a way to take back her words, the attendant answered.

"Of course we can. It's one of the perks of working here. Didn't they tell you? Just tell the cook what you want."

Agata nodded her thanks. As the other attendant turned to her food, Agata ate slowly. She waited until the other woman left and then returned her tray to the station. "Can I get food for my family?" she asked the cook standing on the other side of the counter area.

"Don't ask," the man answered, eyeing her. "Just tell me what you want."

Agata swallowed and stood straighter. "A carrot, an onion, turnips, and a bell pepper. And one of those fish tins."

The man gathered them up and handed them to her. "Anything else?"

"That's all. Thank you."

"What did you say?"

Agata froze.

He chuckled. "Never heard gratitude in this camp before."

"Well," she answered, "maybe it's about time that you did. It consumes most of our lives, doesn't it?"

"It does that," he answered before turning away. "Just don't let anybody else hear you."

The whistle blew, heralding another train's arrival. Agata quickened her pace as she realized that she should have checked back into the last arrival as they settled in. It always took time for the prisoners to adjust to the horrific circumstances they were not expecting. Other prisoners who had been there the longest would sort them out.

She balanced the vegetables while checking her clipboard. She was assigned to take the next group to the same barracks. As she started to pass it by, she slipped in between their barracks and Elsa's. None of these buildings had side windows, and for that, she was thankful. She hurried to the end of the building. As she rounded the corner, she caught sight of one of the women who had been with Elsa standing sentry at the window. Agata made eye contact with her for the briefest of moments before spilling the food onto the ground outside the door. Then she hurried behind the row of barracks toward the front courtyard. When she reached the end of the row, she looked back to discover the food was gone.

36

Hank

The snow and cold were relentless. Hank shivered underneath a mountain of covers despite the perspiration seeping through his skin. He felt as though he would never get warm again.

In their travels, Hank, Rafe, and Matylda had encountered an abandoned home not far from a village that Matylda knew had once been filled with the *Armia Krajowa*. There had been food left on the kitchen table as if the residents had left in a hurry, but the home had not been ransacked. They settled in with the intention of remaining just one night, but Hank became sick that night with a fever, chills, and a cough that had deepened into possible pneumonia.

Matylda brought a tray into the bedroom and set it on the nightstand. She was dressed in layers of clothing she'd found in the home, including two pairs of gloves that made her hands look like boxing gloves and two woolen head scarves.

"Here is your medicine for the day," she said in a cheery tone. It sounded forced, and Hank could tell from the expression in her eyes that she was concerned. "I went into the village and traded for some chicken bones and made a nice, hot bone broth."

She helped Hank sit up, fluffing the pillows at his back, and then arranged the tray in his lap atop the covers. He caught sight of himself in a dusty dresser mirror, horrified to see dark blue circles enveloping his eyes and his unkempt, oily hair sprouting in all directions. He leaned over the bowl, inhaling the steam. His stomach felt so empty that he swore the sides were rubbing against each other. The broth also contained a few carrot tops and turnips that looked as though they'd seen better days.

Hank raised a spoonful of broth to his mouth with an unsteady hand.

"Do you need help?"

He weakly shook his head.

"Lean over the bowl so if anything spills, you won't lose it. You'll need every drop."

He complied. "Are we safe here?"

"As safe as anywhere," she answered. She stepped to the window and pulled a thin curtain to the side to peer out. It was covered in frost, and she rubbed the glass with her gloves to try to peek through. "We can't get far in this weather. It's below freezing, and the snow is deep. Rafe found a small stack of firewood against the house, but it is frozen to the ground. He said when he gets back, he will take apart a chair and burn it." She half-waved her hand toward the cold fireplace.

"When he gets back?" Hank asked. He set down his spoon and held onto the tray as he coughed, lest he spill the contents. He could feel the fluid building up in his chest. "Where did he go?" he continued as the rattling cough subsided.

"Reconnaissance." Matylda glanced over at Hank. "Don't worry, he isn't blowing anything up. Footprints in the snow would lead the Nazis straight to us. Speaking of which," she added, letting the curtain fall as she turned back to Hank, "we've had fewer Nazis in these parts lately."

"What is the latest news?"

"We received an underground paper just this morning. It was left at our front door." She sat in a small wooden chair and rubbed her arms to increase circulation. "The Soviets are at Poland's northern border, and the Warsaw Uprising continues. As you know, the Soviets encouraged the *Armia Krajowa* to stage a revolt in the Warsaw Ghetto."

"Yes," Hank said. "I remember."

Matylda sighed and stomped her feet for additional circulation before continuing. "The Poles thought the Soviets would come to their aid and help them drive the Nazis out of Warsaw, but they didn't lift a finger."

"What? Why not?"

"It is rumored that Josef Stalin ordered them not to advance, because he thought the Nazis and the *Armia Krajowa* would kill each other, and the Soviets could march in to claim the territory without Soviet bloodshed."

"That's callous."

"To say the least." Matylda took a deep breath. "Anyway, the Soviets have advanced to our east and now hold parts of eastern Poland."

"How close are they?"

"They have steadily been gaining ground. I suppose they are no more than an hour from us presently."

"I thought I heard bombs during the night."

"You did. Major offenses are coming."

"What of the other Allies?"

Matylda rose and paced the room, alternately rubbing her arms and torso for warmth. "They are too far to the west of us. The newspaper reported that the Allies currently occupy parts of Italy and wanted to fly supplies to Warsaw, as the Nazis had laid siege to it, but it was over 800 miles. The Soviets refused to grant permission to use their seized airfields." She shrugged. "One never knows the truth, of course."

"Why would the Soviets refuse them use of their airfields?" Hank began coughing again, and Matylda stopped to rub his back where his lungs ached.

"You are asking the woman whose husband was murdered by them?" She asked sadly. She continued without waiting for an answer. "The Soviets are not our friends. They never have been. In many ways, they have been as brutal as the Nazis. When Nazi Germany invaded the Soviet Union, they went from Germany's ally to their enemy quite literally overnight. And the enemy of my enemy is our friend, for now. If they are allowed to occupy us after the war, they will once again become our enemy."

"I have to get out of this bed." Hank started to move, but as dizziness set in, he could no longer hold onto the tray. Matylda rushed in to take it from him and set it on the nightstand before ushering him back against the pillows.

"You cannot move. Once you have rested and gotten your strength back—" she hesitated.

Hank's eyes met hers. Rafe's voice was unmistakable.

Matylda raced to the window and pulled back the curtain, and Hank managed to lean forward to look through. Rafe had walked up the dirt road to the house, a bundle of mismatched layers of clothing that covered his head to his feet. The snow was nearly to his knees, and deep depressions where he had walked left a trail behind him.

He held both hands in the air as three military vehicles surrounded him.

"The Nazis," Matylda breathed. "They can't take him!"

As she rushed out of the room, Hank struggled to get the covers off him and rise. A coughing spell seized him, and as he coughed, a few drops of blood scattered across the bedding.

"We are friendly!" Hank heard Matylda exclaim—in Russian. "We are unarmed!"

Before he could rise to his feet, two men burst through his doorway, carrying the brutal cold with them. Their shoulders and fur hats were covered in freshly fallen snow, but they appeared oblivious to the freezing temperature. "Are you Henry Mullins?" one asked in Russian.

"I am," he answered.

"Hank?"

"Yes."

They peered around the room as if taking in their surroundings and Hank's physical condition. "Sit, sit," one of them directed as Hank attempted to rise. He removed a glove and pulled out papers from an inside pocket. "A letter for you." He handed it over to Hank before repositioning the wooden chair beside the bed.

Hank involuntarily shivered as he accepted the envelope, his teeth chattering. It was addressed to him in Dottie's handwriting.

The man smiled. "I am Major Misha Volkov of the 60th Army of the First Ukrainian Front."

"The Red Army?" Hank asked.

"We don't exactly call ourselves that," Misha said in amusement.

Hank peered at the envelope again. "How did you—?"

As Misha settled into the chair beside the bed, he chuckled. "You didn't think the Americans delivered mail this far east, did you?"

"No, I—I thought—the Poles." His voice faltered.

"Your mail has been coming to us for a long time now. So have your photographs and magazine articles. Good work, by the way."

Hank felt his heart sink. "Did they stop with you?"

"No, no. We passed them along, some of them." As Hank's expression clouded, he added, "You must understand that some facts must remain hidden when at war." He nodded toward the envelope. "We are also the ones who censored your letters and news reports when necessary."

A movement in the doorway caught Hank's eye, and he looked up to find Rafe and Matylda. The soldiers encouraged them inside the room, as one pointedly looked at the cold fireplace.

"You are ill, Hank?"

Of all the scenarios that Hank might have mustered in his mind for meeting the Red Army, he never imagined it would be while he lay in bed in someone else's layered pajamas. "Yes," he answered.

"Ah." He smiled again, perhaps in an effort to be reassuring. "Well, I have to ask you to come along with us. Our doctors will tend to you."

"Why?"

Misha studied Rafe and Matylda for a moment before answering. "We have evidence that you and your companion have information concerning Kraków."

"I don't want to mislead you." Hank began coughing again, and it was another long moment before he was able to continue. "I know little about Kraków, the city center, but I do know the area, especially from Oświęcim to Będzin."

"Yes. Będzin."

"What do you want to know?" Rafe asked.

"What we want to know cannot be gleaned from one conversation. That is why we have transportation waiting just outside. I might add, even our vehicles will be warmer than this room."

"Are we prisoners?"

"Oh, no, no. You are our guest. And we need your skills. We want your photographs." He turned toward Rafe. "We need your journalistic skills. And we need your knowledge of the area."

"I don't understand," Rafe said. "Don't you have Soviet journalists?"

Misha stood and held out his hand. "Of course we do. And now, you both must come with us."

As Hank attempted to climb out of the bed, supported by a soldier, Matylda asked, "What of me? Can I go with them?"

"I'm afraid not. Our orders are to retrieve only these two men."

"But—"

"You must understand, this is an army of men."

"You have women serving in the Soviet armed forces," Matylda insisted.

"And you are a trained soldier?" Misha half-smirked.

Matylda's chin rose as she answered. "I am a nurse. Do you not have wounded?"

"Why should we trust you?"

"With your affiliation, why should we trust *you*?"

Misha's smirk became a reluctant half-smile. "And you are professionally trained?"

"I am. I worked at the Catholic Hospital of the Transformation in Warsaw."

"Ah. It is a shame what happened to it."

"A shame?" she repeated. "Or a crime?"

This caused Misha to pause. "You would not lie only because you wish to remain with your paramour, 'ey?"

"Neither is my paramour. And I know you would quickly discover my lies. Show me your wounded, and I will demonstrate my helpfulness."

Misha walked to the door, turned, and waved his hand. "Come. The three of you."

As Hank was half-carried out of the room, still wearing overlapping blankets over layers of pajamas, he watched as Matylda whispered something to Rafe. Rafe nodded a couple of times as she spoke, then looked back at Hank, concern etched deeply across his face.

37

Max

Max stepped outside his office building and paused to light a cigarette. The stench was overwhelming, and he fought back a wave of nausea. The winds had shifted, and the acrid smoke from the camp's chimneys was belching nonstop. He caught a glimpse of a small cluster of people heading to a business on the other side of the courtyard, their faces covered with scarves as they tried to withstand the smell.

It had been this way for more than two months. He was disgusted. The air in his office was stale, and the four walls had begun to close in on him. Standing outside in the stink was not an improvement.

He didn't know how camp personnel managed it. After the Allies' invasion at Normandy, the Nazi camps stepped up the extermination efforts. The trains ran non-stop around the clock, the whistles blowing at all hours of the night. No one could escape them or sleep through them. More than 350,000 Hungarians had arrived since May, and it was rumored that eight out of every ten were gassed upon arrival. The efforts were expected to continue through mid-summer, if not beyond, and the pressure was on for Max to send more personnel to handle the volume.

He'd written to cities as far away as Berlin, almost begging for reinforcements, but personnel shortages were the norm. Every available male from the age of twelve upwards was needed for the front lines, which meant almost every available female was already working in the war effort.

Meanwhile, late each evening when the day's extermination quota was met, a siren wailed the announcement, and shortly after, the day shift descended upon the local bars, where guards celebrated their accomplishments in drunken stupors. Special, multi-tiered cakes were often ordered in advance, as though the attendees were celebrating a wedding, rather than the destruction of their fellow human beings. Max learned that everyone became looser as midnight merged into dawn. Earlier, he had regularly joined them in celebratory orgies until word spread that syphilis and gonorrhea were running rampant through the guard population. He'd quickly secured an appointment with a local doctor. The tests came back negative, but it was a lesson learned.

The spread of disease had placed additional pressure on him to replace guards who often called in sick or were too ill to be effective. On top of that, several attendants had become pregnant, and it was anybody's guess who the fathers were. That posed additional headaches. The Third Reich forbade those of Aryan descent to use birth control or receive abortions, while those of non-Aryan descent had their fetuses killed and were forced into sterilization.

As if those challenges weren't enough, it hadn't helped that one female attendant was fatally punished for being too nice to a prisoner. Max remembered her, as she'd traveled a great distance to work there. She'd previously worked at a pig farm and still smelled like it, though she was cordial and soft-spoken. Max had known immediately that she wasn't the type who would last, but he'd sent her anyway, hoping they would toughen her up.

Rumor had it that she had stepped in front of a prisoner and made the egregious mistake of saying, "Pardon me," which was overheard by none other than Anke. The new guard was brought into the courtyard, all personnel and prisoners were rounded up to watch, and the guard was tied to a pole and beaten by her fellow guards with any weapon they preferred, though bullets were forbidden. After each took their turn with whips, chains, and batons, the final blows were administered by Anke, who struck her in the head repeatedly with a metal club.

Suffice it to say that the attendant fell into a coma. Once she had regained consciousness, the camp doctor determined she had suffered irreversible brain damage, and she was transported to the gas chambers to go up the chimney with the Hungarians.

Max was disgusted. How was he supposed to attract people willing to work in a slaughterhouse if they kept killing and maiming them? He hadn't met his quota last month, and he was seriously short this month. He'd begun to consider requesting a trip to Berlin to plead for people in person, but that would take

Wilhelm's approval, and he wanted to remain clear of the man. With his mother presumably still in the camp, he believed he was treading a thin and dangerous line. Come to think of it, he hadn't heard back from Agata, which he assumed meant she hadn't yet located his mother.

He caught a glimpse of Katarina crossing the courtyard, a scarf wrapped around her nose and mouth. He rushed to catch up with her before she reached the bar.

"Max," she said in greeting, her voice muffled through the material.

He pulled her into an alcove, but it did nothing to dispel the stench. "I am sending you to work in the camp."

Her eyes widened in shock. "Max, I can't work there, and you know it."

"I know nothing of the sort."

"Who will provide drinks to all the guards every evening? It will have to shut down if I am not there to serve them."

"You can work both jobs. I'll request the day shift for you."

"You're an idiot. Those guards work twelve hours a day. I can't go from that to serving drinks for another eight hours. It would kill me."

"You'll figure it out."

"Max—"

"I will give you twenty-four hours. Provide me with someone to take your place, or I will send your paperwork over tomorrow. If you do not show, they will send SS to get you." Without waiting for a reply, Max turned on his heel and started back to his office.

"Fuck you, Max!"

"Yeah, fuck me!" Max retorted without turning around. "Everybody else is!"

By the time he had returned to his office, his mind was churning. He wouldn't wait for women to apply. He would stop advertising in the local papers and in town centers. There were plenty of farms in the surrounding area. The women who worked there had been protected by the necessity of agricultural work to provide food to the military and locally to camp personnel, but these were extenuating times.

He stopped at his secretary's desk. "Get me a car and driver," he ordered.

"Yes, sir. When would you like to be picked up?"

"Right now," he snapped as he returned to the courtyard to await his military escort.

38

Agata, Late 1944

Viewed from afar, Anke Bauer was considered attractive. Yet when one drew closer to the Ausch-Bitch, her beauty melted away. Her consistent scowl had etched permanent lines around her mouth, nose, and forehead. Once upon a time, her eyes might have been a clear or vibrant green, but they had darkened, and her pupils widened as though a sinister presence had taken hold inside her, leaving her gaze disconnected and soulless. She had two emotions, anger and rage, which she alternated between.

A former milkmaid, she could barely read or write. It was said that she had never left the rural farm of her childhood until she was brought to Auschwitz from Germany, and her knowledge and understanding of people was solely what she had learned from Nazi radio stations. She had a deep disdain for education, books, knowledge, and non-Nazis.

And she had remained Agata's boss throughout her employment in the Auschwitz Hell.

It was also rumored that she was Max Kursell's lover, though Agata never saw them around town together. She was often rushing to grab onto someone else's arm, attempting to cajole them into taking her to dinner or the theatre, laughing in an obscenely cachinnate manner as if she wanted every head turned in her direction. Meanwhile, whatever man was unfortunate enough to be latched onto wore a decidedly repugnant expression until they were free of her. Afterward, Anke's harshness remained as if she had begun to wear the atrocities of her actions on her face.

It had been a year since Agata had discovered Elsa, and everything had changed. While Elsa was nursed back to a stage that would pass for life, she was far from well. She was forced to work as a seamstress for twelve hours a day, seven days a week, to provide uniforms for the men at the front. The seamstress workers were marched in a work column to get their lunch, which consisted of a bowl of soup that may or may not have contained a piece of potato or rutabaga too spoiled to serve in the guards' cafeteria. Supper was 300 grams of black bread, carefully weighed, which also served as their breakfast.

Agata still smuggled food to Elsa, but she had been relocated twice. The women prisoners that Agata had met on that fateful day had died or been dispersed throughout the camp. She'd lost track of Felka and had no way of knowing whether she still lived. One of the guards had discovered she was not Jewish, and she'd been abruptly removed from that sector. Thankfully, Max had not summoned her again, so she assumed that he had either lost interest or discovered the information through another channel.

Getting food to Elsa was always at the top of Agata's mind, as her methods had to vary from day to day and week to week to avoid suspicion. There were days when it was impossible, melting into nights when Agata cried for her sister and for her inability to do more.

Under Anke's supervision, the female attendants had become increasingly more brutal, their actions often rivaling or surpassing those of the male guards. Those who were too soft according to camp requirements were no longer simply dismissed. They were branded traitors to the Nazi cause and punished accordingly. To continue her attempts to keep Elsa alive meant Agata had changed, too.

When she occasionally caught her image in a mirror, something she used to do each morning before work but rarely bothered anymore, she no longer recognized the woman who stared back. She was forced to acknowledge a darkness in her eyes, a stare as if her attention was riveted on an object a hundred yards away, which did not exist in reality. Her skin had aged beyond her years just as Anke's had, the marks of permanent scowls etched for all to see.

When other guards were within sight, she often had to use her baton on prisoners who had done nothing wrong, simply to prove that she was a loyal Nazi. She pulled her arm back to an obscene degree. While holding it above her head, she hoarsely whispered for the prisoner to fall to the ground when they were struck and to remain still. When the baton came down, she tried to absorb its force before it made contact, but she was only partially effective. More than once, she had struck a weakened prisoner and heard a bone crack.

Word had traveled too slowly through the inmate population, so those who were more fortunate met her eyes before the strike in acknowledgement of their feigned role. Meanwhile, word traveled amongst the guards that she had such a wicked strength behind her battering that it often caused the inmates to faint.

At night, she often could not clear her mind of the atrocities she had committed and those she witnessed, as the scenes kept replaying in her dreams as if she could alter their outcome. In the beginning, she had avoided watching the beatings that occurred all around her. Now, she forced herself to observe. She had attempted to memorize who was involved and the dates and times, but the scale of their transgressions made it impossible. She now wrote down the facts each day before she left her post, placing the piece of paper inside her bodice. She had taken apart a seam in a uniform skirt and sewn shut one of the pockets, so she could slide each piece of paper into the skirt from the inside once the paper was complete. All of it was done in the bathroom, the only place she had privacy. As the documents accumulated, they became as weighty as a book, making it impossible to wear. She kept it neatly folded at the bottom of a box in which her clothes were kept, slid under her bed in the room she shared. She knew if it were found, her fate would likely be the same as the prisoners housed at Auschwitz or the attendant she'd seen beaten to death.

But there was a sliver of hope on the horizon.

She heard the news through the lens of Nazi propaganda, but there was no denying that the Allied forces were inching closer to Kraków. As Oświęcim decorated the streets for the Christmas holidays, the

Nazis were being driven back in Ukraine by the Red Army. Meanwhile, the Americans had breached the German border in the west and were fighting near Aachen. The two armies were like an open book closing upon the Nazis in the middle.

The changes in the camp were alarming to Agata. In addition to the requirement that guards become more brutal, the trains had slowed due to tracks damaged from fighting or sabotage. Those who arrived were often taken directly to the gas chambers, with Agata and her coworkers leading the way. By this point, it seemed that everyone knew exactly what Auschwitz was. The prisoner population dropped substantially, either from starvation, illness, or extermination. With the Nazis no longer controlling the vast amount of territory they once did, they could not carry out their final solution on the same scale regarding what they determined was the Jewish problem.

This alarmed Agata because the vast number of prisoners working was no longer needed. Uniforms and shoes piled up. The filled warehouses had nowhere to take the supplies, and the damaged tracks further stymied their efforts. If workers were no longer needed or desired, it meant they must be exterminated.

Agata was on edge with every passing day, her mood shifting from the exhilaration of the Allies' approach to dismay that Elsa might not make it until that day.

~~~~~

Agata positioned herself along the line of prisoners awaiting their evening bread allotment. While
~~~~~

others at the front of the line carefully weighed each slice of bread, which had dropped to below 300 grams due to new shortages, Agata and others walked the line to ensure no one spoke among themselves and that the strict formation was maintained.

She spotted Elsa and casually made her way toward her, her eyes flitting over the other attendants and those surrounding her sister. She shouted for those within hearing range to maintain their line, though they were already in perfect formation. As they shifted, she caught several of their eyes and expressions. She could never understand how they could be grateful for her pittance of food, shared by Elsa, and her brutality, which they had come to realize was an act, when she lay awake each night with mounting and crushing guilt.

"Hold on, Elsa," she managed to whisper. "The Allies are approaching."

At that, several in line gasped and looked toward Agata.

"Silence!" Agata shouted. "No speaking or you will receive no bread!" To drive home her words, she used her baton to separate two of the prisoners in line and push the others into another perfect line, steps from where they'd been. "Americans to our west, Soviets to our east," she whispered. "Hold on. Survive."

As the prisoners moved into their new position, a gap opened between two, and Agata found herself staring into the eyes of an attendant on the opposite side. For a moment, they both stared at one another in stunned silence. Then, Agata shouted at other prisoners further down the line as she quickly put distance between herself and her sister.

She didn't know how she managed to complete her task. She remained until the line had dwindled to only a few. The sun had set long before, and now the lights throughout the camp cast a muted yellow glow across the frozen ground. As she turned toward the building where the food was kept, she caught sight of the attendant she'd encountered. She was speaking to Anke. When they both glanced in her direction, she felt her blood run cold.

Agata turned and strode with purpose toward the front gates. It was the end of her shift, but she fully expected Anke to call her back or stop her from exiting. She could see no future for herself, but she felt an overwhelming obligation to remain alive for her sister. She had been an idiot for speaking to Elsa. She replayed the scene in her head, wondering if Elsa had answered. She didn't think she had. If she had remained mute, there may not have been a way in which Anke could tie the two together. That is, she thought, unless one of the prisoners provided information. It wasn't unusual for several to be taken in for interrogation; she'd seen it too many times in the past.

She had been stupid. She mentally berated herself on the long walk home past snow-covered fields, the ruts in the road frozen and slippery. As she neared the multicolored Christmas lights in Oświęcim, they brought no joy but only hypocrisy, and she prayed that God would bring the Allies soon before it was too late.

39

Hank

Major Misha Volkov had blond hair buzzed so short that, from a distance, he looked bald despite his youthful face. His skin was smooth, his deep dimples making him seem to be smiling even when he was not. In contrast, his ice-blue eyes lacked empathy. Now, he studied the chessboard with the same intentness he might if he were planning his next battle, which Hank considered to be highly likely.

"I don't understand," Hank said after Misha made his move, "why the Red Army did not advance on Warsaw. Surely, they could hear the fighting. Word is that it was quite intense."

Misha did not meet his eyes as he studied the board. "They will advance in time."

"But the Warsaw Uprising failed. The Red Army blew an opportunity." Hank moved his king into the corner.

"The battle was between the Nazis and the Poles. We allowed them to weaken each other." Misha moved his knight diagonally toward the king, stopping two spaces away.

"So, are we to remain here through the winter?" With his king safe for the time being, Hank focused on another section of the board.

"All shall be revealed in time," Misha said quietly. "You know that your friend's lady friend is an enemy of the Soviet Union," he added casually.

"Matylda?" Hank moved his rook, setting up a nice play. He smiled inwardly.

When Misha did not move, Hank looked up to find him studying not the board but his face. "What are your plans after the war?"

Hank couldn't tell whether he was being asked as a friend or a foe. Misha had been cordial and accommodating, providing medical services to treat what was diagnosed as pneumonia. Hank was soon on the mend, but his assignments were few and scattered. He couldn't help but wonder if they had been apprehended. If so, he would be eternally grateful that they had not been sent to one of the internment camps the Soviets had built or repurposed for prisoners of war. He leaned back in his chair. "I want to go home," he said. "I have been stuck in Poland since 1939. What started as an assignment lasting a few weeks has turned into years. I miss my family. It is as if I had joined the military."

"And where is home?" Misha asked as he moved his rook next to Hank's king.

"North Carolina," Hank said as he studied the board. He had to take Misha's rook to save his king. "I think I'll take some time off. Life is too short to be this far from Dottie. But," he added, glancing up to catch

Misha's eyes, "you know where I live already. It was on every envelope."

"And your friend, Rafe? Will he return to Spain?"

Hank captured Misha's rook and then groaned as he realized what he had done. "Rafe wants to get his mother out of France. Then, he wants to take her to America."

"And will he also take Matylda?"

Again, the game was paused as the men locked eyes. "I don't know."

"He should, my friend. Matylda is an opportunist. She fought the Nazis with the Polish Underground. She cooperates with us—to a point—to stay alive. But you must know that when the time comes, she will attempt to rejoin her compatriots to fight against the Red Army. And you must know that we would never allow that to happen."

A chill crawled up Hank's back and across his arms. He rubbed his forearms through his thick clothing. "What would happen to her if she did not go with us?"

Misha shrugged. "She would be sent to a prison camp. Most likely, it would not be in Poland but in Siberia. She would be made to talk, to identify her fellow conspirators." His words hung in the air.

"Why is she not there now?" Hank asked quietly.

"Because of you."

"I am not so valuable."

"Oh, but you are."

The sound of footsteps interrupted them, and both men turned toward the door as a Soviet soldier appeared in the open doorway. "Sir," he said, "Sorry to interrupt. You are needed in the Colonel's office."

"I will be right there." Misha stood, captured Hank's king with his knight, and added, "Checkmate."

As Misha disappeared through the doorway, Hank stood, leaving the pieces as they were. He grabbed a heavy coat with a fur collar slung over a nearby chair. Along with a fur cap, it was much-needed warmth provided by the Red Army. He made his way through the door and onto the front stoop. He paused for a moment to light a cigarette and then studied the surrounding terrain.

The Soviets had established numerous camps in eastern Poland, where they now enjoyed total control. It was challenging to determine what these buildings had been before the war; Hank surmised they were part of a training camp for Polish soldiers. Now, the Soviets fought alongside those soldiers to drive the Nazis out of the country, but the two nationalities remained separated when they were away from the battlefield.

He knew that Misha was right. The Soviets had only two choices when the war was over. They could pull out of Poland, leaving it to the Polish people. Or, they could negotiate with the fellow Allied countries for total control of the country. Due to Poland's proximity to the Soviet Union, it would likely fall under its domination. If history was any indication, and Hank thought it was, the Soviets would be as brutal as the Nazis in rounding up dissidents, including those who fought for Polish independence.

Yet, Misha was in the same set of circumstances. He was Ukrainian, and through a twist of fate, his country fought alongside the Soviets. They, too, could be at the mercy of the Allied powers, who could decide whether Ukraine would be allowed to pursue democratic independence or be dominated by Stalin.

His eyes roamed the tree line. The ground was covered in several feet of snow. Snow stubbornly clung to naked trees so frigid that their bark appeared to turn white. As his eyes followed the branches to the top, he realized the skies were such a close match that it was difficult to tell where the trees ended and the skies began. A few evergreens were scattered throughout, their cone shapes a stark reminder that it was Christmastime.

He wondered what Dottie and the kids were doing. His heart began to ache as he thought of past Christmas trees, the corner of the living room anchored by their multi-colored flashing lights as they presided over brightly wrapped packages. They'd never had much, what with the Great Depression and then the war, but he'd managed to hold onto his job, which was more than he could say about some of his neighbors. The job security, however, came at a steep price, requiring him to leave the country and live in war zones.

He had once thought it was worth it for Dottie and the kids to have financial security. Her last letter mentioned that the checks continued to arrive at the house each week, so he knew they were safe from hunger and foreclosure.

For now, he and Rafe, and Matylda by extension, were safe. They had not received any word of Piotr. Hank suspected he had been tortured and, if he lived, was sent to one of the camps near Kraków. He didn't know why Misha would warn him of Matylda's fate, but he'd been right. Matylda was an opportunist and a survivalist, and it didn't help matters that a Soviet sniper had killed her husband. Maybe Misha warned him because he, too, shared her ideology.

"Bum a smoke off you?" Rafe asked, pulling Hank out of his thoughts.

Hank reached into his pocket with a heavily gloved hand and gave him the pack and a lighter. "Been talking to Misha."

"So, what's the news?"

"I have a strange feeling… I think the Allies are preparing a big offensive."

"Where have you been, Suzie Q? The offensive has been going on for six months now."

"I mean here."

"Well, yeah. That's the way it works."

Hank puffed on his cigarette. He glanced around them to make sure they were alone before continuing. "And Misha wants you to take Matylda out of Poland. She isn't safe here."

"He said that?" Rafe lit his cigarette and handed the half-empty pack and the lighter back to Hank.

"In so many words. Do you think you will? Take her, I mean?"

Rafe peered into the distance. They puffed for a minute or two, their mini-plumes of smoke wafting into the frigid air. "If I pissed right now, I think it would freeze mid-air."

"Shit, Rafe."

"That, too." A long moment passed. "Fucking Vichy fuckers."

"Vichy France is no more," Hank said with a relieved sigh. "I wish I were there right now, entrenched with Americans."

"What do you think the weather is like?"

"Warm. Warmer than here."

"Hell, an icebox is warmer than here."

"Will your mother stay in France now that the Vichy government has been defeated?"

"Fuck, no. I'm taking her to America. I'm going home with you, Hank. May as well leave room in your bags for us."

"And Matylda?"

Rafe peered around them before answering. In the distance, the dark silhouettes of random soldiers churning up the snow in their heavy boots were a stark contrast against the Polish winter. "I don't know, Hank. It's too early."

"You like her, though, right?"

"Yeah. But…" he hesitated. "This is her home. She's a freedom fighter. I don't even know if she'd want to leave. And her husband hasn't been gone long. She hasn't had time to grieve."

"She seems to like you."

Rafe shrugged. "Yeah. Well. War will do that, especially since she's become a widow. Who knows what will happen when it's over?"

When it's over, Hank thought. He took a long puff. The end could not come soon enough.

40

Matylda

The hospital ward was a dismal, dark, open room, filled with cots so closely packed that Matylda had difficulty navigating between them. Despite her advanced nurse training, she was relegated to mopping floors and cleaning up after the wounded and sick Soviet patients. She'd long ago become numb to the sight of vomit and diarrhea. As she pushed the mop and bucket with her foot to the next opening between cots, she realized she had also become numb to the soldiers' cries and screams.

There was something worse than death, she thought as she mopped. It was living with hopelessness. The war had done that to her. It had broken her brain. No longer could she imagine life after the war. With her husband gone and Piotr's status unknown, she tried to picture herself alone, but she couldn't. At one time, she would have thought that there would always be work for good nurses, but doubt had sailed in with a vengeance.

A commotion began at the end of the room as a new patient was quickly wheeled in on a groaning cot.

"Orderly!" the head nurse yelled at her. "Move that bed behind you!"

Matylda dropped her mop and rushed to the other side of the corridor created by rows of cots, quickly pulled an empty cot out, and rushed it out of the way. No sooner had she cleared the way than the new patient was wheeled into the spot. A doctor and nurse remained as the man moaned loudly.

"He's coming out from the anesthesia," the doctor said. "Administer 30 milligrams of morphine as quickly as possible."

"His wound, doctor?"

"I already amputated his leg, but there's shrapnel in his chest. No point in digging around for it. Damn it. We can't afford to lose another sniper." He dabbed at his perspiring forehead before he rushed off to another patient.

As the nurse raced to the medicine cabinet, Matylda slowly picked up her mop. As she moved it back and forth across the cold floor, her eyes were riveted on the new patient. A sniper, her mind shouted repeatedly. A fucking sniper. As she stared, the young man morphed into a killer hiding behind an elevated wall or in a bell tower, his eyes set on her husband as he moved forward to assist the Soviet army. He held a rifle in his hands, his eyes steady on the sight, his finger evenly pressing against the trigger until the bullet escaped from his weapon and found Aleksy. Had he suffered before he died? She wondered. She stared at the soldier. Did you watch him in his last moments?

The nurse returned with two syringes, each preloaded with the requisite amount.

"Nurse!" the doctor called out.

She left the syringes on a tray beside the bed and rushed to the end of the corridor.

Matylda stared at the tray. Sixty milligrams could bring on morphine poisoning, especially in the frigid temperatures. She stepped toward it. An eye for an eye, her mind shouted. You killed Aleksy, and now, I will kill you.

She reached the tray and jerked her head upward to peer toward the end of the room. The doctor and nurse were actively engaged with what appeared to be a patient in full cardiac arrest.

The soldier moaned, and she picked up the first morphine syringe. He opened his eyes and locked them on hers. They were cornflower blue and filled with pain, the irises dilated, the skin around his lips taut and chapped. "Please…" he managed to whisper.

"It will all be over soon," she said gently as she checked the syringe and confirmed the dosage. His arms were naked despite the extreme cold, and she moved a thin sheet out of the way before she removed the cap and plunged the needle into his arm. She watched as the morphine was expelled from the syringe, her fingers steady.

He blinked but otherwise held her gaze.

"It will take a few minutes to take effect," she whispered. "Here, I'll help you along with another one."

She picked up the second syringe and turned back to him. He was staring at her. There was something else in his expression, something she hadn't seen since the war had begun: trust. "How old are you?" she asked.

His lips moved as though he struggled to answer. Finally, he whispered hoarsely, "Seventeen."

She stepped backward and set the unspent syringe on the tray. "How long have you been fighting?"

"Two…" he said groggily, his eyes closing, "…years."

"What are you doing?"

Matylda whirled around to find the nurse standing a few feet away. "I'm a nurse. He was in pain, so I gave him 30 milligrams as the doctor ordered." She picked up the tray and handed it to the nurse. "I don't know where the other medicine should go."

The nurse grabbed the tray from her. "Stick to your mop," she said as she scurried off to another patient.

"You're welcome," she said quietly to no one in particular. She turned around to observe the young man. His breath had deepened. She felt for his pulse and stood there for a moment longer simply holding his wrist. I couldn't do it, she thought as she retrieved a wool blanket from the foot of an unused cot. As she positioned the blanket over his body, she realized that she just couldn't do it.

41

Hank

Kraków was one of the oldest cities in Poland, having been established in the 4th century. It was rumored to have been founded by Krakus, a mythical ruler, who built the city over a dragon's cave, most likely a mammoth's lair. After slaying the creature, the legend went that the city was blessed with the ability to flourish, as evidenced by its rich architecture. As Hank rode into the city on January 18, 1945, he was struck by the elaborate medieval buildings. It was a shock to his system, as he had become so accustomed to seeing structures reduced to overflowing piles of gray rubble that he'd forgotten what proper streets and infrastructure actually looked like.

The fires and smoldering that were currently evident were due to the approaching Red Army and not the Nazis. The Germans had left the city intact, as the leaders surrendered it before shelling could begin. It was subsequently used as the headquarters for the General Government, a puppet government for the

Nazis. Soldiers numbered 30,000 in the Wehrmacht garrison, over three times the number in Warsaw, with more than 10,000 additional Nazi soldiers moving through.

As Hank perched on the back of the open vehicle and snapped pictures while Rafe took notes from his dictation, he was struck by the silent streets. They had approached not from the southeast as the Germans had anticipated, but from the northwest, their attack so swift that the Nazis hadn't the time to destroy the city, as was their custom. Hitler was still making each tactical and strategic decision, regardless of how small, and he had not believed the Soviets would attack in such significant numbers nor move as swiftly as they did in the deep snow. Subsequently, he sent units to Hungary to guard the oil fields there, leaving Poland under-defended. The Germans had no recourse except to retreat. They'd managed to burn a few bridges behind them, but it had not slowed the Red Army's advance.

Hank was struck by the civilians who began to gather on the sidewalks to watch the procession. Some cheered and waved, relieved that the Nazi Army that had subjugated them for five years was finally on the run. Others were more muted, remembering times past when the Russians or Soviets had occupied them with similar brutality, their guarded expressions still capable of revealing their suspicion of any occupiers.

They continued through the city, which had a population of approximately 250,000 before the war, until they reached a very different, eerie section. Hank recognized it immediately. It reminded him of the Jewish sector in Będzin, but far larger. As they passed by barbed wire and stone fences that appeared designed to resemble a graveyard, the streets were nearly empty, and had it not been for the rumble of the Soviet vehicles, it might have been entirely silent.

There were several factories in the Kraków Ghetto, just as there had been in Będzin. As they passed by each one, soldiers disembarked from various vehicles to inspect and clear them. Hank's eyes roamed upwards to find towers that normally billowed smoke, ominously dormant. For a brief moment, he remembered the day the chemical factory was converted to munitions, and how upset he had been that he'd have no drugs for bribes. He recalled how Otto's hands were shaking from the need for more drugs and how despondent he had appeared when sitting on the stump after the massacre. He pushed the thoughts out of his mind as he attempted to concentrate on how the photographs he now took would make their way around the world, but a heaviness was growing inside him.

A lone elderly woman emerged from a stark red building, her movements painfully slow. Her cane wobbled so dangerously with her body that she appeared as though she might collapse at any moment. The convoy halted, and Hank swung his camera toward her as two military officers came to her side. One appeared to stabilize her as the other spoke. She gestured a few times, pointing up and down the street, her kerchief becoming askew. As Hank continued to snap pictures, he realized her feet were not covered in shoes but in so much wrapping material that they appeared several times the average size. After speaking with her for a few minutes, they helped her to the vehicle in front of Hank, her movements so painful that two soldiers hoisted her inside.

The soldiers spoke briefly, one glancing over at Hank. He responded by pointing his camera away from them and toward an empty side street. Out of the corner of his eye, he noticed they were on their radio. A moment later, one of the soldiers approached him.

"You are Hank?" he asked.

"Yes. I am."

"Major Volkov requests that you join him in his vehicle."

Hank and Rafe exchanged glances. "Both of us?"

"Yes. He is four trucks ahead."

Hank and Rafe scrambled out of their vehicle and walked alongside the others, passing the lady. Hank peered at her as they passed and was surprised to discover that she wasn't old at all. There were moments throughout his life when he knew a specific event would remain with him for the rest of his life, and this was one of them. He wondered what her life had been like before the war and what had happened to her that had prematurely aged her.

When he reached Misha, the major signaled for them to join him in his vehicle. Once they settled in, the procession did not begin. Misha glanced behind them before speaking.

"We have been told that Jews lived here. Many were brought here to work in the factories, just as they were throughout Poland."

"Where did they all go?" Hank asked.

"The woman tells us there are others here, perhaps a few hundred, who hid as the Nazis rounded them up. A few hundred, out of tens of thousands who once lived and worked here." He hesitated. "She says the rumor is they were taken to a transit camp near here, called Plaszów. Are either of you familiar with it?"

They both shook their heads.

"She also said there is a very large prisoner camp south of Kraków. It is supposed to be somewhere between Oświęcim and Będzin. Do you know where that is?"

"I have a good idea," Hank said. "I've never been in it, and at the time, I couldn't get close to it because it was heavily guarded."

"Well, it isn't guarded now," Misha answered. "I'm certain of it. We'll have to confirm, of course, but prepare to go with us. We'll want as many photographs as you can take. She says it is as large as a city."

"We'll be ready, of course," Hank agreed. "Whatever you need."

"By the way," Misha continued with a sad smile, "yesterday, the Red Army occupied Warsaw. Before the war, there were an estimated 1.3 million residents. The current estimate is somewhere around 150,000. The city, unlike this one, has been nearly obliterated."

Rafe looked at Hank pointedly.

"Don't say it," Hank said.

"You know I am."

"Don't."

Rafe took a deep breath as he leaned back in his seat. "Revelation 12, verses seven to nine. When Satan was cast out of Heaven, he was hurled to earth and his angels with him. We have been fighting Satan, my friend. We have been fighting against pure and unadulterated evil."

"I asked you not to say it," Hank said with a sigh.

"Fucking Affirmative," Rafe added.

The vehicle gave a small lurch as the convoy started up again, and Hank raised his camera. As he shot pictures of the remaining inhabitants, hesitantly venturing outside while shielding their eyes, he was struck by how unaccustomed they appeared to be to the sunlight. Their faces were gaunt and dirty, their movements painful, their bodies swathed in material that didn't resemble normal attire. He had a sudden sinking feeling that what they had witnessed throughout the war was only the tip of the proverbial iceberg.

42

Max

For months, the radio in Max's office had blasted news of the Americans and Western allies on the European continent. Ever since the surprise invasion at Normandy, the media had concentrated on the day-by-day advance.

Germans had been stunned by the abrupt turn of events. For years, they had been informed that their forces were supreme in every way. They had been led to believe the Americans and their Western allies were knuckle-draggers, talkers who had to discuss and debate every decision in great detail, making them unlikely to make any physical progress at all. Even if they managed to mount an offensive, the superior German troops would quickly and decisively take them out.

When news of the successful Allied invasion reached them, they listened in disbelief, believing it was propaganda. They could not imagine the vast numbers of troops, vessels, aircraft, and tanks. As the war had dragged on, rations had been necessary for everyone, not just the Jews, other prisoners, and civilians. It took months to build a tank, even with established supply chains and slave labor. Now they heard that Americans were building their M3 Lee tanks at a rate of 45 per day. It was mind-boggling and too fantastical to believe. Yet, day after day, the radio spewed more information, and when the camp superiors in Berlin began issuing countermeasures, they knew what they had heard was true.

But the Americans and Western Europe were not Max's most critical concern. It was the Soviets.

Truth be told, he would rather be captured by the Americans or the Brits than the Red Army. This was echoed by others, most particularly the females employed by the Third Reich. The West seemed to have a code of conduct concerning prisoners of war and the civilian population, especially children and women.

The Red Army was out for revenge.

Then, a few days ago, they were ordered to destroy all records.

Germans did not destroy paperwork. On the contrary, they kept meticulous records. People killed in the gas chambers, for example, were painstakingly recorded, unless they were marched directly from the cattle cars to the chambers. Employees had extensive personnel files. When they were ordered to destroy all of it, they couldn't wrap their heads around it. They had celebrated with a massive party, complete with cake and flowing alcohol, after successfully exterminating nearly half a million Hungarians in only three months, a feat captured in every Hungarian's record. Now, they were to destroy them, along with records of Jews and prisoners of war? It made no sense.

Max wiped the sweat from his brow, even though the winter weather chilled the room. Their indoor heat had been intermittent for months, to the point where they all wore coats and mittens while they worked.

Max had attempted for hours to get through to Berlin to confirm the orders, but phone lines were spotty at best and nonexistent at their worst. Especially in Poland, where the *Armia Krajowa,* or Poland's Home Guard, was rising like termites in a decaying woodshed, they never knew if the trains could run, the phone lines were operational, or the roads were blocked. Their process seemed to be "the enemy of my enemy is my friend," so they were joining with the approaching Red Army to hinder the Nazis at every turn.

Finally, he'd sent word to the camp commandant to confirm the orders. To Max's astonishment, he did. He also informed him of procedures underway in the camp, which involved marching thousands of prisoners from Auschwitz-Birkenau to other camps that were not in the Red Army's direct line of assault. He seemed to believe that the Nazis would still prevail. However, Max had begun to feel like a bug who would inevitably get squashed in the Allies' pincer movement.

A month ago, he hadn't even known what a pincer movement, or double envelope, was. Today, he knew precisely. It was an established military tactic in which the enemy attacked from multiple sides, crushing the opposing army in the middle. In this case, the pincer movement consisted of the Western forces rolling over Western Europe while the Red Army moved in from the east. Day after day, they'd heard media reports of the Allies' advance to reclaim all of France and Belgium, pushing the retreating Nazi Army all the way back to Germany. In the meantime, the Red Army had taken Belarus and Hungary. While reports of the Western advance were understandably distressing, reports of Soviet atrocities on German soldiers and civilians were shockingly horrendous.

He frantically sent a message to the camp requiring Agata's presence. He had to know what had happened to his mother and whether she was being marched under guard to another camp. He no longer wished to think about the chimney, which continued to belch black smoke. Many buildings were streaked with the stuff, as if Oświęcim were a coal town, but now the source sickened him.

Max carried another box from the file cabinets and placed it upon a dolly. He had grown unaccustomed to physical labor. Only a week ago, he would have ordered the records disassembled and removed. While Nazi privates, or Waffen-SS, carried out his orders, he would have retreated to a nearby bar for a few drinks.

However, with the Red Army advancing, the German Army was astonishingly in retreat.

The official word was that they were needed in Germany to protect the country from another pincer movement aimed at Berlin. That would have had the troops leaving in an orderly fashion for the west. It did not make sense to Max that they were fleeing in every direction. Desertions were shockingly common. Even camp guards were retreating. Katarina had been one of the first, and Max had no idea in which direction she'd gone. With every guard absent from duty, he received a phone call or a message if the lines were down, requiring him to fill the empty position immediately. Fill it with who? He wondered. Civilians, even those who had supported the camps from Oświęcim and Będzin, were running away like refugees, ripping off any swastikas that had once identified them as proud, loyal Nazis.

Max bounced the dolly down the broad marble stairs of the administration building, at any moment convinced he would lose control and the boxes would fly down the remaining stairs into an unruly heap at the bottom. And at this point, he was beginning to care less. The only reason he was still working even as his own building had emptied was a total confusion as to where he could go. Even if he commandeered a vehicle, there was no petrol. He would be forced to leave it stranded somewhere along the way, and he couldn't imagine himself walking with a band of ragtag refugees.

He miraculously reached the bottom step. He paused while he wiped more sweat from his brow. The stench of smoke and burning paper was nearly overwhelming, and when he stepped outside the building with the dolly, he was forced to cover his face with his sleeve. A scant few civilians from his office remained, and they quickly grabbed the boxes and heaped them onto the pyre.

"How many more?" one asked. Georg was an older man with bad knees and weak lungs. His eyes appeared positively rabid as he stared at Max. Despite their frantic work, none of them could adequately process their present circumstances.

"Hundreds," Max answered.

"Hundreds of files?" He leaned on a pitchfork he'd been using to stir the flames.

"Hundreds more boxes."

"We'll never make it. The whole German army has pulled out."

"Then, fuck it," Max answered. "Let's leave the rest and get drunk."

"Where?" Georg asked. He paused alongside Max and peered at the surrounding courtyard. "Everybody is gone. The booze left before they did. Who knows what the hell we've been drinking?"

"I don't care what it is, as long as it dulls my senses."

Georg tossed the pitchfork onto the ground. "We'll have to break in."

"Hell, they didn't even lock the doors, from what I heard," Max said as they started across the courtyard. "Why bother? The Reds would just break the windows anyway."

They glanced back, but the other civilians had abruptly disappeared. Max paused for a moment as his eyes scanned the courtyard. He had deduced that they were obscured by the massive bonfire when a movement caught his eye. He grabbed Georg's arm and pointed.

Dozens of tanks were rolling into the city's center. With years of Nazi occupation, he knew the telltale lines of a Panther or Tiger I, but these were neither. These were lighter vehicles, and they were surrounding the courtyard, their weapons pointing directly at Max and Georg.

Max whirled about, intent on running, but the rumble of tanks had formed a complete circle. One soldier raced in his direction, a machine gun held in his hands as he shouted in Russian. They stood motionless, trying to decipher the command, as another soldier appeared behind him.

"Hands up!" the second soldier bellowed in German, then in Polish. "Hands high!"

Max catapulted his hands into the air. He caught a glimpse of Georg doing the same thing as the older man urinated across his pants. Max quickly looked away and back toward the approaching soldiers.

In the next moment, he was hurled to the ground, his face scraping the pavement. His arms were wrenched behind him and tied so tight that he thought his shoulder blades were going to be ripped out of him. One of the soldiers kicked him viciously in the side, causing him to empty his bladder alongside Georg.

The first soldier yelled in Russian while he continued kicking him.

"How many?" the second translated, pointing to the buildings.

"I don't know," Max managed to puff out.

He was kicked again with steel-toed boots. "How many? How many?"

"Twenty," Max answered, when in truth the number could have been two or two hundred.

He was kicked dangerously close to the pyre as soldiers fanned out along the courtyard. The smoke was overwhelming, and the heat intense. Yet, as Max attempted to crawl away from the flames, a soldier propped his heavy boot on his back, crushing him down to the pavement. Max's face was unnaturally shoved to the side, and he caught a glimpse of the guard above him as he lit his cigarette and then tossed the lit match onto Max's back. Then a man in a tailored uniform appeared alongside the soldiers. He wore a distinctive cap that was unlike the Nazi helmet. As Max struggled to peer upward, his eyes went to the bright red band and gold insignia, the red braiding on his collar and cuffs, and the team of men standing behind him that appeared to be his assistants.

"I can help you," Max managed to croak.

The officer chuckled. "You don't appear to be in a very helpful position."

"That's where you're wrong," Max said. He spoke quickly. "I was forced to work with the Nazis. I am not German; I am Polish. I am a victim here. But my job was to staff the concentration camp. The guards will attempt to hide among the prisoners; I'm sure of it. But I can identify them for you."

"Lift him up," the officer said.

Two privates lifted him to his feet by grasping his elbows held behind his back. He cried out in pain, and when he was standing once again, it took a moment for him to gather his thoughts.

"What concentration camp are you referring to?"

Max nodded toward the horizon. "Auschwitz-Birkenau. It is a slave and death camp."

"A what?" The officer grimaced as though he found Max's statement hard to believe.

"There are factories there to support the Nazi war effort. You'll want to shut them down, and I can show you exactly where they are and what they manufacture. The workers are slave laborers, mostly Jews, but also some prisoners of war and political prisoners. There are Soviet prisoners there," he added for good measure, though he had no idea if any were actually there.

"Put him in my vehicle," the officer ordered.

Before the privates could comply, Max hurriedly added, "But that's not all. They've been exterminating Jews, prisoners of war, and undesirables—nearly half a million Hungarians just this past summer, and a million Jews."

"Don't lie to me," he retorted. "It is easy to check out your story, and lies will only make your captivity more difficult for you."

"I am not lying," Max insisted. "And I can point out the guards who committed the murders."

43

Agata, January 27, 1945

Agata stepped outside her door to the sound of distant artillery and plumes of black smoke on the eastern horizon. She'd received an urgent message from Max Kursell requiring a meeting with her in town, but she'd been unable to comply for the past several days. An anxious energy clung to the camp while the Nazis fought the Red Army to the east and the Americans in the west, pinning them in place.

The camp had grown ominously still. Over the past week, any prisoners who could walk were ordered on a march into Germany's interior over two hundred miles away, where another camp would continue to work them on behalf of the Nazi war effort. The obvious fact that most of the prisoners would die on such a long, forced winter march seemed to escape those who ordered it, or they simply didn't care.

The guards expressed their confidence in the superior German forces' ability to repel both the Soviets and the Americans, as well as any other potential adversaries. Yet many of those not tasked with guarding the prisoners on their march abandoned their posts shortly after, leaving only a skeleton crew behind.

Elsa was too weak to travel, and Agata did not know whether it would prove a blessing or a curse. Everyone had been moved to barracks closer to the crematoriums, presumably so a smaller contingent of guards could more easily control them. They consisted of the weakest prisoners who had dwindled to flesh-covered bones and nothing else. Some crawled, others used canes or makeshift crutches. Some, like Elsa, were confined to sleeping in their bunks. Even extra food could not pull Elsa out of her malaise, and Agata feared she was giving up.

Agata stepped into the narrow road and looked toward the front of the camp. The absence of any guards in the guard towers struck her as an ominous sign. With her heart beating faster and more frenetically, she continued toward the front courtyard. It was eerily silent. Even birds had always stayed away from this place as if they sensed the evil here. It was now well known in town and throughout the prison population how the crematoriums were used. In the absence of many of the guards and prisoner workers, the bodies were piling up behind those buildings. Yet even vultures stayed away, flying well beyond the borders, perhaps understanding that this place held a human depravity beyond anything recorded in history.

As Agata drew nearer to the gate, she was surprised to find it closed and padlocked. Terror began to sweep through her as she realized they had all been locked inside.

"Agata! Agata!" The voice startled her, and she whipped around to find Elfriede, another female guard, nearing her. When Agata first began working at Auschwitz, Elfriede appeared to be in her early 30s, but now her hair had turned a mottled gray, and bags under her eyes made her appear much older. When she spoke, it was with a snappishness. "You are needed." She stopped for a brief moment to catch her breath. "I've been looking everywhere for you," she added in an accusatory tone. Before Agata could respond, Elfriede pointed toward the barracks. "Get everyone out. No one is to stay behind. Line them up at Crematorium II."

"Even the sick ones?"

"Everyone. No exceptions. They are all to be killed. Orders from the top. Anybody left behind will be shot."

A massive explosion rocked the ground, and Agata and Elfriede both teetered, throwing out their arms in attempts to steady themselves. "What was that?" Agata breathed as debris and acrid smoke filled the air.

"They are destroying the crematoriums. Number two is the last in operation. When all the enemies of the state are killed, they will destroy that one, too."

The reference to the prisoners did not escape Agata, yet she knew that no words she might have spoken would have made any difference in that moment. She felt a strange sensation in her heart, as if it were hardening.

"Hurry!" Elfriede ordered as she clapped her hands. "We are all to move quickly!"

Agata rushed toward the first inhabited barracks. As she opened the door, she found a small contingent of women. It was a miracle that they were still moving, as each one appeared to be more dead than alive. "Form a line outside," Agata ordered. "No exceptions. If anyone is too ill to walk, carry them, drag them."

As the women began to shuffle, Agata rushed to the next building and gave the same order. She found Elsa as still as she had been when she first discovered her over a year ago. "Carry her," she ordered two nearby women. "Keep her at the rear." She met their eyes as she spoke. There was recognition in them; despite their deteriorating physical conditions, their souls were strong. They understood. Somehow, they understood.

When the lines formed in front of the two barracks, Agata ordered them to move toward the crematorium. Although they had been repositioned in the last weeks, there was still distance to cover. Looking around, Agata could see no other guards. "Move slowly," she ordered. "Pass the word down the line. Leave space between you. Move as slowly as possible."

Then, she moved into the next barracks and the next, until a long line of emaciated skeletons somehow managed to put one foot in front of another. When one faltered, others stumbled to their aid. As Agata watched, one woman was partly carried and partly dragged by two others, as they put her in between them with her arms over their shoulders, her head lolling forward.

"God help us," Agata breathed. She walked back through the barracks, checking every bunk. Inside one, she saw these words scratched into the wall: "If there is a God, He will have to beg me for forgiveness."

A moment later, she reemerged. Elsa was about halfway up the line, a tiny bag of bones too weak to stand on her own. As she made her way toward her, Elfriede returned. "Anke has ordered you to the crematorium."

"I have never worked there," Agata breathed in horror.

"We are all doing things we have not done before today," Elfriede hissed. "Anke wishes to speak with you. I'd hurry if I were you." Her eyes were narrowed as she spoke, and her hand went instinctively to her baton as though she intended to treat Agata like a disobedient prisoner.

Something clicked inside Agata. Calmness settled over her, despite the urgency and the frenetic activity. This was ending. The Nazis were not winning, as they'd all been told. If they had been, they would not have been ordered to abandon the camp. They would not be blowing up their own carefully constructed buildings and facilities. Instead, they would be opening the gates to Allied prisoners of war.

This was ending, and it would end with these people, these final survivors, in line outside the crematorium.

The stench as she reached the ovens was so overpowering that she fought to keep from fainting. The skies were filled with smoke so black and roiling that she'd never before experienced anything like it, and she prayed she never would again. It was a mixture of chemicals and building materials smoldering as the explosions continued around them, intermingling with the constant reek of dead bodies. From the male side of the camp, she could see the last of those prisoners ordered into another line converging on the other side of the same crematorium. She quickly scanned the line, but did not see Piotr.

She entered the building to find the lines snaking inside. The hallway was wide and immaculate, as though she had entered a hospital. The floors appeared recently cleaned and waxed, and the walls were pristine, despite the vast numbers that had come through. Many of the people in line were praying, their bodies rocking.

Elfriede ordered those nearest the shower doors to strip despite the frigidity of a building without heat. As Agata hesitated, Elfriede hissed, "Around the corner. Stop dawdling."

Agata hurried away from Elfriede and found Anke in another corridor at the door to the shower room. Her eyes were as cold as ice, and her lips were pursed in an odd, half-up, half-down manner as she stared at Agata, unblinking. Agata had barely reached her before she spoke.

"You are not German," Anke spat, "and your name is not Agata Heinrich."

Shocked, Agata stopped in her tracks. "It is—!"

"You are not from Fürstenwalde, and Henri and Herta Heinrich are not your parents. There is no Henri Heinrich, and Herta never had a daughter named Agata. Herta Heinrich claims not to know you."

The calmness that Agata had felt outside felt like strong arms enveloping her. A sensation like hot liquid coursed through her body, and she became acutely aware of her baton in its holster. Without taking her eyes off Anke, she knew exactly where the other woman's baton was positioned, as well as a loaded pistol Anke always wore.

"You are wrong," Agata stated flatly. Her voice surprised her, sounding powerful and confident as it echoed in the vast, empty hall. She raised her chin in defiance.

"Others will determine whether that is the case," Anke hissed. "You will be tried." Her lips curved into a wicked smile, and her eyes remained cold-blooded and icy. "And executed if found guilty. Of course, you will be punished long before you are transported to trial." She half-turned toward a clipboard on a table.

Agata slipped her hand around her baton and held onto it as if her life depended upon it, which she was sure it did. As Anke half-turned, she raised the baton and, with both hands, slung it against the other woman's head. Blood burst forward, spraying the pristine, white wall.

To her astonishment, Anke did not lose her footing. She turned toward Agata with the strange expression still on her face, as if it was frozen in time. As her hand went to her pistol, Agata leapt forward, pummeling the woman with the baton still held in both her hands. As Anke began to withdraw the gun from its holster, Agata hurled the baton against it, causing it to ricochet off the wall and slide along the floor.

Agata knew that Elfriede must have heard the scuffle. She knew that every second counted. She was determined now to bash Anke's head in, and she went after her like a madwoman. She no longer saw the hallway, even as she assaulted Anke against one wall and then the other. She no longer felt the energy presence of a line of women only a few yards down the hall and around the corner.

Yet, Elfriede did not come to Anke's aid. No one did. It was only Agata and Anke in hand-to-hand combat, as Anke tried unsuccessfully to wrench the baton from Agata's hands. Anke's hands were bloodied as Agata remained transfixed on them. She would not allow the woman to reach any weapon.

They came to be locked against the wall, Anke pinned against it as Agata held her there. The woman was strong to the point of seeming superhuman, and the slightest bit of doubt began to encroach on Agata's thoughts. God help me, she thought as she struggled against her. Anke's eyes held no fear at all but a strange fascination with the unfolding events, which further unnerved Agata.

Anke moved an inch along the wall, forcing Agata to remain with her. Perhaps she intended to reach the corner where she would receive reinforcement. She opened her mouth, and Agata, her hands and arms still locked with Anke's, butted her head full force against her teeth. Anke's call for help became a warbled, bloody wheeze as her front teeth flew across the floor.

The wall was interrupted by a door jamb. Anke's face was bloodied now, and Agata could feel blood rushing down her own face, though the adrenaline had prevented her from feeling the brunt of Anke's blows. A moment later, she lost her grip on Anke as she reached the open doorway. As Anke stumbled backward to regain her footing, Agata grabbed the door handle and slammed the door shut.

Agata tried to lock the door, but it had no lock. She realized it could not be opened from the inside, only from the hallway. Their eyes met through a glass window in the door. Anke's expression had turned to horror as she stared back.

A movement to her left startled Agata, and she whirled around with her baton in her hand. The line of prisoners had been ordered to move up, and now the end of the hall was filling with them. The ones in the front had seen the combat playing out between Agata and Anke. They stood completely still, some trying to hide their naked bodies.

Agata returned her baton to her hip. Her eyes searched the surrounding area. She didn't have to look far before finding something that looked like a breaker near the door. As she reached for it, Anke's face was plastered against the glass. Her lips were moving frantically as if she were begging, but Agata could not hear her. It took both hands to pull up the breaker. There was a slight hissing sound.

Agata backed away from the breaker and the door. Through the glass, she could see Anke rushing around the room as if trying to find a way out. She kept low to the floor, perhaps knowing the gas would escape through ceiling fixtures into the room below.

She pulled the baton from her hip as she started down the hallway, fully expecting to encounter Elfriede. She wasn't sure if she could fight another woman as strong and determined as Anke. Her strength was already ebbing.

One of the prisoners was frantically pointing to something on the ground behind her, and Agata whirled around, expecting another foe. Instead, her eyes landed on Anke's pistol. She hurried back, grabbed the gun, and moved forward. "Run!" she called out. "Tell everyone to run and hide. Get as far away from here as you can!"

She turned the corner with the gun drawn, but Elfriede was gone. The line was falling apart as the women were breaking up. They could not run, Agata realized. They were too weak and too infirm. And there was still a male guard on the other side of the building. It would only be a matter of time before he discovered what had transpired. As bloody as Agata was, anyone with half a brain could quickly identify who had shoved Anke to her death.

As she exited the building, she stopped short. The camp was filled with men, and they were all shouting orders in Russian. Her knees threatened to give way, and she grabbed onto the side of the building to steady herself. In the blink of an eye, she could no longer see the prisoners as scores of soldiers came between them. Several had their eyes on her, fixing her with a stare as though she was now their prey.

And, she realized, in her camp guard uniform, she was.

44

Hank

January 27 was a blustery day. A thaw the day before had resulted in refreezing overnight, and the top layer of snow was blown off the sidewalks and streets, leaving only ice. Hank and Rafe slipped and slid as they made their way to a building taken over by the Red Army. Thankful to find heat as they came through the large double doors, they made their way down the hall to a briefing room.

Misha rapped on a podium. As Hank and Rafe took their seats among Soviet soldiers, he announced, "Quiet, everyone. When we leave here, we will drive in a convoy to Auschwitz-Birkenau, a prisoner camp just outside the city limits."

The buzz stopped as he pointed to a photograph that had been mounted on the wall behind him. "This is an aerial shot of Auschwitz-Birkenau, taken yesterday. As you can see, it consists of rows of barracks; each row is the equivalent of a dozen or more city blocks. We've labeled the rows on the photograph here, and each of you will be assigned to clearing out a specified area. We are looking primarily for Nazi soldiers, guards, or associated personnel, some of whom might attempt to hide or identify themselves as prisoners. If in doubt, consider them as prisoners of war."

Misha pointed to a large courtyard near the front gate. "Bring all Nazis to this point after disarming them. We will have trucks lined up to accept all weapons. At least two soldiers should frisk each Nazi, regardless of age or gender. Recon has informed us that the Nazis have sent children as young as ten years old to the front. You may find some here working."

There was a murmur of disgust at children fighting. "The children have been radicalized, so don't let them fool you. We've been informed they are more likely to shoot to the death than the adults, so remain vigilant." He used a pointer to identify specific buildings. "Other teams will fan out to these buildings. Recon informs us that some are administrative buildings and factories. Our sources also tell us there is a medical complex, latrines, and back here—" he pointed to what appeared to be a heap of rubble "—the enemy has been blasting whatever was housed here. Only industrial chimneys remain there. Assume they have mined the camp."

An older man with a weathered face raised his hand. "Is that why it appears to be deserted? Have the Nazis abandoned it?"

"Yes and no. We have been informed that thousands of prisoners were confined here. Most of them were Poles and Jews, so expect to see something similar to what you've all witnessed in the Jewish Ghettos. However, as the Red Army has advanced, our recon tells us that most of the prisoners were marched out of the camp or placed on trains, presumably for other camps scattered around southern Poland, such as Świętochłowice and Siemianowice. The Red Army will round them up; it is only a matter of time."

He referred to a piece of paper before continuing, "A few days ago, more than two thousand prisoners were placed on trains. For reasons unknown to us at this time, they were ordered off the trains in a rural area. Those too sick to disembark were killed with machine guns. Some who were left behind to die of their wounds were assisted by local residents. What this means to you—expect the Nazis to kill any remaining prisoners. Any that remain should be brought to this courtyard. Units there will separate them from the Nazis. There will also be a large contingent of medical personnel on hand."

"Do we know how many might be at Auschwitz-Birkenau?" another asked.

Misha took a deep breath. "They estimate roughly seven thousand."

"Seven thousand?" A murmur went up. "Seven thousand, after evacuation?"

"That's right, and our sources tell us that the remaining soldiers or guards may be going from one building to the next, shooting all those who are left. So, time is of the essence. A few things before you go: prepare for a stench of dead bodies worse than any battlefield." Misha pointed to an area where the detail was blurred, possibly due to the reconnaissance aircraft's speed. "These are pits. We have been told they are filled with murdered prisoners. Also," he continued as if he didn't want to dwell on that aspect, "those who remain might be starving. This isn't a hard and fast rule, but our recon tells us that if someone is of normal weight, they are likely a Nazi. Any questions?"

As hands went up, Hank raised his camera and took a picture of the room with the photograph of Auschwitz in the background. As the men began to break up, he rose and walked to the wall as he studied the layout.

"Why do I feel as though we are going into the gates of hell?" Rafe asked as he stood beside him.

"If what you've been quoting all these years is any indication, we've been in hell all along."

"See that?" He pointed to the industrial chimneys. "Those are furnaces. Big-ass furnaces."

"Men," Misha said as he came to stand beside them, "I have special instructions for you both. We want as many photographs as you can take. If this means returning there for days or weeks, so be it. The entire camp must be documented. We also need photographs of every person—"

"All seven thousand?" Hank breathed.

"All seven thousand. You must understand that for every prisoner we free, a family is looking for them. You'll find paper and markers in an office down the hall." He glanced up with a half-wave toward a soldier in the back of the room. "Sergeant Novikov will take you there and make sure you have all you need. Have each prisoner write their name, date of birth, and place of origin, and hold it in front of them for the picture."

"We'll need an entire truck filled with paper if we find seven thousand there."

"You'll have it. There will be other photographers there, and at least one videographer, so your area is here, these blocks." He pointed to two rows of barracks-style buildings. "At the most, you may find a thousand prisoners there. Sergeant Novikov will remain with you, so if you become overwhelmed, he will radio to us, and we'll bring in assistance."

"And if we find someone who needs medical assistance?" Rafe asked.

"The sergeant will radio us. We have teams of medical personnel arriving—doctors, field nurses, and supplies. They will triage and treat the wounded or ill." Misha hesitated. "Men, you've seen battle before."

"We're pretty battle-hardened," Rafe offered.

"Well, we're told this could still be a shock. These won't be soldiers captured in battle. These are civilians—women and children, old men, the feeble. Put your emotional armor on, because you'll have to work through any conditions you find there."

"You can count on us," Hank said.

"Your pictures—and those taken by the others—will be provided to all the Allied nations, including America." He took a deep breath. "Very well, then. Get moving."

Before Hank and Rafe reached the doorway, Sergeant Novikov had already moved into the hall and was marching briskly down the hall. As they hurried to catch up, Hank felt a heavy weight descending on him. He had been to battlefields before, covered the atrocities at Guernica, and photographed Poles massacred outside their villages. Yet, something was gnawing at him. He glanced at Rafe as they rushed into the supply room, where reams of paper awaited them. Rafe felt it, too. Hank could tell by his darkened eyes, furrowed brows, and pursed lips. This would be a day they would never forget, and something told him that the world would never forget it, either.

45

Max

It was nearly 3:00 in the afternoon before a convoy of Soviet vehicles made its way to the camp. There had been sporadic fighting in the area surrounding Auschwitz-Birkenau, but it was unclear to Max who was doing the fighting, as the Nazis had retreated before the Red Army's advance.

Max rode with the 322nd Rifle Division. It was the first time he had ventured this close to the camp, as he'd made it a practice to keep his distance. It gave him plausible deniability, as he could always claim that he only filled personnel vacancies and had no idea what was occurring in the camp. That was true, to an extent, as he heard figures and anecdotal stories each night in the bars, but he had never witnessed the brutality himself.

Now, he could use that plausible deniability to try to save himself from a Siberian prison camp.

He was astounded at what he witnessed. The guards who customarily remained in the towers overlooking every foot of the camp were all gone, and a chain that had been locked across the gates was removed; the gates were thrown open. Hundreds of walking skeletons were in the courtyard. Those with enough spirit left cheered as the Soviets lined up their vehicles outside the fence. Others helped to carry those who could not walk. Several buildings had been destroyed, presumably by the Nazis, before they fled and were still smoldering.

A military officer, Sergey Zaytsev, arrived at Max's vehicle as soon as it pulled to a stop behind the others. "Max Kursell?" he asked in Polish.

"Yes," Max answered.

"Come with me." He opened the door for Max and led him through the wide gates. They moved past hundreds of prisoners who watched them with growing curiosity. They stopped in front of a group of Soviet soldiers who were using bandanas to cover their noses and mouths. Sergey handed one to Max. "It is up to you whether you use it, but we have been warned there is disease in the camp—typhus, tuberculosis, dysentery, to name a few. Do not touch anyone. They carry lice and skin diseases."

Max accepted the bandana, disgusted that he would be exposed to such an array of germs. He hastily tied the material around his face, but it kept slipping, which further annoyed him.

Sergey pointed toward a group of people with medical armbands. As he continued, he slipped back and forth between Russian and Polish while providing instructions to the group. "The doctors and staff are taking care of everyone, but it will take a while and a lot of personnel. In the meantime, you may be asked for food or water. Do not provide anything."

Max thought he saw the slightest tear in the man's eyes as he continued. He wondered why, as he shouldn't have known anyone there. It occurred to him that Felka might be there, but he still couldn't muster a tear over it. An idea popped into his head; if Felka was there and he reunited with her, it would prove that he had been an unwilling pawn during the Nazi occupation. Then again, he thought, his mother might say something that would ruin everything. It was far better to hope she didn't see him there at all.

Sergey continued speaking, and Max tried to concentrate on his orders. "The doctors tell us that in their condition, random food can kill them. They will all be removed to medical facilities, where they will be properly fed and nursed back to health… those that survive," he added. "Do you understand?"

Max nodded along with the others. No one else was dressed in civilian clothes as he was. They were all soldiers and lower-level soldiers at that. He puffed out his chest. He had been important with both the Polish and German armies; the least they could have done was team him up with higher-level officers.

"Several groups are searching for camp personnel who may attempt to hide among the incarcerated," Sergey continued.

Max's heart dropped when he realized he wasn't the only one, and he wondered who else had turned allegiances.

"Our group has been assigned a specific area. Come with me." Sergey led them several blocks away, which was more exercise than Max had encountered in ages. They stopped in front of a series of buildings. "Our job is to go through every building on both sides and all the way to that far corner, there." He pointed to an area in which prisoners had gathered to watch them. "Identify every person. Every building must be emptied. Max, you are to identify any Nazis or Nazi sympathizers. They will be arrested and brought to a designated area in the courtyard." When he turned to Max, his face hardened. "Do not attempt to escape. If you do, my orders are to shoot to kill. If you encounter a Nazi sympathizer and fail to identify them, your fate will be the same as theirs. Am I understood?" With the last words, Sergey almost seemed to grow in height as he towered over him.

A chill began in Max's toes and moved upward to the top of his head. "I understand," he managed to respond.

Before Sergey could continue, a ruckus began about fifty yards away. Several prisoners in striped, grimy uniforms had surrounded another person and were pummeling him. Max and the others in his group moved toward the crowd. Sergey abruptly stopped his charges, raising his arm to prevent them from gathering closer as they discovered the victim was a male guard. The prisoners had managed to disarm him and were using his weapons, consisting of a whip, a cat-o'-nine tails, and a baton, against him. He must have been three times heftier than any of the prisoners, and yet, the onslaught was ferocious enough to keep him doubled over as he vainly tried to shield himself.

"Aren't you going to stop that?" Max asked, incredulous.

Sergey was silent for a moment before turning to Max. "Why?"

Before Max could answer, the guard whistled. A German Shepherd appeared seemingly out of nowhere, raced down the dirt road, his teeth bared, his eyes riveted on the guard. As the prisoners began to scatter, leaving the guard on his knees in the dirt, Sergey stepped forward and withdrew his pistol. Just as the dog reached him, his eyes still on his master yards away, Sergey shot him in the head, killing the dog with one bullet. Then he quickly marched to the guard, with the rest of the group following.

Sergey pointed his pistol at the guard. "Get up," he said in German. "To your feet. The next bullet is for you."

Max cowered behind the others. The prisoners kept their distance as Sergey ordered a Soviet officer to bind the guard's wrists, ensure he was disarmed, remove his shoes and socks, and march him to an area in the courtyard where he would be lined up with other prisoners of war.

Then Sergey turned to Max. "Can you identify him?"

Max avoided looking at the guard as he answered. "Hans Wagner."

The soldier who was binding his wrists looked up and repeated the name.

"His position?" Sergey asked.

"Camp guard," Max replied.

"A supervisor?"

"No." Max looked around. "I would assume all the supervisors have fled."

"Your job is not to assume." Sergey's jaw stiffened.

Max nodded. As Hans was led away, Max asked, "What will be done to him?"

"That is for someone else to decide." He pointed to the closest building. "Clear the building," he ordered the soldiers in his group. As Max started to move, he grabbed his forearm and unceremoniously pulled him back and nearly off his feet. "You stay with me at all times."

As the prisoners were informed that they were free, they hobbled outside the building in varying stages of incapacitation. Max was forced to study each one and determine if they were Germans attempting to hide among them. It was not a difficult job, as every prisoner was no more than walking bones, so thin and emaciated that Max didn't understand how it was humanly possible to remain alive. As their task continued, the soldiers were assigned to gather stretchers to transport the feeblest among them to medical tents set up at varying intervals, which were already overflowing.

"There!" Max shouted, pointing his finger. "She is a guard!" He felt himself grow taller with his newfound importance.

The woman was not dressed in prison stripes, but she walked with her chin held high in a crisp, form-fitting uniform. The prisoners gathered to watch her pass them by before one picked up a rock and tossed it at her, hitting her in the head. Though blood spurted outward and the guard stumbled slightly, she quickly righted herself and wordlessly continued.

"Arrest her," Sergey ordered.

As the soldiers surrounded her, ordering her face down to the ground, the look of astonishment was palpable.

"You are arresting me?" she bellowed with indignant authority. "I have kept order in this camp!"

One of the soldiers removed her baton and cracked it across her lower back, slamming her to the ground. "Shut up!" he thundered. As they continued removing her weapons and shoes, one raised her skirt to her waist as if searching for hidden weapons there. When they lifted her to her feet, they did so by grabbing her arms tied behind her back. She uttered an involuntary scream as a bone cracked.

"Who is she?" Sergey asked.

"Auguste Heinz. Camp guard," Max answered flatly. He pointed to her epaulets. "The officers wear insignia."

"And who is to say they will not remove it?" Sergey spat.

"Straight to the holding area?" one soldier asked with a malicious grin. "Or is a side trip necessary?"

"The holding area," Sergey answered curtly. "We have much work to do. Later," he added, waving his hand. "Perhaps you will have time later."

Another bloodied female guard came around the corner, half-carrying a prisoner who appeared to be unable to walk on her own. As one soldier led off Auguste, the others surrounded the second guard and ordered her to release the prisoner. When she didn't appear to understand, Sergey shouted the orders in German and then Polish.

A group of female prisoners rushed in, all talking at once. Two gently took the weakened woman from the guard, while others attempted vainly to reason with soldiers who did not speak their language. Once the guard was separated from the sick prisoner, the soldiers thrust her to the ground to perform the same disarming and binding they had just completed with Auguste.

Max was astounded to see the female prisoners attempt to rush in while other soldiers held them back. Unlike the scene he'd witnessed earlier, where the guard was attacked and beaten, these women argued with the soldiers attempting to arrest her. He was nearly tempted to interpret, but he was too mesmerized by the unfolding scene.

"Name?" Sergey asked. He now carried a notepad and pencil as the guards began to add up.

"Agata Heinrich."

One of the soldiers brought her to her feet by her hair, pulling out a substantial clump of it in the process. As they shoved her past Max, he noticed the pebbles in the dirt had skinned the side of her face. He wondered why her clothing was covered in fresh blood. She did not look at him as she passed, and the female prisoners started to follow her. The distance between them grew as the soldiers were fast and efficient, while the prisoners were feeble, their gaits halting.

The hours dragged on with about a dozen guards rounded up in the section Max had been assigned. Though he performed the duties assigned to him, he had increasing difficulty processing the scenes before him. His mind felt as though it simply had ceased to function, as if he had been plunged into another realm that was not of this earth and which the human brain was not equipped to handle.

And yet he knew somewhere in his soul that his nightmare had only just begun.

46

Matylda

The medical vehicle was filled with personnel, including doctors, nurses, and orderlies. As they bounced along in a long convoy, it was difficult for Matylda to imagine that anyone was left to treat the Soviet patients left behind. For as far as she could see, light-tan boxed vehicles with their distinctive red crosses against white backgrounds rolled forward along the road to Auschwitz-Birkenau.

They had precious little daylight left, she thought as she peered out a small flap window in the otherwise closed vehicle. They had been forced to cool their heels most of the day as Soviet soldiers combed through the camp, ensuring it was safe for additional forces to enter. Still, they had been briefed that suspected Nazi employees remained embedded inside, though the army was confident they would root out every last one.

Matylda was roused from her thoughts as a Soviet nurse said, "It's unusual for us to be transported into the field."

"I wonder why they're not bringing the wounded to us?" another chimed in.

"Calm down, everyone," a doctor interjected. He appeared tired and had kept his eyes closed for much of the trip. As the nurses grew silent, he continued, "You were all in the briefing. This is a situation unlike any of us has ever experienced."

"But, how is this different?" a woman across from Matylda asked. "Wounded are wounded."

"Your jobs are to stabilize the patients for transport, as many as seven thousand," the doctor said.

"How are a few hundred of us going to treat seven thousand wounded?" a young nurse whined.

"Are you serious?" Matylda recognized the older nurse supervisor. She was a stout, no-nonsense woman, and now she leaned forward to glare at the younger nurse. "Where the hell have you been while we've been fighting for six years?"

The transport rolled to a stop, abruptly ceasing all conversation. When the rear flap doors parted, the doctors were the first to disembark, followed by the supervising nurses. Matylda was one of the last to step onto a road packed into a solid slab of hardened snow. Her first reaction to what lay before them was one of horror.

All the medical personnel, herself included, were clothed in layers. The Soviets were accustomed to temperatures far lower than those in Poland, and they knew exactly how to keep from freezing. They had carefully arranged woolen undergarments next to their skin to hold in warmth and keep perspiration out, as any moisture would chill them. Over the wool, they wore an insulating layer meant to trap the warmth between it and their heavy undergarments. On top of that, they wore water-resistant outer garments. Their gloves covered a good portion of their forearms and were tucked inside the outer clothes, and their feet were clad in two layers of wool and skid-proof boots. It was the Soviets' ability to thrive in winter that eventually made fools of the Nazis during Operation Barbarossa.

Yet, when Matylda surveyed the camp beyond the fence, she spotted people as far as the eye could see, dressed in thin clothing as though it was the middle of a brutally hot summer. They were barefoot, the luckiest among them wrapped in threadbare blankets. And they were all walking toward the front gates.

"Hurry!" the head nurses called out. "Grab the supplies! Go through the gate. We must keep moving!"

Matylda shook off her horror and hurried to the supply wagon, grabbed what she could carry, and joined the line of medical personnel rushing through the gates. Once through, she had no time to stare, as she was instructed to dart into the courtyard, where tents were being erected. As quickly as a tent was declared stable, it was filled with cots, sheets, blankets, pillows, and all manner of medicine and paraphernalia.

"Line them up outside," a doctor ordered. "Sickest ones first. This tent is for triage. Anyone who can't stand in line or is carried forward is to be seen first." The order was repeated down the rows of medics until order was established amidst the chaos.

Matylda swiftly began lining up the patients and quickly discovered that it was rare to find someone walking on their own. Most appeared to be starving. They scratched at lice, mites, and fleas to such an extent that they seemed to have infected every living thing, despite the brutal cold. Many were held up by others or dragged on blankets; those were placed near the front of the rapidly growing lines.

She was only vaguely aware that the medical transports had pulled away from the gates immediately after the personnel had disembarked and the supplies were retrieved, to make room for a convoy of military vehicles and soldiers. Soon, the courtyard was swamped with patients and soldiers. Shortly after, the medical transports reappeared, facing in the opposite direction, and the sickest patients were steadily moved on canvas litters with wood poles into their cavernous interiors. Once fully packed, they set off toward the Soviet field hospitals for urgent care.

"Orderly!" someone called. "Orderlies needed!"

Matylda rushed to the tent opening to find a line of litters waiting for transport. She quickly picked up one end, while another orderly, a young woman, picked up the other. As they hurried through the chaotic courtyard to another waiting transport, she glanced down at the body in the litter. It was a young woman so emaciated that she might have appeared to be a pre-teen but for her withered face. She lay in a fetal position and was so still that Matylda wondered whether she had already succumbed to death.

They reached the ambulance and stood in line for a moment as others were placed inside, where patients were arranged to maximize the space.

Matylda leaned toward the woman. "What is your name?" she asked. The litter was as light as a feather; the woman couldn't have weighed more than sixty pounds. She balanced the poles in one hand as she leaned forward and gently rapped her cheek. "What is your name?"

After a long moment, the woman attempted to open her eyes.

"What is your name?" she repeated.

Her lips moved, but no sound escaped.

"Your name?" she asked again.

"Siostra Mamo?" The whisper was so low and labored that Matylda couldn't be sure she heard it correctly. "Is it you?"

"Do you know where you are?"

"In hell." Her fluttering eyes stopped trying to open, and she appeared to slip into sleep.

"You have been rescued," Matylda told her as she handed the litter poles to personnel inside the ambulance. She wanted to say more, but the litter was whisked away too quickly. Another orderly handed her an empty litter and instructed her to hurry.

As she rushed back to the tents, she overheard a supervisor announcing, "All ambulances will continue their rounds between the hospitals and the camp until all patients have been transported out of this putrid hell."

The work continued for hours, but it seemed more like minutes. Only the darkening of the skies told her that night would soon be upon them. In anticipation, soldiers were already bringing up portable lights that would illuminate the tents throughout the night.

Matylda finally stopped to catch her breath after too many trips to count. The packed snow had turned to slippery mush under the constant trampling, making every trek to the waiting ambulances an exercise in balance control. Yet the lines grew ever longer as more were found and informed of their unexpected freedom.

Everyone was famished, and it broke her heart that they had nothing for them. Again and again, she explained that they would be transported to a hospital, where they would be assessed and fed. Despite strict orders, she witnessed more than one soldier handing out candy bars, but she couldn't bring herself to object.

As she wiped her forehead of perspiration despite the cold, she spotted Hank and Rafe emerging from one of the many streets that surrounded the courtyard. They raced to another staging area, a destination clearly in mind. Her eyes followed them until she realized that Nazis were being rooted out, frisked, cuffed, and lined up. She had been so busy with patients that she hadn't noticed the bedlam beyond the courtyard. Former prisoners who were strong enough to fight were pummeling the Nazi guards, as Soviet soldiers stood by watching. Occasionally, a soldier would join in with the butt of their rifle if the Nazi appeared to be gaining the upper hand.

Once they joined the group of Nazis, Hank began busily snapping pictures as Rafe scribbled notes. Then, patients who had stood in line for hours started to break away from the tents and rush as best they could to a point where Soviet soldiers were forced to hold them back. One woman called out, "Agata!" The name was repeated among the people until it became a constant chant.

Then, a male voice joined the fray, shouting, "Agata! Agata!"

Her blood ran cold. She knew that voice. Frantic, she rushed through the throngs of people, calling, "Piotr! Piotr!"

Matylda's search was abruptly interrupted by a massive blast in the area where the Nazis had been assembled. The ground trembled under her as women began screaming. The air was filled with rainbow colors produced by a grenade, the metal casing and incendiary materials flying out in all directions. Matylda pulled a mask over her nose and mouth as she tried to wave away the smoke, while she continued to call out for Piotr between coughing fits.

As the air began to clear, several medics raced toward the site of the blast, and Matylda was caught up in the rush to help the victims. As her feet flew across the ground between them, she caught sight of bodies lying in a tight circle. It was not difficult to discover who had set off the grenade, as a Nazi guard lay in the midst of them with his arm and side blown away.

She was still yards away when she went down to her knees on the hard, packed snow.

That's funny, she thought. I must have slipped. She tried moving her hands to push herself up, but she couldn't feel the ground.

As Matylda looked up from her position in the cold muck, several faces were turning around. The medics' rush forward halted as they stared at her in horror. Surely, she thought, they must know that I didn't fall on purpose. Why are they looking at me like that?

47

Matylda

Matylda could hear the commotion all around her, but the smoke was too thick for her to see anyone else. Their voices shouted in all directions in distinctly female and male tones, but she was unable to decipher their words.

It dawned on her that there was too much smoke from one grenade; a second detonation must have occurred as she rushed toward the victims of the first blast. She whirled around, her equilibrium lost as confusion set in. Then, a pinpoint of white light shone from a distance and grew larger as it drew near. Help was on its way; the military was shining its floodlights on the scene, and they would soon find her.

A figure began to form inside the light, the gait so familiar to her that she was speechless. As he came closer, his clothing came into focus. He wore brown, slightly baggy slacks, an off-white linen shirt, and a warm tan vest. His hair was chestnut and cut short, a few stray locks escaping beneath an umber flat cap. As he became more focused, a broad smile emerged across his face, reaching to his aquamarine eyes.

His arms spread wide, and she threw herself into his embrace. "Aleksy!" she cried.

"Maty," he said, holding her so close that her face was pressed against his neck. "Oh, Maty, how I have missed you."

She could have remained in his embrace forever. He was huskier than he had been during the war, and her hands roamed across his back and hips as if she could pull him into her. When at last she pulled away only far enough to look into his face, he appeared more youthful than he had during the Nazi invasion. Gone were the worrisome lines between his brows and the downward turn of his lips.

It dawned on her that Aleksy appeared as he had before the war, the imminent danger, and the hate-filled rhetoric. He was the man she knew and loved when peace was taken for granted, food was plentiful, and they were free to plan their futures together.

"Aleksy," she cried, tears of joy rushing down her cheeks, "I thought you were dead. They said—I received word—"

"No, Maty, my darling," he said, wiping the tears with his thumb. "I was never gone. I was always beside you, even when you couldn't feel me."

"But—how is it possible—you surely were not a prisoner here?"

"No, darling. I was never a prisoner here—or anywhere." He turned toward the light that had shone behind him, wrapping his arm around her. "I'm here, sweetheart, to help you transition to your new home."

"What are you talking about?"

Although he continued to smile, a sadness swept over his eyes. He wordlessly pointed to something beyond them.

Matylda did not want to see what he pointed to; intuition told her that it would change everything. And she did not want anything to change. Now that they had been reunited, she wanted and needed to remain in his arms. Nothing else mattered now.

As if reading her mind, he said softly, "It's okay, Maty. I am not leaving you, now or ever. Just look, and then I'll explain everything."

She reluctantly turned in the direction he pointed and gasped as she spotted several medics in a circle. They knelt on the uneven ground, their heads nearly touching as they labored over someone she could not see. "I should help them—"

"No, sweetheart. They've done all they could do."

"What happened?" she breathed.

"One of the Nazi guards had not been properly searched and disarmed," he said sadly. "It was a small grenade, but it was so close to the others that it inflicted casualties."

"Yes," she said, "I remember. I was rushing to help them."

"Yes, you were."

"But, then…" she paused. "I'm confused."

"You won't be for long, darling. I promise." With his arm still around her, he squeezed her waist. "A young soldier panicked, you see. He thought he was firing into a crowd of Nazi guards."

"How could he think that? We were all wearing white—"

"Yes, but you weren't the only ones rushing in to help the victims. He panicked, Maty. He was young and inexperienced, and he panicked."

"Did he hit anyone?"

"Yes, he hit one."

"Only one?"

"Only one. And then he was disarmed."

She continued to watch the medics until one leaned back on his haunches and shook his head. They all rose to their feet in unison. Her eyes fell on black boots splattered in slush and mud. The standard-issue attire might have belonged to any Soviet soldier or medic, yet somehow she knew. "Don't let go of me."

"I won't let go of you, Maty. You'll never be without me again."

A strange sensation began to envelop her. Her chest felt compressed as though someone was sitting on it, and her mind fought to understand the scene unfolding before her. The medics dispersed, vanishing into a peculiar mist. Only the body remained. It was dressed in olive trousers, the matching top obscured beneath a wool jacket splattered in blood across the chest. The strap from a medic bag was still across one shoulder, the bag itself lying beside the body, its contents spilled beside a fallen beret. She didn't want to look at the face, but her eyes seemed to have a mind of their own.

The hair was shoulder-length and straight, as it spilled around her face and neck. The eyes were open, staring at the heavens, the shade of blue vivid. Her cheeks were still flushed with the frigid cold.

"It's me," she whispered.

"No, Maty. It was only a small part of you."

She turned to look into Aleksy's eyes. "Am I dead?"

"Death does not exist," he said softly. "Matylda Wiśniewska is no longer alive in her earthly body. But I am looking at her right now. She is as alive as she has ever been."

"I don't understand." She tried to peer around him. "Is this heaven? Where is everyone else?"

"Come," he said. "We'll walk together to the other side."

She took one hesitant step and then another. "Aleksy," she said suddenly.

"Yes, my darling?"

"My limp, the one the Gestapo gave me. It's gone."

"Yes. It's gone." He smiled reassuringly. "And you are in your prime, Maty. Just as I am."

She glanced down at her body to find a younger, fitter version of herself. She was dressed in a floor-length, red silk dress. As she held out her arms, she realized they were covered in long, pristine white gloves. One hand moved to her head, where she found a wide hat with a broad silk band. She didn't need to see it to know the silk matched her dress. "It's my Christmas outfit," she said as if dazed.

"Yes," Aleksy said. "You wore it on the night I proposed. Those were good times, weren't they, Maty? Before the war?"

"Yes," she said, fighting back tears. "Those were good times." She wiped at her eyes and gazed at him again with an overwhelming sense of love. "Don't leave me."

"I won't leave you. I promise."

They walked toward the light, their arms wrapped around one another. With each step she took, she felt lighter and freer. The orb appeared to pulse as they neared, as though it were alive. The energy it emitted felt like unconditional love, the kind a parent has for their newborn or the kind she had for Aleksy.

When the mists surrounded them, she kept her arm around Aleksy, his solid presence helping to guide her. It was over, she thought. It felt surreal that it was all over—the Nazi threats, invasion, and occupation, the Soviets, the Home Guard. It was all over, and yet, here was Aleksy, his arm still around her, drawing her next to him as if he would never let go.

~~~~~

The voice abruptly cut into Matylda's conversation with Aleksy. It was neither male nor female; yet, somehow, it was both. He rose at the sound, and she reached for him to bring him back down to her. "Did you realize we have been together for months?" he asked.

"No," she answered. "It's been seconds."

"Seconds in our time," he acknowledged. "Months on earth."

Matylda sensed a new presence approaching, and she tried to grasp Aleksy to hold him to her.

"It's okay, Maty," he said. "I'll be just over there, and I'll be back as soon as you're finished."

"Finished with what?"

"It's part of your transition. Everything will be fine. You'll see."

"But, I thought I was in my new home."
~~~~~

"You are, darling. I am only a small part of it."

"More than a small part," the voice said, "and perhaps the most comforting part."

Matylda stood as Aleksy faded. She stepped forward and tried to grasp the space where he had stood, but her fingers only floated through thin air.

"Don't worry," the voice said reassuringly. "He will be back. He promised, and I will make the same promise to you now."

She turned to find a being standing a few feet away. He was at least a foot taller than she was, willowy, and dressed in a flowing violet garment that reached the ground. The hair was copper and short, framing delicate features. The green eyes were stunning in their intensity.

"Who are you?" Matylda asked.

"My name is Jerahmeel. I am here to guide you through your life review."

"I don't understand."

He waved toward a field in which Matylda and Aleksy had been sitting. "Please, sit." They sat across from one another. As his long, slender fingers flitted around the fabric and caused the threads to glow, Matylda was intrigued. Even this close, the creature defied explanation.

"You have reached the other side," Jerahmeel said, "as Aleksy has already explained."

Matylda looked around them. A gate had appeared behind her that she was certain had not been there before. "This doesn't look like what I thought heaven would be."

"That is because we are not in heaven."

"This can't be—!"

"No," Jerahmeel answered with a gentle smile. "You are in between. This is where your life is reviewed."

"I was baptized—"

"Yes, yes," Jerahmeel said, cutting her off. "But this is a *review*."

In the blink of an eye, Matylda found herself at the farmhouse that had belonged to her family for generations. It was a crisp autumn day, the kind of day that apples are gathered from the trees, and pumpkins and gourds littered the fields, their rounded bodies tethered to the ground by serpentine vines. It was the season of apple cider and hot chocolate, of baked fruit pies, sweaters and caps, and sunny days that melted into chilly evenings.

Yet, she stood on the ground outside the farmhouse, her heart breaking as she watched Piotr and Aleksy prepare to rejoin the Home Guard. Then a strange sensation came over her; she felt the men's angst at leaving her.

Piotr was in doubt whether he was doing the right thing. She saw the scenes playing out in his head. On the one hand, he was itching to get to his unit and defend his country. On the other hand, he was leaving his sister at precisely the time she needed him to help bring in the harvest.

"Please stay safe, Piotr," she called out. "Don't worry about anything here! I'll take care of everything. You just take care of yourself."

She felt his emotions as if she were inside his mind. *Please stay safe* translated into *I love you, and I don't want to lose you*. The rest told him that she was strong enough to be on her own, which gave him the fortitude to leave her.

Aleksy stepped toward her, pulling her into his arms and kissing her. "I'll be back soon, darling," he said. Unable to suppress the tears that rose, he turned his face away from her, pulling her to his shoulder.

"I know you'll be back," she said. "I'm counting on it. We have our entire lives ahead of us."

"Yes, we do," he said. He pulled back and took a deep breath. "Yes, we do," he repeated.

Again, she felt as though she had somehow managed to enter his mind. He knew he would not return. He'd had a dream that he had died, but he didn't tell her about it; he didn't want her to worry. Yet, he'd experienced a premonition that this was the last time he would see her.

"I'll be in Warsaw soon," Matylda added. "I'll be helping to care for patients at the hospital there, just as soon as I get things squared away here at the farm. We'll meet up there. The invasion will be over soon."

"Yes. I'll see you there." He kissed her again, more deeply, and as if he did not want to go.

Matylda turned to Jerahmeel. "He knew he was going to die."

"Yes," Jerahmeel answered. "He did."

"Yet, he didn't tell me."

"Your courage in seeing them both off without tears gave him the strength to go. He carried that image of you waving him off."

"It must have been so traumatic for him." She looked around, her heart heavy with grief. "When will he be back?"

"Soon," Jerahmeel answered. "Very soon. You see, every word you ever uttered and every action you ever took impacted someone else. The good that you did fluttered outward to create more good in the world. Negative words and actions also ripple outward, creating more turmoil. All souls are interconnected. All energy is shared."

"I cannot have been connected to the Nazis—or the Soviets."

"Ah. But you were and still are."

The scene changed again, and she found herself in the Soviet hospital. She watched as she moved forward to stand beside the soldier's bed and eyed the two vials of morphine. This time, however, she felt the soldier's eyes upon her. She felt the intensity of his pain, of the shrapnel left in his body, of the wounds that made him want to cry out every time the sheet touched him. She felt the emotional weight of losing his leg, wondering how he could ever return home and face the girl he'd left behind, his mother's face, or his father's dashed expectations. He would never be able-bodied. She felt his angst and even a desire that he had been killed in battle rather than live out his days as an invalid, a weight on a family that was already hand-to-mouth.

"He wanted me to kill him," Matylda said in awe. "It was as if he knew what I was contemplating."

"Yes," Jerahmeel answered.

"It would have been better for him if I had given him a fatal dose."

"Ah, but it would not. You see, the war was coming to a close. He would have a time of convalescence, but the girl he left behind would still be waiting for him. They would go on to marry and have children. His father's expectations would adjust, and his son would become valuable in the family business in other ways. His infirmity would cause him to pursue accounting and finance, and through those fields, he would turn his father's business into a profitable venture that neither could have imagined."

"You speak as though it has already happened."

"It has, and it hasn't." Jerahmeel cocked his head. "Linear time is purely an earthly experience. Here, there is no time. There is no future, no present, and no past. We travel freely between them." He took a breath. "Had you killed him, his girlfriend would have married another but been unhappy. His father's business would have faltered, leading to dissolution. His parents would have buckled under the strain and blamed each other. Everything you do ripples out, you see."

"I want to see Aleksy."

"In due time, my child."

"And my parents—I haven't seen them yet!"

"Ah." The creature smiled. "It is not yet time."

"Please, don't make me wait—!"

"You will wait because your father and his wife are not on this side." With a wave of his hand, a circular window opened up.

As Matylda leaned forward, she found herself peering at the farmhouse where she had lived, but it seemed different somehow—smaller and newer. The crops were tall, the stalks waving in a gentle wind, and the clouds puffy and white. Her stepmother stepped outside the back door to ring a bell affixed to the side of the house. "Suppertime!" she called out.

Almost instantly, two men emerged from the barn. They laughed and joked as they joined her stepmother before all three disappeared into the house.

"My father and Piotr," Matylda said, tearing up.

"Your stepmother, too. They all survived the war. They rebuilt the old farmhouse that had been destroyed." Jerahmeel smiled. "You'll be pleased to know they have an indoor bathroom now, and the kitchen has been upgraded."

In a garden just beyond the house, two women picked flowers. As Matylda leaned in to identify them, she was unable to see them clearly. They both wore pale garments that fluttered in the summer breeze. The sound of laughter wafted up to her as their grainy figures disappeared inside the house with their bouquets.

"Who are they?" she asked.

"In due time, you will learn everything, my child."

"What of my mother? My natural mother?"

"She is here and waiting for you. You'll only have to wait a little longer. For the others, you will be the one they each see as they cross over to this side." He began to glide away from the farmhouse, and Matylda followed. When she glanced back, the scene was gone as though it had never existed.

"But for now," Jerahmeel was saying, "we have an entire lifetime ahead of us. You must see how your words and actions have impacted everyone you have ever come into contact with. You'll see how those people were affected by you, and how that, in turn, influenced their interactions with others."

"That will take another lifetime!"

"Not here. It will take what it takes." Jerahmeel shrugged. "Some souls move through this stage in an instant. Others take the equivalent of centuries."

"Who could possibly take centuries?"

"Are you sure you don't know?"

Matylda shook her head.

"Someone designed the gas chambers that killed millions. For every member of that team, from the architects to the workmen who assembled them, the weight of every person killed by their invention is a life they must experience as if it were their own. They will perish time and time again, feel the horror, the terror, and the pain of being separated from their loved ones and murdered through hate."

"But," Matylda said, "what of the workmen who only did what they were told? What of the men who connected the gas lines, but didn't know what was coming? Surely, they would not experience such a hell."

"Oh, this is not a punishment. They will experience exactly what I've described to you, over and over, until every person's life has been reviewed through them. They will feel every emotion, from the love of their families to the hatred hurled at them. They will feel the suffering from their inventions."

"If it isn't punishment, what is it?"

"It is understanding. It is compassion. It is empathy. You are displaying this right now. You could hate the Nazis and all they did, yet you ask about one who is possibly innocent of crimes against their fellow human beings. Everyone involved in the process of harming another—even if they are at great physical distance from them—must understand the consequences of their actions. If they feel like they are in hell, they have created it for themselves."

Jerahmeel's figure vibrated as he continued, "We have your life to review and all those whom you impacted. Let us get started so that you can begin the next phase of your existence with Aleksy. He is waiting."

48

Max

Max stood on the central road in Będzin's Jewish ghetto, his eyes riveted on the guard gate. He blinked twice as if the scene unfolding before him would change when he reopened his eyes. Not only did the surroundings remain the same, but a roar of voices clambering over one another threatened to overwhelm his senses.

He turned slowly to discover a silent line of Jews snaking down the center road for as far as the eye could see, while Nazi soldiers barked orders as if they were competing against one another in their ferocity. He watched as some civilians were abruptly struck with a rifle butt, spat upon, or pushed to the ground. With each transgression, he felt the victim's distress. Unlike the pain he felt when he was alive, this was far more intense, as if every torment vibrated outward to create more suffering.

Max sensed a breath upon the back of his neck. It was so hot that it felt as if his skin was being scorched by a malicious sun. An unexplained terror seized him, causing his breathing to become ragged and shallow, and his heart to palpitate. He wanted to run as far away as possible to escape this place and time, but his feet were rooted to the ground as if they belonged to a statue. The sensation was shared by all those in line, their inward cries taking on physical shapes that surrounded and taunted him.

He was steadily pivoted around. He hadn't turned himself; he hadn't possessed the ability to move. He was revolved as though he existed on a rotating pedestal. A tall figure loomed before him, too colossal to be human, yet it wore a cloak with a strange head covering that appeared to be both a hat and a hood. The graphite-colored cloak was so long that it covered the figure from head to toe, and as his eyes became riveted on its lower extremities, it appeared to vibrate and levitate.

"You were here." Max's voice sounded odd to him, as though his voice had become separated from his body. "I saw you here, on that day."

"Yes," the figure answered. Its face was entirely shrouded in pitch-blackness, the depths so complete that it was as though it had no face at all.

"You are Abaddon," Max said.

"Yes. I am Abaddon." The voice was heavy and harsh, as if it belonged to an apex predator. As he turned and raised one arm, the cloak undulated like thick, murky smoke had been disturbed. The tip of a finger pointed from under the cloak's arm.

Max felt as though he no longer had control of his body but was turned to face the direction in which Abaddon pointed. He found himself staring at the long line of people. Unlike the original time, he could not prevent himself from staring into each face and registering each emotion. He felt intense fear, overwhelming sorrow, unimaginable distress, consuming anxiety, depression, and hopelessness. With others in the line, he felt a glimmer of hope, prayers, a yearning for clean water, and enough food to reverse starvation.

Mrs. Weiss began walking along the line, inquiring about its purpose from fellow Jews, and her daughter, Celina, stepped behind her. Max recoiled as they approached him.

Abaddon cackled, his voice sinister. "They cannot see you. You see, Max, they are dead. But you knew that already, didn't you?"

"I am in hell," Max croaked as his throat constricted.

"Do you recognize them?" Abaddon pressed. Without waiting for a reply, he continued, "Of course, you do not, because you turned your face from them. There are a few you know, such as Mrs. Weiss and her daughter. Over there, you see that young man?"

"I've never seen him before."

"Are you sure? Look more closely. It is the child who dropped an apple on you on your way to the bakery. He was only seven years old."

Max instinctively reached for his forehead where the apple had struck him. "It hurt."

"Yes. It did. But, was it worth paying for it with his life?" Abaddon vibrated in shades of gray and black as he continued. "He was only a child, and he regretted his action as he matured. He was trying, like the rest of them, to forge a life and a future for himself and his loved ones."

"I didn't know he was Jewish."

"He wasn't. But, you identified him as Jewish, didn't you, Max? You wanted to appear important. You condemned him to death for throwing an apple as a child. You sent him to this ghetto, and then you ordered him marched out of the city to be murdered in the woods."

Max attempted to turn away, but he was held facing the scene unfolding before him.

"It also did not matter whether he was a Jew or a Gentile," Abaddon continued. "Religion is a façade created by cultures. It is the soul that truly matters. You see, if you are earnest and sincere, you pray to the same God, regardless of the rituals surrounding you." He waved a cloaked arm to encompass all those in line. "The rest, you will soon know."

"What are you saying?"

"You determined your afterlife by the life you led while living." As Abaddon spoke, his words appeared to turn to black smoke, which encircled Max. "Every deed, thought, and word created energies that you must experience on this side. Had they been positive, you would experience happiness, lightness, and gratitude. Above these are love and hope, which sit at the pinnacle of all you should strive for. These ripple outward, creating higher vibrations and more encompassing love and hope. It is strange how that works, isn't it? The more love you give away, the more love comes back to you."

"I committed good deeds," Max insisted.

"Yes. It is impossible to find a soul that hasn't acted with, thought, or verbalized occasional positive intentions. But, you see, Max, all that you ever said or did was weighed on a cosmic scale. A good deed must have been the result of unselfish love, understanding, and compassion for another. Times when you acted in kindness will come back to you here, and you will see how your altruism positively affected others."

Max puffed out his chest. "I am sure we can find many instances."

Abaddon chortled, the sound echoing until it surrounded Max. "You cannot bargain with us here, Max. Your soul is transparent." Before Max could respond, Abaddon continued, "You will experience those times after you encounter the others."

"The others?" Intense terror began to form inside him. He felt helpless. He was no longer a human being but a creature lower than a cockroach, something that must be annihilated.

"Feel that, Max? Each person standing in this line is a soul. Yours is no better than theirs; all souls were created equal. The facades that are worn in an earthly existence—skin color, languages, money, privilege... They mean nothing here. Absolutely. Nothing," he emphasized. "The moment you crossed over the threshold into the afterlife, your soul exists only in love or the absence of it."

"I don't understand—"

"Then I will explain it to you. Very soon, you will find yourself in the body of one of these people in line. Yes, Max. *These* people." Abaddon began to move alongside the line, pulling Max with him as if they were bound by an invisible cord.

"You will experience their existence from the time they were born. You will see and feel their families, friends, and all those who loved them. You will move through life with them, through them, experiencing the constellation of their schools, churches, and communities."

"That doesn't seem too bad."

"It won't be. Until you experience the unadulterated hatred of someone who never knew them, someone like you, who decides their fate without looking in their faces or learning who they are. It will be undeserving hatred, and all hatred is undeserving."

The emotions were reaching a crescendo, bordering on insanity, as all the souls turned to look at him in unison.

"And you will find yourself in this line," Abaddon continued, "selected by you or a soldier you ordered here, and you will march out with the others. And there will be a time when you will understand why you were selected and the fate that awaits you. You will feel their horror, their alarm and panic, their complete helplessness as you are ordered into the woods. You will feel their physical pain, but it won't end there. You will fully comprehend the lives you ruined, as every person in this line was loved by others. You will feel their terror and overwhelming sadness as they discover the fate of the murdered one. You will hear their sorrow as they ask the heavens how anyone could completely lack compassion for other human beings. And," he concluded, "that someone will be you. For you had a hand in their murders to the same extent as the person who pulled the trigger."

Max began to speak, but his words were silenced as if Abaddon's hand was wrapped around his throat.

"Ever wonder what it felt like to 'go up the chimney,' Max? None of these people did; neither did the people who were gassed first; not even your mother, for they were murdered before they were incinerated. But you will feel it, Max. You will feel every excruciating second of it. There is no concept of time here, Max, which means every second will feel like an eternity. And when that is finished," Abaddon continued, "you will find yourself back in line as the next victim. The process will repeat again, and again, and again..." He pointed to the long line again. "You will experience every drop of pain you inflicted on every soul in this line, including Mrs. Weiss and Celina."

Max tried to object, but Abaddon's figure grew taller and bulkier, the black smoke swirling with the same intensity as Max's terror.

"When you have experienced each soul's journey, you will begin again with every soldier who experienced trauma from your order; all fifty of them. Then, with every soul you sent to a camp, thousands of them, Max. Thousands," he growled. "You will also experience your mother's sorrow at her son's role in these atrocities. And did I mention, you will experience the atrocities that each guard perpetrated, each guard that *you* sent?"

"I am in hell," Max moaned.

"It is a hell that you created, action by action, word by word… For, with every person you harmed, you must experience what you caused them to experience, repeatedly, until you understand."

"You said that you hold the secret to the gate," Max said. "I will do whatever you wish if you will open it for me now."

"Open it for you?" Abaddon mocked. He smiled with red teeth that shone from the depths of the darkness beneath the hood. He turned and pointed in the opposite direction. As Max turned to peer behind him, Abaddon continued, "You are on the other side of the gate now."

Sheer panic enveloped him. "Then, get me out of here! Please! I beg you! I will do anything!"

"You cannot bargain with me, Max, and I have grown weary of your attempts. You will remain here until you have experienced every soul's journey that you impacted in life. It makes no difference how physically close or far you were from their fates. You were a cog in the mechanism that perpetuated hatred and harm. You could have been the broken link in the chain of hatred at any time, at any point."

Max felt a sudden shift in the air and an urge to look down at his body. Instead of the jacket and trousers he was accustomed to wearing, he found himself staring at the belly of a pregnant woman dressed in dirty, thin rags. His hand was drawn to the stomach, but it was not the masculine hand he knew, but a petite, frail, and bony hand of a half-starved woman. The baby feebly kicked inside her, and she knew it would not be long before she would go into labor.

"Wait!" he cried out, surprised to find his voice undulating between his own and the young woman's.

Abaddon had reached the gate, and now he turned in the entrance.

"Are you Satan?" Max shouted.

"I have told you that I am not."

"Then, who are you? What are you?"

The hood grew larger with soot that caught on the air and swirled around the figure. Two red eyes emerged above snarling, red teeth, causing Max to recoil in horror. When Abaddon spoke, the voice was fathomless and blood-curdling.

"I am the mirror of your soul."

49

Agata

The evergreen needles of the Scots pines soared above Agata, their uppermost branches dancing with a light, airy breeze. The sky was the most consistent shade of azure she'd ever seen and so devoid of clouds that it appeared more like a painting than reality. She barely made out a family of soaring birds in the distance, circling one another as if in play, their wings alternately dipping and rising.

As she traced the treetops downward through the hefty trunks to where they disappeared among a heavy blanket of needles on the forest floor, a strange sensation began to envelop her. She knew this thicket. In fact, she doubted that she could ever forget it, no matter how hard she tried.

"It was you, wasn't it?" she asked softly.

"Yes," Celeste answered.

Agata turned to face Celeste. "You were here."

She nodded.

"You gave me food and told me the way to the village and the clothing factory."

"Yes."

"But, how can that be? The food was real. I ate it. The village was exactly where you said it would be."

"Yes." When Celeste smiled, her gown shimmered in gold and silver. "There were always angels around you. We don't live in the distant clouds. We have too much work to do on earth."

"I don't understand," Agata insisted. "How is that possible?"

"Why do you believe it is impossible?" She began to stroll through the woods, and Agata followed. "I am the seagull directing the lost mariner to a safe port," Celeste began. "I am the deer that alerts the wanderer to danger. I am the red cardinal who sat on the windowsill at a camp devoid of birds."

"Wait," Agata said. As Celeste halted and turned to face her, Agata pointed. "It is there, through those woods, that I found the villagers. They had been murdered, even the children. If angels are always among us, why weren't they protected?"

Celeste's eyes saddened. "We were there, but there are times in which we must work through the living. For example, you had a choice when we met in the woods. You could have continued waiting for a ride. Another came this way three days later. Or, you could have returned to Warsaw or set out directly for southern Poland. It was your choice to go into the village, where you found appropriate clothing for the rest of your journey."

"I met two men there."

"Yes, you did. Again, you had a choice. You could have traveled with them. Had you made that choice, you would have been reunited with Piotr."

Agata gasped. "Why didn't you tell me when we met?"

Celeste cocked her head. "And then, what would have happened to Elsa? No," she said without waiting for her reply, "you were single-minded in your journey to save your sister."

"I don't know if I was successful." She sat on a fallen log, her shoulders slumped.

"Yes," Celeste said, coming to stand near her, "you were successful. Elsa was days away from dying of starvation. You saved her with the food you provided. And, in so doing, you saved many others."

Agata's eyes filled with tears. "I did so very little. The power that invaded Poland was so strong, so formidable. What difference could I alone have made against such evil?"

"Enough difference to save your sister's life. Along with the others you saved, the resistance rippled outward to encompass others. You were only a grain of sand against a sea of evil." Celeste waved her hand. The woods transformed into a vast beach that stretched as far as the eye could see. "But there were millions of grains of sand just like you, and together, they repelled the immoral and corrupt forces."

Agata was silent for a long moment. "Why did so many people follow those evil forces? It only resulted in heartbreak and hatred, and eventually, in murder and destruction."

"Because," Celeste answered patiently, "every person on this planet is an eternal soul living a momentary existence in a human body. Every soul has a choice that will not only change the course of their eternal life but also the course of others' lives. They can reject malevolent forces in all their forms and spread love, tolerance, and understanding. Sadly, some choose to follow figures that lead to hatred, catastrophe, division, and disaster."

"Why?"

Celeste shrugged. "Because they make promises that some were waiting to hear."

"There were millions of us—millions of Poles, Hungarians, and ethnic groups from across Europe. Allied forces were fighting to free us from an evil empire. Why was that not enough?"

"Ah, but it was enough. For you see, dear Agata, evil was defeated. The invaders were purged."

"But, at what cost?"

"Is there any cost too high to repel dark forces?"

"Why did it have to happen at all?" Agata pressed.

"It didn't." Celeste sighed, and for the first time, she appeared weary. "War is never inevitable. Hatred, division, and intolerance are learned." Two dogs began walking along the beach as if they had appeared out of thin air. "Do you see them?" Celeste asked.

"Yes. I do."

"One is white with short fur, while the other is tri-colored with long fur. Neither one cares about the other's color. Neither one cares that while one was carefully bred for herding sheep, the other is a mongrel of unknown lineage. Each has love for the other. Each provides companionship and permissiveness. They play, eat, and sleep together in harmony. Oh, they have brief spats. But it never rises to the level of hatred."

"Are you saying that dogs are better than humans?"

"At the moment, the species is. Perhaps, humans have a lot to learn from the animals around them."

A tear escaped and raced down Agata's cheek before she could stop it. "I am guilty of atrocities."

"Oh?"

"I struck prisoners in the camp, too many times to count or remember. I hated my little sister when I first saw her, thinking that, if she weren't there, my mother would still be with me. I made a promise to return to her and my father, a promise I couldn't keep. And," she added between sobs, "I killed a guard on the morning the camp was liberated." She looked Celeste in the eyes. "I committed murder."

"That's a lot of confessions."

"Yes. I suppose it is."

"You have suffered from tremendous guilt," Celeste continued. "Guilt is the first step toward grace and redemption."

"I don't understand."

"To feel guilt means you must feel empathy. To feel guilt means you must care. It means you wish you had made a different choice."

"But I can't go back and change things."

"No. That much is true. However, the weight of guilt is the first step in making better decisions and becoming a more highly evolved soul. If you do not feel the consequences of your choices before you reach this side, you are destined to experience those events through those you impacted. Because you are truly sorry, repentant for the things you did that hurt others, and resolved not to repeat those actions in the future, the gift of grace may be bestowed upon you."

"I don't understand."

"Everything boils down to lessons. For those who don't acknowledge the evil they wrought or the bad decisions they made, they are fated to experience them until they understand the effects their thoughts, words, and actions had on others. When you experience guilt, you already understand how you negatively impacted others. The lesson is learned. Grace and forgiveness may be offered. Provided," she added, "that the guilt is sincere and the soul is determined not to repeat it."

Celeste began walking again. Reluctantly, Agata rose to follow her. The beach morphed into a busy avenue lined with buildings and people. "All of the villagers in the woods, and all those who perished in the camps and beyond, were met on the other side with unconditional love and an absence of pain. Angels provided safety and security for their souls, even though their bodies were lost. They are in a far better place, to put it mildly." She stopped and pointed. "Do you remember this place?"

Agata peered at the building in front of them. It was a formidable brick building, just as imposing and menacing as it had been when she was a child. "We are in Fürstenwalde," she breathed. "That is a hospital."

"I was there, too," Celeste said quietly, "on the day your mother passed into the afterlife."

"You mean on the day she died."

"Ah, but she is not dead." Celeste stepped back. As her figure began to glimmer again, she added, "The soul is never dead."

Before Agata's eyes, Celeste's figure became a swirling mass of lights that glistened in all directions as though she were coming apart. In the next instance, she vanished, leaving Agata with an overwhelming sense of love and unconditional acceptance. She stepped forward into the void left, but sensed someone behind her.

As she turned, she found herself staring into her mother's face.

"Agata," Anna said, stepping forward. To Agata's astonishment, she appeared exactly as she had before her body had blossomed with Elsa inside her. She looked so young; her face was radiant, her skin glowing, and her eyes filled with compassion. Her slender arms were outstretched, and as Agata fell into them, they encircled her with an embrace that she wanted to continue forever.

"Why did you leave us?" Agata cried.

"I was never actually gone," Anna said, stroking her daughter's hair. "I was always right there beside you, even when you couldn't feel my presence."

"But—"

"I had to pass over to this side," she continued. "Had I remained, we would have stayed in Fürstenwalde. All of us would have been placed in a camp, Agata. None of us would have survived."

"I don't understand! We needed you!"

"Fürstenwalde did not remain the town of my youth, nor of yours," Anna said sadly. "It became the site of a subcamp of Sachsenhausen, a labor and death camp. Because I passed away, your father was able to take you and your sister to safety in Warsaw."

Agata was openly crying, her body wracked with her sobs. "We suffered anyway, Mama. And Papa—"

"Yes. Ira. What a good father he is. I always knew he would be."

"But, Mama, he—"

"Take care of him, Agata. Take care of him and your sister."

"What are you saying?"

"He has traveled far to be with you," she said. She held Agata at arm's length from her as she smiled. "He has crossed the country in every direction."

"What?"

"Take care of our little family, Agata, my dear child. And know that I am with you. Even when you can't feel my presence, I am there."

The words that were ready to escape Agata's lips were lost on a dizzying blast of wind that spun her into a light more brilliant than the sun. Agata wrapped her arms about her face in a vain attempt to shield her eyes from the radiant orb. As she drew closer, she was overcome with weakness and lightheadedness, as though she would faint at any moment. The last thing she remembered was being laid upon a soft, warm bed as if she had truly collapsed.

50

Agata

The light was so bright and unyielding that it threatened to burn her eyelids.

Agata blinked several times as she struggled to open her eyes fully. For the first time since the explosion, she experienced pain when she moved. Her left side felt as though every nerve was on fire, and her eyes watered and throbbed with the light's intensity. Each inhale was laborious, and she struggled to make even the slightest move.

She longed to return to Celeste's side, where she hadn't experienced physical pain or discomfort, and she wondered where her angel had gone. She tried to call out to her, but her throat was parched, and no sound escaped her lips.

Agata eventually managed to open her eyes and found herself lying flat on her back, staring at an annoying, bright light hanging from the ceiling. She lay there for a moment as she attempted to get her bearings. An antiseptic odor filled the air, irritating her nostrils. It smelled as though someone had mopped the floors with a too-strong solution, and she desperately wanted to open a window.

Noise filled the air. Men's and women's voices seemed to come at her from all directions, and yet, they sounded faint, as though they were a distance away. Someone coughed. Wheels groaned against the floor.

Agata managed to turn her head and was astonished to see Elsa half-reclining on a bed only a few feet from her. She appeared as though she had fallen asleep while reading a well-worn copy of *To Have and Have Not* by Ernest Hemingway. She was afraid to close her eyes, concerned that when she reopened them, her sister would have disappeared.

Elsa appeared small and frail, but she was clean. Her hair was almost shoulder-length, not the buzz cut that all prisoners endured. There was color in her cheeks; gone was the thin alabaster skin Agata had become accustomed to seeing in the camp. She wore a clean, white hospital gown that reached from her neck to her ankles, where her feet emerged wearing socks. Socks! Agata wondered about the last time she'd seen socks, but she couldn't remember.

She slowly began to realize that she was lying in a busy hospital ward. If she managed to peer toward her feet, she noticed a row of beds across from her, filled with people suffering from various ailments. Unlike the camp with its dark, foreboding walls and inadequate lighting, this room was filled with sunshine intermingling with overhead lights. The voices she'd heard were nurses and patients, primarily speaking in hushed, reverent tones as if trying not to disturb the others.

A cart approached Elsa's bed, pushed by a young woman in a long-sleeved blouse and crisp white apron, her dark hair almost entirely covered by a white cap. The aroma of hot chicken stock and cooked vegetables tickled her nose, and Agata realized she was famished.

Heavier footsteps sounded behind the cart. "Here, allow me to take that tray from you," a male voice said softly. "She's asleep, but I'll make sure she awakens and eats it."

Agata's heartbeat quickened so abruptly that she thought she was having a heart attack. She knew that voice. In fact, she could never forget it.

She tried to turn toward the voice, but her arm was tethered to an intravenous drip, and every movement sent her body spiraling into pain. As the cart wheeled past her, a man stepped between the beds and placed the tray on the nightstand between Elsa and her. He leaned forward and appeared to be gently shaking her sister.

"Elsa," he said, "my little angel, wake up and eat." As Elsa began to stir, he continued, "They've brought you fresh chicken soup, a roll, and a salad. Look, there are radishes and carrots and peas!"

Agata's throat felt as though she'd walked through a desert under a hot, unrelenting sun. She strained to call for her father as he helped Elsa sit up in bed. Finally, a croak managed to escape her.

Startled, Ira nearly dropped the tray he was attempting to balance in front of Elsa. When he turned, his face went as pale as if Agata were a ghost manifesting in front of him. He quickly returned the tray to the table as Elsa peered around him. Her eyes lit up at the sight of Agata.

"Nurse! Nurse!" Ira called out, his voice sounding too loud and animated in the staid, clinical room. As the attendant turned around, her lips pursed as if to shush him, he leaned over Agata and continued, "My daughter's eyes are open! She's come out of her coma!"

Agata fought to remain awake, but the effort was too great and the pull of sleep too strong. The faces of Ira and Elsa, leaning over her, blurred as a doctor and a nurse rushed to her side. Their voices mingled, Elsa's young, high voice seeming to merge with Ira's soft, gentle baritone. As they were replaced by a doctor's calm, deep tone, she succumbed to the heaviness descending on her.

~~~~~

Two weeks had passed, and Agata could now be propped up in bed against layers of decadent pillows. She wore a bandage that wrapped around her shaved head, concealing jagged wounds and incisions. The bandage was meticulously changed every day when the doctor inspected her injuries. In between, she had visits from medical personnel intent on asking her the same questions as they wrote in their notebooks. The prognosis was good, as she was able to recall much of her life, though she had forgotten details of the day the camp was liberated. She would likely be bothered by debilitating headaches, but it was a small price to pay to be reunited with Ira and Elsa. She had somehow returned from the dead.
~~~~~

While Agata was in a coma, Elsa's organs had begun to shut down, likely due to starvation and repeated infections. Under the care of the Polish and Ukrainian nurses, however, she was flourishing. The infections were effectively treated, and she was slowly adding back the weight she'd lost. It wouldn't be much longer before she would be released from the hospital.

Ira had miraculously survived the occupation. After he'd been placed on a cattle car heading for the north side of Warsaw, the tracks were blown up by the Polish underground resistance. In the heat of a skirmish between the Nazis and Poles, several cars were opened, and the prisoners rushed out. Casualties were heavy among the resistance fighters, and most of the prisoners were recaptured, but he'd managed to evade them. He had then set out on a grueling journey to find his two daughters.

"Is the war over?" Agata asked as Ira and Elsa perched on her bed.

"It is for us," Ira said. "The Polish Resettlement Corps is working to relocate us, just as soon as it's safe and you're cleared to move."

"But for the rest of Europe?"

"I have heard the Allies are days away from defeating the Nazis. They've surrounded Berlin, where Hitler is rumored to be hiding."

"Hiding?"

"Yes, hiding. He has been living underground for months now, supposedly safe from the bombing. It's called the *Führerbunker* and is now what is left of the *Führer* Headquarters. Can you imagine? He has been reduced to hiding in subterranean tunnels like a mole.

They will find him and capture him," Ira added. "I am sure of it."

"And Piotr?"

It was Elsa who answered. "When the camp was liberated, Piotr joined the Polish First Army. They are playing a huge role in capturing Berlin. I am so proud of him!"

Agata laughed, but her head throbbed with the effort. "How can you be proud of him, when you hardly know him?"

"He was here with you when we were first brought here. Papa and I got to know him. Piotr never stopped fighting, Agata. Never. He never gave up."

The sound of wheels reached their ears. "It's too early for supper," Agata mused.

As they turned toward the sound, a wheelchair was pushed down the long corridor between beds. A woman was behind it, her crisp, gay blue dress in contrast with the white hospital gowns and medical uniforms. From this distance, she looked like a movie star with her gleaming, shoulder-length hair and svelte figure. As they drew closer, Agata was drawn to her round face and wide smile.

Behind her were two younger women who were similarly dressed and who appeared like younger versions of her, though with darker hair. But, as Agata's eyes moved from the women to the person in the wheelchair, her heart began to race.

The man was thinner than the last time she'd seen him. His face was gaunt, but he wore the same wide smile as the others. As her eyes moved across his figure, she realized both his legs were missing. One ended just above the knee, while the other ended halfway up his thigh.

"Agata!" he called out as they reached her bed.

"Hank?" she asked incredulously.

"I didn't know if you'd remember me," he said.

"How could I ever forget you?"

Ira rose and shook his hand. "I'm Ira Goldstein, Agata's father."

"Hank Mullins. This is my wife, Dottie, and my girls, Mary and Susanna. And you," he added, locking eyes with Elsa, "must be the infamous Elsa Goldstein."

"I don't know how infamous I am," she laughed as she shook his hand and those of each family member.

"Infamous enough for your sister to walk through the Gates of Hell to find you," he answered.

"Did you lose your legs on the day the camps were liberated?" Agata asked gently, nodding to his body.

"I did," Hank said, slapping his thigh. "But you know, in the big scheme of things, I'm doing okay. I'm alive, and I have my lovely wife and beautiful daughters. With any luck, my son and son-in-law will soon come home from the Pacific, where they've been fighting. Anyway, I heard that you had opened your eyes, and I had to come by to see you."

"You've been here in the hospital this whole time?"

"Yes. I must have suffered a concussion; they told me I was out cold for a time."

"When did you awaken?"

"I don't recall, exactly. When I woke up, Dottie was here with my girls."

"We were told he might not make it," Dottie interjected. "He was near death when we arrived."

"We kept talking to him," Mary said, "begging him to come back to us."

"I must have heard them on some level," Hank said, shaking his head, "because I had some pretty vivid dreams while I was out."

"Dreams?" Agata asked. "What kind of dreams?"

"Well," Hank said, scratching his head, "I just remember asking an angel of God to get me back home to my family."

"An angel of God? Was she, by any chance, named Celeste?"

"Joe. Did you have dreams also?"

"I did."

"Well," Hank laughed, "they must have been giving us some mighty fine medicine while we were out. I think I dreamt in Technicolor."

"I have a feeling that my dreams have changed my life."

"They certainly have changed mine."

"You had a partner when I saw you last," Agata said. "Was he injured in the explosion, too?"

"Rafe," Hank offered. "No. Thank God, he had cleared the blast area. In fact, directly afterward, a young, inexperienced soldier opened fire. Rafe forced him to drop the rifle."

"Did the soldier hurt anyone?" Elsa breathed.

"One, a nurse," Hank said sadly. "Unfortunately, she didn't make it."

"How did Rafe stop the soldier?" Elsa asked.

"With a slingshot. He's pretty good with it. The soldier was knocked off his feet, long enough to be disarmed, and he gained a nice bump on his head. Otherwise, he was fine."

They all marveled over Rafe's slingshot prowess before Agata ventured, "Where is Rafe now?"

"Right about now, he should be closing in on the outskirts of Berlin."

"He's in Germany?"

"That's where the action is. He made a good friend in the 60th Army of the First Ukrainian Front, a guy named Misha. Anyway, after liberating the camp, the Ukrainians continued west with the Red Army. They successfully pushed back the Nazis all the way to Berlin. The Americans, Brits, and other Allies are advancing from the west. The German lines are collapsing, and Berlin has been heavily bombed."

"By the way," Dottie interjected, "Japan surrendered. Ray and Buck are still in the Pacific, but the war is over for them. They'll soon be coming home."

The conversation veered into a discussion of a new atomic weapon dropped on Hiroshima and Nagasaki, ordered by America's new president, Harry S. Truman. There was a long moment of sad silence as they spoke of Franklin D. Roosevelt's death. Throughout the war, there was tremendous hope and faith in Churchill, Roosevelt, and Stalin. Eventually, the conversation ventured back to Rafe.

"Did Rafe have a family?" Agata asked.

"Yes," Hank answered. "His mom is in France, freed from the Vichy government. After Berlin, he plans to keep moving until he reaches her in France. He wants to move her to America. The magazine editor I work for said he'd be proud to hire him."

"What will you do now?" Ira asked.

"I'm going home," he said, grasping Dottie's hand. "Flight leaves tomorrow, which is why I wanted to swing by and say hello."

"What will you do when you get home?" Agata asked.

"The magazine I work for wants a series of articles regarding my experiences. I'd sent a slew of them, but they were heavily redacted, and most didn't make it through. The magazine seems to think Americans will be interested in what has transpired over the last five or six years. What will you do?"

"I don't know yet," Agata answered thoughtfully. "We really haven't discussed it yet."

"We're waiting," Ira said quietly. "Agata was in grave danger for a long while, and she's still got a long recovery ahead of her."

"Well, I wish you all the very best." Hank pulled a card from his pocket and handed it to them. "That's my address. Please write to me and let me know how you're doing. If you ever want to visit America, I'd be honored to show you around."

"Thank you," Ira said, accepting the card.

"I won't offer to show you around Poland," Agata laughed. "I wouldn't be surprised if you never wanted to see it again."

"Oh, I'll be back someday," he answered with a broad smile. "I want to see the progress made now that the Nazis are gone."

"Then, look me up. I'll send you my address as soon as we know where we'll be."

After shaking everyone's hands again, Hank signaled to Dottie to turn him around. They had only gotten a few steps away when Hank suddenly signaled to be turned back toward Agata. He removed a blanket that had lain across his lap to retrieve a small bundle.

As Dottie handed the bundle to Agata, Hank said, "I almost forgot to give you this. When the Ukrainians were going door-to-door in Oświęcim, they came across your things in a place you must have rented."

Agata accepted the bundle, running her hands over the smooth leather duffel. "I didn't think I'd ever see this again," she said. "I took it from the village where we met."

"Yes," Hank said, "I remembered it. I told them I would get these things to you. It's mostly just clothing, and I doubt you'd want to wear those items again." He smiled briefly before continuing, "But there was something else hidden inside one of the garments."

Agata rifled through the things until she heard the crunch of paper that she'd hidden so long ago.

"Hang onto those notes," Hank said. "There's talk of trials when the war is over. You could testify to what you witnessed, and the notes will corroborate your testimony."

"Yes," Agata said quietly. "I would be honored to testify, and you're right; these notes have dates, times, and names in them."

"I know. I read them." With final good-byes, his family wheeled him back down the aisle toward the wide double doors at the far end of the room.

As Agata watched, a nurse who had been standing next to a patient raised her head and locked eyes with her. Her platinum hair shone from underneath the cap, and her starched white uniform began to twinkle in shades of gold and silver. She smiled broadly at Agata as though they shared a secret. The patient appeared to sit up, though his body was translucent. The nurse wrapped her arms around him. They swirled into a gentle vortex, and in the blink of an eye, they were gone.

Notes from the Author

Thank you for taking the time to read *Padlocked*. It has always been readers like you who buy or borrow my books that allow me to continue doing what I love. If you enjoyed this story, please tell your friends or post a review on Goodreads, Amazon, or other sites.

As with all my historical novels, I have made a tremendous effort to remain true to the facts of the era. However, there are two glaring instances in *Padlocked* where I took literary license. The first is the explosion that occurred in Chapter 1 during the liberation of Auschwitz-Birkenau. To my knowledge, there were no such explosions at any liberated camps.

The second instance concerns the gas chambers. In order to remove evidence of crimes against humanity, the gas chambers were dismantled in late 1944 and completely destroyed before the Allies arrived on January 27, 1945.

Nazi Germany renamed Oświęcim to Auschwitz after the region was annexed. However, to avoid confusion between the city and the camp, I continued to refer to the city as Oświęcim.

As Agata was ensuring that all prisoners had emptied the barracks, she came across this sentence etched into the wood: "If there is a God, He will have to beg me for forgiveness." That text was truly inscribed next to one of the bunks and remains at Auschwitz for visitors to view. Other details, such as Agata dropping food on the ground for the prisoners to make soup, were inspired by true stories of guards who risked everything to help their fellow human beings.

Anke Bauer's character was inspired by brutal female guards, including Ilse Koch (known as "The Witch of Buchenwald"), Ilse Grese, and others. Some of the guards were put on trial, convicted, and sentenced to imprisonment or execution. Ilse Koch was convicted of life imprisonment. She became delusional while incarcerated, convinced that the prisoners she had abused had returned and were forcing her to endure what she had perpetrated on them. She eventually committed suicide by hanging herself in 1967.

Other resources involved in the stories of Agata, Max, Rafe, and Hank include:

10 of the Most Famous War Correspondents https://www.warhistoryonline.com/featured/american-war-correspondents.html

11 Nations Conquered by Nazi Germany in World War II https://www.warhistoryonline.com/world-war-ii/11-countries-invaded-nazi-germany-invaded.html

60th Army of the First Ukrainian Front https://en.wikipedia.org/wiki/1st_Ukrainian_Front

American Foreign and War Correspondents https://encyclopedia.ushmm.org/content/en/article/american-foreign-and-war-correspondents

Auschwitz-Birkenau Topography

https://www.auschwitz.org/en/history/kl-auschwitz-birkenau/the-topography-of-the-camp/

Auschwitz-Birkenau Commandants
https://www.auschwitz.org/en/history/the-ss-garrison/commandants/

Auschwitz Crematoria
https://www.jewishvirtuallibrary.org/crematoria-and-gas-chambers-at-auschwitz-birkenau

Auschwitz Guards
https://www.politico.eu/article/auschwitz-guard-germany-holocaust-history-world-war/

Będzin
https://www.jewishvirtuallibrary.org/bedzin

Będzin Ghetto
https://www.jhi.pl/en/articles/the-bedzin-ghetto-we-remember,37

Będzin Holocaust Historical Society
https://www.holocausthistoricalsociety.org.uk/contents/ghettosa-i/bedzin.html

Eastern Front
https://www.britannica.com/event/World-War-II/The-Eastern-Front-June-December-1944

Female Concentration Camp Guards
https://rarehistoricalphotos.com/female-guards-concentration-camps/

"Final Solution" – Britannica
https://www.britannica.com/event/Final-Solution

"Final Solution" – Holocaust Encyclopedia
https://encyclopedia.ushmm.org/content/en/article/the-final-solution

George Patton's Role in D-Day
https://www.historyonthenet.com/pattons-role-in-d-day

How the Red Army Captured Warsaw
https://www.historyhit.com/1945-red-army-retakes-warsaw/

Inside Nazi Germany's Drug Use
https://www.history.com/articles/inside-the-drug-use-that-fueled-nazi-germany

Jungdeutsche Partei
https://en.wikipedia.org/wiki/Jungdeutsche_Partei

Men and Women in the Polish Resistance
https://polandatwartours.com/unsung-heroes-the-brave-men-and-women-of-the-polish-resistance-during-ww2/

Nazis Were Not Socialists
https://fullfact.org/online/nazis-socialists/

Normandy Invasion
https://www.nationalww2museum.org/students-teachers/student-resources/research-starters/research-starters-d-day

Operation Barbarossa
https://en.wikipedia.org/wiki/Operation_Barbarossa

Poland After the War
https://warsawinstitute.org/post-war-war-years-1944-1963-poland/

Profiles of 21 Nazi Leaders on Trial at Nuremberg
https://www.upi.com/Archives/1946/09/30/Profiles-of-the-21-Nazi-leaders-on-trial-at-Nuremberg/2178534120119/

Vichy France
https://www.worldwar2facts.org/vichy-france-facts.html

Warsaw Deportations
https://encyclopedia.ushmm.org/content/en/article/deportations-to-and-from-the-warsaw-ghetto

What Poles Ate When There Was Nothing to Eat
https://culture.pl/en/article/what-poles-ate-when-there-was-nothing-to-eat

While Hitler Snored

https://www.military.com/daily-news/2019/05/31/while-hitler-snored-d-day-rommel-and-panzers.html

World War II Chronology for December 1944
https://www.onwar.com/wwii/chronology/1944 12.html

Additionally, please visit my website at https://pmterrell.com for a link to a YouTube playlist entitled "World War II Research," which includes hours of verified footage taken during the war, camp liberations, trials, and aftermath.

With regard to the afterlife and near-death experiences endured by Agata, Hank, Matylda, and Max, events are based in part on recorded near-death experiences and religious beliefs held by several major religions.

I had not intended to write this book, as it is a different genre from my other writings. However, one night I dreamed this story in its entirety. The next morning, I decided it had to have come from a higher source. When I prayed and asked God how I could possibly remember the thousands of details across multiple main characters, I heard Him answer, "You won't remember. But I will."

The result is the story you hold in your hands.

About the Author

My full name is Patricia McClelland Terrell, and I have been writing under the pen name p.m.terrell ever since a publisher presented me with my first fiction book cover. The graphic designer had also entered my name in lower-case letters; my editor hated it, and I loved it. It's been p.m.terrell ever since.

I began writing when I was nine years old, inspired by a schoolteacher and elementary school principal. Scott-Foresman published my first book, a computer instructional for universities, in 1984. Scott-Foresman, Dow-Jones (Richard D. Irwin branch), Palari Publishing, Paralee Press, and Drake Valley Press have published 26 books to date.

Before embarking on a full-time writing career, I founded McClelland Enterprises, Inc. in the Washington, D.C., area in 1984, specializing in workplace software instruction. I opened another business, Continental Software Development Corporation, in 1994, which focused on custom application development, programming, website design and development, and computer crime. I held two Top Secret security clearances, one with the United States Secret Service and the other with the CIA. My favorite assignment was detecting Medicare fraud and abuse, which helped recover millions of dollars for the federal government.

I was honored to be the first female President of the Chesterfield County/Colonial Heights Crime Solvers. I also served as the Treasurer for the Virginia Crime Stoppers Association. Since moving to North

Carolina, I served on the Robeson County Friends of the Library and the Robeson County Arts Council.

I launched The Book 'Em Foundation with Waynesboro, Virginia, Police Officer Mark Kearney, and assisted in Virginia, New Hampshire, and South Carolina events before establishing the Annual Book 'Em North Carolina Writers Conference and Book Fair, chairing it for several years before turning it over to Robeson Community College in Lumberton, NC.

Other Books

Stand-Alone Books:
Dani's Decision
A Struggle for Independence
The Adventures of Blade and Rye
Checkmate: Clans and Castles
A Thin Slice of Heaven
The Banker's Greed
Ricochet
The China Conspiracy
Kickback

Black Swamp Mystery Series (in order):
Exit 22
Vicki's Key
Secrets of a Dangerous Woman
Dylan's Song
The Pendulum Files
Cloak and Mirrors

Hayley Hunter Paranormal Mystery Series (in order):
April in the Back of Beyond
The Misremembered Lighthouse

Ryan O'Clery Mysteries (in order):
The Tempest Murders
The White Devil of Dublin

Mary Neely Historical (in order):
River Passage
Songbirds are Free

Non-Fiction:

Take the Mystery Out of Promoting Your Book
The Dynamics of Reflex
The Dynamics of WordPerfect
Memento WordPerfect, Progiciel de traitment de texte
Creating the Perfect Database

www.ingramcontent.com/pod-product-compliance
Lightning Source LLC
LaVergne TN
LVHW020039110826
845155LV00029B/556

9781935970576